HEAP HOUSE

IREMONGER
BOOK 1

HEAP HOUSE

written and illustrated by

EDWARD CAREY

First published in Great Britain in 2013 by Hot Key Books
Northburgh House, 10 Northburgh Street, London EC1V 0AT

Text © Edward Carey 2013
Illustrations © Edward Carey 2013

A CIP catalogue record for this book is available from the British Library.

ISBN: 978-1-4714-0156-5

1

Typeset by Palimpsest Book Production Limited, Falkirk, Stirlingshire
This book is typeset in 11pt Sabon LT Std

Printed and bound by Clays Ltd, St Ives Plc

Hot Key Books supports the Forest Stewardship Council (FSC), the leading
international forest certification organisation, and is committed to printing
only on Greenpeace-approved FSC-certified paper.

www.hotkeybooks.com

For my brother James (1966–2012)

The Ill Child Clod Iremonger

A UNIVERSAL BATH PLUG

Beginning the narrative of Clod Iremonger,
Forlichingham Park, London

How It Started

It all really began, all the terrible business that followed, on the day my Aunt Rosamud's door handle went missing. It was my aunt's particular door handle, a brass one. It did not help that she had been all over the mansion the day before with it, looking for things to complain about as was her habit. She had stalked through every floor, she had been up and down staircases, opening doors at every opportunity, finding fault. And during all her thorough investigations she insisted that her door handle was about her, only now it was not. Someone, she screamed, had taken it.

There hadn't been such a fuss since my Great Uncle Pitter lost his safety pin. On that occasion there was searching all the way up and down the building only for it to be discovered that poor old Uncle had had it all along, it had fallen through the ripped lining of his jacket pocket.

I was the one that found it.

They looked at me very queerly afterwards, my family did, or I should say more queerly, because I was never absolutely trusted and was often shooed from place to place. After the safety pin was found it seemed to confirm something more in my family, and some of my aunts and cousins would steer clear of me, not even speaking to me, whilst others, my cousin Moorcus for example, would seek me out. Cousin Moorcus was certain that I had hidden the pin in the jacket myself and down a dim passageway he caught up with me and smacked my head against the wall, counting to twelve as he did it (my age at the time), and lifted me high up onto a coat hook, leaving me suspended there until I was found two hours later by one of the servants.

Great Uncle Pitter was most apologetic after his pin was found and never, I think, properly recovered from the drama. All that fuss, accusing so many people. He died the next spring, in his sleep, his safety pin pinned to his pyjamas.

'But how could you tell, Clod?' my relations wondered. 'How could you know the safety pin was there?'

'I heard it,' I said, 'calling out.'

I Heard Things

Those flesh flaps on the sides of my head did too much, those two holes where the sounds went in were over-busy. I heard things when I shouldn't.

It took me a time to understand my hearing.

I was told that as a baby I started to cry for no reason. I'd be lying there in my crib and nothing would have happened at all but suddenly I would be screaming as if someone had pulled my scant hair or as if I had been scalded with boiling water or as if someone had sliced into me with a knife. It was always like that. I was an odd child, they said, unhappy and difficult, hard to calm. Colic. Chronic colic. The nursery maids never stayed long. 'Why are you so bad?' they asked. 'Why will you not settle?'

The noises upset me; I was always jumpy and scared and angry. I could not understand the words of the noises at first. At first it was just sounds and rustles, clinks, clicks, smacks, taps, claps, bangs, rumbles, crumblings, yelps, moans, groans, that sort of thing. Not very loud mostly. Sometimes unbearably so. When I could speak I should keep saying, 'Who said that? Who said that?' or 'Be quiet. Shut up you, you're nothing but a washcloth!' or 'Will you be silent, you chamber pot!' because it seemed to me that objects, ordinary everyday objects, were speaking to me in human voices.

The maids would be so cross when I slapped about

some chair or bowl, some handbell or side table. 'Calm down,' they kept telling me.

It was only when my Uncle Aliver, recently made a doctor then, took notice of my upset that things began to improve for me. 'Why are you crying?' he asked me.

'The forceps,' I said.

'My forceps?' he asked. 'What about them?'

I told him that his forceps, which were something that Aliver always carried about him, were talking. Usually I was ignored when I spoke of the talking things, sighed over, or I was given a beating for telling lies, but Uncle Aliver asked me that day, 'And what do my forceps say?'

'They say,' I said, so pleased to be asked, 'Percy Hotchkiss.'

'Percy Hotchkiss?' repeated Uncle Aliver, all interest. 'Anything else?'

'No,' I said, 'that's all I hear. "Percy Hotchkiss."'

'But how can an object speak, Clod?'

'I do not know, and I wish it wouldn't.'

'An object has no life, it has no mouth.'

'I know,' I said, 'and yet it persists.'

'*I* do not hear the forceps speaking.'

'No, but I do, I promise you, Uncle, a muffled, trapped voice, something locked away, saying, "Percy Hotchkiss."'

Afterwards Aliver would often come to me and listen for a long time about all the different voices I heard, about all the different names, and he would make notes. It was just names that I heard, only ever names, some spoken in whispers, some in great shouts, some singing, some screaming, some sounded with modesty, some with great pride, some with miserable timidity. And always, to me, the names seemed to be coming from different objects all about the great house. I could not concentrate in the school room because the cane kept calling out, 'William Stratton', and there was an inkwell that said, 'Hayley Burgess', and the globe was rumbling, 'Arnold Percival Lister.'

'Why are the names of the objects,' I asked Uncle Aliver one day, I was but seven or so at the time, 'these Johns and Jacks and Marys, these Smiths and Murphys and Joneses, why are they such odd names? So different from ours.'

'Well, Clod,' said Aliver, 'it is certain that we are the ones with the less usual names. And that it is a tradition of our family. We Iremongers have different monikers, because we are different from the rest of them. So that we may be told apart from them. It is an old family custom, our names are like theirs that live away from here, beyond the heaplands, only slantcd.'

'The people in London do you mean, Uncle?' I asked.

'In London and far away in all directions, Clod.'

'They have names like the ones I hear?'

'Yes, Clod.'

'Why do I hear the names, Uncle?'

'I do not know, Clod, it is something peculiar to you.'

'Shall it stop ever?'

'I cannot tell. It might go away, it might lessen, it may get worse. I do not know.'

Of all the names I heard, the one I heard most of all was James Henry Hayward. That was because I always kept the object that said 'James Henry Hayward' with me wherever I went. It was a pleasant, young voice.

James Henry was a plug, a universal plug, it could fit most sink holes. I kept it in my pocket. James Henry was my birth object.

When each new Iremonger was born it was a family custom for them to be given something, a special object picked out by Grandmother. The Iremongers always judged an Iremonger by how he looked after his certain object, his birth object as they were called. We were to keep them with us at all times. Each was different. When I was born I was given James Henry Hayward. It was the first thing that ever I knew, my first toy and companion. It had a chain with it, two feet long, at the end of the chain there was a small hook. When I could walk and dress myself, I wore my bath plug and chain as many another person might wear his fob watch. I kept my bath plug, my James Henry Hayward, out of sight so that it was safe, in my waistcoat pocket while the chain looped out U-shaped from the pocket and the hook was attached to my middle waistcoat button. I was very fortunate in the object I had, not all birth objects were so easy as mine.

While it was true my bath plug was a thing of no monetary value, such as Aunt Onjla's diamond tiepin (that said Henrietta Nysmith), it was in no way as cumbersome as Cousin Gustrid's skillet (Mr Gurney), or even my grandmother's own marble mantelpiece (Augusta Ingrid Ernesta Hoffmann) that had kept her on the second floor all her long life. I did wonder over our birth objects. Should Aunt Loussa ever have taken up smoking had she not been given an ashtray (Little Lil) at birth? She began her habit at seven years of age. Should Uncle Aliver ever have been a doctor if he was not presented with that pair of curved forceps designed for child delivery (Percy Hotchkiss)? And then of course there was my poor melancholy Uncle Pottrick who was given a rope (Lieutenant Simpson) tied into a noose at birth; how miserable it was to see him mournfully limp through the unsteady corridors of his days. But it was deeper than even that, I think: should Aunt Urgula have been taller if she had not been given a footstool (Polly)? It was very complicated, people's relationships with their birth objects. I used to look at my own and know it fitted me perfectly, my bath plug. I couldn't say exactly why but I knew it was true. I could never have been given anything else other than my James Henry. There was only one Iremonger's birth object in the whole family that did not speak a name when I listened to it.

Poor Aunt Rosamud

And so, despite their distrust and mutterings, despite the fact that I was generally left alone, I was called for when Aunt Rosamud lost her door handle. I never liked entering the domain of Aunt Rosamud, and as a rule I should not be permitted in such an uncomfortable pasture, but it suited them that day to have me there.

Aunt Rosamud, truth be told, was old and grumpy, a bit lumpy, and quick to shout and point and pinch. She distributed charcoal biscuits to all us boys willy-nilly. She was apt to trap us upon the stairs and ask us questions about family history and if we got the answer wrong, confusing a second cousin with a third for example, then she should grow itchy and unpleasant and take out her particular door handle (Alice Higgs) and knock us upon the head with it. You. Stupid. Boy. And it would hurt. Exceedingly so. She had bruised, bumped and banged so many young heads with her particular door handle that she had given door handles a bad name and several of us might be cautious when turning such objects, bringing back such memories as they did. It was not a huge wonder then that we school fellows were held especially suspicious that day. There were many among us that should not mourn for the door handle should it never be recovered, and many of us were terrified at how active it should be if it was. But surely all of us felt some sympathy for Rosamud in her loss, never forgetting that Aunt Rosamud had lost something before.

Aunt Rosamud was supposed to marry a man I never met, some sort of a cousin called Milcrumb, but he got caught beyond the wall of the mansion in a great storm and was drowned in the heaps that surround our home.

His body was never recovered, not even his particular plant pot. And so Milcrumbless Aunt Rosamud shifted about in her unmarried rooms and hit at the world with her door handle. Until one morning the door handle was, like Milcrumb before it, not about.

Rosamud sat on a high-backed chair that morning, full of misery, and with nothing about her saying Alice Higgs at all, as if she'd been suddenly silenced. She seemed a half thing to me then. There were many cushions stuffed around her and some uncles and aunts hovering beyond the cushions. She didn't talk, which was unlike her, she only looked ahead, dolefully. The others, though, made much fuss.

'Come, Muddy, dear, we're certain to find it.'

'Take heart, Rosamud, it is not such a small thing, it shall surface soon enough.'

'Bound to, bound to.'

'Before the hour is out, I'm sure of it.'

'Look now, here is Clod, come to listen out for us.'

This latest information did not seem to cheer her especially. She looked up a little and for a small moment regarded me, with anxiety and perhaps a very little hope.

'Now, Clod,' said my Uncle Aliver, 'shall the rest of us step outside while you listen?'

'That's all right, Uncle,' I said, 'no need at all. Please don't put yourselves out.'

'I don't have a care for this,' said Uncle Timfy, the senior House Uncle, my uncle whose birth object was a whistle that said Albert Powling. Uncle Timfy blew his Albert

9

Powling so very often when he found something not right. Uncle Timfy the sneak, Uncle Timfy of the plump lips, who never grew above child size, Uncle Timfy the house spy, whose business it was to creep and creep and find disorder. 'This is wasting time,' he protested. 'The whole house must be searched and searched at once.'

'Please, Timfy,' said Aliver, 'it can do no harm. Recall how Pitter's pin was discovered.'

'A fluke, I call it, I've no time for fancies and lies.'

'Now, Clod, please, can you hear your aunt's door handle?'

I listened hard, I walked about her rooms.

'James Henry Hayward.'

'Percy Hotchkiss.'

'Albert Powling.'

'Annabel Carrew.'

'Is it here, Clod?' asked Aliver.

'I hear your forceps very clearly, Uncle, and Uncle Timfy's whistle, most particularly. I hear Aunt Pomular's tea tray right enough. But I cannot hear Aunt Rosamud's door handle.'

'You are quite sure, Clod?'

'Yes, Uncle, there is nothing here by the name Alice Higgs.'

'You are certain of it?'

'Yes, Uncle, most certain.'

'Stuff and nonsense!' snapped Uncle Timfy. 'Get the unwholesome brat out of here; you're not welcome, child, go to the schoolroom at once!'

10

'Uncle?' I asked.

'Yes, Clod,' said Aliver, 'run along then, thank you for trying. Don't tire yourself, tread carefully. We must mark this officially: date and time of loss, 9th November 1875, 09:50 hours.'

'Would you care for me to listen out about the house?' I asked.

'I won't have him snooping!' cried Timfy.

'No, thank you, Clod,' said Aliver, 'we shall take it from here.'

'The servants shall be stripped,' I heard Timfy saying as I left, 'every cupboard tipped out, everything emptied, every corner disturbed, every little thing!'

The Orphan Lucy Pennant

2

A LEATHER CAP

Beginning the narrative of the orphan Lucy Pennant,
ward of the parish of Forlichingham, London

I have thick red hair and a round face and a nose that
points upwards. My eyes are green with flecks in them,
but that's not the only place I'm dotted. There's punctuation all over me. I'm freckled and spotted and moled and
have one or two corns on my feet. My teeth are not quite
white. One tooth is crooked. I'm being honest. I shall tell
everything how it occurred and not tell lies but stay with
the actual always. I shall do my best. One of my nostrils
is slightly bigger than the other. I chew my fingernails.
Sometimes the bugs do bite and then I scratch them. My
name is Lucy Pennant. This is my story.

The first part of my life I do not remember any more with
perfect clarity. I know that my parents were hard people,
but showed kindness in their own ways. I think I was happy
enough. My father was a porter on the Filching–Lambeth

border of London in a boarding house where many families lived. We were on the Filching side but would sometimes go out into Lambeth and from there walk into London itself by way of the Old Kent Road right into it, hearing all the business of the Regent's Canal. But those in Lambeth sometimes came to us on the borders of Filching and smacked us around about and told us to keep out, to stay in Filching where we belonged, if we were ever caught out of Filching without a pass there'd be trouble.

It used to be a nice place, Filching, so they say, a long time ago, before the heaps were brought here. Forlichingham it used to be known as once upon a time, but no one from here would ever call it that, not if they wanted to be taken seriously. Just Filching, that's all. Everyone here grew up with the dirt heaps and around them and along them and in them and should serve them one way or another all our lives, either as part of the great army depositing it, or among the tribes that sort it, we're all of us in Filching one way or another serving the heaps. My mother worked in the laundry of the boarding house cleaning the clothes of so many heapworkers, scrubbing the rubbers and leathers. One day, I told myself, one day they might measure you for leathers and that would be that, you couldn't expect anything else after that, not once they'd actually measured you for leathers, or 'married' you for leathers. That was what they called it, 'married', because then you should really give your whole life to the heaps. There wouldn't be anything else for you after you'd been married. It'd be wrong to expect it.

I would walk about the building where we lived, seeing all the people, all that life. Sometimes I helped clean the different lodgings and then if I saw something that shined particularly or would easily fit in a pocket, I might find it essential. I stole a bit. I remember that part. Just a bit of food sometimes, or maybe a thimble, there was once a fob watch which later in my excitement I overwound. Its face was cracked when I got it, no matter what Father said. If ever I was caught, Father should get his belt out, but I was not caught that often. I learnt to hide these little bits of mine in my hair, I'd conceal them beneath my thick locks, under my plain bonnet, Father never found them there, he never thought to look in that red nest.

There were other children in the building, we used to play together, we went to school in Filching, and most of what we learnt there was about the Empire and Victoria and how much of the globe we were, but also we had lessons in Filching history and about the heaps and their dangers and their greatness. They told us the old story about Actoyviam Iremonger who was in charge of London heaps, of all London's rubbish brought into our district, a hundred years ago and more, back when the heaps were smaller and manageable, and that he drank too much and fell asleep for three days and so never gave the heap sifters the order to sift and so the heaps just got bigger and bigger, all the used stuff, all the filth of Londoners pouring in, and the job got huger and huger, and ever afterwards the heaps have always had the advantage of us. The Great Heap sneaked ahead and became the gross wild thing it is. Because of Actoyviam and because of gin, and how they worked in partnership. I don't think I believed a word of it, they just told us it to make us work harder, that story had a message: don't be idle or you'll drown in it. I never wanted to be married, I'd rather stay in the building with my parents and work there, and there was no reason, not then, if I worked hard, why I shouldn't.

It wasn't a bad life, all told. There was a man upstairs in one of the top rooms who never came out at all, but we would hear him wandering about. Sometimes we put our faces to the keyhole, me and my friends in the house, but we never exactly saw him. How we spooked ourselves about him and then ran downstairs laughing and screaming. But then the illness started.

It was seen first upon things, upon objects. They stopped behaving like they used to. Something solid would turn slippery, something shiny would grow hairs. Sometimes you'd look about and objects wouldn't be where you'd put them. It was a bit of a joke at first, no one entirely believing it. But then it got out of hand. You couldn't get things to do what you wanted them to, there was something up with them, they kept breaking. And then some of them, I don't know how else to say it, some of them seemed so unwell that they were shivering and sweating, and some had sores on them or spots or horrible brown stains. You could really feel that some were in pain. I can't remember it very well. Only that shortly afterwards, people started getting ill too, they stopped working, their jaws

16

wouldn't open or they wouldn't shut, or they'd grow great cracks upon them, or they'd look somehow busted, and they just stayed in a heap and wouldn't do anything. Yes, that's it. People started stopping, even as they walked down the street. They'd just stop and they couldn't be started again afterwards. And then when I came home from the schoolhouse one day there were men outside our basement room, official men with gold braid bay leaves embroidered on their collars, not the green bay leaves that most of the people I knew wore on their everyday uniforms. They wore gloves, these people, and had spray pumps, and the ones that went into our room put on leather masks with round eye windows in them that made them look like some sort of monster. They said I couldn't go in. I kicked and shrieked hell and smashed my way through but there were Mother and Father, leant up against the wall, quite neatly, as if they were bits of furniture, no life in their faces at all and Father's ears which were always quite big anyway looked like jug handles. Just for a second, I only saw them for a second, because then other men were screaming that I must not touch, that on no account must there be any touching, and I was pulled away then. And I hadn't touched.

To see them like that. Father and Mother. I wasn't allowed to stay. They grabbed me. I didn't fight so much then. And I was taken away. They asked me if I'd touched, again and again. I said I hadn't touched, neither Mother nor Father.

I was put in a room on my own for a while. There was a hatch in the door; every now and again someone would look in, to see if I was getting ill too. Some food would appear once in a while. I banged on the door, but no one came. After a long bit, some nurses in high white hats marched in to look at me. They knocked on my head with their knuckles, they listened to my chest to see if I was going hollow. I don't know exactly how long they kept me in the room waiting, but in the end the door was opened, and men with gold bay leaves looked me up and down and nodded to each other and said, 'Not this one. For some reason, not this one.'

Some people it took, the illness. And some it didn't. I was one of the lucky ones. Perhaps, perhaps I wasn't. It depends which side you come down on. It had all happened before. Heap Fever, as it was called, came and went; this was the first bout of it since I was born.

There was a place for children like me, those made orphans by the illness. It was situated against a bit of the heap wall that was said to have been built just after Actoyviam's time, and sometimes, if there was a bad storm in the heaps, some object might lift up and dash itself upon the roof. It was a place full of snivelling and yelling, a lot of cowering and swearing went on in those soiled rooms. Every one of us it was certain should be married to the heaps when we came of age, there was no escaping the heaps from that place. And we listened to them smashing and shifting and groaning in the night and knew that, soon enough, we'd be out there in the thick of it. We were got up in very worn black dresses and pointed leather caps that was the uniform of the orphanage; the leather cap was a sign that we belonged to the heaps, that soon enough we'd be out there. Before the illness came, I'd often seen the orphans being marched through Filching in their leather caps; we were not allowed to speak to them, they were always so silent, and there were always unhappy-looking adults marching alongside them. Sometimes, one of us might whistle out to them or call to them, but there was never any answer, and now, there I was, in a leather cap myself, marked out.

There was another redheaded girl in the orphanage. She was cruel and stupid. That ruddy miss was of the opinion that there should only be the one girl with such hair in the place. We fought but no matter how I walloped her there never seemed to be an end of it. I knew given half a chance she should always come at me again, for the spite of it. She was that angry.

There then.

I think that's all right. I think it is. I find it hard to remember, always harder. We never left the orphanage once we were in it, and those old bits of our lives grew so far away and the further away they grew the less we could be sure of them. But I think I'm right. I do think so.

I can't remember what they look like any more, my own mother and father.

What else was there?

The next big thing.

A man arrived at the orphanage, particularly to see me. He said his name was Cusper Iremonger. 'An Iremonger?' I

19

asked. 'A proper?' Yes, he said, an actual one of those. He had a golden bay leaf on his collar. It's their symbol, I should probably explain, the symbol of the Iremonger business, the bay leaf to represent them, because they are powerful bailiffs among other things. This Cusper person said something about my mother's family, about how her family was related to the Iremongers a while back, a long while back. 'All right,' I said, 'so what am I then, an heiress?' He told me that I wasn't but he said there was work, should I want it, in a great mansion. By which he meant *the* great mansion.

I knew about the Iremongers of course, everyone did, everyone from Filching and all the other wheres beyond too, I suspect. They owned it pretty much. They owned the Great Heap. And they were bailiffs, had been for always, and it was said they owned all the debts of London and called on them when they had the itch for it. They were very wealthy. Odd people, cold people. Never trust an Iremonger, that's what we always said in Filching, amongst ourselves. Shouldn't say it to their faces. Lose our jobs for that. No question. I'd heard stories about their house far out in the heaps but I'd never seen it. Just a fat blot in the distance. But now I might. I was being offered employment. It was a chance for me to get away from the heapwork, to leave that leather cap behind, the only chance I was ever likely to get. I should be very glad, I said. Obliged of it. What a bit of luck. 'I shan't be married, then?' I asked.

'No,' he said, 'not to the heaps.'

'You're on,' I said.

'Please to hurry.'

He took me in a dull one-horse carriage away from the orphanage, the nag was thin and shivering, the carriage was old and bashed about. We travelled through the sorting lanes, it was a sunny day, I do remember that, and the heaps were so quiet you could barely hear them, there was blue in the sky, the haze was relatively thin. So there it is: blue in the sky, me smiling as we bumped along to Bay Leaf House, actually to Bay Leaf House itself.

'What, here?' I asked.

'Even here,' he said.

'Am I going in?'

'You are. Momentarily.'

'What a business!' I said.

We'd always talked about being inside Bay Leaf House, me and my friends, but none of us ever had. We hadn't got within a hundred yards of it, we'd be moved on pretty sharp if we did. Family only it was. All the rest, keep out. And here I was in a carriage being driven in, family too. Me an Iremonger! The gates were shut behind me and the Cusper fellow was urging me to hurry. And then we were inside the actual place, and there were offices and desks and people with paper and noises and strange pipes everywhere and clanging noises, and distant thuds. People all done up in collars and ties and all of them yellowish.

'Show us around?' I asked.

'Don't be impertinent,' he said, 'don't touch anything. Come with me.'

So I followed him down some corridor, people busy either side of us, all of them men. And then at a door that had written upon it TO FORLICHINGHAM PARK we stopped, the next door over said FROM FORLICHINGHAM PARK. Cusper rang a bell that hung above the doorframe, there was a creaking cracking sound and then he opened the door TO not FROM and we stepped inside a cupboard-sized room. He told me to hold onto the railing there. I held on, the man pulled on a rope that hung down from the ceiling, I heard a bell sound somewhere and then the cupboard-room began to move. I let out a scream, the world seemed to shift and we were moving down, down, down, I felt my heart rise into my mouth, I thought we should surely be killed, I thought we were plunging to our deaths. There was a sudden burst of light, the man had lit a small gunny-lamp, he wasn't even holding on, but smiled at me, and told me not to worry. The cupboard-room stopped with a bump, and went downwards no further.

'Where are we?' I asked.

'Under,' he said, 'deep under. You must go under to get where you are going.'

We were at a station. There were train tracks. There were signs painted against the wall saying WELCOME TO BAY LEAF HOUSE STATION and there was an arrow pointing one way which said TO GREATER LONDON and another that said TO IREMONGER PARK. The train was already there and stoked up too, steam pouring out, I was hurried along the platform past many men in dark suits and toppers looking nowhere in particular. There was a goods van at the back with baskets of things and boxes and supplies. I was pushed up inside by Cusper Iremonger; I was the only one there, only me and a lot of things.

'Sit on a basket, someone will fetch you when the train arrives. Behave yourself.'

And then he slid the door closed and a bit later I found that it was locked. I sat there a good half hour, then I saw through the wire mesh window – there was no glass – a very tall, old man, all dressed up in top hat and long black overcoat with fur collar, marching forwards, and other smaller people rushing and bowing behind him, what a size this old man was, what a grim determined look he had about him as he got on the train. I think the train must have been waiting for him because almost immediately a man in a cap came running along the platform, waving a flag, blowing a whistle, and off we shunted. I looked out of the mesh but soon enough there was nothing to see but black and more black and only black. And smells and fogs came into the goods van which wasn't sealed and as the train sped on I was dripped upon a good deal, spray coming through the mesh window, and the smell of it wasn't good. At last the train slowed down and stopped with a screeching whistle which deafened me for a while, and I looked out but could see very little until a while later, when the goods door was slid open and a woman, tall and thin in a plain dress, was saying to me, 'You're to come this way and to hurry yourself.'

That was the beginning of it. I had arrived.

The Prefect Moorcus Iremonger
(doctored daguerreotype)

3

A MEDAL (MARKED 'FOR VALOUR')

Clod Iremonger's narrative continued

My Cousin Tummis (and Moorcus)

Before I had quite reached the schoolrooms I was met by the approaching noise:

'Hilary Evelyn Ward-Jackson.'

That was the particular cry of the birth object of my cousin Tummis, and indeed he rounded the corner a second later.

'Clod, dear man,' he panted, 'so glad to have intercepted you.'

'Good morrow, old Tummis, you look fair puffed out.'

'Indeed, I do, I do, and I shall tell you why: school is abandoned for the day, on account of Aunt Rosamud. The teachers have all prodded and patted us down, emptied our pockets and poked us all aboutwards, looking, one and all, for the missing handle, and, it not being found, we've been hurried out to be in our own rooms until further notice and not to be in anyone's way whatsoever, but to holler loudly should we see Aunt Rosamud's brass headacher.'

I was very often in the company of my cousin Tummis, it was most usual for us, mucking about, chewing the fat, ruminating, cogitating, philosophising, mumbling, tumbling, peaking and troughing. My cousin Tummis was very tall and very thin. Tummis always had Hilary Evelyn Ward-Jackson about him, which was a tap, a tap that would not be out of place in a bathtub; it had a small enamel disc in the centre of its tap-wheel inscribed with an H for hot. It was a very fine object and had had a profound effect upon Tummis because the dear fellow did leak a lot and there was very often a drop of liquid snot hanging from his nose; that drop had such a long way to fall, all the length of Tummis, it must have been quite dead before it hit the ground. He was quite a sensitive fellow, Tummis was, and very concerned for a great many things. He had yellowish hair – it always looked rather uncertain as if it hadn't quite made up its mind to be hair yet and thought it might really be a cloud, of methane say, it was so very thin, you could see his skull beneath it.

Even though he was already seventeen by the time Aunt Rosamud lost her door handle, Tummis had not married. At sixteen an Iremonger should change from wearing corduroy shorts to long trousers made of grey flannel. At sixteen an Iremonger should marry a wife who has been chosen for him, an Iremonger girl, not a sister or first cousin but certainly a relation of some sort. At sixteen an Iremonger should put away all school things and commence proper work at home in one of the departments in the house, or, if we were particularly gifted, to be employed beyond the dirtheaps in London itself, at least in the borough of Forlichingham, which we could sometimes see in the distance from the windows higher up in the house. It was certainly unlikely that I should be allowed to work in Forlichingham on account of my being ill from a young age, and poor Tummis was being held back from marrying Ormily and from grey-flannel trousers; he was not thought ready.

Tummis loved animals, he loved all the animals that were so numerous about the house, cockroach or rat or bat or cat or blat, and he collected them, he brought them into his rooms, and whenever he had collected too large a family Cousin Moorcus should come to his room and disperse them, often smiting one or two or ten in the process. This may have been the cause of his still wearing corduroy shorts a good year longer than was usual and his knees, still on display, were rather knobbly and embarrassed and they so longed, longed for grey flannel that he kept his hands upon them whenever he could, as if to cover them up, but which actually made them appear all the more naked with those big hands (something like boiled tripe) about them. I suppose Cousin Tummis was rather an anxious creature altogether.

'No school then,' I cried to Tummis. 'A day of rest!'

'Yes, but, Clod, man, listen up a moment; I should not go home if I were you.'

'It may be two rooms unkempt and unclean to you, but to me, it's a palace.'

'It's not that, Clod.'

'Shall we go to your menagerie, then, to caw and shriek with it, old drip?'

'It's Moorcus, Clod.'

'Oh,' I said, 'Moorcus, is it?'

Cousin Moorcus, school prefect, my first cousin, the biggest and most handsome of the Iremonger boys, had about him a medal with ribbon that said FOR VALOUR which he wore most unusually out on permanent display. This was the only particular object that had never spoken to me, not a whisper, not a sound; it was most stubbornly silent. But this was a relatively recent phenomenon, just six months ago Moorcus had kept his birth object hidden about his person, and I had often heard it groaning the words 'Rowland Collis.' But suddenly, half a year since, Moorcus sported a medal upon his chest, declared this his birth object, and had many locks put upon the door of his apartment. And after that I never heard Rowland Collis no more.

'Cousin Moorcus,' repeated Tummis, and held up his hands which were bloody about the knuckles.

28

'What has he done?'

'Not much at all this time, as you see,' said Tummis, casually examining his small wounds. 'He was busy enough though, he's been denting top hats and banging heads, right in front of the masters, and they did nothing to stop him.'

'They never do, Tummis, they are frightened of him.'

'He was a little cruel to a couple of the younger cousins, but, and this is most, he was especially disappointed not to search you. He made comments about it, in particular terms not exactly pleasant, that he would, you know, turn you inside out. He remembers, and retold the history, of finding you after poor Uncle Pitter's pin. Well, dear plug, that's the story, a penny dreadful to be sure; but don't go home, lose yourself a bit, be quiet until evensong and then maybe he shall have forgotten.'

'Thank you, Tummis,' I said, shaking his hand and apologising as the dear fellow winced, 'ever so.'

'I shall head to my home, which will be underpopulated without you. But to my fur beetles and fireblats, to my mealworm beetles and my cockroaches, to my woodlouses and my clothes moths and my phorids, my darkling beetles and flesh flies, my thrips and sowbugs and my pill bugs and midges and grainbugs and earwigs and bot flies and of course to my gull, I shall pass your salutations.'

'Thank you, my dear tap, I'll find you later.'

'Off you go then, plug,' he said, 'and be obscure about it.'

Grandfather

So into higher corridors I went, but not quite so high as the attics where the ceilings are thick with disease-carrying bats, kicking up the dust which was deep here and there, watching the progress of a snail or two in damp back rooms, stepping over the slugs, listening out for the rats, hoping to avoid Cousin Moorcus. Cousin Moorcus had broken arms and legs on five different occasions; it was not uncommon for an Iremonger cousin to end up in the Infirmary after Moorcus had been about him. Indeed it was most regular. I was particularly eager, profoundly eager, to avoid him.

I had so often been through the great hulk house, chamber by chamber, in the regions where I was permitted, and through some that I was not, up and down, through long winding staircases, listening to its talking objects, that I knew quite well where I might hide myself. Our home, Heap House, as we called it, was not an original structure; it was built up of other former places. When Grandfather bought up new places, he should often have the buildings dismantled, brought across the heaps, reassembled once more, only this time at a different address, clamped, and bolted, braced and steel-girdled onto our home. Out here deep in the heaplands we had London roofs and turrets, ballrooms and kitchens, outhouses and stairways and many, many chimneys. Huge carts had pulled great masses across the heaps – back when the heaps were still navigable. So

I felt, in my way, I was discovering London by walking into those transplanted bits. I sought out London by walking in London rooms, by reading books, by touching places Londoners had actually been. I looked for names scratched on walls and furniture, for people did like to write their names, they liked to leave a proof of themselves, they were all wonderful to me, those names, clues of a greater world. I loved to wander through all those bits of London, there must be many gaps then, over there. It must be something similar, I have often thought, to when a person loses a tooth, only London must have so very many teeth you might not be able to tell. There were small shacks and pieces of palaces in our heap home. It was an enormous building, our place, made up of many other ones. But the original structure, hard to find now, had been in our family for several centuries.

My family lived only with its own kind, Iremongers with Iremongers, full-blooded Iremongers, all steely and grim and poker-faced. There were so many cousins and uncles and aunts, great aunts and great uncles, hordes of us, Iremongers of every age and shape, all connected by blood. And to keep those plentiful people fed and dressed a whole army of servants was needed. These servants were Iremongers too, but they were part-Iremonger, Iremongers of a lesser hue: one of their parents somewhere down the line married someone un-Iremonger and each generation afterwards kept on doing just that. I cannot say exactly how many servants there were, there were many that worked downstairs in the deep honeycomb of the cellars or out in the heaps who never came upstairs.

I was up in a high corridor, much of it taken from a former caulking factory of Tilbury, when the house suddenly shuddered. I held onto the wall waiting for it to finish. There followed a loud and horrible scream. And that was quite usual. It was the scream of Grandfather's steam engine.

The engine travelled from Heap House into London every morning, and came back at night, with the same horrible screaming and thumping that shook the entire house. The train stopped in the cellar and Grandfather was taken up into the house by a lift pulled by unhappy mules that lived down there in the darkness and never came up. There was a tunnel that ran from the house under the dirtheaps into the distant city.

My grandfather, Umbitt Iremonger, his birth object a silver cuspidor, a personal one, for Grandfather to aim his very own sputum into, ruled over us all. Grandfather came in and went out into the city to do his great service, and when he was out there was a sort of relief in the house, the longer the day wore on the more anxious we would become waiting for the house to scream again, waiting for the noise of his returning locomotive.

The scream fading, I went onwards again. I wandered through the leaking corridors, turning into small cubicles, smaller rooms brought in from here and from there. I often visited these hints of a greater world, for all I had ever known was Heap House. I had never been anywhere else, just Heap House and the heaps themselves.

I thought I should be safe up there, safe and alone, safe with the insects busy about, the rodents in the walls, and the odd maggoty seagull that had somehow found its way into the house but not back out. But up there, in a room originally belonging to a tobacconist's from Hackney, I heard a hurried whispering that meant I was not alone.

'Thomas Knapp.'

And then there was a sudden light, a lamp came into view and was shone in my face.

I Am Hunted

'What are you doing there? Who is it? Come out into the light.'

Ingus Briggs, the underbutler, a distant relative of some sort, his birth object a tortoiseshell shoehorn (Thomas Knapp), was suddenly beside me. Mister Briggs had a great collection of pincushions in his sitting room (a girl he once loved had a pincushion birth object). He once showed me his pincushion collection while in a sociability fit, and even begged me to push pins into them, an activity which I believe he did every evening when his duties were finished. He pushed hundreds of pins and needles into materials of varying compliance and this gave him great comfort. Briggs was a small, shiny person; I think in his youth he must have been very highly polished by his parents. I think those old Briggses must have rubbed him night and day with brass rub or silver shine until they could see their own loving reflection in him.

'What are you doing, Master Clod?' he asked.

'I am wandering the house,' I admitted.

'Do not let them catch you at it. For they do not like it, they will not have it.'

'Thank you, Briggs, I will try. But you do not mind, do you?'

'I mind the candles and gas lamps, I mind the carpets and brooms and shoeblacks, I mind things, things I mind. Not people. People under me, surely. But never do I mind them that are above me, not for me to mind them above, not done, not done at all ever. Have you seen your Aunt Rosamud's door handle?'

'No, I am sorry, Briggs, I have not.'

'It is a great distress.'

'Briggs?' I asked. 'Have you seen Cousin Moorcus?'

'Not long past he was on your landing, and since he has come into contact with Master Tummis.'

'Oh, poor Tummis. Where are they now?'

'I couldn't say, but you might be wise not to enter Marble Hall, or the refectory, you might not approach the morning room, or even yet any of the downstairs parlours. I should, in a general way, keep yourself more silent. I heard someone walking up here, footsteps above me, that was why I came up. Master Moorcus is very certainly looking out for you,

Master Clod. Whilst others seek your aunt's door handle, he looks for you in the larger cupboards, under stairs. I should, in a general way, move more quietly.'

'Thank you, Briggs, thanks awfully.'

'I never said a word,' said Briggs as he left.

The View From Our Windows

I moved along, I kept in unpopular places, listing rooms with bubbled or peeling wallpaper. In a former barber's shop, bolted to the third floor, originally from Peckham Rye, a room that I had not been in for several months, and where I thought I should be quite safe from Moorcus, I stood before a window thick with grime, but with a small crack in it, through which the outside whistled in, and, when I put my eye to the slight hole, there was a small view to be had of the outside of what lay beyond our home, of the heaplands in all their majesty. The heaps were calm that day and peaceful, it should have been a perfect day for sorting had not the loss of Aunt's door handle kept everyone inside.

But with Aunt's great loss the heaps went unpicked. I should have liked to go out into them. I should like to have got myself all togged up and set forth with Tummis beside me. We were all of us Iremonger children to be very well dressed when we went out. We wore new boiled collars and starched shirts, and perfectly tied black bows, our suits were cleaned and pressed, our top hats were dusted, and white twill gloves were placed upon our hands by a servant. We must always be properly dressed to go out into the heaps, it was a house rule, it was important to show respect to the heaps, for the heaps, as we were endlessly reminded, had made us what we were. And what we found out there we must hand over to our seniors who accepted these objects and put them in piles to be taken back to the city and resold, or to be crushed or boiled down or stripped bare and made into something else. So many things were to be used again. For as long as the weather allowed it we were to sort in the heaps, but not to go too far, for if we waded out too far for safety then we might not get back in time if the wind got up, or some terrible gas escaped from down below. Many cousins had been lost deep in the heaps, my senior Cousin Rippit among them. He was Grandfather's favourite, Rippit was, he went out one day into the heaps with his body servant and he never came back. And many more servants besides had been lost out there, taken by surprise by some wave of objects crushing down upon them, or having climbed too high and plunging down deep, deep, deep. It was a wonderful danger. How I should have loved to wade further, to be out of my depth, to feel the heap deep beneath me, cold and enormous. Out in the heaps, there were such *things*, things from far beyond our home, things from other lives. So we sifted and found for the family and brought things back, lugged the bits and pieces over to the Iremonger walls, and took them inside for salvage. Woe betide the Iremonger child that came back clean from a morning or afternoon spent out in the heaps. Our clothes were most carefully inspected at the end of a sifting day, our gloves must be black, our shirts thick with grime, our top hats dented or ripped, but not missing, our knees bruised and bloody, and our snot full of dirt. If we were in the least clean or unscuffed we were beaten.

Only on the very stillest days was I allowed out to exercise in the heaps, with wadding stuffed up my ears and with a scarf wrapped around my head like a big bandage even if it was hot summer outside and the heap haze was impenetrable. So I stood there that day of the lost door handle, my face at the cracked window, wondering in my fancy about all those other people a huge dustheap away, wondering if I could somehow get word to the city beyond, to Forlichingham, to London, and imagining that there was someone beyond of all those people, someone who might like the look of me.

'Is there,' I whispered, 'anyone there? Who are you? What do you look like?'

And then reflected in the glass came a face, and with it was a smile and with it were the words, 'Got you, scabrat!'

My Cousin Moorcus.

The Heap House Serving Girl Lucy Pennant

4

A SEALED BOX OF SAFETY
MATCHES

Lucy Pennant's narrative continued

The stench of the place. It stank so much way out in the dirtheaps it was as if you were always crowded over, the smell of it was so big and so shocking it felt like something solid, something you could touch and hold, was creeping about you, sweating on you, breathing hard on you. Back in Filching I had seen new people arriving, foreigners and such, coughing and weeping at the smell, a smell that I being a native didn't take much notice of, and I should laugh at those complaining greenhorns, thinking them very delicate and weedy. But now, here was I far out, coughing and wincing, and the woman looking at me how I looked at Filching foreigners.

'What a pong, however do you live with it?'

'No talking, hurry yourself.'

I followed her out from the rail line inside some other

sort of station which at first felt darker yet than the tunnel, but then there was someone waving a lamp and I began to make out six sweating donkeys heaving on a treadmill, a man in livery whipping the beasts so that they might pull harder. From there we moved upstairs into a vast chamber as big as a church and I supposed that now we must be inside the mansion itself at the bottom of it, full of clanging and shouting, and everyone there wore white, or something approaching white, and steam rose up from many different places. This was one of the kitchens, the evening meal was being prepared and all was great action. I was marshalled beyond, still reverberating from the strange bumpy journey and the shrieking whistle, so that though my aching head might have realised the journey was over and we had arrived, my body was still trundling along. I followed the thin figure out of the steaming chamber up more stairs and into a study of some sort with a desk and a pleasant armchair with a flowery pattern. Seated in the chair was a lady, quite handsome, who smiled at me as I came in.

'I am Mrs Piggott,' said the woman, 'the housekeeper here.'

Mrs Piggott's hair was done up at the back in a very neat tight little bun, everything about her was tidy, but her teeth, when she opened her mouth I saw her teeth were worn almost to nothing.

'Do you know where you are?' she asked.

'The man who came for me said Forlichingham Park.'

'It is, child, though here we call it Heap House. There's nowhere else for miles around, should you travel out beyond the gates you'd get very lost and it would be devil hard to find you. We are in the dumps, dear, far out in the waste dumps. There's no map that has this place on it. We're quite sealed off.'

'Can I sit? I'm a bit wobbly,' I said, 'that train, the smell out there . . .'

'Sick it up then, poor dear, whatever it is. Get out of you all that's not from here, best if you do. For now, young lady, you are from here. Keep standing though. You may not sit.'

'Is there a window?' I said. 'I want to look out of a window.'

'No windows down here, only upstairs. Though it is true candles and gas must be lit day and night, even there. You'll get the hang of it soon enough.'

She tenderly laid a hand on my cheek. She smelt of lavender. Some other servants came into the room then, women all of them and in plain dark uniform.

'Thank you, Iremongers,' said Mrs Piggott.

'Thank *you*, Mrs Piggott,' they all said.

'In this house,' Mrs Piggott said, smiling at me, but with a certain sadness in her eyes, 'you shall be called Iremonger, you mustn't think anything of it, it's just our way, it is the custom here, you understand, and I am not the maker of customs. You shall be called Iremonger like everyone else, only I and Mr Sturridge the butler and Mr Briggs the

41

underbutler and Mr Smith the lock and Mr and Mrs Groom the cooks have their names, for we have high positions and they have need, those upstairs, to summon us by our names, but everyone else is just and only Iremonger. There now, do you understand, Iremonger?'

'My name is Lucy Pennant,' I said.

'No. You are not being quick, my dear. It hurts, I know it hurts, but we are a family here, and not without our kindnesses. It will seem strange for a little while, but then, soon enough, it shan't any more, dear Iremonger.'

'Lucy Pennant,' I said.

'No!' she said now with a little more force though trying to keep her smile. 'That person is not to be mentioned . . . we'll call you Iremonger. Iremonger is what you are now. You should not want me to be unhappy, Iremonger, should you? I am quite a personage, when unhappy I am a spirit, a force, a character. You should not want that, should you?'

'No, I shouldn't, but . . .'

'No, Mrs Piggott,' she said.

'No, Mrs Piggott,' I repeated.

'Very good then. Your duties shall be explained to you. What sort of an Iremonger are you, I wonder? What do you have to recommend you? Whatever you have shall not surprise me. I have seen everything. We have Iremongers here who try to claim attention in all the most foolish of ways; there are Iremongers of mine who don't walk, and Iremongers who don't see, and Iremongers who can't

42

hear, we have Iremongers that say they talk to ghosts, and Iremongers who predict things, Iremongers who climb up chimney flues, we have Iremongers who never stop sleeping, and Iremongers who do not go to sleep. We have short Iremongers and long Iremongers, we have Iremongers that laugh and Iremongers that don't, we have Iremongers, we certainly do, all sorts. All here. And now we have you. And that's very nice, isn't it? And we'll soon get to know you, and you to know us. Well then, and there you are near the bottom, and higher up am I, and what sort of Iremonger am I? I'm Claar Piggott, full Iremonger several generations back, but still holding liquid of that inextinguishable spirit. Claar, but you must refer to me as Mrs Piggott.'

She put her own dry finger to my lips.

'Now then,' she said, 'empty your pockets. There are to be no things here, none whatsoever, it is an uncluttered haven down here.'

I stood still, dumbfounded, as the various servants came at me as if all of one mind and delved in and out of my pockets in a matter of seconds. I tried to push them away but there were so many of them.

'Is that all?' asked Piggott.

The women nodded, and all looked very disappointed.

'It's not much, is it? A handkerchief, a pencil, a comb.'

'I wasn't allowed to collect my things,' I said in defence of those few bits I'd helped myself to at the orphanage, 'they never let me back home. Said they burnt everything.'

43

'I shall take these now,' said Mrs Piggott.

'They're mine,' I said.

'And they shall be looked after, my dear.'

'That's theft,' I said.

'Calm please. Now it is time for your medicine.'

'My what?'

'You shall be inoculated, child. Everyone out here has been inoculated, it is to keep you well. It is to stop you from catching any sickness, there are many maladies, you know, to be picked up from the heaps. Iremonger, if you will,' said Mrs Piggott to one of the servants who came forward with some sort of metal tube with a point to it.

'Roll up your sleeve,' said Mrs Piggott.

'Why should I?'

'It is for your own good,' she said, 'everyone here must have it.'

'What is that thing?' I asked her. 'Whatever shall you do with it?'

'It is, child,' she said, 'a very advanced piece of business, a thing of great scholarship, very modern, it is a brass oil gun syringe with leather washer. Upstairs of course, theirs is of pewter and with a fruitwood handle. It shall pump some physic into your arm.'

'I don't like the look of it.'

'Nor does anyone very much, but you should like the look of yourself even less with weeping sores and swollen limbs I dare say. Come now.'

'I don't think I will.'

'Hold her,' said Mrs Piggott very calmly, and two Iremongers took hold.

'Let me go! I'll take my chances with any sicknesses if it's all the same to you. I never got ill like Mother and Father, I never . . .' but before I could tell them Mrs Piggott had come at me with that brass thing and she'd pressed it against my skin, and something sharp had gone right into me. 'Ow!'

'What a fuss you make,' said Mrs Piggott, returning the brass thing to the servant.

'That hurt!'

'It is all over,' she said, dabbing at the drop of blood upon my arm with a bit of wadding.

'I didn't like that.'

'Never mind now,' she said, busy wiping the wadding on something upon her desk.

'You stabbed at me!'

'Now then, your birth object.'

'My *what*?'

'Your birth object, poor ignorant of new Iremongers, has been selected for you I have it here. There, you may hold it a moment.'

She took up a kidney-shaped dish from her desk, laying in it was a box of matches, it was an ordinary box of matches such as I've seen many times before. There was a band of paper glued around the box to keep the drawer sealed. Written on the paper were the words SEALED FOR YOUR CONVENIENCE. There was a smudge upon

45

it, a reddish-brownish smear on the cardboard, and one of the corners, I noticed, was missing a little bit. It looked like it had been snipped off neatly with scissors, but not making enough hole to see into the box. I shook the box, the matches inside rattled, that hole was not big enough for any of them to fall out. I suddenly felt exhausted. Just then, all of a sudden. I thought I should faint.

'I don't feel so well.'

'That is quite usual.'

'I feel a bit sick.'

'Not to worry, child, you are liable to feel a little strange for a day or two. Your arm might ache.'

'Because of what you did to it,' I said.

'The aching is nothing to be concerned about, it means the medicine is working. Well then, enough, my dear?' Mrs Piggott asked.

'Enough what?'

'I think that's enough time spent together for now; you may see it again, if your behaviour is up to the mark, in a few days' time and thereafter once a week.'

'To see this matchbox?'

'Yes, indeed. But only if you are very good.'

'Why should I want to see it?'

'You will, you will. That matchbox has been chosen particularly for you. It represents you perfectly.'

'Who chose it?'

'Upstairs chose it. My lady chose it. Ommaball Oliff

Iremonger herself. It is just for you; we all have our birth objects. Each is perfectly selected to describe us exactly.'

'Whoever chose it never met me,' I said. 'It's all madness!'

'How she strikes like a match. She is such a deep one, my lady is.'

'It's all nonsense,' I said.

'Now then, give it to me,' said Mrs Piggott. 'Hand it over please.'

'Take it for all I care,' I said and gave her the matchbox, dropping it back in the bowl.

'And now,' said Mrs Piggott, 'it *shall* be sealed for your convenience. It's going somewhere very safe. Mrs Smith!'

In came the strange sight that was Mrs Smith.

She was a big, flat-faced woman, with flushed cheeks. There were keys clanking and clinking all about her, around her large waist was a thick belt from which hung many rings from which hung many keys. At first impression it seemed she was wearing a skirt over her dress, a strange jangling metal skirt, but it was all the keys of Iremonger Park; she looked after them, every one. Keys hung from her hips and from a great necklace, and several smaller keys she kept in the loops of her earrings.

'Mrs Smith,' said Mrs Piggott to the clanking golem before her, 'the new Iremonger here wishes her birth object to be locked away safely, if you please.'

Without pause, Mrs Smith drew out a particular key from one of the many key branches and walked to the back of Mrs Piggott's office which was entirely made up

47

of many drawers of varying sizes, each with a lock to it, and each with an identical brass knob and a small brass bell suspended by a stiff wire which sounded whenever the drawer was touched. And beside all these drawers, like a warder staring at convicts, loomed a metal safe as tall as the ceiling and as wide as Mrs Smith. Mrs Smith unlocked a drawer, its little bell rang, she pulled it open and took from inside it a small wooden toy train, which she handed without expression to Mrs Piggott.

'Ah, yes,' said Mrs Piggott, 'that belonged to poor Iremonger, didn't it? Well, unhappy thing, she shan't be needing it now. Here, Mrs Smith.'

She handed the other woman the matchbox, it was put in the drawer and locked away, the bell of my drawer growing quiet very quick. Well, I thought, so what.

'And thus, Iremonger, all is concluded. I bid you good luck. Welcome to Heap House.'

Solly Smith the Lock of Heap House

5

A COMB CUT BIT KEY 1⅝'

A statement by Solly Smith, Lock Keeper,
Forlichingham Park, London, discovered after her
death, locked in a cellar strongroom inside a safebox,
within an iron box, padlocked

Count of Myself

I Solly. Solly the lock.

Very private. All locked up. I don't say nothing. I keep
it in. Locked. Too many words. If you ask me. Far too
many. Lock 'em up. Never tell no one. Solly don't let a
word out. All those secrets. Keeping them private. I locked
myself up years ago, haven't let myself out. Was unlocked
once. That was nice, lovely yes, name of William Hobbin.
Died soon after, dry cholera, locked away for ever from
me, vault.

I did the locks with Father. Father did locks. Father got
the poison at last, lead in his blood, locking him away

from me too. Then not a word ever, all shut up. No words from me. I shut up. Then Piggott comes at last. She gives me the keys, she turns the movement in me, she makes the play with oil, gains the strike, she looks at my face as if to say, 'A brass escutcheon, let's polish that up.' She gives me keys. Never to be locked out ever again. Nothing locked from me.

Upstairs. Infirmary. Objects. Locked up. I seen them! They're alive, ain't they? Moving they were. But locked up, locked alive. I shan't tell, keep it safe. But I'll burst with it. Things, things are breathing! Won't keep still. Won't tell anyone. Master Moorcus needed five new steel rim locks. Mustn't tell anyone, he says. Why so many? Why so much? And he wanted all the keys to them, none for me. But I keep extra, just in case. And when he was at his schooling. I looked, I gandered. Something in there, something in there I didn't like! I heard it in Moorcus's room. Heard it moving! Mustn't tell, mustn't tell. But must tell someone, must tell someone, must tell or burst. So I made a decision, decision to tell this paper, only this paper and then lock it up good. Lock it in Piggott room, in safe there, the tall one what says CHATWOOD'S DOUBLE PATENT BOLTON, lock it in there. The safe shall know the secret. Big safe. Bolton. Bolt. That safe looks at me. Knows, it does.

Lock it, lock it.

Safe.

Solly.

The Extinct Ayris and Puntias Iremonger

6

A KEY TO A PIANOFORTE
AND A CHALKBOARD RUBBER

Clod Iremonger's narrative continued

The Silent One

Cousin Moorcus had me by the ear.

'I haven't done anything, Moorcus; you should let me go.'

'It's Mr Moorcus to you, maggot.'

'You've no right.'

'I've every right. Keep your foul gob shut.'

'I haven't got the door handle.'

'Whoever said you had? Straighten up, toerag,' he said and as he said it he punched me in the stomach.

'Straighten up, I said!'

When I tried to stand up he kicked me.

'Can you not keep upright, Clod? Are you not capable?' He kicked.

'Why?' I gasped.

'For being Clod, what else? And that's enough all on its own.'

I lay on the floor. Moorcus bent over me, he quickly put his hand in my waistcoat pocket, pulled something out.

'James Henry Hayward.'

'No, Moorcus, please!'

'Get up,' he said, 'come on, you mutt, let us run!'

He had hold of James Henry, he pulled the chain.

'No, Moorcus, it's expressly against house rules!'

'Don't talk to me of rules, I'll make the rules with you, dog, up, up! Get up!'

He pulled me by my plug and I ran along beside him, hurrying to keep up, lest some damage occur to my poor plug.

'Come, mongrel pup, trot, trot!'

He marched faster so I should run beside him, fretting so. He took me back down the stairs and then into the prefects' common room where the promoted Iremonger boys hung about. Stunly and Duvit were there, hair slicked back, smoking clay pipes, drinking sherry and putting on the usual show of adulthood and prosperity.

'Look what I found,' said Moorcus and only then did he let go of my plug, dropping it suddenly to the ground as if it were something repellent. I cupped James Henry quickly in my hands, and hid it away back in my pocket.

'Oh God, Moorcus, must you really bring that thing in

here?' sighed Stunly. It was Stunly's general condition to sound bored and weary.

'No doubt he'll start snivelling and hearing things and we shall have to listen to him spout nonsense,' said Duvit, taking hold of me by an ear. 'Admit it, Clod, you're batty and broken. Why don't you just get yourself lost in the heaps, do us all a favour and drown yourself out there, why not set off now? Clod, answer me once and for all, what's the use of you?'

'I've a task for the weird thing,' said Moorcus, 'it's inspection tomorrow.'

'Tomorrow,' said Stunly, 'when was that announced?'

'The Little Uncle just declared it.' He meant Uncle Timfy. 'Part of the shake-up about Rosamud's bloody door handle. So the weird thing here, this odd bit, can polish our objects for us, can't you?'

'Oh, no, please, Moorcus. Not that.'

'Mr Moorcus.'

'Please, Mr Moorcus. I'd rather do your shoes.'

'I don't care what you'd rather anything, Clod, get cleaning, and stop talking. We don't wish to hear you.'

And so I was given their birth objects to clean for inspection. Touching someone else's birth object is a very discomforting thing, it never seemed right, it's all together too personal. I sat at a table and with varnish cleaned Duvit's wooden doorstop which said to me in a croaked voice Muriel Binton and Stunly's fine folding pocket rule (Julius John Middleton) and last of all Moorcus's medal marked FOR VALOUR with its red and yellow striped ribbon which never said a word to me unlike the doorstop and the pocket rule, and despite its shine and swank it always seemed a very poor, characterless thing. It frightened me more than a little, this silent thing, I never wanted to be near it. It made no sound. It seemed to me utterly dead, as if I were touching a corpse. They kept me at it until the train came screaming back, and that, as always, got everyone nervous.

'What do we think?' asked Moorcus. 'Shall we let the foul thing go?'

Duvit retrieved his doorstop and put it back into his inside jacket pocket where it usually lived. Stunly took his rule, and snapped it open and shut a few times,

'Thank you, Clod,' he said, 'good work,' and went back to his book.

'Cut along then,' said Moorcus, 'before I change my mind. Say "thank you".'

'Thank you,' I mumbled.

'Thank you, Mr Moorcus,' said Moorcus.

'Oh God, Moorcus, give it a rest will you,' said Stunly, and I blessed him a little for it. 'Let the monstrosity go. Can we not have a little peace?'

'One thing more, Clodfreak, there's something else the Little Uncle told me, something for me to pass on,' said Moorcus, grinning. 'Just a small thing, barely worth the mention: it's your Sitting tomorrow.'

'My Sitting!' I cried. 'Are you sure?'

'Yes, dishcloth, it is announced.'

'You're not just saying that to be cruel?'

'Get out.'

'Really, Moorcus, are you telling the truth?'

'Get out.'

'Run along, Clod,' said Stunly, sighing, 'and think of Pinalippy.'

'No!' I cried, because of the Sitting and because Moorcus had just kicked me hard in the rump.

'I shall murder you one day, Clod,' said Moorcus, 'and I shall enjoy it. Yes, I really think I shall.'

Oh, Our Cousins on the Other Side

I ran from the common room as fast as I could, round the corner and far from the silent medal, spitting and cursing and wiping my hands on the wallpaper, on anything, not satisfied until I was at a sink and with a jug of water and scrubbing my hands until they hurt. But that shouldn't wash the memory of it away. And worse even than that was the thought of my Sitting. Of the Iremonger cousin called Pinalippy.

Cousin Pinalippy was much taller than me. She had a little dark hair on her top lip. There was a voice that came out from Cousin Pinalippy's pocket which said 'Gloria Emma Smart' but I had no idea what Gloria Emma looked like. Cousin Pinalippy could thump and pinch. She had a particular entertainment which was to go up to some young Iremonger and, opening his black jacket, seize a pinch-hold of shirt exactly where the nipple was, and twist it; this was uncommonly painful. It was this person, this tweaker of boys' breasts, who I was to wed on the unhappy birthday when I moved from corduroy shorts to full-length black trousers. It was this same Pinalippy who I was to be shut up in a room with the next day, for my Sitting. It was family law that, some months before a marriage, sometime during the male Iremonger's sixteenth year, the betrothed were to be left in a room together, no one else would be there, only him, only her. Me and my James Henry, Pinalippy and her Gloria Emma.

I did not know what Cousin Pinalippy's birth object was because Iremonger boys and Iremonger girls were taught and lived separately. We did not dine in the same room, we saw each other only out in the heaps. We did not know each other's birth objects but always there were attempts to discover them, to reveal who the cousin really was. Sometimes it was obvious: poor Cousin Foy had been given a ten pound lead weight at birth (Sal), so she never moved very fast, for she must always carry her weight with her, and once Cousin Bornobby managed to tug out the hot-water bottle cover (Amy Aiken) from poor sickly Cousin Theeby to her absolute distress and shame. For ever afterwards she was always known, as if Bornobby

60

had taken every bit of clothing from her, her privacy gone for ever. He was given such a thrashing for that. Afterwards, Cousin Pool, who was to marry Theeby – Pool had a foot pump (Mark Seedly) – felt that there was nothing for him to look forward to any more, that his life was in ruins, because Theeby had been so compromised.

On the day of the Sitting the betrothed are to show each other their birth objects. The thought of seeing Gloria Emma Utting filled me with certain dread. So to Tummis I went for a shoulder to lean on, but when I got there I discovered he needed comforting of his own. I found Tummis, moist about the nose and eyes, in his room. Moorcus had been there before me and all his beloved creatures were gone. Tummis had a roach in his lap.

'They missed Lintel here,' he said, 'and that's something.'

They had missed Lintel, but every other creature had been dispersed or smitten. There were a few telltale smearings on the floor, but most of all Wateringcan, Tummis's precious seagull, a black-legged kittiwake to be specific, had escaped out of the room and was missing somewhere about the house.

'Oh, my Wateringcan!' Tummis groaned.

Poor Tummis did try to be more Iremonger, but he found it monstrous hard. Tummis could not stop himself, a dead rat was a dead friend to him. He preferred the company of animals to Iremongers, and loved the house very much, especially at night when he might observe the wildlife. He named all his cockroaches and petted them, and was very fond of his second family. Once, a few seasons ago, Tummis had acquired, after long saving his pocket money, an ostrich egg, an egg which he wrote for and had delivered in a special wooden crate from near London where a man kept such huge fauna. He treasured that egg, and tried very hard to hatch it, keeping it warm and safe. But one day, when Tummis was away from his room, it is supposed Moorcus came in there and smashed the egg. When Tummis returned there was nothing there but eggshell. Some of my relatives told stories that the ostrich egg had not been smashed by Moorcus, but that it had in fact hatched of its own accord and let itself out, thumping away into household myth. They said the noises in the night were made by Tummis's errant ostrich. But I did not believe one animal could make all those sounds. For myself, I was certain that it was Moorcus who did for Tummis's ostrich, and now Wateringcan was lost alongside it and should join the great list of Tummis's missing.

Out in the heaps I had observed Tummis standing up to his shins, cooing at the seagulls and pretending to glide like them by moving his arms and flapping a little; often he brought the gulls crumbs and buns. But mostly, even above all those animals, even above his lost ostrich, it was Ormily who Tummis he loved.

Cousin Ormily was small and sweet and shy, she was

62

quite quiet and unassuming, her hair was so blonde it was almost white and she had white eyebrows, and she was very fond of Tummis. It was all very odd, this Iremonger love match, no one knew what to do with it. Ormily's birth object, Tummis told me, was a watering can. She had told him so herself, and what greater proof of her love could there be than that? Tummis had named his seagull after Ormily's birth object, calling it Wateringcan.

'Sometimes, I do think I shall die in corduroy shorts,' he said, 'and never be with her. I was going to see her, very quickly tonight, before Evensong. She was to wait for me in the chest of the Grand Grandfather. But now, how can I tell her that Wateringcan got out? She'll think I don't care.'

He was so miserable, something had to be done.

'Tummis,' I said, 'go and see her. I'll keep watch for you if you like.'

'Really, Clod? You'd do that?'

'You will not be disturbed.'

'Oh, quick, then, and thank you, a million thanks.'

'We'll not let Moorcus ruin another thing.'

So we hurried down the marble staircase to the Grand Grandfather before the gong sounded, tiptoeing past Grandmother's porter snoozing at his desk, he who admitted or refused entrance to Grandmother's wing beyond. Towards the bottom, at the turn of the stairs, was the Grand Grandfather, a very considerable timepiece originally from a blacking factory in Tooting, with a huge face and a long body, and a door into its workings; a case large enough for two people to hide themselves inside and whisper. There waited Tummis within the clock, and I stood a little way away endlessly tying my shoelaces and doing what I could to appear innocent. A slight creak in the stair, a mumbled name from a covered object, and a light small personage appeared, saw me and was about to run away or else burst into a thousand pieces at the embarrassment of it all.

'It's all right, Ormily,' I said, 'go in, he's waiting, I'm keeping watch.'

And in she went, her cheeks a red beacon, and the door shut behind her. I crouched and waited. They shouldn't be more than a minute or two; very soon the staircase would be clacking under the weight of Iremongers all rushing for Evensong. I kept there, crouching, listening out for anyone coming, but hearing nothing at first except the small whispering of a gas lamp kept just beside the enormous tickage and this I heard at last to say in a very uncertain voice, 'Ivy Orbuthnot? Ivy Orbuthnot?'

And seeking to cheer the gas lamp, I whispered to it, 'Yes, that's quite right, as you say, Ivy Orbuthnot.'

'Ivy Orbuthnot?'

'Ivy Orbuthnot, definitely.'

But soon there were other sounds to be heard beyond the lamp. These were coming from inside the clock. It took me a little while to catch the watering can's name.

I had heard it whispering on the rare occasions I had been by Ormily, but I could never catch what it was saying, it seemed such a shy thing. Now, crouching by the clock, I heard the following, 'Hilary Evelyn Ward-Jackson.'

'Perr . . . Br . . . ate.'

'Hilary Evelyn Ward-Jackson.'

'Perdita Braithwaite.'

'Hilary Evelyn Ward-Jackson.'

Etcetera. Hilary etcetera Braithwaite. Onwards and onwards though so soon the Evensong gong must sound. A tap and a watering can in ballad together. To escape those private sounds I stepped down the last few steps of the marble staircase and into Marble Hall and there in the great hallway of Heap House, the absolute centre of the whole colossal edifice, was the enormous glass-fronted famous furniture, the Great Chest which stood on eight large carved feet shaped like a lion's. Inside upon the numerous shelves were kept the various objects of the late Iremongers. Each object had a piece of string tied around it and a paper tag on which was written someone's name, the name of the person who had once belonged to that object. Here were some of my ancestors, as seen through the thick glass of the great chest:

Idwon, inkpot
Agith, pillbox
Arfrah, washstand

Robitt-Fridick, penknife
Slibolla, fish kettle
Borrid, ewer
Naud, tweezers

When each Iremonger died their birth object was placed in the Great Chest in the hall, all of them never made a sound, I couldn't hear them, they'd stopped talking. There on the fifth shelf were my mother's and father's.

Ayris, key to a pianoforte
Puntias, chalkboard rubber

I look a little like Mother I was told, and so my presence caused distress. When I was born my mother died. My grandmother found it particularly difficult to observe me and so I did not see her for months at a time. My mother had been the favourite of the house, she was my grandparents' youngest child and their first daughter after twelve sons. I know very little about her. I know that she sang. Her voice, I have been told, was extraordinarily beautiful. Now, since my birth, there was no singing any more. Grandmother had forbidden it.

My father was not very much talked of at all. He was a quiet, peaceful man, born with a weak heart. Wrapped in cotton almost all his existence, carefully fed sugar cubes in muffled rooms, and brought out every now and then to visit my mother, for Grandfather had decided shortly after

Mother was born that she should marry little Puntias, before it was discovered he had a weak pump. He had been kept carefully until he could marry Mother, he never went out into the heaps. Two weeks after I was born, in grief at Mother's death and in joy at my birth, my father's heart stopped.

I would often go to Marble Hall and think of Mother and Father, of their objects and of all those other ones besides theirs, of all those finished people.

Standing there admiring all the dead, I had quite forgotten Tummis and Ormily and only remembered them because of the rumbling in rooms above me, people were moving upstairs, they were coming this way. The gong, the gong should sound any moment. I ran back to the lumbering timepiece, tapped on the door.

'Hilary Ward-Jackson.'

'Perdita Braithwaite.'

'It's time,' I said, 'it's time already!'

And indeed the stairs were hammering with the stirring of my relatives, jostling and crowding and swarming towards the great family chapel. They must come out, they must come out now, or they should be caught. Upstairs, just one flight above, I heard the clarion cry of Albert Powling.

'Little Uncle.' I knocked in warning. 'Little Uncle!'

And just in time, for the stairs were yelling then, the door of Grand Grandfather opened and out fled Ormily and Perdita Braithwaite and they were down the stairs in a moment, and then followed Tummis and his Hilary, banging themselves against the door as they exited and only just in time. Yes, there was Tummis transported to a dreamland, all huge smile and a redness about his mouth and the declaration, none too quiet, 'Oh, I love her!'

'Oh, shut up,' I said, 'and act unloved, for God's sake, here comes Moorcus.'

Moorcus tripped Tummis down the stairs, but he did not fall far, it was nothing very much, there was not far to fall, and all the little cousins laughed as they always did in Moorcus's presence. Tummis picked himself up. He still had a smile upon his face, love his anaesthetic. All of us gathered to our pews, all aunts of us and uncles of us, all cousins by the tens and twenties, trousered ones and bedressed ones, and the shorts people towards the front, myself amongst them, boys on the west nave and on the east the girl cousins, Ormily somewhere about them. A great gathering of crows and jackdaws and ravens. Being in the swollen chapel was like having my head in a great dinning bell, it was upsetting and I always had a terrible head fever afterwards and would go and lie down, thankful that evensong is only once a week. In such a noise I could not hear a thing.

The old Iremonger dirge, Old Broken, was sung out, and I mouthed the words along with the others,

In the spring's early blue morning
At the beginning of my days
A perfect gold was adorning
My skin was alight, ablaze,
I was hopeful then and youthful,
On the shelf I was atop,
I was happy then and useful,
When you bought me from the shop.

In the summer's lovely bright light,
I was for ever at your call
I was polished, I stood upright,
On the shelf in the front hall.
Ent'ring visitors would gasp then
At this piece you did call 'mine',
You would very quietly ask them,
Had they anything so fine?

In the autumn when the cold comes
And when the wind is wont to caw
Then a sudden urgent someone
Slammed so hard the old front door,
And I fell then and I tumbled
All the way unto the floor
I was broken then and humbled,
Never needed, never more.

It was mid-singing that I looked up a bit at my dark family mass all groaning along, and there I saw all those backs of head, all that Iremonger hair out and combed or else under bonnet, but one head was not pointed down at all, one was up and turned back and looking exactly at me. It was Cousin Pinalippy. There was not much love in that face as it stared and stared and found no approval. It turned at last but I remembered it as our family hymn persisted.

> *Watch me, keep me, please remember*
> *I am not something to be lost,*
> *In the howling dark December*
> *In the winter's rubble frost,*
> *I am useful, I am needed,*
> *Do but hear me now, I moan.*
> *My entreaties are not headed*
> *On the heap ground I've been thrown.*
>
> *Now there's nothing left to speak of,*
> *Now there's no one to say my name,*
> *Do you hear the last small creak of*
> *A thing only full of shame,*
> *A nameless and faceless no one,*
> *Lies out here upon the mound,*
> *So smashed, so trodden, so undone,*
> *Who shall ne'er again be found.*

Then the family dispersed for the night to its own corners. I waited for all to flood away, shook Tummis's hand, wished him goodnight, and at last retreated for the day, too shocked by the thought of Pinalippy and tomorrow's event to mingle more.

The Underbutler Ingus Briggs

7

A TORTOISESHELL SHOEHORN

Lucy Pennant's narrative continued

The women servants took me along a passageway and into a different room with pegs and benches. I was given new clothes, the simple black dress and plain flat shoes and white cap that they all wore. The white mob cap had a red bay leaf stitched into it. They told me I should change now. There was a little stall they showed me to, there was no door to it but a small curtain. I changed. One woman folded my old clothes and took them away. I didn't care, they belonged to the orphanage. Goodbye to that leather cap, I shall not miss you a jot. The remaining women, some of whom were girls of my age, patted me and brushed my hair, and nodded at me, purring almost, saying again and again, 'It's all right. It's all right.'

'Whoever said it wasn't?' I replied.

One of the older of the women whispered, 'How lucky!

A new relation! We're all one family here. You are at home now, you're where you're supposed to be at last. No doubt you've been other places, never mind, you're home now.'

I was told it was time for me to come and meet my family. I was ushered back into the kitchen and all the cooks and serving men and girls all came over and looked at me with considerable thoroughness, I was moved on, one after the other after the other.

'Welcome home,' each said to me.

'Ah, welcome, here she is at last, home! Home!'

'Home!'

'Home!'

And they looked so pleased to see me, and many of them were tearful and kissed me as if I really was a very dear person to them, a beloved one at last returned, that I thought all right, I don't mind a hug now and then, and soon I was hugging them back. One by one they all hugged me, young men came up and held me close to them, and some seemed to smell me. But then in all that warmth and kindness there was the sound of someone clearing his throat and all the Iremongers darted back to their various stations and I was left on my own before a very tall man with considerable eyebrows, in very smart dress clothes, black tie and tails, who ushered me towards him, and I went forward.

'I,' came a voice so low it was almost hard to make out, his noises like rumbles, 'am Mr Sturridge, the butler. I sing the song of Heap House, it is a song of order and correctness, it is the noise of right and dignity. It is the noise of these halls, these many stories, it is the sound of every chamber in this great palace which is, though undeserving, our home too. We live amongst these pillar roots, underground beneath them that move above us and are above us and that is how it should be. Heap House sticks into the ground like a mighty flagpole, and thus a part of it must be buried from sight. Our part is for ever in the deep and its only light is candle and gas lamp. We are the roots, the great roots of the plant that grows above. We dwell beneath the earth where we belong, and here we labour, each at his station. I am the keep, I am the keep-it-in-place, I am brush and dustpan, I am polish and bite. How do you do?'

I bowed to the huge man.

'Welcome. Tomorrow, Iremonger,' he said, pausing a moment before announcing, 'fireplaces.' The serving Iremongers around me bristled at that word, and several patted my shoulders in approval, and said with great encouragement, 'You work above ground, above ground!'

'Now,' said the butler.

A man stood out from behind him, I hadn't seen him before. This I would learn was the underbutler, a very greasy-looking man, who nodded at me and then rang a bell.

We were all gathered into a dining hall, there were several long tables, and one raised on a dais where Mr Sturridge sat with Mrs Piggott. Upon the tables all ready and waiting was a bowl filled with some steaming food and also two spoons at each place, one empty, the other holding a small quantity of something brownish-grey. I saw the head cooks then, Mr and Mrs Groom, shortish and pale, very similar-looking as if they were brother and sister, not man and wife. But people often grow to look like one another, I had seen that before. They were of a shape, the Groom couple, hard to tell exactly one from the other, both had breasts, both had hips, both had big hands, and were dressed in the same white clothing that marked their employ.

No one sat down, they all stood before the bowls and spoons looking at them longingly. Another bell was rung and then everyone began to chant from memory a strange little poem, or grace, in low voices, some closed their eyes, some put their hands together in prayer,

In this house
Where we live
In the love
Which we give
In the time
Where are hid
All the secrets
Of our blood.

All our organs
And our bones
All our lungs
And liver

And blood,
Thick and thinner
Thank o thank
For this dinner.

Once more a bell was rung, and now all hurriedly went
to their places and very carefully picked up their empty
spoons, and all ate the soup. It was salty and thick and
far better than the food at the orphanage which had small
chips of bone in it and once a rusted nail. But no one
touched the other, larger spoons, which were serving
spoons. As soon as the bowls were empty they were taken
away by other servants in coarse grey outfits but no one
left their places, each sat only with the filled spoon before
him, but not touching it. Then another bell was rung and
another grace chanted,

Our piping and our plumbing
Our right and our wronging
Take a spoonful of comfort
Sugar sweet and crunchful
To last us all the long nightfall.

Then they began, in so many different ways, to eat from
the other spoon. All was very quiet and concentrated as
this business was done, there were some noises of crunching,
but very small sounds. Some opened their mouths as wide
as they were able and pushed the whole spoon in, others

77

hunched over their spoon, sniffing and then carefully lapping it up with their tongues, others went at it spoon-tip first and slowly and methodically worked their way over the bowl. I lifted my spoon, I could not exactly tell what it held. It was rather grey, something thick and grimy, and had a strong smell that I couldn't quite name, but was not far from the great slap of stench I smelt when I arrived.

'What is it?' I whispered to my neighbour.

'We have it every night. It's *so* good,' she said, a stout girl with a nose that was askew.

'Yes, but I cannot tell what it is.'

'If I told you, you might think strangely of it, perhaps you should eat it first and then I should tell you. I think there was a time when I thought it a little strange, I do seem to remember that, but actually it's really quite something. Eat then, do eat.'

I raised the substance to my mouth, but my nose protested, I could not do it. 'I'm not hungry,' I said.

'Then may I have it, may I?'

'Help yourself,' I said, but then, 'if you tell me what it is.'

'We're not supposed to tell new Iremongers, they're to learn it later.'

'Then you shan't have it.' I raised the spoon to my mouth as if I was going to eat.

'*No*, wait! I'll tell you, I'll tell you.'

I lowered the spoon.

'It is,' said the girl, 'city dirt, London dirt. Collected

from dustcarts and haulers and pounded in the kitchens. One spoonful every night-time.'

'Truly,' I said, 'what is it?'

'City dirt,' said the girl, offended, 'what I told you.'

This girl, I thought, shall be no friend of mine, to bait a person who's just arrived, a person that's such easy prey, no sport in that. In any case, I wasn't going to eat that muck. Around the room I saw all those serving Iremongers licking their spoons and their lips.

A bell was rung again, and I was taken by some Iremongers to a dormitory, one of the women's dormitories. By then I was very tired and hoped that after some rest all might seem better and less strange. It was a peculiar place sure enough, filled with peculiar behaviour, well so what, I thought, people are peculiar. And people with money are at liberty to be as peculiar as they like. And so what, too, if this place was such a long way from anywhere else, people are private are they not, and people with money may be as private as they like. And so what even if it was below ground, and we lived like rabbits in a burrow, and these cellar halls and rooms were very like a warren, so what when I, tomorrow, should go up the stairways and be above the ground. And I must never forget, I told myself, that I was out of the orphanage, I had a job, the food but for that spoonful was good, I had even perhaps something of a future. I lay down, stroked my arm which did ache a bit, but it was all, I told myself, for my own good, and then very soon I was quite asleep.

I dreamt of matchboxes, of the matchbox I had been shown, I dreamt of breaking the seal, of slowly pushing the cardboard drawer open and hearing then that there was something in there, something other than matchsticks, something living, something muttering, something horrible. I woke up frightened. I don't know how long I had been sleeping, my arm was very stiff. There was whispering in the dormitory, perhaps it was the whispering that had woken me.

'She hasn't said much,' came a voice.

'But she will, she'll give it up, she'll tell us everything. The stories. The news.'

'She must give it up.'

'What a thing to keep to yourself.'

'I cannot believe she'll be so selfish.'

'She's very fresh.'

'I like her.'

'I'll like her if she tells us, not until.'

'But she does look new, doesn't she? Very new.'

'So, so fresh.'

'But she's asleep. Totally sleeping. Out and out, we shan't get nothing tonight.'

'So then, what do we do?'

'Tell some history or other.'

'Piggott's definitely sleeping?'

'Think so.'

'Then I'll be Grice. My name is Grice W—'

'You were Grice Wivvin last week.'

'It's not her turn, it's mine, and I don't want to be Grice, I want to be Helun Parsinn. My name is Helun and I was born –'

'No! Not you and not Helun, it's me and I'm going to be Oldrey Inkplott. Hello, this is little Oldrey, I am from London –'

'How about being *her*?'

'Who, the new Iremonger?'

'Yes, why not? I'm sick of the old stories.'

'Yes! Her! But . . . but we don't know her story.'

'Guess it. Guess it. Let us have a new history!'

'What was her name, her name! Does anyone remember it?'

'I do. I do!'

'Say then. Go on.'

'It was . . . oh it was . . . ah it was . . . Lossy Permit.'

'Oh, Lossy! Lossy Permit!'

'My name is Lossy Permit.'

'Where are you from, Lossy? Oh, Lossy, do tell us.'

'I am Lungdon born and bred, I am from Spittingfeels.'

'I, Lossy Permit, grew up in a mansion smelling of soap.'

'I, Lossy, am from the circus – my mother had a beard and my father was as tall as a house.'

I sat up then, I'd have no more of their nonsense. I cleared my throat and said, 'I have thick red hair and a round face and a nose that points upwards. My eyes are green with flecks in them, but that's not the only place I'm dotted. There's punctuation all over me. I'm freckled and spotted and moled and have one or two corns on my feet. My teeth are not quite white. One tooth is crooked. One of my nostrils is slightly bigger than the other. I chew my fingernails. My name is Lucy Pennant.'

'Oh yes, oh yes please. Can you tell us?'

'Tell us, do please, your history.'

And I told them. I remembered much more back then.

I told them and I told them and still they were not happy, they wanted to hear it again. Everything about Filching and Lambeth, the Old Kent Road. One girl just wanted to hear about the kite I once had made of an old straw hat, a crunched boater, blown from the heaps into our courtyard. And from that I must tell them about my old doll (made of bits of piping) and how I played in the dirt park, and my friends at school, and the building I lived in and everyone who lived there and how my parents suddenly stopped, and all the rubber suits of men and women who worked in the heaps.

'We have rubber suits when we go out here too,' one of them told me.

'And anchors,' said another, 'did you have anchors?'

'So that we can be pulled back in if need be.'

'But sometimes no matter how hard the rope is pulled –'

'Stop it!' one of them called. 'That's not for now. We're talking of the new girl.'

'How often do you get to go out into Filching?' I asked. 'Into London?'

'What do you mean?'

82

'How often do you leave the house?'

'Leave it? To go out in the heaps do you mean?'

'No, no, I mean for a break, go out into the city, see London, stretch your legs.'

'Oh, we don't go out.'

'Talk sense,' I said.

'We stop here, why would we go out into London?'

'Well, I'll be going out, after a bit,' I said, 'when I've found my legs. A bit of a wander. See my friends.'

'Friends!' cried one. 'How lovely!'

'You were saying, new Iremonger, about your home.'

'Do tell us please.'

And I told them. One quiet person liked most of all the end of my story, the part when I had arrived in Iremonger Park, when the servants had come to me and took my things, she liked that part best because she was in it.

'I am in your story,' she told me very quietly, 'I am a part of it. To think of it, there I am, right at the end and that's good, isn't it? *Me*, I found my way into a history!'

Asked of her own history she couldn't remember it. Others could drag out very little things, such as having their hands slapped with a ruler, or being picked up, or a balloon popping, or a man with a beard, or a dress, or someone holding their hands, or being read to. The younger Iremongers in the dormitory could remember more, but many of these had been born in the house and talked of nothing else but playing in the cinder box, but one or two tried very hard and could almost remember a mother or a father, but these were shadows of parents, they were only hats or dresses trying to be parents, an occasional floating moustache, a necklace. They were parents made of faint smells and whispers.

There were two old women Iremongers, dressed in the same white nightdress as everyone else, their creased and bent bodies put into the same cloth as the young lively ones. These women did not join in the excitement, they did not listen to my history even though one of the girls went over to their beds to whisper some of it to them, but the old women shifted over turning their backs, they closed their eyes and put their prunish hands to their large ears and would have none of it. One of them kept telling us to pipe down, even threatening to call out for Mrs Piggott.

There was a girl too, like the old women, who did not come out to see me. She was a little thing with a great nose that looked as if it should've been someone else's.

'And who's that one?' I asked.

'Don't worry about her. You mustn't let her upset you.'

They told me that before I came she had been the last new Iremonger to arrive here, and that they had used to go to her bed every night and listen to her stories, but now, she was left alone, she was no longer news.

'Come along,' I called to her, 'I'd like to hear your story.'

She put her head and her nose beneath the covers and it did not come out again until morning.

'Your birth object is a matchbox,' said a girl beside me and with great pride as if she was bursting to tell me a secret though I had told her, and others talked of seeing it not half an hour before.

'What's all this fuss,' I asked, 'about a matchbox?'

'They're very important, birth objects are.'

'They are, I didn't feel myself till I had my birth object.'

'And what is it,' I asked, 'that it's so important?'

''Tis a handbell.'

'So much fuss about a handbell,' I said.

'Well mine,' said another, 'is a ladle.'

'And mine is a dustpan.'

'Mine a clothes brush.'

'Mine an iron.'

'Mine a needle.'

'Mine poultry shears.'

'They're all there in her sitting room and Mrs Smith has the keys. And we're allowed to see them once a week.'

'Wonderful day!'

'Upstairs they keep their objects with them, they're always with them. But not down here, down here Mrs Piggott looks after them.'

'But Madam Rosamud's lost her object just this morning. And they've searched the whole house but still it's not been found.'

'A door handle it is.'

'A lovely brass one.'

'Then why not just give her another?' I said.

'Oh, it wouldn't be the same.'

'It wouldn't be *her* door handle at all.'

'It was a lovely thing, I've seen it myself. Once, there being a shortage, I was upstairs and allowed to be a body servant for her in her rooms.'

'A body servant?' I asked.

'A body servant is an Iremonger from below who is allowed to dress them above us, to wait on their bodies. It's a very privileged thing. No one in this dormitory is a body servant, body servants each have their own room.'

'With chamber pot.'

'Yes, while we share ours.'

'But now we are especially not allowed to be in the presence of upstairs Iremongers, not since Madam Rosamud's door handle went walkabout.'

'They've looked everywhere. Mr Sturridge's very nervy about it all, everyone's unhappy. We'd all really love to find the handle, but no one knows where it's got to. They've searched our rooms thoroughly, gone through the mattresses, turned out our pockets, everything, lord knows we've encouraged it too, but it's not anywhere to be found. It's such a small thing and the house so big.'

'Do you know what Mrs Piggott's birth object is?' I asked.

'Mrs Piggott's is a corset, Mr Sturridge's a ship's lantern and Mr Briggs's a shoehorn.'

'Mr Groom's is a pair of sugar cutters and Mrs Groom's a jelly mould. Mrs Smith's is a key, one key among all those others. I wonder what happened if you found it, I wonder if then you could unlock Mrs Smith!'

'Think of what would come tumbling out.'

'I shouldn't like that at all.'

'Oooh! Look out, Iremonger, you're being eaten to death!'

Everyone then in a terrible panic started swiping at their nightdresses. I looked down at my own bare legs, there were insects climbing all around them. I had felt something before but in the darkness I presumed it was the gentle touching of some Iremonger's fingers, because they had touched and petted me so, but now there was a whining and buzzing about my ears and small things crawling on me.

'What are they?' I cried. 'Get them away!'

'She's been bit.'

'Bit bad.'

'All that new blood. They do like that.'

'We'd better get to our own beds now. Pull the netting over you, Iremonger, or you'll be so red and swelled up tomorrow you shan't do anything but moan and weep.'

'And scratch. Scratch and scratch.'

As we all ran back to our beds I watched our shadows dancing in the candlelight, but then I saw it wasn't our shadows moving but great congregations of insects scattering about the floor, hurriedly fleeing.

'Thank you for telling us your story, Lossy Iremonger.'

'Lucy Pennant.'

'Thank you.'

'Thank you.'

'I'll tell it to you whenever you like,' I said.

'Will you?'

'*Will* you?'

'Yes, of course.'

'We'd love that.'

'I shall never forget it,' I said.

'That's the spirit,' someone called.

'Everyone says that at first, but they always do in the end.'

'Maybe she won't.'

Somehow, at some point, though my legs were scratched and bleeding a little, and my arm so stiff, I found more sleep.

The next morning my arm still ached, one of the Iremongers looked at the spot where Mrs Piggott had poked that thing into me and said I was doing well, that there was barely any mark to speak of. In truth, it did not worry me so much as the bites on my leg. After breakfast, when we lined up for inspection, I heard the steam engine howling, heading back towards London, back to everything I knew. My duties were described to me, I was to clean certain of the fireplaces in the upstairs of the house. This I learnt was a privileged position, far better than being sent out into the heaps. They tried me out on the below-stairs fireplaces to begin with, so that I might get the hang of them before I was sent upstairs in the night-time when the family had gone to bed. They watched over me and made many comments. I had a wire brush and buckets and shovels and a hunk of lead to scrub the grates with. I had brushes and must carry with me also stacks of old London newspapers that I must roll into balls and fill the fireplace with after I'd cleaned it and then I must put some sticks on top of the paper and a few pieces of coal on top of the sticks. They were very particular about how it was to be done. Any part-burnt bits of coal were to be put back on the fire to be used another night, any large cinders were to go in one metal bucket, and the remainder of the ash was to be sifted into the largest bucket to be collected downstairs in the ashroom, where all the ash of the house was gathered up. It was a great sooty place and all who worked in it were smudged and begrimed, and coughed mightily, and had weeping eyes, and black streaks beneath their noses, but were cheerful and thankful to be in the house. Better to be inside, they said, than out beyond in the heaps.

I was so busy with my learning, which took up most of my first morning there, and was always timed: 'You could be faster,' the underbutler Mr Briggs insisted, 'Iremonger, faster still,' so that there were many moments when I forgot myself and became only one of the people who laid the fireplaces and no one else, and an hour might pass before I remembered who I was before I came to Iremonger Park and that I once had a father and mother. When I worked, more and more, I found myself thinking of that matchbox in Mrs Piggott's room. I found myself yearning for it. Such a fuss over a matchbox, I told myself, pull yourself together.

When I go upstairs, I told myself, into the greater part of the house, I shall be alone then and then I shall whisper to myself everything about me, over and over again, and so doing keep myself to myself and not let me go. I shall keep my brain busy, I must stray off their rules a bit, I shall go about exploring, I shall go places I am not supposed to, I shall creep into rooms, I shall do all that. I am Lucy Pennant, that's who I am and there's no call to fuss over matchboxes.

At lunchtime, towards the end of the meal, Mr Briggs came up to me, he had kept his eye on me all day, and he asked me why I wasn't having my spoonful.

'City dirt, is it, sir?' I said. 'I don't really want it.'

'City dirt?' he repeated. 'Who said that? It's sugar and spices, expensive stuff that we're very privileged to have, it'll keep you strong and stop you from getting ill, but tastes something marvellous. Try it.'

'No thank you, sir,' I said, 'rather not.'

'Try it,' he said.

'I'm not hungry,' I said.

'Try it now, Iremonger, or I shall be forced to get someone to really encourage you. It's very important you eat it, it'll keep you well.'

'Really, sir, I don't want it.'

'Want? Want? What have you to do with want? You're a serving Iremonger, it's them upstairs that can have wants. Take a bite now or I shall have to shove it in your mouth myself, and I'll ram it down and I wouldn't want to hurt but I'm not always so exacting. Just a taste,' he said, 'now.'

And so I raised the thing to my mouth and took the tiniest crumb of it into my mouth. And it was sweet and warming somehow. And felt, a little, like kindness.

'Swallow,' he said.

And I did, and I felt happier then than I had in a long while.

'Well,' he said, 'what do you think?'

'I like it,' I said.

'I knew you would,' he said, grinning, 'I just knew it!'

'I do like it,' I said, eating the rest.

'Course you do,' he said, 'what's not to like?'

After an afternoon and an evening still practising firegrates, keeping at it until the train hollered back from London, there was a break for supper. I sat beside the girl in our dormitory who'd refused to listen to my story, the one with the nose, I forced a place on the bench beside her.

'Tell me about yourself,' I said, 'I want to know.'

She was a small, pale and bony girl with a downturned mouth and with that nose, but she did not yet have the grey skin of many of the Iremongers, her lips were even a touch reddish. When I sat down she kept eating, pretending I was not there.

'Do you remember your name?' I asked.

'Iremonger,' she said.

'My name is Lucy Pennant,' I whispered.

'God, don't I know it.'

'Will you tell me your name?'

'Do you know there are a herd of Lucy bloody Pennants, common as dirt they are. The girls have got it bad, I hear them whispering to themselves in the scullery or the kitchens, in the scrub room, in the laundries. Lucy Pennant, or variations of it, they often get it wrong, I heard one Iremonger muttering all about Lurky Penbrush. Well, Lurky, I'm quite sick of you if you want to know. I'm ill with it!'

'Tell me your name then, if you still know it.'

'I *do* know my name. I *do* know it! Who the hell do you think you are?'

'I'm Lucy Pennant, who are you?'

'I wrote it down somewhere.'

'Did you? Well then?'

'Yes, I wrote it down so that I should never forget it. But when I try to remember my own name I can't, all I come up with is Lucy Pennant. For five minutes I was sure *I* was Lucy Pennant. But I'm not, I'm certainly not, I've my own name and I've written it down.'

'Where did you write it?'

'Oh, Lucy Pennant,' she said and there were tears in her eyes, 'I can't remember. I just can't remember. Though I know I wrote it somewhere, I *know* that I did. With a knife I scratched it. I was looking for it, you see, when Mr Briggs found me. I was taken to Mrs Piggott straight off and put to the heaps for two whole months as punishment and I'm not to see my tea strainer for two weeks neither, I do not know how I shall make it. And two months in the heaps!'

'Just for looking about a bit?'

'They don't like it, they want you where they put you. And now I don't think I'll ever find my name.'

'You and me,' I said, 'we'll keep looking, we shan't stop until we find it.'

'They'll put you to work in the heaps at the slightest thing,' she said.

'Well, they can go to hell, can't they.'

'That's good,' she said, 'go to hell with them.' When she smiled, which was rare, she looked so much more pleasant, even a bit pretty.

'We shall find your name, I promise it,' I said.

'It's all I can think of, even when I'm out there.'

'What's it like in the heaps so far out?'

'It's hell, that's what it is, hell.'

'Tell me.'

'You never know if you'll come back or not. You have to be so careful, suddenly the ground gives under you and you start sinking down. I don't know what I'll find tomorrow. P'rhaps I'll find my own death. You stick to your firegrates, you hold onto them firm for all your life. But be careful up there and do exactly as they say and don't run into any of the upstairs Iremongers, any of the family, or you'll find yourself out in the heaps with me. When are you going up?'

'As soon as Mr Briggs rings the bell.'

The Betrothed Pinalippy Iremonger

8

A LACE DOILY

Clod Iremonger's narrative continued

The Last Breakfast

I didn't sleep. I couldn't sleep. Pinalippy was in my head, and when, next morning came at last, with its thin light, I was already up and moving mournfully towards breakfasting.

It was my habit to head to the mess hall as early as I could before too many of my fellow corduroy shorts arrived because if I left it too late then the din of their birth objects was too much for me, and my head should be pounding. I usually was the first to appear, the first to leave. That morning Tummis was there already, we shook hands.

'Given all the business with Rosamud,' I said, 'maybe I shan't have my Sitting today, maybe it shall be cancelled.'

'And the pair of us remain behind in shorts? That should not be so bad.'

'One day, Tummis, your trousers are certain to come.'

'I dreamt of Ormily last night. May I tell you of it?'

We were interrupted then by a plain woman's voice announcing, 'Cecily Grant.'

Here was Cousin Bornobby beside us, Cecily his women's size four shoe swinging in a leather pouch around his belt so that it hung between his legs. Cousin Bornobby had a great collection of drawings and prints of women wearing very little clothing, all were found out in the heaps – somehow he always knew how to find them, he smelt them, he said, he had a particular snout for it. Bornobby was always extremely tired-looking, there were always brown and grey circles around his eyes. Bornobby washed with some sort of scented soap and you could always smell him coming, but always there was an undersmell with him, as if the ghost of a fish was following him about, swimming in his air. He had recently found something new in the heaps, and bored of it himself he now wondered if he could rent it out to us, it was an advertising pamphlet, it said:

CHAS. THOMPSON COMELY CORSETS
Glove-Fitting. Long-Waisted Perfection!! Sold by
drapers. One million pairs annually.
Made in lengths 13, 14 and 15–inch. Fits like a
Glove!!
If your draper cannot supply you write direct to
49, Old Bailey, London giving size, and enclosing
P.O.O. and the Corset will at once be sent to you.

'Not today, Bornobby,' said Tummis, 'it's his Sitting today.'

'Today is it?' said Bornobby. 'Then all the more reason. Come on, Clod, have a look at these corsets, do think of Pinalippy so attired.'

'Bornobby, please not now,' said Tummis, 'don't upset him.'

'How about this one, this is something special, just for you, Tummis.'

PULVERMACHER'S 'ELECTRIC SUSPENSOR BELT'
Muscular vigour is around the corner, Pulvermacher's
Galvanic Establishment,
194 Regent Street, London W. Established over 40
years. Every appliance warranted.

'No, Bornobby,' said Tummis, 'I'm really not in the market today.'

But Bornobby was not to be so easily put off. He took hold of Tummis's arm, but just at that moment the advertisements were plucked away by a different hand. Moorcus.

'Thank you, gentlemen, I'll look after these!'

'Please, Moorcus!' begged Bornobby.

'Albert Powling!'

Turning about a little before Moorcus, Bornobby and Tummis, I saw Albert Powling, the whistle, and the Uncle Timfy that belonged to it. Then the others jumped because Timfy was blowing hard upon his Albert.

My Cousin Pinalippy

'Clod Iremonger!' called Timfy.

Albert Powling whistled me out of the dining hall, up the stairs, and all the way to the Sitting Room.

'Nervous?' Uncle asked.

'A little,' I admitted.

'Know what's on the other side of this door?'

'One Cousin Pinalippy,' I murmured.

'How do you look?' asked Timfy. 'Pale and sweaty. What a prize you are. There'll be many another cousin weeping for lost love now, I shouldn't wonder. Surely you're a heartbreaker, Clod.'

'Is it time?' I asked.

'Very nearly.'

'What's it like, Uncle Timfy, what is marriage like?'

'I was only married to Cousin Mogritt for two months,' said Timfy sadly, 'before she caught bleaching fever and all that was left was her little mouth-harp.'

'I am sorry, Uncle, were you happy, was it everything you had hoped for?'

The train screamed below the house, Grandfather going into the city, the whole house shaking in acknowledgement, it did little to improve my spirits.

'It's time,' he said. He blew his Albert once, so weak now in comparison, he opened the door, propelled me inside, closed it after.

'Gloria Emma Utting.'

'James Henry Hayward.'

Inside, in the half-light, seated at the far end of the room on the particular small red sofa that was used for these occasions I knew, without looking, by hearing alone, was sat my Cousin Pinalippy Iremonger with her Gloria Emma. It was the same sofa that my own mother and father had sat upon years ago. No other seat in that room. Never was, never shall be.

How, in the past, had each male Iremonger cousin chosen to approach his female cousin? Some may have run at it. Some may have pounded at the door, begging for it to be opened. Some may have shaken hands. Some straight to the kiss. I stood there by the door. We could not be the first for whom this was true, the whole half hour going by without contact, keeping each as far from the other as could be, looking even in opposite directions until someone should come to let us out and break the horror. Cousin and cousin, close so close, cousins every day, cousins in the night, cousin with cousin, cousining. I kept as still and as quiet as I could.

'Gloria Emma Utting.'

And then another voice, 'I'm waiting.'

Statue. Like a statue. But the voice came once more, and terrible it was, 'Do you require directions?'

Statue.

'Gloria Emma Utting.'

'Must I fetch you?'

The voice required movement. And I began the awful

expedition to the small sofa, not directly across the room, but rather, crablike, following the walls, in little steps, side by side, so that the journey might be twice the length.

'Well, this is you then, is it?' she said.

I thought it was.

'I'm to marry you.'

'Yes,' I managed, 'but not yet.'

She was much taller than me. She had a little hair on her upper lip.

'You *are* nervous,' she said.

'Yes. Yes,' I said. What else?

'We knew it was going to happen, it wasn't as if they didn't give us warning. You're shaking. Are you very ill?'

'Yes, I am.'

'You won't die if I touch you, will you?'

'I couldn't be certain.'

'So then I'll be a widow.'

'We're not even married yet.'

'But we will be. There's no getting out of it.'

'Well,' I said, 'no.'

'Will I have to look after you?'

'I hope not.'

'I don't know that I'll be very good at that.'

'No.'

'Could you grow, do you think?'

'I might,' I said, 'I'll try.'

'Well then, Cousin Clod, you had better listen to me. If we remain in Heap House after you're trousered we shall be allotted two rooms and in those two rooms, you and I are to confine ourselves. They may be very small rooms. They may be really only one room with a false wall made of little more than board. That's what happened to my sister Flippah when she married Cousin Crosspin, but she found that after a while she could move the wall. And the more she despised Crosspin the more she pushed the wall. She stayed in one room, that room was getting bigger and bigger, and he was in the other always decreasing room. In the end he had to sleep standing up. I wonder if we'll get a moveable wall. Do you fit in a cupboard? I think you would. I hope we get a cupboard. If not you might go under a bed. Upon a mantelpiece? No, you'd be too conspicuous there. Don't look so miserable.'

'I am miserable.'

'I'm lying, you mophead,' she said, 'I do lie. I'm going to lie to you. I'm a terrible liar, I can't stop myself. Never believe a word I say. That's my advice. I'm doing you a favour telling you that, often people have to work it out for themselves.'

'Erm,' I said, then, 'Thank you.'

'I'm older than you.'

'I'm fifteen.'

'Seventeen.'

'For six more months.'

'I don't love you.'

'No!'

'But I am capable of love.'

'Oh.'

'I've loved a lot in my time.'

'Yes?'

'Shall I tell you about it?'

'Yes?'

'I'm for ever falling in and out of love,' Pinalippy told me, in very secretive tones. 'I'm in love at the moment, but not with you. I'm thick with love, but not with you. We've been *together*. We couldn't stop ourselves, one with the other, leg over leg over leg. What a fumbling! Buttons all over! Hooks and eyes! What panting. All that skin and things! Oh, but it's hopeless, I'm supposed to marry you.'

'Cousin Pinalippy?'

'Cousin Clod?'

'Are you lying?'

She did not answer that.

'*Are* you lying?' I tried again.

'Well then,' she said after a moment, 'let me see it. Bring it out. Come, come. You know that you should. I'll have a look at it now. Show me.'

Slowly, carefully, I brought out my James Henry, and laid it flat in my hand, I held it away from her but so that she could see it.

'A plug is it?'

'Yes,' I whispered, 'a universal plug. It fits most sinks. It's called James Henry Hayward, that's the name I hear it saying.'

'They've told me about your hearing things, my Aunts

102

Noona and Curdlia did, and they've told me to snap it out of you. A plug called James-whatever to your mind, Clod Iremonger, is still only a plug.' After a moment she added, 'A plug is not very romantic, is it?'

'No,' I said, 'not much. I suppose.'

'A plug,' she said.

'Yes,' I said, 'a universal plug.'

'I am to marry a plug. A plug. Is that my life? A plug. I had thought it might be all sorts of things. You're quite mysterious I thought, being so ill and pale, and hearing voices. It could be something very extraordinary. I'd quite settled my mind on it being a pocket watch. I'd have been happy with a paper weight, a magnifying glass, but a plug, a plug. A nice shoe perhaps. Yes, a well-turned shoe would do very excellently.'

'*Did* you think I was mysterious?' I said. 'There *is* mystery in a plug.'

'Now who's lying?'

'With a plug you keep things in, or removing a plug you let things out. A plug in a boat can stop a man from drowning.'

'You'll find that's called a bung.'

'Taking away a plug all bad and poisonous things can disappear. You pull out a plug, who knows what will happen, what will escape, what has the plug been keeping shut up? A plug can keep in good nourishing things. A plug is an opening, a closing, a small, circular door. A gateway between worlds.'

103

'Oh *really*?' said Pinalippy.

'Really,' I said.

'Here's what I know about plugs,' said Pinalippy, 'I use a plug when I take a bath, but I don't have contact with it myself, it's a servant thing, a plug is. The servant puts it over the drain, then pours in the water, then I step in. I'm naked in the water, Clod, do note, altogether naked. I wash myself and get out, the water, do note, Clod, dirtier now but much more interesting, is let out when the servant uses the plug. It's very servant-class, your plug. You'd like to see mine too, I'm sure.'

'No, no,' I said, 'it's all right.'

'You'd like to see mine,' she said very strongly.

She carefully took out something rolled up in a tube she kept beside her. She spread it out upon her lap, upon her thigh. Upon the thigh of Pinalippy.

'There!' she said.

'Gloria Emma Utting.'

Gloria Emma was, like my plug, round. But it was larger and flatter though less substantial. It was very thin and had many holes in it, at first I feared she had not looked after her birth object at all, that some species of moth – we had so many – had nibbled at it, had bitten into her, but then I saw that the holes appeared regularly in a pattern and that they were quite deliberate.

'What is it?' I asked.

'Do you not know?'

'No,' I said, 'I've never seen one before.'

104

'It is,' she said, 'a doily!'

'A doily?' I said. 'A doily called Gloria Emma Utting.'

'So you think it has a name, do you?'

'Yes, yes it does.'

'I've never heard it.'

'I can't help that.'

'You hear it quite clearly?'

'Yes, very clearly.'

'Gloria?'

'Gloria Emma Utting, that's what it says.'

'Anything else?'

'Nothing else, only the name.'

'Gloria Emma Utting.'

'That's right,' I said. 'A doily.'

'A doily!' she proclaimed with emphasis.

'And what is a doily?' I wondered.

'You do not know?'

'I never met one before. What is its purpose?'

'A doily is for putting upon a table.'

'Oh yes?'

'And making the table pretty.'

'Oh yes?'

'Things may be placed upon it, a plate of little cakes for example, or a vase of flowers. Or! It can be left alone, upon a table. It transforms a table, does the doily. The simplest plainest table can be made lovely-looking by a doily.'

'But what does it do?'

'It goes on any table and makes it look pretty.'

'But it doesn't actually do anything.'

'It is a little portable piece of beauty!'

'And then you put things upon it?'

'You can. It is not necessary.'

'But then it would be covered up. I do not think I entirely understand. But perhaps I do, is it to protect a table? So that it doesn't get water damage, or crumbs upon it? I think I see. A small tablecloth but then why the holes in it?'

'It is a piece of rare beauty. *Very* delicate.'

'It might rip easily?'

'If not properly loved.'

'It is not very practical, is it?'

'It will not hold bath water if that's what you mean.'

It seemed to me a most unnecessary object. Could I love a doily? It had so many holes in it, as if it was shy of existence, as if it wanted not to be.

'You may touch it, if you like,' she said.

'Touch it?'

'If you like.'

She put the doily in my lap, it had no weight to it, this whisper of an object. She in her turn sat now with my plug upon her lap, we sat silent for a long while, at last she muttered, looking at my plug, 'Something toad-like.'

So we remained getting accustomed to each other's James Henry and Gloria Emma, until at last Uncle Timfy's whistle sounded outside, and then she took her doily from me, and I, my fingers briefly over her lap, brought James Henry back home. I was glad it was over, I do not think we were a very good match. But she whispered to me, 'I think that went very well, don't you?'

There were tears in her eyes. And then, for a moment, I thought it might be all right after all, but then I heard the sigh, 'A bath plug.'

And I decided it probably wouldn't. As I stood up I heard the sofa say something, it said, 'Victoria Hollest.'

Well, I thought, so the sofa is called Victoria Hollest, there was nothing especially remarkable about that. There was a newel post downstairs called Victoria Amelia Broughton and I once heard a candlestick call itself Victoria Macleod and there was a croquet mallet in the games room called Vicky Morton. Very well, another Victoria, so be it. But then Victoria Hollest, the small red sofa, said, 'Where's Margaret?'

And that was something else wasn't it? That was something very big. No object had ever spoken anything but a name to me before now. It was so strange and uncomforting, this new and sudden communication, that all my insides felt wrong and I thought I might be sick there and then on the sofa, or worse still upon Pinalippy and her Gloria Emma, but I kept it in. What was happening? What was happening to me? Was I going mad? Would my heart, like Father's, suddenly stop? I staggered to the door. I promised myself that as soon as I could I would come and listen to Victoria Hollest again, but for now I must leave it alone, for Uncle Timfy was not famous for his patience.

My Head and a Coal Scuttle

We were supposed to position ourselves somewhere separately and think of our futures together for the rest of the day, Pinalippy and I. I was to go and sit in the Elephant Room, and Pinalippy was to sit in the White Room. Just sit, sit and think of our lives together, our cold lunches waiting for us on a tray. I should stay put for several hours. So I sat trying not to panic about the talking sofa and not to think of where or who Margaret might be, and so for a while I did think about Pinalippy and for some of the time I did try to concentrate on the feel of her doily, but that sofa kept calling to me in my head and so I wandered about the room, worrying, trying to distract myself. It was dusk when I heard Albert Powling coming and Timfy at last sent me packing.

'Run along, Clod, and behave yourself; no time for your mishaps today, we're all at hackles up.'

I ran back all the way to my room, avoiding the main corridors where Iremonger traffic was at its thickest. I did not wish to meet with jeers and whoops about me and my Sitting, any name calling and singing and all the clothes being pulled off, and being tossed up into the air, I should like to avoid all the business that often happens after a Sitting. I shouldn't go to supper that night, I had a tin of squashed fly biscuits, that would do, and I wouldn't come out till morning, when my Sitting would be less fresh and hopefully likewise their enthusiasm for it. I made it home just a short while before the train was back in from London.

My two rooms were not very large but they were all mine. Clod through and through and generally in a bit of a heap. Perhaps I was not the cleanest of all Iremongers. I had no parents to adjust me, to give me rules and see that I grow to their interpretation of how an Iremonger should grow, I had no sibling to steal or to be stolen from, to pry and talk and have in common. I am Clod and this was my kingdom. It was not very large perhaps and it was not so grand, but it was my sty and I wallowed in it nightly.

I should never have had my hair cut, never have clipped my nails, have eaten what I liked, got up late, slopped and slooped about in my mash, were it not that I had a body servant, who though only a serving Iremonger, and so not to be particularly thought about, came once a week and aired me out. Then I must make sure all was very well hidden, for he searched so well and was a terrible nose. I was steamed in that laundry day, I was scrubbed and snipped and rubbed and boiled and dipped in smells, my hair was bullied into obeisance and I was made white again and blank until the next week by which time I would have scribbled all over myself, creased me and blurred me and filthied myself in exactly the way I liked. Anything that I had not hidden well would not be there, nor would the body Iremonger mention it, he would just take it; it would go for ever and for ever. Sometimes to have a feeling of even greater independence and total me-ness, I might light a clay pipe or even puff on a cigarillo if I had found one, or then if not have rolled myself a quick cigarette of clippings and dried dust mites, only then should the body Iremonger remind me that such things were not permissible and then Briggs would come to me and, begging my pardon, should pinch my ear quite hard or rap my knuckles, then I should have to say twelve Hallo Moorries (Moorrie was a very good Iremonger who was a wonder at sifting and found many lost treasures, before perishing in a methane explosion, lighting up a fat cigar out on the heaps. NOT A BEANY (which is how Tummis and I say '*nota bene*'): NO SMOKING ON THE WASTEGROUND. HIGHLY FORBIDDEN.) But otherwise I was mostly left alone to my own stink.

That night, when the night bell was sounded, when all was quiet along the corridor – except for the noise from Cyril Pennington, a fire bucket, which was perpetual – I headed out in search of Victoria Hollest.

I was very nearly at the Sitting Room when I heard a new mumbling coming from the schoolmasters' common room. Looking in I saw some serving Iremonger busy about her night-time tidying business and thought nothing of it to start off with, I have little enough time for the serving Iremongers but do prefer it when they are less conspicuous, and I was about to move on, but then I heard that there was something very wrong with this Iremonger. I thought serving Iremongers never made noises, yet this one did. This one definitely was saying something with its serving mouth shut. Why was this one making noises, what was it saying? As I listened out for the words, the serving Iremonger, who I saw now was young and had quite some red hair visible beneath her bonnet, came at me with maddened looks and struck me upon the head with a coal scuttle.

Doctor Aliver Iremonger

9

A PAIR OF CURVED FORCEPS

From the medical journals of Doctor
Aliver Iremonger, G.P.

Wednesday 9ᵗʰ November 1875
The patient Rosamud Poorler Iremonger, aged fifty-seven,
is distressed. Yellowness to the eyes. No comfortable position can be obtained. The patient describes aching all over
her corpus. She keeps reaching out to hold something, but
whatever is placed in her hand is not a comfort. I have
had other brass door handles brought before her but these
have only quickened her terror. She believes that she shall
become something other than she is now. There is no
quietening her, save with physic.

Thursday 10ᵗʰ November 1875 – 10 a.m.
Great prostration of strength. She has not left her bed all
day. She fears she shall be struck into something any
moment. The patient wails about a return of the Old

Disease. Her brother, she says, fell to it aged seven; he folded into a possing-stick for tub washing. Patient cannot be comforted. Surely, her fears are exaggerated. If she would but calm herself, but the patient has it in her mind that the terrible malady is returning and nothing shall persuade her otherwise.

Thursday 10th November 1875 – 11 p.m.
Features much altered. A coldness now about the surface of her body. Eyes sunken in sockets. Body is changing colour, a blue-blackness to it now not present before. She has not spoken these past five hours. Patient sleeps at last and is to be considered comfortable. Pulse imperceptible.

The House Aunt Rosamud Iremonger

A BRASS DOORKNOB

Lucy Pennant's narrative continued

A surly Iremonger, middle-aged and heavy, with many insect bites all over her legs, guided me, took me up from the underhouse, up all those stairs. At the turn of each staircase there was a hatch.

'Why so many hatches?' I asked.

'In case it floods,' the iremonger said. 'In case the heaps pour in, to seal the house up, stop the flooding coming up any further.'

'But what about those beneath the flooding?'

'They're flooded in, aren't they, what do you think? Come along, come up.'

She shifted fast and it was hard for me to remember exactly the routes back down. Each set of stairs was different: one was stone, one was rusted metal, one was wooden and very chipped and broken, one was wooden but dusted and polished with a carpet runner all the way up and brass carpet rods.

'It doesn't make any sense,' I said.

'Not to you,' said the Iremonger.

'Why is it built like this?' I asked.

'It is how they like it, them that live here.' The Iremonger wiped her nose with her wrist. 'Many are sick the first few times they come up, it's quite usual. Some are sick each time they come up no matter how often they've come up previous, no matter that they do it daily, still they will be sick. You're holding a bucket, Iremonger, you can always use that.'

'No, I don't think I'm going to be sick,' I said, 'I should like to see more of it.'

'Not to! Stay in the rooms I take you to, not for you to go about. Mustn't. And if you get lost don't head upwards, you keep heading upwards and you come to the attics, see, and in the attics are all the bats, and they are biting bats and dangerous. Don't get lost. Mustn't. Mrs Piggott!'

'How much of it is there?'

'Much.'

'They must be very rich, the Iremongers. And are they also,' I wondered, walking around so many empty places, 'quite small in number?'

'Mrs Piggott!'

'And perhaps a little shy?'

'Piggott!' she snorted, stopping, turning around. 'Have you ever seen one of the family, a proper one?'

'I have,' I said. 'Cusper Iremonger.'

'Ah, but he doesn't live in, so he don't count.'

'Have you seen one that does?'

'Not close to,' she said. 'I saw one once from a great distance coming forward, gave me a terrible turn. I managed to hide away behind a sofa, I was there several hours, until I was certain he had gone.'

'Why, what would happen if you hadn't hidden?'

'I don't like to think on it.'

'Why not?'

'They're deep!'

'Well, and what does that mean?'

'And they're fast!'

'Well, so am I.'

'And they're wicked!'

'Are they? What do they do?'

'Take. They take.'

'I *should* like to see one.'

'Mrs Piggott!'

'What happens if I come across one when I'm making a fire?'

'You must hide yourself.'

'And if there's just one there before me and I haven't had a chance to hide?'

'Won't happen.'

'Why not?'

'Because they're sleeping now or we shouldn't be allowed up,' she said. 'You mustn't think about them, not for a moment. Just get your job done, quick as you can, and then back downstairs as fast as you like. And then you've done it, the night's over. And if you see anything, if anything starts coming, then you hide, don't you. As fast as you like. And you don't get seen and you keep hold of your scuttle and if anything comes at you, you hit it, my girl, you hit it and hit it.'

'But what *would* come at me?'

But she only said, 'Mrs Piggott!'

I was left alone shortly after. I didn't mind it at first, the space, the emptiness, just me there. But then of course it wasn't just me there at all, there was the house as well.

I saw one of the withdrawing rooms and a morning room, the breakfast room, the Sitting Room with just one old red sofa in it, and what was called the Sun Room which was a room with more windows than most but which had a most dismal feel about it, all the glass panes thick with dirt. The other thing I had not properly understood with the old Iremonger beside me, giving directions, hurrying, panting, was that even though I was on my own in those rooms upstairs still it was far from quiet. The plumbing got very angry, and then there were all the noises of the animal life busy about the house, different things somewhere in the walls, chewing away, and I could see why I was instructed always to keep my coal shovel close by, but only to hit out if I was absolutely provoked, in genuine self-defence, but that if I killed a rat or seagull

120

I must afterwards be sure to clean up the mess. And not to throw the bodies away for there was use in the body, they could be skinned and the skin contribute to a coat, or feathers for quills or for stuffing, their meat could be used, their carcasses could be boiled down for glue, nothing must be wasted.

Far worse than the animals were the other sounds, the noises of the Upiremongers asleep. Upiremonger, that's what the servants called the family members who lived above ground. Their breathing came down through the flues and into my face. I was certain the house held many ghosts, I should not have been surprised if all the ghosts of London congregated there and made a great playroom of the mansion, I did try not to think of that. But when you work at a fireplace your back has to be turned to the room, and there is no escaping the feeling that someone is watching you. I kept my head low, the coal scuttle in my hand, I lit candles and in the light, I told myself, made little pockets of safety. I tried to remember the songs I used to know.

I found a little tuppence,
I kept it for myself,
It was a magic tuppence,
It ate up all my health.

But that didn't help much.

Spit spat sputum,
Whither are you walkin',
Forlichingham Mound
I am bound.
Crick crack sternum
You shall fall in.
Slip and trip and smack your head,
Filching Mound, that's your bed.

And nor did that, so I kept myself pretty quiet after. Mrs Piggott, I said to myself, and somehow that made me feel better.

There were so many *things* upstairs, so many little bits and pieces that I didn't know the name to. I liked to pick them up and hold them, odd objects on mantelpieces or side tables, things, just things, that fitted into the hand so nicely. Small portraits of unhappy-looking people, framed silhouettes of oddly grown men and women, with locks of hair tied up in black ribbons, twisted up in the back of the frames. Carved snuff boxes, miniature buildings made of toothpicks, silver compasses, an ivory baton, tiny books with gilt edges.

There were so many things of sadness and delight around the uphouse rooms. I felt miserable to leave them behind, once or twice I put them into my pocket just to know what they felt like, and they felt very good, the weight of them. They were such a comfort. Most of all, though, what

I felt my hand longed for was something small and box-like, that rattled when you shook it, *that* I felt should be the perfect thing to hold.

I was in the Sun Room when it happened. I cannot get it exactly straight even now. I was by the fireplace, I don't remember wobbling anything, or hammering on the floorboards especially, but somehow it must have come lose, I must have dislodged it someway or other, no explanation otherwise, because suddenly there it was. Something clanged upon the floor and rolled towards me. Gave me ever such a turn at first. Nearly called out, nearly struck at it. It stopped rolling right in front of me. As if it was aiming for me. As if it wanted me to find it.

A door handle it was, a brass one. A small one, with a rod. I knew that it must be the one they were looking for, that it belonged to someone called Rosamud. I thought she should be very pleased to have it back. But then I thought I might keep it a while, not for long, I'd give it back soon enough, just let me keep it for a few days. It was something to hold onto. It was only a door handle, of course, just a door handle. It was something shiny, it was something to hold, and somehow life feels much better when you have something to hold onto. I'll give it back soon, I thought, I certainly shall, but not just yet.

I did like it. There was something about it, something personal.

I went on, then, with the door handle, I wrapped it up in my thick hair, twisted my hair around it, then pinned it down, I quite covered it with hair like I had with those other things back in Filching, and put my bonnet over so it couldn't be seen, not even really if you took my bonnet off. Perhaps my head was a just a little bit bumpier, just a bit. Just for a little while, I told myself, then I'll give it back. So I went on, doing my labour, feeling better now that I had the door handle.

I was cleaning the fireplace of the schoolmasters' common room, a very thick place indeed, when I had the sudden feeling that someone was watching me. I turned to the door and there *was* someone there, someone horrible.

It was a ghost.

A ghost of a short ill-faced boy. I was so certain he had come to haunt me. He stood there in the doorway, a horrible boy with a neat parting and great circles under his eyes, with a very wide mouth and a head that seemed a little big for his shoulders. And I thought, no, I'm not going to stand it, I've been so terrified all this time about seeing a ghost that actually seeing one isn't so bad and I'm not going to have this unhappy creature skulking around me each time I come upstairs so I shall have to tell it to shove off, that I won't stand for it. So I stood up then and took hold of the coal shovel and marched towards him, hands trembling, and I hit, just as I had been told to. I hit him with the shovel. And my shovel struck. It made contact. It found something, not the doorframe, no, it hit the boy around the ear. There was even a very little blood.

Perhaps this wasn't a ghost.

Perhaps it wasn't.

It wasn't.

No, not a ghost. And if he wasn't a ghost then he was surely one of the family. I'd struck an Upiremonger. There was just a drop of blood but this Upiremonger made a terrible fuss and I kept telling him how sorry I was and he kept holding his precious ear as if I'd chopped the damned thing off.

When he was a bit quieter I begged him not to tell anyone. 'Don't report me, promise me that.'

And he stood with his hands around his lug and said, 'My name's Clod. You've heard of me I expect; Ayris's son.'

'My name's –'

'I know your name,' he said impatiently, 'your name is Iremonger of course.'

'My name is Lucy Pennant.'

'Is it? Is it really? Are you sure? I wasn't aware that there were names for the servants downstairs, except the butler and such.'

'Well there are, and mine is Lucy Pennant, and don't you forget it.'

'You're awfully sensitive about it, aren't you.'

'Yes I am!'

'You needn't be so cross.'

I thought it was clever of me at first to tell him my name, what a place to keep it, inside the head of one of the upstairs Iremongers. Then I wondered if it wasn't actually incredibly stupid. What if he told Mrs Piggott that a maid called Lucy Pennant had not only talked to him which was expressly forbidden but had used her own outlawed name and had actually struck him with a coal scuttle?

'There's something else that's different about you, isn't there?' he asked.

'I expect so,' I said.

'You've got a birth object.'

'Yes,' I said, 'yes I do, it's –'

'But servants don't usually have birth objects.'

'We all do, they're kept downstairs, in Mrs Piggott's room.'

'Maybe it's the scuttle then,' he said, and a moment later, 'no, it's not the scuttle, not the bucket. Could it be your bonnet?'

He was frowning so, he somehow knew I had the door handle under my cap, but how could he know? It's just as the old Iremonger had said, they're deep.

'How long, Lucy Pennant, have you been in Heap House, for you don't seem to know the rules?'

'Since yesterday evening.'

'And before yester evening you were somewhere else then?'

'I've got to be somewhere all the time, haven't I?'

'Well, yes.'

'Everyone's in one place or another aren't they?'

'Yes they are.'

'You're never not anywhere.'

'Yes, yes, steady on. It's not you that's got a bleeding ear. And please to remember that you are a servant and I am not. But to return to the conversation, there are so many somewheres, aren't there? So many places altogether, but I, you see, I've only ever been here.'

'There's a lot of here, masses of it.'

'Yes, it is big, I suppose, but I was wondering, Lucy Pennant, of that place that you were just yesterday. What was it like?'

'Smaller.'

'Oh was it, that's interesting, and was there anything else about it at all?'

'What do you want to know?'

'Everything.'

'That's a lot then, isn't it?'

'Yes, well,' he said, 'if you wouldn't mind. You could start now.'

'And what about me? What do I get out of it?'

'I don't know. My not telling anyone that I was struck by a servant?'

'Show me the house, I'm new here, I get lost. Show it me.'

'Were you in London?'

'I was.'

'Do you know London?'

'Course.'

'Could you tell me about it?'

'An exchange is it then? You'll show me the house, and I'll tell you everything about London?'

'Oh yes, all right. Let's start straight away, this is the Masters' common room.'

'I know that already. Tell me something else.'

'I will. There are seven floors, well, eight in places. Six main staircases. I'm not certain how many back ones. Four dining halls, three long galleries. Many treasures here and there, great collections.'

'Show me.'

'Tell me,' he asked, 'what's your birth object?'

'A box of matches. Show me a collection.'

'What sort of a box, big, small, how many matches inside?'

'I don't know, I didn't see, there was tape around it which said "sealed for your convenience". It's got nothing to do with me really.'

'A sealed box of matches.'

A bell sounded underneath and I knew I must hurry.

'I should go now. We've made a deal, haven't we, come to terms agreeable to both parties?'

'Yes, indeed.'

'There we are then. But it'll have to be another night. I must get on now.'

'Tomorrow night?'

'Tomorrow, yes, if you like.'

'I'll come and find you.'

'Yes, well, all right.'

And I thought, what's that on the chain he has going into his dressing gown pocket, what's at the end of that?

'Goodnight,' I said to him.

And he said, 'Goodnight.' He said, 'Goodnight, Lucy Pennant.'

Yes, that was the first time I met Clod Iremonger.

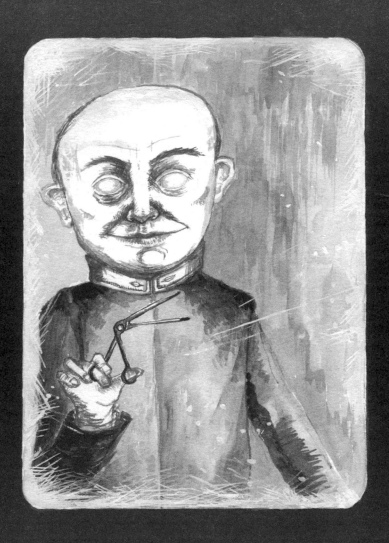

The Governor Extraordinary of Birth Objects
Idwid Iremonger

A PAIR OF NOSE TONGS

Clod Iremonger's narrative continued

Lucy Pennant is in My Head

She is called Lucy Pennant. She cleans the fireplaces in some of the rooms after we are horizontal in our bedpits. I had not spoken to many of the cleaning, spic and spanning, smelling soapy, polishing up, whitewashing and scrubbing scrubbers, bleaching or blacking, ironing-Iremongers, crisp and starching, un-fleaing family branch members that lived, by day, out of sight somewhere down beneath Heap House, with dustpan and with brush. They were nocturnal, I supposed. They did not like us to go downstairs into the service rooms, Uncle Timfy would blow his whistle so and Mr Sturridge would be most unencouraging. So I did not see them much, those people. And they had no sounds to them, no names called out when they went by, not generally. And months would probably pass by without me having given them so much as a thought, as if it were the rats themselves that tried to clean our uncleanables, polished our palace and took all the ash and dead skin away. But now I had seen one of them, caught one in the candlelight. A brilliant moth.

Back in my room, in my space, I whispered, 'I saw Lucy Pennant tonight. She struck me with her scuttle. She comes from London. I heard her birth object, but couldn't catch its name.'

What else? She had green eyes. Was a very little older than me. Bit taller. I might grow, I thought, it probably was not tremendously important. Pinalippy had asked me to grow, but I didn't want to think about Pinalippy then. I wanted to think about Lucy Pennant. She thought I was a ghost; I frightened her. I didn't think I had ever frightened anyone before. I must learn the name of her birth object; I knew a person so much better when I knew what their birth object was and what it called itself.

A Secret From Tummis

Cousin Tummis knocked on my door early next morning.

'Tummis,' I said, 'Tummis and Hilary, come in and close the door. I've something enormous to tell you. Something very wonderful. Close the door.'

'What is it, Clod?'

'Hilary Evelyn Ward-Jackson.'

132

'Your nose is dripping. Hello, Hilary.'

Tummis smeared his nose on the cuff of his shirt.

'I think Wateringcan might come back tonight,' he said, 'I think he might, don't you? I did try to look for him, I did go about a bit, but I found no traces, and I didn't want to be caught by Moorcus, he was on duty last night. Tonight it's Duvit so perhaps I'll have more luck. But I do think Wateringcan will come home, once he's tired himself.'

'I'm sure he shall,' I said.

'Clod, tell me your news, that's what I'm eager about.'

'Tummis,' I said, 'have you ever waited and waited, patiently scratching, itching yourself, wiping at your nose, looking at the door waiting for it to open and there in front of you to appear, an excellent story. Your very own story, mind, not someone else's, not some minor role in some other body's opera. But your own. Your own story. Have you ever wanted your own story in which you're the leading part?'

'How you come at me, Clod, so early in the day.'

'Your own story, Tummis, think of it, your very own. What might it be?'

'A Tummis story? How would that be?'

'My story has come to me, Tummis. I think it has.'

'Oh, Clod!'

'Oh, Tummis!'

'You must tell me everything. How is she? How was the Sitting? I know that she seems quite big and tough but she wasn't after all then?'

133

'Stop! Stop right there, Tummis Gurge Oillim Mirck Iremonger. Pinalippy isn't my story. It's not Pinalippy I'm talking about. My story is something else altogether.'

'No it's not.'

'It certainly is, Tummis. (Your nose is dripping.)'

'(Thank you.) What's this story?'

'Well,' I said, then I hesitated, I didn't want to ruin it. I suddenly thought it was such a delicate thing, very new and small, and I didn't tell Tummis, not yet, though usually I would tell him everything. Suddenly I felt a great gap opening up between us as if he were growing far away, I felt that, but still I didn't close the gap. I left it there. 'I haven't quite got all the parts right yet, I don't want to smash it before I'm certain. But I can say, it has some red in it.'

'Some red, does it?'

'Some red and also some green.'

'A muddy sort of colour then? Brownish?'

'Not exactly.'

'Well, what then?'

'I can't say exactly.'

Down below the train screamed for London.

'Tell me, Clod, please tell me.'

'Percy Hotchkiss.'

'It's Aliver,' I whispered, 'come for my check-up.'

'Do tell me, Clod, quickly. Please do.'

There was a knock at the door.

'Clod,' came a voice, 'may I step in a moment?'

134

'Oh, flotsam,' whispered Tummis nervously, 'oh, flotsam and pokeum.'

The door opened; Uncle Aliver was before us.

'I thought I heard voices,' he said. 'Tummis, are you supposed to be here?'

'No, Uncle.'

'You'll wear him out, Tummis, he's easily tired.'

'I'm quite well today, Uncle,' I said.

'You are no more substantial, poor Clod, than a dandelion.'

'What's a dandelion?' I asked.

'It need not concern you. Some of us, Tummis, are not so robustly fashioned, unlike you, you great bell tower, great walking advertisement for upwards.'

'Is he like the Monument, Uncle?' I asked. 'Is he like the statue built to commemorate the Great Fire of London, built in 1677, two hundred and two feet high, that stands upon the junction of Monument Street and Fish Street Hill?'

'Indeed,' he said, 'very like. You have been reading, Clod.'

'Yes, Uncle, many books on London.'

'I'm sorry, Uncle,' said Tummis, 'it was his Sitting, you see, and I –'

'Don't let me catch you in here again.'

'No, Uncle.'

'Cut along then.'

And away went the dear stork, hurt and snotty.

135

An Uncle Called Aliver

My Uncle Aliver, deliverer of syrups and potions, of foul-tasting pills that looked like animal droppings and smelt as much, Uncle Aliver the doctor, the plumber of human innards, his thoughts all heading inwards, he who looking at every person could only ever see their underskin, their dripping and clotting, their blackening and blueing, he whose imagination was all boils and rashes, he who was companion to pain and swelling, joint-ache, colds and moulds, blisters and twisted testicles, tooth rot and foot rot and gut rot and stomach knot and ingrowing toenails and outgrowing skin flaps, his company, his sociability, his interaction, his hellos and howdoyoudos, his Iloveyous, were all and only with the unwell. Well people, young and sprightly and sleeping tightly every night, he could not comprehend at all. They were not interesting to him. Aliver could only recognise a person by his ailments. He was close friend and admirer of everything from colds to calluses to catarrhs to cataracts to cancers to carbuncles to cysts to catalepsy to cretinism and sat beside them and worried over them a great deal. With someone ill he was loving and tender and patient, with a well person he was rude and blind and baffling and horrible. When his patients recovered he turned his back upon them, hurt and miserable, already missing the disease which he, in his sadness, had helped to dismiss. He had been married, Uncle Aliver, to Aunt Jocklun (cake knife) and the marriage had not been a happy one until poor Aunt Jocklun picked up black lung and then he never left her until she left him for ever and for ever.

With me, Uncle Aliver was generally very attentive and excited, he spent a good deal of worry over me and was so very fond of my head, and I wished he were not so much. On the days he was quick with me and gruff I knew I was doing better. He was a first-rate medical man and knew everything about the stop and go of the human unit.

'You appear very underslept,' said Uncle Aliver to me that morning; he felt my head and listened to my heart. He laid out my pills for the week and there, save for a few brief questions, his visits would usually stop.

'Poor Rosamud, Clod, she suffers so. Her hair is falling out. Her skin has darkened.'

'Indeed, poor Aunt.'

'The whole house is set off by her. How busy I have been. My brother Wrichid thought he saw his own pelmet sliding about his bedchamber, but I think it's more likely the claret cup. Mr Groom has reported a sudden curdling of substances, from milk to marzipan, and a pig carcass hung up in the cold room has grown strange blue lines all over its pelt. Not to mention the birth of Cousin Lolly's latest; she's calling him Kannif after her own father, very frail indeed. And Great Aunt Ommaball Oliff, your venerable grandmother, foul-mooded without cease, presented the poor child with a single curved pencil shaving for a birth object, so it's unlikely to last the night. And of course the heaps are up and that's enough to make anyone tense. I haven't known such distress since Rippit was lost to us. But you, Clod, at least you remain constant, constantly Clod.'

'I have listened out for the door handle, but I haven't heard it.'

'And yet it must be somewhere. Clod, perhaps we might run you around a bit, up and down the house, see what you can hear. We'll not make a parade of it, there's no need for Timfy to know. Yes, perhaps we might. Worth a shot. Would you be up to that? It would get you out of school.'

'Certainly, Uncle.'

'And how was your Sitting anyway? I forgot to ask. Nice girl?'

'It was all right, I suppose. And, Uncle, at the Sitting –'

'A doily, I believe.'

'A doily, yes. And, Uncle, there was something else. The sofa in the Sitting Room, it spoke, quite quietly, it said its name was Victoria Hollest.'

'Victoria Hollest, did it?' said Uncle perfunctorily.

'Yes,' I said, 'and I shouldn't mention anything about it especially except the fact it said something else, something other than its name, it was asking where someone called Margaret was. I'm pretty sure that's what I heard, I could go and have another listen if you like.'

'Clod, you clot!' he said in a passion. 'You should have told me right away. I'd better have a look at your birth object.'

This happened but once or twice a year and Uncle Aliver made it very clear it was not something he enjoyed doing, there were other doctors for birth objects. I brought my plug out and placed it on top of his opened hand, the chain stretched out as far as it would go. He took a magnifying glass from a pocket and used it to observe my plug most fully, he put the magnifying glass away, he took out a pair of tweezers, he turned the plug over. 'Breathe in,' he said, I did, 'Breathe out,' he said and I did.

He tapped my plug lightly with his fingers, it made me very anxious.

'Is anything the matter with my James Henry?' I asked.

'I don't think so, but you may need to see someone else.'

He gave me back my plug.

'How do you feel?'

'Quite well, Uncle.'

'I want to hear what you hear, Clod, about the house.'

The Talking House

Up marble stairs down iron ones we went. Into small cupboards, into great halls, turning here and there at random, trying to hear the door handle Alice Higgs calling out, somewhere those two words picked out from all the cacophony of the building. How to catch it amongst all those other rumblings? The house talked and gabbed, it whispered, it bellowed, it sang and warbled, croaked, cracked, spat, tittered, flapped, panted, tooted and groaned. Young voices, high and lively, old voices, cracked and shaking, women's, men's, so many, many voices and not a one of those from a person, but all from the things of the talking house, here and there a curtain rod, a bird cage, a paperweight, ink bottle, floorboard, banister, lampshade, bell pull, tea tray, hairbrush, door, nightstand, basin bowl, shaving brush, cigar clippers, darning mushroom, mat and carpet. I did come upon a talking doorknob but this one was of Whitby jet and opened the door into the Mourning Room – where dead Iremongers are cleaned and dressed after dying, a room originally part of a mortician's house in Whitechapel – and that doorknob said Marjorie Clarke. We did visit Victoria Hollest, site of yesterday's Pinalippy encounter, but the room was empty now save for the sofa which was indeed still wondering in whispers, 'Where's Margaret?'

'Is that all?' asked Aliver.

'Yes, Uncle, and "Victoria Hollest", those four words.'

'Then perhaps any future Sittings must be delayed. I'd say we should replace the sofa but it has been sat upon for over a hundred years, and, besides, we have only your word on it.'

So continued our rounds. We even went beyond a door marked EEF on one side and ODOM on the other – to represent the separation of the sexes, named after the unfortunate couple expelled from the Garden of Eden, though we use the Iremonger variation of their names. I saw something of the girl cousins' establishments, and, in truth, they were not so very different to the Odom side of things, the classroom was just about identical, except different objects said different things. It was in one of the classrooms, the one for the senior girl cousins, where at one of the desks sat Pinalippy staring at me peculiarly, and so many other girls staring at her and then at me, that the second incident occurred. Uncle spoke to the form mistress, the mistress ordered silence and I went about doing my hearing, and I very nearly missed it, but kneeling down at the desk of Cousin Theeby I heard just under the noise of her hot-water bottle cover (Aimy Aiken) which in itself was not loud, a porcelain inkwell called Jeremiah Harris saying, along with its name, 'I should be much obliged.'

Uncle asked me if I was absolutely certain. I was.

'It's probably nothing,' Uncle told the form mistress, 'but have that inkwell sent downhouse. Label it first.'

I felt very important then, with all the girl cousins watching me, until I heard Cousin Horryit muttering, 'Send him downhouse while you're at it.'

Horryit was considered the most beautiful of all the Iremonger cousins. She had a loud birth object called Valerie Borthwick, I had no idea what Valerie was. Horryit was due to marry Cousin Moorcus the next month.

Later on, in the long gallery, there was a carpet beater that said, besides Esther Fleming, 'Whooping cough.' And in Grandfather's great dining room there was a decanter, Alexander Fitzgerald, that said, 'I'd rather not.' But there was no Alice Higgs to be heard anywhere. At last Uncle Aliver said we might stop now. We sat down upon the marble steps of the grand staircase near the bottom between Grandmother's dozing porter and Grand Grandfather.

'What's happening to the objects, Uncle?' I asked.

'I've no idea, Clod, we may need to call in help. How are you feeling? I haven't tired you out too much?'

'No, sir.'

'Thank you, Clod,' and then, I think it must have been the pressure of the day, all those objects making such new sounds, that, after a sigh, Uncle Aliver spoke out of turn, 'Clod, your grandfather has asked me to take particular care of you.'

'Grandfather?' I asked. 'Grandfather mentioned me?'

'Yes, Clod, he speaks of you often. He will say as I tend to him, "And tell me, Aliver, how is our Clod these days, we have such hopes for him."'

'Does he?' I asked. 'Does he really? I haven't seen Grandfather for over a year. I hear the train coming back of course and going out. Grandmother won't see me, she said she might in the summer, but it's far from certain. And I always thought Grandmother was fonder of me than Grandfather.'

'He has not forgotten you. Only the other day he said to me, "Clod shall be trousered soon I think?" I tell him yes. And your grandfather says, "I must see him before then."'

'Grandfather wants to see me, he actually said that?'

'Yes, Clod, he did. You're a special case, the one that hears things, and so we must be careful with you. We must keep you safe until your grandfather reveals his plans.'

142

'Grandfather,' I whispered, 'when will I see him? I shan't be alone then, shall I? Will you be there, Uncle Aliver?'

'You must not upset yourself, I've probably said too much already. Go back to your room now, Clod, get some rest. I'll sign a chit and have it sent to the schoolrooms. And, Clod, do not spoil yourself over Tummis Iremonger, Tummis is not the kind of friend that you should have, so keep him at a distance, such a person can do you no good at all. You might cultivate, say, your Cousin Moorcus instead.'

'But Tummis –' I protested.

'I shall tell your grandfather how good you are. You do want that, don't you? A good report.'

'Yes, Uncle, of course.'

'Off you go then, my little germ. I must send a message to Bay Leaf House. Tread along carefully.'

In the Sun Room

So dripping, minute counting, second hauling, the rest of the day slowly ebbed. I'm done with the sun, I said to myself, and did a sort of stomping dance to it. I caught naps here and there, shut off bits of daytime, pulled the curtains of my eyes on them and tried to store up a few borrowed minutes, took time from the day and gave it to the night, only when I slept Grandfather stalked my dreams and I sat up in a sweat. At last Grandfather's steam scream engine sounded throughout the house. Not long, not so very long now.

143

I waited for Lucy Pennant, I was dressed and ready though all Iremongers around me were undressed of the day and surely in pyjamas and under sheets and hair nets and moustache nets and mosquito nets. I was waiting, I had brushed my hair in the mirror, pulled my socks up, tightened my shoes and lay on my bed waiting for the house to quieten down. I heard a footman up and down the corridor making sure nothing else was needed, that we had all gone to bed. As I waited and waited I must have fallen asleep. I woke up suddenly, something had just come running past my door, cawing.

Whatever it was had woken me up. How long had I been asleep? I couldn't quite say. Was I too late? I didn't know. I brushed myself down a bit, parted my hair, telling myself if I'm to have any chance of seeing her I must hurry. I opened my bedroom door. What was outside? The night was. I walked into it.

I could not find her at first. She was not in the common room, that fireplace had already been laid. She was not in any of the schoolrooms. At last, down a deep corridor so thick with night that my small candle was nearly choked on it, there she was and there was the quiet, so quiet, words coming from her bonnet, I heard amongst the other objects in that room Patrick Wellens and Jenny McMannister (a fire grate and a bell jar) some other slight whispering. She was in the Sun Room, but she was not making the fireplace, she was wiping the windows.

'Whatever are you doing?' I asked.

'Don't creep up on me like that! Not unless you want a shovel across your ear.'

'I thought you did the fireplaces.'

'I wanted to look out,' she said.

'Should you be doing that? I mean, is it right? I mean, won't you be in trouble?'

'Who does the windows in this house? They're shocking.'

'They probably thought it wasn't worthwhile. It all gets covered over so quickly.'

'I just want to see out, I can't open the window, it's bolted down . . .'

'Well, you see, otherwise the gulls will come in.'

'I thought if I gave one a good scrub maybe I'd see something, anything really, just something, out.'

'You do know that it's probably worse on the other side.'

'I hadn't thought of that.'

'That's one of the problems, living in a dustheap as we do, there's so much dust and soot and ash, it does tend to get everywhere. If you step out just for a minute and then come back inside and blow your nose, well then your snot is rather black. It gets everywhere, the dust, all over, not just the house, people too.'

'So there's really not much point then in cleaning the window.'

'Not much I shouldn't think.'

'But it might make the room just a little lighter. Mightn't it?'

'I suppose it shouldn't make it any darker.'

'Let us try then.'

'Me? You can't mean me, I'm an Iremonger.'

'Yes, you can help.'

'Oh,' I said, and, 'all right then.'

And so I did, and so we did. Clean a window. We wiped it down with old rags and the rags which were not exactly white to begin with were very soon utterly black, no matter how many newish rags we used they were soon all as black, so much night mopped up, but still so much more to go. And as I scrubbed so close beside her I listened out for those muted words, they seemed a little quieter than before, but at last I understood the first word, 'Alec!' I said. 'I think it's Alec!'

'What did you say?' she asked.

'A lec,' I said, 'er . . . I like to clean windows.'

'Idiot,' she muttered. 'Where've you been anyway? I thought you weren't coming.'

'I meant to be here much earlier, I really meant to, but it didn't quite happen. Another night I'll be much quicker.'

'You'd better, I can't stay up here all night waiting for you.'

'No, no, one wouldn't expect that.'

'Things to do.'

'Yes, yes,' I said and for a while we were quiet, scrubbing along.

'I'm sorry about your ear,' she said at last.

'It's quite well now, thank you.'

'The bell will be rung soon enough, I should go down. You'd better be quicker tomorrow. If you want me to tell you anything.'

Our hands were very filthy by then and I didn't mind at all. We stood back to look at the glass. It looked just the same to me, though I told her that it surely was a little lighter, and she seemed glad of that. She made me promise to come back into the Sun Room during the day and see if it was at all different, and I promised her that I would.

'Do you know that what we're doing now,' I said, 'I'm really not supposed to do at all.'

'Clean windows?'

'Not supposed to do that either actually, but most of all, not to talk to you.'

'Why not.'

'Not allowed. House rule.'

'Who said?'

'Grandfather did.'

'Who's Grandfather?'

'Umbitt Iremonger of the dustheaps.'

'I'm one of you lot too,' she said. 'An Iremonger. On Mother's side.'

'I'm Iremonger through and through, mother and father.'

'Then I know what that makes you.'

'What does it?'

'It makes you grow up to look all odd and crooked.'

That stung a bit. 'I'm not very tall, am I?'

'You're a little shifty, aren't you?'

'For my age? I'm fifteen and a half, when I'm sixteen I have to marry.'

'Well, good luck to you.'

'I don't want to marry. I'd rather not.'

'Then say no.'

'Can't.'

'Why not?'

'Rule. Everyone marries at sixteen. Well, nearly everyone.'

'You do like your rules, don't you?'

'No, I don't. They're just there, aren't they, I can't get over them.'

'Because you're so small?'

'Because I'm an Iremonger.'

'I'm sixteen already and not married. Nor likely to be. Came close to it though. Was going to be. Narrow escape.'

'Really? Were you really? Do you mind my asking to whom?'

'The heaps, you dolt.'

'Oh.'

'Oh, he says.'

'Will you tell me about it?'

'What's on the end of that chain you've got there?'

'It's my James Henry Hayward.'

'Your what?'

'My Ja— My plug, my birth object. Do you want to see it? I'll show it to you.'

'You called it something else just a moment ago.'

'Ah . . . well, I may as well tell you I suppose. I hear voices.'

'You do what?'

'Objects, you see, some objects have voices, they have names, they tell me their names. That bell jar over there. Do you see it?'

'Yes.'

'It's called Jenny McMannister.'

'What are you talking about? Are you ill, is that it?'

'Yes, I am ill. Uncle Aliver gives me pills.'

'Is there something very wrong with you? I thought there was to begin with, I had that feeling. Are you dangerous? You don't look that dangerous.'

'No, no, I'm not dangerous at all.'

'You better not be, I'll thump you if you're dangerous.'

'I'm not dangerous,' I said, 'I just hear things.'

'Well, you can hear things away from me. Don't you spook me or I'll get my shovel out again.'

'No, no, I shouldn't dream of it.'

'I'd better get back downstairs now, before I'm missed.'

'Goodnight then. Thank you for talking. I'll come sooner tomorrow.'

'Better had.'

And off she went with all her cleaning business, but she turned around at the door.

'What's my name again?' she said, quite fiercely too.

'It is Lucy Pennant of course,' I said.

'Thank you,' she said, and was gone.

'And Alec something,' I whispered.

And that was it. What a night. I felt quite light as I walked back to my room, I even swung my James Henry around on its chain. I ran the last part, and as I rushed up the stairs I saw, moving fast with me, something just above, for the smallest moment there was a bird moving about in the shadows.

'Wateringcan!' I called.

But then he was gone, out of sight, up into the rooms at the top of the house. He'd better not get into the attics, the bats would do for him there.

I went to bed thinking that it was a shame I had no keepsake of Lucy Pennant, some small thing, something to help me through the day, something to remember her by. A portrait should be best though, a likeness.

Uncle Idwid

Quite early the next morning, just after getting dressed, not long after Grandfather's engine had left for the day, I heard Percy Hotchkiss coming down my corridor and with it something unfamiliar called Geraldine Whitehead. Uncle Aliver knocked and entered, looking very nervous, beside him stood a man I had never seen before and yet felt I had known all my life, there was something very familiar about him. He was wearing official uniform, a gold braided bay leaf on his collar. He was a little man, his sparse hair was stuck hard to his large white skull, and there were veins on his temple clearly visible. Who was he? Why did I seem to know him?

'May I present,' said Uncle Aliver, but nervously, 'your Uncle Idwid Iremonger. I do not think you have met him before; he is your Uncle Timfy's twin brother.'

'How is little Timfy?' asked Idwid. 'He is my *younger* brother, you know, he arrived after me, by some twenty-two minutes.' He said all this smiling, he seemed to smile a lot. His voice, unlike his twin's, was very gentle. I had heard of Uncle Idwid before but never met him. He was a Governor, one of the highest of all Iremongers, but he lived in the city and did not come home.

'Here is the boy at last, is he?' said Uncle Idwid, his face opening up to reveal his clean teeth, but he was not looking at me as he spoke, his face was pointed away. Only then did I see that the orbs in his head were wrong, they were all milky. Uncle Idwid was blind. He was smiling widely around the room and breathing deeply as if to take in all the air. 'Sit me down please, Aliver.'

Uncle Aliver showed him to one of my chairs.

'Make me close to him, draw me very close, and you, dear Clod, come to me. Sit with me, shall you?'

I was sat beside him, very close, both of our feet not quite reaching the ground.

'How lovely it is to be here in Heap House once more,' he said. 'Now, what do I hear?' He cupped his small mani-cured hands to his ears and hummed a little to himself, then smacked his lips. 'I hear James Henry Hayward! Hallo! Hallo! Come, James Henry Hayward, come, come to me!' He opened his hands out. 'I know you're here, come, I want to know you. Let it out, Clod, let me see, do let me see.'

I couldn't help smiling, he could hear like me! Aliver nodded to me and I slowly put my plug into his hands. Idwid brought it very close to his nose and sniffed it, patted it, and stroked it all over.

'James Henry Hayward,' it said, quite happily I thought.

Idwid turned it upside down, he tickled it on its underside.

'James Henry Hayward!' it seemed to giggle. I had never heard it laughing before. And as James Henry called out his name ever more speedily in sheer joy and happiness I became aware of another voice coming closer and that voice was saying in a cool whisper, 'Geraldine Whitehead.'

Geraldine Whitehead I saw now was some metal implement with a long thin twisted snout, a strange skinny clamp of some sort. James Henry immediately shut up.

'My plug!' I called.

'Hush now,' Uncle Idwid said, smiling, 'hush, it's quite well, it's just being looked after by my clippers a moment.'

'Geraldine Whitehead,' I said, 'that's its name.'

'Yes indeed, what a clever one you are! I heard you hear all the names too!' said Idwid. 'Geraldine Whitehead is a pair of special clippers, designed for extracting nasal hair, ear hair too. Very fine and very helpful. Now let me see.' He very gently held onto my plug with his Geraldine

Whitehead, and then just as delicately released it and put the clippers away again, and James Henry said, 'James Henry Hayward.'

'Aliver,' asked Uncle Idwid, 'you have recently examined Clod?'

'Yes, Governor, very recently.'

'And there are positively no cracks upon him, you have checked?'

'Indeed, Governor, none at all.'

'And you have listened to him? And there is no hollowness?'

'There is no hollowness, Governor, I have listened indeed.'

'So then,' said Idwid, quite content, 'I was called in good time. It's something exceptional, my dear Clod, to have a Listener. I'm a Listener and I became Governor Extraordinary of Birth Objects.'

'I didn't know there was anyone else. No one ever said.'

'Clod, we shall keep each other company.'

'I am very glad you are here, sir.'

'We are meant for one another.'

'Is there something wrong with James Henry?' I asked.

'Nothing in particular I shouldn't think, but we shall keep an ear on him,' said Idwid, grinning. 'Tell me, young Clod, what have you been hearing? You've heard Victoria Hollest asking for Margaret? What else then. Tell me, please do.'

'I do hear voices,' I said. 'I think I always have; objects calling out names, always names. I don't know what it means exactly –'

153

'It means you're a very clever one.'

'I just hear names, not everything has a name.'

'To be sure.'

'But some things do, some things whisper their names and some things shout their names, and many birth objects have names, but not all –'

'Not all, you say? How interesting.'

'And the fire bucket in the hall has a name, and a newel post to the marble stairs. All over the house different objects with different names.'

'What a perfect joy you are!' said Idwid, still holding my plug. 'How lovely to have found you. I'm going to be here until all the objects have settled down, because you see,' he said, leaning in very closely so that his shiny moon-face was close to mine, 'the objects have grown a little jumpy. Nothing to be alarmed about, they do get ideas in their heads from time to time and then they need to be reminded gently what they are. I can do that for them. Clod, my little lugs, we shall hear much of one another, very much, and it shall all be splendid. Now, Clod, it seems, according to your Uncle Aliver here, that the unrest amongst certain objects began with the loss of a doorknob called –'

'Alice Higgs!' I cried, having suddenly worked something out. Not Alec. Not Alec at all! I had been so stupid!

'Alice Higgs? And what do you know of Alice Higgs the doorknob?'

'That she was Aunt Rosamud's and she lost it.'

'Nothing more?' he asked.

'Nothing,' I said, though I was shaking. I mustn't tell him, but I wanted to tell him. There was something about him that made you want to please him very, very much. I so nearly told him everything. But though I liked him so, I must keep the whereabouts of Alice Higgs a secret, just for now.

'Well, well, we shall find this Alice Higgs, wherever it may be. It's hiding, but we'll find it. There's no place that a doorknob called Alice Higgs can hide from me. I, Idwid Percible Iremonger, find all things, whether they want to be found or not. Whenever something's lost they often send for me.'

I didn't like him so much then. He handed me back my plug.

'Thank you so much,' he said.

'James Henry Hayward,' it whispered.

'Goodbye, James Henry Hayward, I will hear you again shortly. And goodbye, dear Clod. We shall speak, more, you and I, of so many things. We that hear so much have so much to tell one another. Lead me on, please,' he quietly whispered and Uncle Aliver stood him up and then the shining little man, a smile upon his face, was gone and I was left in my room to my own thoughts, thoughts of Lucy Pennant, who I understood only now in my foolishness was keeping Alice Higgs in her bonnet. I must get it from her before Uncle Idwid finds it, because if Idwid heard Alice Higgs first there was no knowing what might be done to Lucy.

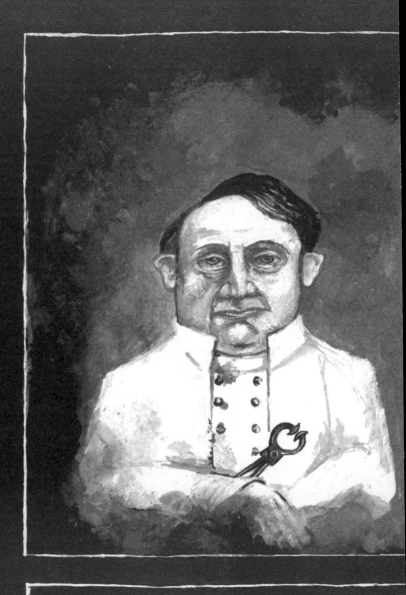

The Heap House Cooks Mr Orris

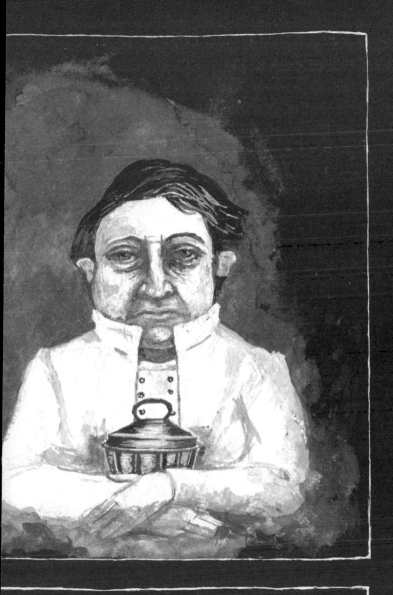

... and Mrs Odith Groom

12

A PEWTER JELLY MOULD AND A PAIR OF CAST IRON SUGAR CUTTERS

Extract from the menu book of Mr Orris and Mrs Odith Groom, head cooks of Forlichingham Park, Forlichingham, London

Entry for 12th November 1875

LIST OF LOSS: Thief in the kitchen. The large brass five and a half gallon fire extinguisher. Palette knife. Two pastry jiggers. Four Iremonger spoons (twelve ounces). Thirteen icing tubes of best nickel silver missing. Thief among us. Don't know who. Will find out. Knives sharpened, keeping on our own persons. Odith a cleaver, Orris his block carver.

LIST OF SPOILED: Twelve haddock even though curried. Hung pigs stained and maggoty, one turned bright turquoise. Seven brace of pheasant as solid as porcelain, can't be thawed. Mushrooms, shattered. Carrots, elasticated. Apples, gone black and hollow. Cured bacon, puddled. Porridge oats, not oats but moths, all suffocated in their jar. So little left to send up the house by the dumb waiter.

Upstairs lunch: pickled pig feet, pickled cabbage, salted lettuce.
Downstairs lunch: chitterling sausage, rescued tripe, snail and spoon.
Upstairs dinner: roast of cormorants, black skimmers and osprey, boiled turnip.
Downstairs lunch: dredged rodent and spoon.

NOTES: Today we saw a cup move of its own volition, actually witnessed it. Is the world coming to an end? There's nothing, nothing to be trusted. Only Orris. Only Odith.

The Heap House Serving Girl
Florence Balcombe

13

A MOUSTACHE CUP

Lucy Pennant's narrative continued

When I woke the next morning, after horrible dreams of my matchbox sparking alight and setting fire to me, I found everyone in the dormitory in a tizzy. The Iremongers were huddled in corners, whispering, but none of them gone to work.

'What's happening?' I asked.

'What's happening?' came back. 'Where'vc you been?'

'Upstairs firegrates. In my bed, trying to get some sleep. The usual.'

'There are new people, come from the city. We're all to be questioned, they came last night with Umbitt.'

'Something's up!' one said.

'Something terrible,' shrieked another. And then they all sounded off like a bunch of shrieking poultry, squawking and nipping, and making lots of movements with their hands and faces.

'I saw one of the city Iremongers shouting at Mr Sturridge,' yelped one.

'And what did Sturridge say?' I asked. 'He wouldn't have stood for that.'

'Wouldn't he though? He did nothing! He bowed his head.'

'And Piggott's in a fury! One Iremonger saw her weeping!'

'Mrs Piggott! Why? What has happened?'

'Things!' they chorused. 'Oh, things!'

'What things?' I asked.

'Last night, Lorky Pignut,' said an Iremonger, smoothing her dress down and standing forward, appointing herself mouthpiece, very important now, chest forward, 'you must have been doing the firegrates, it was after the bell had rung. It happened down the corridor to the ashrooms. There came a terrible screaming, just one Iremonger screaming at first but then afterwards more screaming from other Iremongers, so we all went running, in our nightgowns, just enough time to slip on our clogs, and we rushed down the corridor, serving Iremongers from every room, body Iremongers too, the lot, so many white faces, and pushing through a little, I managed at last to see what is was all about. And then, oh yes, I certainly saw it, with my own eyes! And I screamed too!'

'Oh, the terror!' called the Iremongers around her, ruffling their feathers.

'What?' I asked. 'What was it?'

164

'It was,' said the Iremonger, and very slowly, her face quite white, her hands shaking, 'it was a moustache cup!'

'A moustache cup?' I asked. 'What on earth is that?'

'To be honest, we didn't know at first. Never seen the like. But a moustache cup has a special lip over the rim of it so that a gentleman –'

'A distinguished gentleman very like,' added another.

'Yes, a distinguished gentleman,' continued the first, reclaiming her position, 'may not disturb his well waxed and shaped moustache when he is a-drinking his tea. That's a moustache cup for your information. And there was one last night! On the corridor. A cup with a strange shelf over its rim, white porcelain, no markings. No one knew where it came from, no one had ever seen it before.'

'But what,' I asked, 'is so terrifying in that?'

'Because, Looky Pineknot, if you want to know, it was moving!'

'Moving?' I asked.

'Moving of its own accord, I saw it, I should not have believed it otherwise, but it was rolling along on its bottom, around and around in circles. Sometimes it stopped for a while and then hopped a little forward like a robin or a sparrow or some small bird. Sometimes it rolled itself almost to the feet of some Iremongers and then there was such a screaming or a scrambling to get away from it. One Iremonger threatened it with a poker and it did scuttle away a bit then.'

'There must have been some creature inside it, a mouse, perhaps, or a shrew,' I said, 'a large bug even.'

'No! No!' she said, 'there was just a cup, only a cup, nothing more, and that cup was wild and clinking here and there. Until Mrs Piggott came a-roaring, 'What are you all doing?' and then in that parting of the Iremongers to let her through, the cup took its chance and rolled and clinked and slammed itself along the way, had a direct hit with the fire extinguisher there, and clattered away from it out of the corridor towards the kitchens. And then Mrs Piggott was so white! And then the screaming, "Catch it! Catch it!"'

'You should have seen all the rushing about,' chimed in another. 'Some Iremongers on chairs and tables screaming, as the cup rushed hither and thither in a terrible state, until at last Mr Groom the cook, holding a copper saucepan upside down, managed to trap the thing beneath it. And Groom sat there then, on top of the pan, but you could still hear the cup beneath clanking against the sides making a terrible din. Desperate to get out.'

The train drowned her out a moment, off to London.

'Where it is now?' I asked.

'Still just there, under the saucepan, only Mr Groom's moved now and in his place has been put a great kitchen weight.'

'Twelve pounds!' added another Iremonger with considerable excitement, stepping forward and then stepping back again.

'And there it stays, clinking now and then, but much quieter than before, almost, you might say, sorrowfully.'

'I should very much like to see it,' I said.

'It's being guarded, round the clock, there's always at least four of Groom's kitchen lads there, and each armed with something blunt and heavy – a rolling pin, a thick wooden paddle, a spit pan – just in case the cup gets free again.'

'I'd like to see that all right,' I said.

'Well you can't, Iremonger!' said Mrs Piggott, standing in the doorway. 'Line up everyone! At the foot of your beds. General inspection!'

Mrs Piggott was gripping a tea strainer. It was my friend's tea strainer, the Iremonger who had scratched and lost her name, I felt certain of it. And her bed was empty, she wasn't in the dormitory. Where was she?

We were to stand before our beds, and wait to be called. It was happening in all the dormitories downstairs, there was such a flap on, a general inspection, all the servants were going to be questioned. One by one we should be summoned into Mr Sturridge's office where the interviews took place. The roll call was taken, numbers of servants reported and added up and marked down in the register.

We were asked where my missing friend was, who had last seen her, and one of the Iremongers said that she'd been worming in the ashrooms, that she had bits to haul there after being out in the heaps. More official men came in, city Iremongers with their dark suits and hats and all wearing the golden bay leaf upon their collars. They'd come from Bay Leaf House. They directed some serving boys to take her bed away, her stool, her spare clothes, all of it. As to where it went we heard clearly enough, 'Incinerator.' Shortly afterwards, another Iremonger came in and she had a mop and bucket and she scrubbed the floor where the Iremonger's bed had been.

'What's going on?' I whispered to the scrubber. 'Where is she, do you know?'

'Don't know. Shut up. Not to talk.'

A little later an Iremonger boy came with some whitewashing and scrubbed the wall.

'Do you know what's going on?' I asked him.

'Not allowed to speak. Particular instructions not to.'

After he had gone a further Iremonger entered with a big metal tank on his back and a spray pump.

'Close eyes!' he bellowed.

He sprayed some liquid into the air, all over us and our beds, like it was raining in the room, and when we called out in protest, a city Iremonger swung around some hand crank, a klaxon, an enormous hideous sound, and commanded, 'No talking! Silence! Silence during cleaning!'

And so we were sprayed. And stood there dripping, not just us and our clothes but our beds and the walls, everything sodden.

'Now, ladies, it is no matter,' said the city Iremonger, 'all this spraying, no matter at all. Just precaution. No alarm please. For your safety. Please now, to stand and slowly to dry by air, all is well. And please, a favour to ask of you. Please to shuffle the beds together and fill in this gap here. It looks, don't you think, somehow out of place.' He had us move the beds so that very soon it was as if it had never been there at all. 'So good! So good! Breathe in!'

'Excuse me, sir,' I said.

'What?' said the Iremonger. 'What is your point?'

'I clean the firegrates, sir, upstairs in the night.'

'And?'

'The Iremonger,' I said, 'who used to sleep here, where is she?'

'Why, why care?' He looked so interested now, he took a notebook from a pocket, muttered 'firegrates.'

Look out, I told myself, these men in their black suits will surely do whatever they want with a person, throw them into the heaps without so much as thinking about it.

'She . . . she,' I said, 'took a handkerchief from me, borrowed one. I should like it back.'

'Can't!' he said. 'Handkerchief's gone.'

'Is she well?'

'She is missing, suspected lost in heaps.'

'But she was in the ashrooms. She was worming. She'd come in already. She can't have been out in the heaps.'

'What is your purpose?'

'I clean the grates, upstairs, sir, as I said.'

'Well then, not to worry, are you? Nothing to do with

169

you, is it? You shall be reimbursed: one handkerchief. And now, all present, wait please, a while longer. In silence is best.'

He left.

'*You* wouldn't ask about her,' I whispered to those others in the dormitory. 'She's gone, and you didn't lift a finger. You just stand there. You just do whatever you're told.'

'And how brave were you, Iremonger?' said my neighbour.

'Can't recall you doing so very much,' said another.

'I asked, I did ask,' I said.

'Didn't look like much from here.'

'Didn't look like much of anything.'

'No, not very much,' I admitted.

'No, I should say not.'

'But I will find her, I will find out what's happened.'

'Hark at the hero.'

'I will,' I said, 'I will.'

'You'll clean the firegrates and shut up, that's what you will.'

'I won't let her fade away. I have friends, upstairs.'

That set them cackling.

'I do! Just you wait!'

More cackling.

'What a fuss she makes!' said one.

'And is it worth it?' wondered another.

'All the fuss over a heap.'

'Come on, Iremonger, what nonsense over nothing.'

'You're a firegrate, that's something to hold onto,' one said, and in a kinder voice, 'and we do so like to hear your stories.'

'Can you even remember her?' another asked gently.

'Of course I can.'

'Can you tell us what she looked like?'

'She wore a black dress and a white cap, and there were clogs on her feet,' I said, doing my best.

'And so have we all.'

'She had a big nose, her eyes were brown.'

'And tell us, will you, what was her name?'

'Iremonger,' I whispered.

They had us wait there, by our beds, all morning, drying out. At last, one by one, an Iremonger would be called and escorted out to be interviewed and would not come back afterwards, so that we who were left could only wonder at what was going on. Slowly, so slowly, the day ebbed on. Another Iremonger, a sink Iremonger, poked his head in to whisper that the moustache cup had managed to escape, that one of the kitchen boys, eager for a look-see, had lifted the pot, just a little, and the cup had rushed out, he's out in the heaps now, the boy, and all are looking for the moustache cup. What a fuss, I thought, what a people. I hoped they'd never find that moustache cup. I thought of Clod then, who though a bit strange and creeping, though his head was large and his skin pale, though he was short and peculiar, showed some kindness.

Perhaps Clod, perhaps odd Clod could help me find out what had happened to the Iremonger who had scratched her name. I'd find her, with his help. Together we would find her.

'Iremonger!'

I was called for, upstairs to Mr Sturridge's parlour.

Outside Mr Sturridge's parlour many objects had been stacked. There was the ship's lantern which was the butler's own particular object, and beside it various other odd things, a glass paperweight, a large pencil sharpener with handle, a pen nib, a bookend, a length of skirting board, an unwrapped bar of carbolic soap, a belt buckle and a boot scraper. Other people's birth objects I supposed, but quite why they were kept outside I had no notion.

I was summoned within. Mr Sturridge was in a corner, his great height nearly at the ceiling so that he appeared a sort of pillar to the room and that should he walk away the parlour would collapse. He looked very unhappy, he looked very put out. Various city Iremongers stood around the butler's desk, and behind the desk, raised high on pillows, sat some other type of Iremonger that I'd not seen before. This one was short and shiny and round-faced and in a very fine uniform with a gold bay leaf on its collar, he seemed a very happy man, with a big grin on his face. The eyes were the most peculiar thing about him, they were all white and milky, no dark in them at all. A blind man.

'This room,' he called, 'still is so noisy, still so very

talkative. There! What's that?' He sat upright, his head leaning now this side, now that. He raised his little hands up. 'Silence everyone! Not a sound. I've located it, there, there! There!' He pointed. 'What's there?'

'It is a wall sconce, sir,' said a city Iremonger.

'That wall sconce, quiet at first, timid certainly, is talking now. I hear you, you are called Charlie White. I knew it! I knew there was something tickling at my ears, I knew I heard something! Wait, stop that! Charlie White, be quiet!'

The little blind man took some metal tool from his pocket and began to wave it in the direction of the sconce. 'I will have silence, Charlie! I will!' A city Iremonger stepped up to assist him.

'Mister Idwid, sir, Guv'nor, may we help you at all?'

'Yes, you may indeed. Kind of you. It's Charlie White there! I've woken Charlie White and he's that disturbed, I cannot catch me another thing to hear while Charlie White's Charlie-ing and White-ing. And I know, I do so know it, there's something other than Charlie White and my Geraldine in this chamber. Butler!'

'Yes, sir,' said Sturridge.

'Someone's just come in. Who is't?'

'It is,' said the tall gent, exhaustion in his voice, 'another Iremonger, sir.'

'Without equipment, just in her own clothes?'

'Exactly so, sir.'

'Come here please, new Iremonger,' he said, leaning himself forward, his head at an angle so that his left ear

173

was entirely pointed in my direction, 'there's nothing to be afeard of. What's that, now?' he whispered, a huge smile coming to his fleshy lips. 'Come here, I think I hear you!'

I tried to step back, but a city Iremonger pushed me a step or two forward, closer to the blind man's ear, somehow, he seemed to know I was hiding something, though I cannot say how he knew.

'Closer, please,' he called, 'step closer!'

I was pushed further towards the desk, but just as I came so very close, as I was up against the desk, and as the city Iremonger behind me began to push my head a little over the desk, the little man cried out.

'Charlie White, I cannot hear with all your babbling. You, Dunnult!'

'Guv'nor,' said the city Iremonger beside him.

'Take that sconce away.'

As the taking was going on the little moon-man sat back, muttering to himself, his hand now and then stretching out in the air before him, quite in my direction.

'Something's there! I hear you! Not you, Charlie, not you. Be calm, Charlie, be silent!'

It took them some time to pull the sconce from the wall, but at last it was out, much plaster coming with it, and just as the little man had taken his, very neat, fingers from his ears, someone else came running in.

'There's a Gathering, Guv'nor! A Gathering! Two brooms missing, a fire extinguisher vanished, chimney rods disappeared, three gunny lamps and a water pump handle!

The Grooms have just handed in their report. In the cold room two hooks are unaccounted for. In the kitchens a ladle, a colander, a clove grater. In all it makes a path of disappearance, a map of missing!'

'I'll have no Gathering on my watch!' replied the little man, the smile for a moment falling off his lips, though it was back again a moment later.

'Upwards of thirty items, sir.'

'Guide me, Dunnult, guide me now, my dear fellow, propel me forward instantly.'

Within a minute he was gone and all the city Iremongers with him and I was left with Mr Sturridge in his parlour.

'Yet here, Iremonger?' said the butler. 'Proceed to your duties. The circus,' he said distastefully, 'is over!'

'Yes, sir, thank you, sir.' I was gone in a moment and soon at my day duties. I kept myself well mixed in with other Iremongers through the long day, and whenever I heard any talk of Idwid Iremonger, or Governor Iremonger, I was quick to be out of his way, he was close once only, in the bootroom, where I had a shift polishing, he came in there briefly, but backed out soon enough, complaining that there was too much noise in that place, though there was only me and two other Iremongers cleaning shoes at a trestle table. He never even looked in our direction.

'Too loud, too loud in here by half!' he cried. 'Who was it who dispersed the domestics to their stations?'

'Mr Sturridge, Guv'nor,' came the one called Dunnult.

'He doesn't know his position, wait until Umbitt's back,

then he'll know his position. Then –' big smile – 'he'll be positioned!'

'Yes, sir.'

'Guide me on, then, guide me!'

'Yes, sir, certainly, Guv'nor. This way.'

'A needle in a haystack! And no one can tell servant from servant. And forty-two objects unaccounted for.'

On he went, and, I suppose, up above stairs. I didn't see him again, not that day anyway. Later I should.

The train came back, same as usual. We had our food, like every night. And I was ready at the same old time, my fellow firegrates anxious beside me. I was up the stairs and shifting as soon as the bell was sounded.

I'll wait in the Sun Room, I thought, he'd be certain to look for me there. But then I wondered if the Masters' common room might not be better. I made some half-hearted attempts at the firegrates but I couldn't concentrate, I kept listening out. It seemed to me that there were far more noises that night, and as I was listening out at the fireplace in the Elephant Room, hearing some muttering coming down the flue, thinking I could just about make something out – some distant sound that may have been 'Ach, Umbitt!' – suddenly there he was right beside me.

'I told you not to creep up!' I said.

'Oh, yes, sorry,' he said, 'I was in such a hurry. I mean, I was so worried, I mean, I'm so glad to see you. I've been waiting all day, I should have been to the cellars myself were it not that I knew he was down there and I didn't want to draw attention. I've been *that* worried. I'm so glad to see you!'

'Yes, all right,' I said, 'that'll do. You needn't stand so close.'

'Ah! Sorry,' he said, he was so nervous.

'Truth is,' I said, 'I'm glad to see you and all.'

'Are you? *Are* you?'

'Don't overdo it.'

'I can't help it.' He stroked back the parting in his hair, stood up a little, tried a smile, gave it up, tried a sentence, gave it up, put his hand out towards my head, drew it back in, slumped a little, seemed to be putting off being brave till later. 'I'll show you some more of the house, if I may, come with me.'

I should have told him there and then about the blind man hearing me, I should have told him I was a thief, I should have told him about the Iremonger missing too, but I hesitated and let him draw me on, around and about the ugly palace.

'Dear Lucy Pennant,' he said, stopping at a room, it seemed to me quite at random, 'this here is called the Clip Room.'

'And what happens within, you are given your clips around the ear?'

'No, it is in here the family has its nails cut.'

'Fair enough. Something more. Show me more.'

Onwards we went but not far, Clod in the lead, listening

out, it seemed to me, so very carefully, and then suddenly he pulled me behind a tall vase. I heard something coming, scratching and swooping; there was a high shriek, I nearly answered with one of my own, but Clod put his hand over my mouth, and then a seagull came into view. It was a big raucous bird, and came pattering along the floorboards, poking at this and that. It waddled very close to us, padding right up.

'It's only Wateringcan,' Clod said. 'Shoo, Wateringcan, shoo.'

'Wateringcan?'

'My cousin Tummis's pet seagull, he's a black-legged kittiwake,' Clod explained, 'he got out. Go home, Wateringcan, go home!'

But Wateringcan did not go home, instead he let out his wings and hopped from foot to foot as if he was doing a dance, and then made some unpleasant throaty caw as if he was singing a song.

'He's going to get us caught,' I said. 'Go away, bird, scat!'

Clod took something from his pocket.

'It's all I have, my last squashed-fly biscuit, I'm going to throw it as far as I can and then we'll run in the other direction. Are you ready?'

'Ready!'

He threw it, the bird hopped after it and we rushed away. Along another corridor, Clod stopped suddenly, and had us hide behind a fire screen.

'What is it?' I asked.

'Ssssh!' he said.

We sat there for a long time. I heard nothing at all and just as I was about to tell him there was nothing there, there *was* someone. Footsteps. And I could just see a tall boy with very bright fluffy hair in his dressing gown walking along. He stopped for a bit, wiped his nose on his cuff, and called out in a quiet voice, 'Wateringcan? Are you there?'

Before rushing on again.

'It's Tummis,' he said, 'looking for his Wateringcan. He's a fine fellow, shall we go and meet him? He'd be very surprised to see you. But he'll be with Wateringcan by now and there's certain to be a great deal of cacophony. We used very often to be out together, there was a time we'd be out night after night looking for an ostrich chick.'

'An ostrich, here?'

'In truth, there was never much hope for it, Cousin Moorcus is to blame. Another night you must meet Tummis. I should warn him first.'

I must tell him now, I thought, will he help, can he help? He is an upstairs Iremonger, that's got to mean something. But what am I doing, hanging around with an Iremonger anyway, anyone in Filching would tell me that's a terrible thing to do. You can't trust an Iremonger, everyone knows that, you must keep them at a distance always. Spend too much time with an Iremonger and you're sure to come to harm, stands to reason, anyone in Filching would have said so, and yet there I was, me and Clod.

'Please come in, Lucy,' he said, at another doorway. 'This room here is called the Smoggery.'

'And why is it called that?'

'It is here in the Smoggery that the adult Iremongers come to smog.'

'Smog?'

'Yes, smog. Shall we smog, you and I, Lucy, in this room? It is what it is for after all. Shall we smog upon a leather sofa?'

'I don't know, generally I'm not asked like that, a boy comes at you, doesn't he, and gets closer and then, well there it is, you either do or you don't. And I'm not sure, Clod, I like you and that but . . .'

'You sit down on one of these chairs, they're very comfortable, a man comes and gives you a pipe and he lights it for you, and you smog, you make smog. Sometimes it's been so smogged up in this room that you cannot see from one wall to the other, sometimes there's so much smog the whole floor is obscured, it's a very smoky, foggy, thick place. Fancy a smog?'

'Yes, all right then, I'll have a smog.'

He got a pipe from a rack and we shared it together, the clay pipe passed from my mouth to his.

'I like this smogging,' I said.

'Me too,' he said, 'I do like a good smog.'

'Excellent it is.'

'And that's the truth.'

'Too right.'

'Well then, Lucy, here we are, comfortable too. So then, can you tell me?'

'What, tell you what?'

'Well . . . well can you tell me . . . is there anything you'd like to tell me . . . from your own lips . . . about yourself, I should like to know, there's still time, there's still night left.'

I should have told him all about downstairs, but I couldn't, not yet, and he sat so close to me, and I didn't mind then, and we passed the pipe between us and it was so good for a bit, so good in particular that I didn't want it to stop. What shall he do, I wondered, what shall he do when I tell him, he shan't call out shall he? These Iremongers are so particular about property, but I don't think he shall. I quite liked him then, sitting beside me, his head close, yes I liked him in a way, if things had been different, if it'd been at home say, in the boarding house, we might have done things together. And then I thought, why don't we anyway? So I began to speak, passing the clay pipe between us, and I told him of everything but that which mattered most, as a start to get us going, building up to it, so to speak.

I told him of the orphanage and the other red-haired girl there, the bully, something of the house I lived in before, and the many families that dwelt there on different floors, and that I lived in the basement with Father and

181

Mother, that Mother washed clothes and Father was the porter for the house. And then I told him that there had been a great illness and that objects seemed to get ill and then afterwards people did, and there was a great shutting off of doors and landings and that one particular day when I came home from school my mother and father had, I said, 'Stopped, sort of,' I hesitated there, 'they'd been objectified, they were all stiff and weren't themselves any more.'

'No one told me anything about that!' he said at last. 'Not even rumours!' We were silent a while, then he said quietly, 'So you have no parents either, just like me.'

'But you've got all those cousins and aunts and uncles.'

'I could live without them, pretty much, save Tummis,' he said. 'Lucy, I know about London too, though I've never seen it.'

'You think you know London, do you?'

'The Monument. Elephant and Castle. Lincoln's Inn Fields. Threadneedle Street! The Strand! High Holborn!'

'But do you know what any of them look like?'

'Seven Dials! Whitechapel! The Bloody Tower! Harley Street!'

'What does that all prove?'

'What I know. White sewing machines are got at 48 Holborn Viaduct. Horle's ink powders at 11 Farringdon Road. W. Waller, theatrical costumier and wig maker, 84 and 86 Tabernacle Street, Finsbury Square. Liebig Company's extract of beef, 9 Fenchurch Avenue. All that, that's London.'

182

'But they're just words, said like that they don't mean anything.'

'Bird's custard powder, no eggs required, sold everywhere!'

'That's enough.'

'What else? There's more, much more. Worth a guinea a box, Beecham's pills for nervous and bilious disorders.'

'All right, all right.'

We smogged on a while in silence.

'Do you know anything, Lucy Pennant,' he asked, 'about my Aunt Rosamud?'

'Never so much as a whisper,' I said, reddening up.

'Well you see, how to say, my Aunt Rosamud, well she was . . . no, that's not it . . . I'm not very fond of Aunt Rosamud . . . yes, but how to go on from there . . . when we're born, we Iremongers, born here in Heap House, we are given, each of us, something . . . something to hold onto . . . this isn't quite the way to swing at it. I'll start again. Lucy?'

'Yes, what?'

'Lucy!'

'Yes?'

'Be very quiet. Behind the sofa, quick!'

Again I heard nothing but Clod held his hands to ears and went terrible pale. And again he was right. Long, long before I heard it, he knew something was coming. Whatever it was seemed very large, there was a great rumbling before it was very close, the whole room seemed to shudder, it came closer and closer till everything was shaking, and there was a terrible stench of gas. Clod was in such a panic and about to call out that I held him close to me to keep him shushed. But it did go away again, the great clanking noise, it went quieter and quieter and then at last I released Clod, he looked up and was in such a terror.

'What was that?' I asked.

'It was,' he said in a weak voice, 'it was someone carrying something very loud by the name of Robert Burrington.'

'Who's Robert Burrington?'

'I don't rightly know, I've never heard it before, I don't know what it's doing or who has it. But I don't think we'd better stay here, it's not safe now.'

He took my hand again and rushed me onwards out of the Smoggery and down some stairs, very silently past a man in uniform asleep at a desk, past a monster clock, and into some new huge place I had never been before, nor knew existed.

'This, dear Lucy.'

'*Dear* Lucy?'

'This is the Marble Hall of course.'

'Very grand, isn't it?'

'Here is the Great Chest. In here are kept all the birth objects of the Iremongers that have died. I shall tell you about one or two if you like. See that blackboard rubber there on the third shelf? That was my father's. Beside it is a small key which is to unlock a pianoforte, that was my mother's.'

'You're showing me your parents?'

'Yes.'

'Thank you, Clod,' I said, very sincerely, 'honoured.' I was.

'I didn't know them, either of them. But I often come here, to look at their objects, wondering about them, as if I'll understand them more by studying these bits and pieces. All those old lives. That's Great Grandfather Adwald's swordstick up there.'

'And what is that one?'

'That's Great-great Uncle Dockinn's narwhal horn and next to it is his wife Osta's nautilus shell. And there is the red coral that was Great Aunt Loopinda's.'

'Who got the little clock there?'

'It is an ormolu clock, that was Emomual's, he died over a hundred years ago. And there is his brother Oswild's broadsword, they came from a time when birth objects were such beautiful things, not brushes and ink bottles, not blotting paper and plungers, but carved ivory olifants and gilded armillary spheres and clockwork birds and elephants' feet. But not any more because Grandmother says we need everyday objects, because we live in a utilitarian age.'

'The case is all locked up, is it?'

'Oh yes, it's always kept locked, and opened only when someone dies.'

'A baby's bootie, that's sad.'

'Not really, that was Great Uncle Fratz's and he lived

to be ninety-three. What's sad though is that cloth cap there and that spinning top, that cigar clipper, all died very young, and the salt and pepper pots there, they are sad.'

'Twins?'

'Yes, that's right. Typhus.'

'What are those ones kept in this small mean chest beside the great one, a pillbox, a skipping rope, a glass vase, a glass eye – what's that about?'

'Those are the Iremonger suicides,' I said.

'Poor beggars. No, I prefer the bigger chest, thick glass isn't it?'

'As thick as the glass used in deep-sea helmets worn by men who venture underwater, there's a marking on the bottom right corner – PREBBLE & SON GLASS MANU-FACTURERS FOR THE DEEP. Well, that's the Marble Hall and the Great Chest.'

'Thank you. Very much.'

'I've shown you several rooms now, haven't I?'

'Yes, you have.'

'And now I'm going to ask something, and be very blunt about it.'

'Do it then and all in a rush.'

'I think you have my Aunt Rosamud's door handle in your hair beneath your bonnet.'

'I . . . how . . . well . . . I don't say it isn't so.'

'I know you do, Lucy, and it isn't right.'

'How do you know? Maybe I haven't.'

'I can hear it.'

186

'It's a doorknob! You can't hear . . .'

'It's very faint now . . . quite a whisper, I hear it talking, saying its name.'

'All guff, isn't it? Don't you try to frighten me.'

'It's saying "Alice Higgs", very weakly, it's barely audible now.'

'So you say. That doesn't prove a thing.'

'Then take off your bonnet.'

'Shan't!'

'Please, please, Lucy. It isn't safe, not any more.'

'Finders keepers! I found it!'

'And they'll find you but I doubt they'll keep you.'

'I don't have anything else! Nothing at all! Nothing in the whole world! Not a single thing, Clod, not one object! You wouldn't take it from me, would you? It's such a weight, a perfect little weight.'

'I must take it from you and get it to Aunt Rosamud, and then it'll all stop I think, all will be back to normal, the city Iremongers will go back to the city and all will be well again, and I'll come and see you every night, without fail. And you'll be safe, quite safe. You'll be safe just as soon as you give me the door handle, but if you don't give it to me then they'll keep searching for you and they'll find you, and then, oh Lucy, if they find you with that door handle I've no notion what they'll do with you, but it shall be awful dreadful, and whatever it is they do to you, it will mean one thing for certain, that if they find you with that in your bonnet then they'll not forgive you, and then, for certain, for an absolute certainly, you shan't be coming upstairs any more, and I shall never see you again. And the thought of that is so terrible to me. Give it to me, Lucy, give it to me now, Lucy Pennant, and let me help you!'

What a speech it was. I found my hands undoing my bonnet, but stopped a moment.

'On one condition,' I said.

'Now, Lucy, you ought to hurry! You know you should!'

'There's something you must do.'

'Anything! Only name it and give me the handle!'

'I'm looking for a friend of mine, an Iremonger downstairs, she was out on the heaps, or in the ashroom, and she's disappeared and they're making such a fuss about it, and I want to know where she's gone, I think she's in danger, and I want you to help me.'

'Anything, just give me the handle.'

'You'll find out what happened to her?'

'Yes, I'll try what I may, what was her name, how will I know her to talk of?'

'That's the easy part,' I said, 'she's the Iremonger that's gone missing.'

'Right then!' he said and held out his hand.

'She lost her name, she scratched it somewhere here in Heap House, but she can't remember where she put it.'

'I've probably seen it. You should have asked earlier. People have written their names all over the shop.'

'Tell me!'

'Some have been burned with a magnifying glass like

188

Jaime Brinkley, 1804, but that is on a window seat that was made before it got here.'

'A female, Clod. Seen any female names?'

'Helen Bullen, Form 2B.'

'Where was that?'

'It's on a ruler in the schoolroom.'

'I don't think that's her.'

'This is the Property of Prunella Mason, Keep Off. That's on a chest in the Long Gallery.'

'No, no I don't think so.'

'Florence Balcombe, 1875.'

'Where was that?'

'Um, one of the back staircases. On a step scratched in.'

'That's it! You've found her, Clod, you've bloody found her!' I gave him a kiss then, right on the lips for the joy of it. He looked punched afterwards, as if I'd struck him. 'Got her name!' I said. 'Now we need to find her. You'll ask about, Clod, won't you, find out what happened?'

I took the bonnet off and my hair came down, and I heard Clod whispering, 'I shall start flying. Oh, I'll bump on the ceiling!'

'What?'

'Nothing, nothing at all, Lucy Pennant,' he said. 'It's very red, isn't it, your hair. You kissed me.'

But then he went all white again.

'Just a kiss, Clod.'

'Albert Powling!' he whispered. 'Hurry!'

We hid behind the Great Chest, which now had twelve

feet when only a moment ago it stood on eight.

Footsteps, then more footsteps, different footsteps. Then speaking too.

'I heard something,' came a man's voice.

'Yes, Uncle Timfy, what was it?' This one was younger.

'I think it was voices. Stunly, Divit?'

'Yes, Uncle.'

'I want you very alert, I'll not have these city Ires telling us what's what. I'm the what's what around here. I don't care that Idwid's back, what's Idwid to me? He's always putting me down. So what that he's a Governor? I'm the one that looks after Heap House, I'm the one with eyes that work. I'm a House Uncle, I am, and I will have my respect. Well then, you've done your rounds, who's missing, who's out when they should be in?'

'Tummis, Uncle.'

'And Clod.'

'There'll be no trousers for them if ever I have a say in it. Where's Moorcus?'

'On the task!'

'What's that now?'

A rustling sound, a patter of feet upon the marble slabs.

'It's that bird again.'

'Catch it! Trap it!'

And from our hiding place I heard Clod whispering, 'Oh no.'

A great shriek.

'Got it, Uncle!'

'Good boys, good boys.'

'Hilary Evelyn Ward-Jackson,' whispered Clod, 'oh no!'

More footsteps, more people arriving. 'Look what I found!'

'Tummis Iremonger!'

'Wateringcan! Wateringcan! There you are at last!'

'Wring it, snap it!' yelled the one called Uncle.

And then there was a noise like a stick being snapped in half.

'Wateringcan!' someone yelled in pain.

'Well done, Moorcus. Take him, upstairs now, to Umbitt himself!'

And then they all went away again. And panting, shaking, we crawled out, there was the seagull on the floor.

'Oh, my poor, poor Tummis,' said Clod.

'And poor Wateringcan,' I said.

'It must all stop, it's all going wrong,' he said. 'Give me the door handle, Lucy, for good and all.'

I untied my hair then, and handed it over.

'We'll meet tomorrow?' I asked.

'Yes, yes,' Clod said in a panic, 'you know the Sitting Room?'

'With the red sofa?'

'That's it, we'll meet there, tomorrow night without fail.'

'Why there?'

'It must be there, I should so like to see you there. Oh,

everything's going wrong. I'll get this to Rosamud, that'll help, I know it will. Tomorrow night, Lucy, dear Lucy!' he cried, holding my hands, kissing me hard on the lips and then he was off. I don't suppose he'd kissed many people before. I didn't mind, he might try again if he liked.

I ran off too, back to my buckets and things and quickly down the stairs. I was very late, so late, because there was a very slight light coming up from the windows, some day trying to get through. I thought in all the chaos they shouldn't concern themselves over me. As I went back down, all was quiet as it should be, some noises from the kitchens as breakfast was ready, but nothing out of the usual. I've made it, I thought, I'm safe now, no harm should come to me now, all over with. Clod will help, bound to, he's all right he is, after all. Yes, I like him. And knowing that and the pleasure of thinking it, was something of sudden and curious delight. I like him, Clod Iremonger. I couldn't stop my smiling. I put my buckets in their place, and went to the dormitory, all safe, all better now, try to sleep maybe. I'll see him again tomorrow, all will be well. Florence Balcombe, I said to myself, Florence Balcombe and Clod Iremonger. I opened the door, all was quiet, in the many beds all those lumps sleeping. I moved quietly along the line of beds, and all was well. Quite well. Nearly at mine. Nearly there. Then I thought, that's a bit odd, there's someone sitting beside my bed, on the stool there, I must be mistaken, it's some other Iremonger's pit, surely, an Iremonger sitting up and getting ready for the day, some other Iremonger, not to worry, my bed must be further along, and I went on further a little, and that person at the bed watched me as I went on, and then that person, whoever it was sitting on the stool, said, 'Good morning, Iremonger, I've been waiting for you.'

And I said, in my horror, 'Good morning, Mrs Piggott.'

The Wretched Alice Higgs

14

AN ICE BUCKET

Clod Iremonger's narrative continued

In the Corkscrew

We were like some fleas or bees or small flies or croak beetles, or shrink blats, or scarab ants, or horned moths, that live only for a short time, flutter, scurry, creep, eat, live, love and then die within brief moments and then are all done with and then are only flecks of dirt. A whole life pushed into such little time. Oh, she's a thought, the best of thoughts. The best thoughts I've ever had are all Lucy Pennant. I shall see her again tonight, I told myself, when it is dark again, that's not so very long away and she shall be in the Sitting Room, and we shall sit together upon Victoria Hollest and I'll tell her then what I think of her. I'll kiss her again then.

'Aaaaleeesss Heeeeeegssssssss.'

'James Henry Hayward.'

'Right you are, Alice, on we go,' I said to the door handle, rubbing it a little in my waistcoat pocket. It sounded so faint, so unsteady.

It was at least a half hour's journey to the Infirmary. I must hurry this door handle back to Aunt Rosamud before Uncle Idwid found me, or, worst of all, found Alice Higgs in my possession. I could not go the direct way, the main staircase would be shrieking with birth objects any moment. It was the start of a new day, the Iremonger family was getting up, the middle floors were already swarming. I would go the back way, up the winding stone stairs called the Corkscrew and take the door halfway up which would come out onto the Long Gallery – formerly a covered bridge over the Fleet River – and then climb down the other side, until at last I might achieve the Infirmary, which was, once upon a lifetime, a Turkish baths near St James's Square.

Up the Corkscrew I went and round and round, my steps making clanks and shocks and hallo-here-I-ams upon the old stone stairs. It took so many ups and rounds to get to the door halfway up, but at last it was there, only when I tried it, it did not open. There was something the other side of the midway door, something with a name. I couldn't catch it at first, the door was so thick. Was someone guarding the door – had Idwid had a sentry posted? Perhaps, I thought, it was Tummis's ostrich come to surprise me. Then the handle turned and the door began to open, and then the name was quite clear enough to me:

'Robert Burrington.'

That did it. That had me moving. And in my terror, not thinking properly, instead of going back down which would have been the right thing to do, I went up and up, north up the Corkscrew which was not a place to go. Quietly. So quiet at first and slow, slow as I dared, and the door, I thought, is the door still opening? As I slipped on upwards there came an answering thump, an answering clank from below. I prayed it was only my echo, only it seemed to be growing, that echo, it seemed to be stamping out on its own and coming to its own life and to be its own thing entirely. I caught the name in that horrible clamouring and it was, fast and faster, speeding onwards like Grandfather's engine did through the heaps:

'Robert Burrington. *Robert Burrington! ROBERT BURRINGTON!*'

Whoever carried the it that called out 'Robert Burrington' was scaling the twisting stairs through the darkness towards me. On I went then, gasping and panting, that deeper heavier clanking beneath me. There was no door now but the one at the top that gave onto the space where the bell of the bell tower once stood, but the bell had been moved down into the house, it was the bell that now summoned us to mealtimes.

At the top was a door into the attics, and it was that door, that terrible out-of-bounds door, which now I and James Henry Hayward and, though fainter, Alice Higgs fled, slipping and sliding on those ancient steps worn by so much foot treading over the centuries, making it dipped and cupped and smoothed out and treacherous at even the slowest pace. On I scrambled, on and up, on and round, to the deafening roar of Robert Burrington, closer and louder, but there was the door at last, arched and ancient, a turn of the screw above me, and on I went, slipping, on hands and knees now, as that Robert and that Burrington bellowed so much, and there was the door, I touched it now, and there, just one turn below, was the bellowing of Robert Burrington, and a heave, and a Robert, and another heave, and a Burrington, and at last the door gave way and I was out of that horrible stone throat and into a different peril.

The Attics of Heap House

The attics of Heap House were never to be visited, for in those rotting chambers lived bats. Tens of thousands of them, they bit at living things with great determination and could cause monstrous infections. There were at least seven cases in my lifetime of an Iremonger succumbing to rabies after bat bites. Unto these regions, with something shrieking Robert Burrington behind me, did I come, in my terror beyond the door of the bell tower ignoring the moulding sign that said TRESPASSERS WILL NOT BE.

I slammed the door behind me. Into the thick, stinking,

damp darkness I sank. Above me there was rustling. I mustn't wake them, I must be very quiet. I shifted onwards as carefully as I might, sliding once and feeling a thick dampness and muddiness along my arm, but on I went, in desperation through the dung field to try and find myself some sort of hiding place.

There was a great mound, slightly luminescent, which was especially tall and funnel-shaped, and there I crouched and waited. I could not hear Robert Burrington yet. The attic door remained closed and dark. Perhaps the holder of Robert Burrington shan't come, I thought, perhaps he knew all about the attics and was thinking twice about it, and was sensible and wanted no part of it, yes, perhaps he was not so foolish as to try the unstable upper storeys. Only then, as I considered this, there was a certain small creaking and with that creaking came a sound, and whoever he was that carried Robert Burrington stood in the doorway. I could just make out a shape, of a man, a long tall man with a black topper, taller and thinner than any man I had ever seen before, eight foot tall perhaps, and so little width about him. I waited behind the mound. What shall he do?

'Robert Burrington?'

From deep in my pocket I could just make out the muffled response. As if my plug longed to reply.

'James Henry Hayward.'

I shoved my plug deeper down.

'Robert Burrington?' came again.

'Al . . . Al . . . Al . . .' was all the poor door handle could manage.

'Robert Burrington?' once more.

Now as the stretched man waited, something very curious began to happen. I began slowly to hear other names coming from him, to hear that other names existed beneath the loudest and certainly dominant Robert Burrington. I heard Edith Bradshaw talking and Ronald Reginald Fleming and Alasdair Fletcher, there was an Edwin Brackley and a Miss Agatha Sharpley, there was Cyril Pennington. Cyril Pennington was the fire bucket from my landing, for some reason this man had taken it. I had never heard so many names before on a single person, and still, listening carefully, there was another wave of names behind the first. I caught a Matron Sedley and a Tom Packett and a Jenny Rose Finlay and a Stoker Barnabus and then ever so faintly a Nobby. Yes, something was very quietly saying, 'Nobby.' And there were other names yet, I could make them out bit by bit as if they were coming in and out of hearing, as if they were breathing in and out. Amongst them I caught another familiar name. I heard, rumbling slightly, 'Florence Balcombe.'

Florence Balcombe, why should she be calling with the objects? It made no sense, and yet, under the waves of names, I heard it once more, 'Florence Balcombe.'

I was so struck by hearing Florence Balcombe's name that I almost forgot my predicament, but James Henry called out as if it wanted to talk to them all. And then, above everything else, it came once more, 'Robert Burrington!'

And my own plug cried, 'James Henry Hayward!' I stuck my hand in there and shoved it deeper down, covering it with my handkerchief to deaden its cry.

'Robert Burrington?'

Had the long man heard my plug? Could he hear? He stood there, and then I thought he seemed to sniff very slightly. I kept so still and quiet, a statue, a statue, I thought, I'm a statue, I'm made of marble, nothing in the world shall make me move.

'Robert Burrington? Robert Burrington? Matron Sedley? Alasdair Fletcher?'

Can the bats hear them, I wondered, oh, please let the bats hear them. But there was only the faintest rustling from that vast dangerous ceiling above me. The stretched man stood in the doorway and from him something wondered loudly once more, 'Robert Burrington? Robert Burrington? Edith Bradshaw? Nobby?'

From another part of the room there was a new voice, 'Freddie Turner.'

'Robert Burrington?'

'Freddie Turner!'

Something flew over my head, in the dim light I thought it to be a hobnail but surely it was some insect, and whatever it was flew directly at the long man. It hit the long man and as it hit there was a very slight ding, and the cry, 'Freddie Turner!'

'Robert Burrington!' Much louder.

'Freddie Turner?' A whisper now.

'Burrington!'

'Freddie?'

'Burrington!'

'Fred . . .' and then all was still again.

All except a sudden crying out from my bath plug.

'James Henry Hayward! James Henry Hayward!'

My plug was calling to it! And in answer there was a great roaring from the doorway, 'Robert Burrington! *Robert Burrington!*'

What happened next happened at such speed that I could only afterwards piece it together. When I looked back at the doorway, the long man was not there, the doorway was empty. I could not see him at first, but in my panic I moved backwards, scuttered backwards on hands and feet, as if I were an upturned beetle, my hands scrabbling in the bat drop, sliding a little in its chalky crumbliness, and, as I moved, up above me, as if a wind had suddenly blown through the attic, the ceiling began to fidget most urgently. I tried to get up but kept losing my footing and sliding back down, and then I saw the great long figure approaching fast.

The principal object held by the stretched man announced itself louder than ever before, as if the mouth of a volcano had just opened, or a cannon calling, a holler, '*ROBERT BURRINGTON!*'

There was a sudden definite smell of gas, and also of some tar, and then the stretched man lunged forward.

'*ROBERTROBERTEDITHMATRONEDWINMISSNO-
BBYFLORENCEBURRINGTON!*'

And all went suddenly and entirely dark.

I am dead.

I am dead now.

I am dead now, I thought.

I am quite and very dead now, I thought, and yet, I thought, and yet, I reasoned, and yet, I fathomed, I'm thinking this. And yet I feel myself breathing on and yet I seem to be in the same place, and yet there are my feet before me, and yet here are my legs and yet here is my chest, still waistcoated, and yet then, am I not dead? And what then is that terrible blackness just in front, and that great screeching and flapping and yipping in and out, and swooping? And is there between the flaps and shrieks still yet some Roberting? Still a definite evidence of Burringtoning? Indeed, indeed, there was.

As the long man stamped towards me, he had awoken the ceiling and he was now thick with it. Robert Burrington was bat-battling, and there I was scrambling up at last and was upright and heading away from the terrible screams and yelps and I found a ladder and climbed it, and then a skylight and shoved it and then was gasping upon the roofs of Heap House and then, in an instant, I could hear nothing, nothing at all.

On the Top of Things

I could hear nothing out there, nothing at all, because I could hear everything. Everything was calling out at me, every object that had a voice was roaring and wailing and singing, whispering, laughing, jeering, sneezing, talking and ranting, and I could discern no one noise out of so many, all was a hideous rush, a wall of sound, a great tidal wave that turned me deaf. I was an in-house thing, meant for the indoors. It was best for me to see the world through a window but not to step out, not to come so close to so many, many things. I was deaf, out there on the roof of Heap House, the heaps swirling beneath me in storm.

The rooftops of Heap House were the great province of the birds, the wattle and daub of this highest landscape were feathers and excrement. There were other feathered things beside the seagulls, there were pigeons too, scabby city pigeons with one foot or one eye. Though not as dangerous as the bats, it would not be good to upset the seagulls. They had terrible tempers. This was their home, after all, not mine. I should scramble over the top of a dome or two and find my way to the outside spiral staircase which ran the length of the building and was taken from libraries all across London. I looked about. I looked down. And all the view was rubbish.

Such peaks and troughs, such mountains and valleys, such deep depths. To look at it all shifting and moving, stinking and cracking, it was such a thing! Heaving and humming! It is not possible for an Iremonger not to be proud of the dirtheaps, proud and of course fearful. I could have stayed there and watched it in its glory, I could perhaps have caught the Heap Blindness that so many Iremongers before me had succumbed to. My Second Cousin Roota who, unhappy in her school hours, bullied and shunned, sticked and stoned, word-hurt and bruised, took herself up to these roofs day after day for comfort, until at last, she fell in love with the heaps and gave her heart to them, and one day, bully-bled and hurting head and heart, she wandered the rooftops and looking out at the waves of rolling filth, she gave herself entirely up to them and threw herself from the rooftops. She sailed wonderfully, soaring at first but then the grace was over and turned into a hurried plummeting down.

Then, suddenly, there was something other than the heaps, something else moving. The hatchway where I had escaped was opening up once more and a top hat began to emerge, like a chimney breaking through a roof. More top hat came and more yet; though the hat was certainly scratched and dented it continued to sit atop the long man.

The long man, the long man was coming.

I scrambled on then, as fast as I could. I prayed he had not seen me. How could he have survived the bats? On I rushed, on and on, scuttling seagulls who snapped at me in complaint, and I made it at last to the Forest on the roof.

The Forest on the Roof

The Forest was what we called all the chimney stacks that Grandfather, in his wisdom, had had gathered up from all over London town, small pots or great organ pipes, so many, many stacks, only some of which connected to the vertical passageways down below. There were several thousand of these upright dominoes and among them I now rushed, screaming, as behind me, through that fog of seagulls and their things, the long man with his long hat and long face, long arms and long legs marched.

I set off down a lane somewhere in the middle of the Forest and charged on, kicking the birds out of the way. I did not stay in that one lane of chimney stacks but kept switching, diving further in, turning left here, then right, then right again, once more a right, then a left, count three four five now turn, back up a bit, left, left, down this one a long way, switch lanes again, down another path and left here, on a bit and turn around, quickly quickly, anyone there, birds and chimneys, quick get behind one, which one, this one. A tall multiple stack with five pots at its top, here I crouched and heaved and panted. I stuffed James Henry further down just in case, and waited and panted, panted, waited, and wondered. Who is that person? What is he? Where did he come from? How did he come to be like that, so strange and stretched?

There he was again. He wasn't in my lane, he was three or four lanes away, but so tall that he was longer than the chimneys and the top of him peeked up above them. He was pushing at some of the chimneys, knocking them down; at larger ones he leant over to look inside, inserting his long hands into the limited interiors and pulling out, on occasion, birds' nests and a gull or two and when the birds bit and shrieked at him he smacked them away, not hurt at all, undeterred. He selected chimneys, one here, one over there, stamping among them and peeking within, coming closer to me until I saw his shadow upon my own lane. He was only two chimneys away, the shadow darkening all before me, but then his long legs hurried him on again, and I waited and shook, my face hard against the rough clay, and each time when I thought him gone, I would catch him again, his tall hat seen above the Forest.

At last I thought I must try it, I should have to or my head would explode. I stepped out a little, I could not see him, I looked down the path of stacks east and west, I could not see him, I trod out, I could not see him. In the distance was the rusting dome that marked the top of the spiralling staircase that would safely deliver me back down into the house, but between me and the metal stairway were whole streets and lanes of chimneys and he might be waiting for me, behind or to the side of any one of those.

I couldn't see him. Now or never.

He's gone, I said to myself, whoever he was, he's certainly gone.

I ran.

And then, suddenly, there he was again.

He was sitting in line with the chimneys, he was sitting up. I saw the long stretched body, his top hat at chimney height, just another chimney pot I thought at first, one with a thicker stack. But this stack had thin arms crossed around it and long legs drawn up, had a long body and, most terribly, a stretched face. Before he had always been in the dark or at a distance, but now there he was a few small steps away, keeping still amongst the chimney stacks. Waiting. Biding his time. It was then, with him so close, that I saw him properly for the first time. The horror of it.

The long thin man wasn't a person.

He wasn't a person at all.

He, it, *it* was a great collection of things. It, it was made of metal, of pipes and springs, of gears and pistons, a mechanical being consisting of so many, many things brought together, with some sort of engine inside it. Its top hat was a long pipe with a lid and a little steam was coming out of it, and there were many small objects attached to its larger metal pipes, like barnacles upon a ship's hull. There was a corkscrew, a clay pipe, there was a magnifying glass, there was a ball of string, an apron, a great hook hanging down from its hat swinging before the face like a monocle. I could see quite clearly what its face was now, it had no real face, the face was a polished brass plate, and the plate had writing upon it: UNDERWRITERS LABORATORIES INSPECTED, 5 ½ GALLON HAND FIRE EXTINGUISHER, CLASSIFICATION NO. 650859 – this stamp I had mistaken for eyes. What I had taken for the mouth in much larger stamped letters read: TO PLAY ON FIRE TURN UPSIDE DOWN. What previously I had believed to be the long man's nose was in fact the hose of the fire extinguisher, a length of thick black piping and at its tip a bronze nozzle. This then, this terrible collection, this was the long man and I stood right before it, appalled – appalled and fascinated. Has it stopped, I wondered. Is it broken now? Surely it was never really moving, surely I had just imagined it. Whether it moved before or not, it was certainly very still now. There, I told myself, your imagin-ation has done this to you. And I put a finger out to prod it. And as I did it started up again.

The nozzle began to move, to sniff so it seemed to me, and with the sniffing I could just make out a whirring coming from inside the creature and a thumping. It began to stand up.

I stayed not a moment longer, but plunged onwards, yelling loudly, screaming, hurting, terror-turned, and hurled myself towards the rusting dome. As I ran on, a basket, surely pulled up from the heaps by the birds, rushed past me, spinning itself back in the direction I had fled, towards the creature, desperate to join it. It was not only the basket but suddenly other things were moving too, so many things were skipping about, smashing towards the mass of objects whose principal name was Robert Burrington, and Robert Burrington that great collection was growing larger and larger. I looked back, it was up again, and with great long strides hauling itself onwards, growing as it went, smashing chimney stacks as it rushed, great long hands of rakes and pistons and pipes and tubing feeling out before it and the nozzle nose bouncing to and fro in high alert and excitement, and, I think then, had not a lightning rod launched itself directly at the eager collection, and briefly felled Robert Burrington, I think I should very likely have been crushed, but it lay stunned a moment trying to make sense of this latest addition and in that moment I was beneath the dome, I was at the rusting metal staircase and had seized the railing. I began jumping and leaping downwards, screaming still, screaming all the way, and then there was the door and I was through it, somewhere high up in Heap House.

I was inside again. I could hear. I could hear myself screaming.

It won't stop, that thing, all those things, it cannot be stopped, I thought, it'll come down any moment, it'll bring the whole roof with it, it can't be stopped, the bats couldn't stop it, it's just growing and growing, it'll have everything, it wants everything and everything runs to it. It knew I had James Henry and it knew I had Alice Higgs and it wanted them so badly. It shan't be stopped. It shall never be stopped. How can things do that? How can things move on their own?

Don't stay there, I told myself, don't stay there by that door so close to the outside stairs. That door shall open soon, right enough, and all those objects shall come smashing in, sniffing for James Henry and Alice Higgs. Quick, quick, move yourself, the house is rumbling isn't it, isn't it? Is it upon the stairs now? Is it winding its way down?

On, on, Clod, to the Infirmary, give Rosamud back her handle and then, by God, get help, cry for help. Up I got, on I ran. To the Infirmary.

The Infirmary

My hearing was coming back though the rumbling still thundered on in my head, but ever a little less and a little less. I could not hear Robert Burrington, I kept looking behind me for the clanking of that thing of things, but it had not come yet, but soon, I thought, surely soon it would. I must return the door handle Alice Higgs to Aunt Rosamud. It had all started with the door handle, perhaps it might stop there too. That once I had delivered the handle back where it belonged somehow the whole upturning of Heap House might stop, that all the pieces of Robert Burrington might disperse, that everything might settle down once more, and that, most of all, in the night I might see Lucy Pennant. And so, the Infirmary.

I could not march into the Infirmary and loudly announce myself, this must be done carefully and quietly. Nothing could be achieved until the matron Iremonger, a great white handkerchief upon her head, was away from the desk in the entranceway. She sat there with seven watches pinned upside down upon her bosom. I waited. Come on, come on, always looking back for Robert Burrington. Come on, come on. At last some sickened Iremonger hollered out, and away the matron went, her footwear clattering upon the floor tiles. Then I was in the Infirmary and seeking out Aunt Rosamud.

The name of the patient within each chamber was posted upon each of the doors and so I hoped my aunt should very soon be found. She was not down the first corridor I crept, nor yet the second, on the third all was much busier and I had to shelter a while behind a great basket of filthy linen. There were so many names calling out upon that floor, some groaning, some moaning, some in complaint, some in whispers, some hurt, some crying, it took me a time to isolate them, for my hearing to come back, for the thudding to cease, but then at last, among others, I caught the words, 'Geraldine Whitehead!'

Uncle Idwid was just beyond the door with the greatest commotion inside it. But that was not all, and that was not least, because then I caught another name amongst the jumble of names and that name was slow and serious, sharp and spiteful, 'Jack Pike.'

Grandfather was within. Grandfather himself was here though Grandfather should be in the city by now. Only then did I understand that for the first time in my life I had not heard the train leaving that morning.

Grandfather himself and his portable cuspidor Jack Pike

and also Uncle Idwid and his nose tongs Geraldine White-head were all four parked together beyond the door just before me. And then I heard the shrieking, an awful howling, a painful bellowing: screech, scratch, terrible bellow. And the worst was the name it called out in its absolute misery, 'Percy Detmold! Percy Detmold! Percy Detmold!'

What were they doing to poor Percy Detmold, whoever he was? What was happening inside the room? I crept up to it and saw through the keyhole Grandfather, sat with his huge back to me and beside him Uncle Idwid, holding Geraldine Whitehead in his hand. But there was no one else in the room, no one at all, and yet the screaming went on, made worse each time Idwid pushed his nose tongs at something just out of my view. Idwid shifted and I saw that the whole agony and misery was coming from nothing more than a tea strainer. A very scratched and dented tea strainer lay on the table, which Idwid was clinking now and again with his Geraldine.

'Percy, Percy Detmold!'

A tea strainer, a tea strainer in agony.

'You shall stay as you are, Percy Detmold,' Idwid said, his voice not so gentle now, I could hear the Timfy in him. 'You're nothing but a tea strainer! You know nothing of a moustache cup, nothing at all. You are, and shall be, a tea strainer. Here then – Umbitt has you now!'

'PERCY DETMOLD! PERCY DETMOLD!'

Why were Grandfather and Idwid bullying the object

213

so? What has happened to my home, what has happened? How will anything ever make sense again? Get rid of the door handle, I told myself, at least get rid of the door handle, and quickly before Idwid hears it or my James Henry.

There were so many doors with the wrong names – Nareen, my Great-great Aunt, and my Aunt Shorly, and Second Cousin Lorry – but then near the end in a back corridor barely lit was the little sign IREMONGER, ROSAMUD, and in I went, shutting the door fast behind me.

It was a simple room, a stool, a table, a bed, a lump in the bed that surely answered, 'Present,' if asked, 'Rosamud?'

I went to the stool, it was quite a high stool. I could just make out on the side of it: PROPERTY OF STRANGERS CLUB, LONDON I placed Alice Higgs upon the stool, but to my abused ears Alice said not a word.

'Hello, Aunt R.,' I said. 'It's me, Clod. How are you? How have you been these last, however long it is? I have something for you, Aunt Rosamud. Here it is. Upon the stool. Are you there?'

There was no response, no movement, no sound at all.

'Are you there, Aunt Rosamud, are you there? I have something for you, something you shall be very pleased to see. Wherever are you? Which bit, precisely, is you? I don't remember you as a pillow, no, you never used to be a pillow.'

I could not make her out. There were so many sheets

and blankets piled up and crinkled here and there, many pillows too but I could not discover Rosamud in all that. I could not see Aunt Rosamud. I could just about picture her in my head, as I remembered her, angry and wielding her door handle, and as I began to remember her so I began to make sense of the mound on the bed. I could tell a sheet from a pillow case, a blanket from a quilt, then out of that mound very slowly I began to comprehend a figure. There at last was Aunt Rosamud, she had been lying upon the bed all along but her body, it seemed to me, it seemed without question, was made from sheets and quilts and pillows. She was made of the stuff from a bed, stuff which had been haphazardly arranged, thrown rather upon the bed, in the rough shape of poor Rosamud, but looking now I felt quite certain very like Rosamud, that poor Rosamud herself had become a mound of material.

'Aunt Rosamud!' I called. 'Aunt Rosamud, you're nothing but bedding!'

I think I may have begun calling out then, I think I must, because it seemed to me that it was certain the bedding was Rosamud and that the bedding had indeed just moved of its own volition and a single unhappy duck feather had been briefly launched by the moment. My Aunt Eiderdown, my Aunt Comforter, dear Aunt Pillowcase, poor dear Aunt Blanket, oh help, oh help.

I pulled at all the bedding trying to find my aunt within, I scrambled through it, getting myself caught and knotted in it, but at last I had it all pulled from the bed and there was no aunt there at all, not a single aunt. She must be away, I thought, she must have gone away; the only thing that was in the bed was a metal bucket, a cold bucket, like the buckets used to keep ice chippings in, with a lid – a sad-looking bucket that had something so familiar about it. As if I had seen the bucket before, as if I knew the bucket very well and was a little frightened of it. Then it seemed to me I heard a noise, a small noise, but gaining in confidence, the noise was, 'Rosamud Iremonger.'

'Aunt,' I called, 'Aunt! Where are you? I hear you well enough. Aunt! Aunt!'

'Rosamud Iremonger.'

'I hear you but I do not see you. Where are you hiding yourself? Come out. It's me – it's Clod. Oh, where are you, Aunt?'

'Rosamud Iremonger,' came the sad voice again.

And then there was no hiding it any more. The voice came from the bucket in the bed. It was the bucket that was talking. My Aunt Rosamud was a bucket. And then came another voice.

'Hello.'

It was not the bucket speaking, this new voice came from somewhere else, from the stool, there was someone sitting on my aunt's stool, a small very dirty girl in a threadbare dress, very thin and pale, great smudges beneath her eyes, some poor starveling, some mudlark heaved from the heaps. I had never seen this urchin before and yet there was something, like the bucket, that seemed so familiar to

216

me. The dishevelled girl had a large head and a thin body, like an afterthought, trailing from it. But the head was very solid and prominent, a round head, quite shiny, were she an object, something like a . . . and then she said it, she said her name, 'Alice Higgs.'

And then I fainted away.

The Housekeeper Claar Piggott
The Butler Olbert Sturridge

15

A CORSET AND A SHIP'S LANTERN

Lucy Pennant's narrative continued

'Good morning, Mrs Piggott,' I said to the figure sitting on the chair beside my bed.

'Is that what you call it, Iremonger?' replied the house-keeper as she approached. 'I should call it rather a very bad morning, for you. I should call it the worst of mornings, for you. Where have you been?'

'Upstairs,' I said, 'cleaning the firegra—'

Before I could finish my sentence the white bony hand of Mrs Piggott struck me hard across the face.

'No,' she said, 'I won't have that. That won't do at all. Where have you been?'

'Upstairs, Mrs Piggott.'

'That much is certain. Where upstairs?'

'Please, miss, doing the firegra—'

Again the hand struck.

219

'I'll ask one more time, and take very good care with your answer. I am a loving person, I am warm and lively, I thrill with emotion, and that emotion can be over-stoked, and I can become very hot, I can bubble over, you should not want that, should you, my dear?'

'No, Mrs Piggott, I shouldn't.'

'And so, Iremonger – I shall not call you Firegrates now, not since your firegrates have been inspected and found wanting, some have not even been touched, but a moment yet before we consider that – where, pray tell me, and what? Out with it!'

All the other Iremongers in the dormitory were awake now, and all sitting up, watching, taking it in, smelling some blood.

'Mrs Piggott . . .' I said.

'Go on.'

'The truth is . . .'

'Go on.'

'I got lost.'

'You've never been lost before, why were you lost this time?'

'There was a noise, a terrible noise, a clanking, a hissing, a great clattering, and I ran from it.'

'That's a Gathering!' she cried. 'You've seen a Gathering! They've been looking everywhere for a Gathering, they knew there was one, they need to stop it before it gets too big.'

'A Gathering, Mrs Piggott?' I asked.

'A great collection of pipes and whistles, of brass tubes, handles and bolts, all sorts, piecemeal, made of a thousand bits, this and that all over it, pilfered, got together, ganging up, getting bigger. There's one been reported, seen somewhere about the house and then lost again, it's in hiding. Where did you see it, my child?'

'Outside the Clip Room, on the third floor.'

'Outside the Clip Room? Whatever were you doing there? You're not supposed to be there. There's something very foul going on, something deceitful and nasty, something treasonous or my name's not Claar Piggott. I don't think I like you, Iremonger, I'm just coming round to disliking you this minute, I'm nearly there, a few seconds longer and I shall probably really despise you. Come,' she said, pinching the back of my neck and pulling me onwards, 'if you've seen a Gathering there are others that shall need know of it. You're coming with me.' She pinched me hard.

'My neck!' I cried. 'You're hurting me.'

'I mean to do it, lovey, that's exactly my intention.'

She dragged me along to Sturridge's parlour. I was in a panic, trying to fight her off. But I needn't have struggled so much, that blind man was not there. Grim-faced city Iremongers were keeping the butler company, some wearing shining brass firemen's helmets.

'She's seen a Gathering!' Mrs Piggott announced as we entered.

'Where? When?' the men called, getting all worked up.

'On the third floor,' said Mrs Piggott. 'Clip Room.'

221

'How long ago was that, Iremonger, be quick and tell us, how long since?'

'Two hours ago it was, I think,' I said.

'Two hours!' a man cried. 'It'll have moved on for certain.'

'But we must look all the same. See what's missing. Get an idea of its size.'

'Perhaps it's heading upwards.'

'It may still be there. There is a chance.'

'Grab the hammers, take the crowbars, the weights, gunpowder. Be sure to have the fuses. The magnets too! Up we go!'

The men took all manner of heavy instruments and rushed from the room and I was left alone in the company of Mrs Piggott and Mr Sturridge.

'This house is falling to bits, Olbert,' she said to the butler, 'how could a Gathering have been allowed to happen? What damage shall it do?'

'It may do a great deal, and they might too with all their weaponry. They have no understanding of this house, no love for it at all.'

'And then there's this Iremonger for you, Olbert, she has been wandering around the uphouse, her firegrates have not been done.'

'That's fresh villainy,' came the butler's deep reply. 'These are uncertain days and nights, oh wandering Iremonger, and in them what are you doing walking boulevards that are not yours to walk. What do you mean by it, to tread about so? Well now, my pedestrian, where did you go exploring? Did you see anything new, anything magnificent? It is magnificent, this Iremonger Park. What did you find to excite you, what made you gasp and wonder? Please, do tell, I should so like to hear it, I cannot gather enough good opinion of this mighty mansion.'

His words, though so deep they felt chiselled upon stone, were so much gentler than the housekeeper's scratching noise, and he looked at me with what I thought was kindness. He so loved the place, I wanted to tell him something good of it, I wanted to make him happy. I wanted his favour against hers.

'I saw, Mr Sturridge, sir, the Clip Room with all its scissors hanging up, hundreds of them there must be.'

'Yes, oh yes, it is such a sharp place. Some of the nails of the older Iremongers do grow a little tough and some are let advance to great twisting lengths, some are sharpened as keen as any knife, but in the Clip Room there are jaws to trim 'em, to bring them to order. Very good, what else did you see?'

'The smoking chamber with all its leather seating.'

'You've been in the Smoggery?'

'It smells of places far away.'

'Indeed it does, it does. Of Turkey, of Afrique, perfumes of Arabie. Quite right. And what else did you see?'

'I saw, most of all, a huge place with marble flooring and a great chest filled with the most beautiful treasures.' But this last admission was not well taken.

'She's been in Marble Hall! A firegrate in Marble Hall!' the butler thundered.

'I told you I didn't like her,' said Piggott, 'what trespass!'

'There's never been a common firegrate in Marble Hall, it's Briggs himself that does those fireplaces. Never allowed. Not permitted. Out of bounds!'

'I'm sorry, Mr Sturridge, Mrs Piggott, I didn't mean –'

'Ingrate, firegrate, dirty, thieving little vermin!' shrieked Piggott.

'Never before! Oh, never before!' yelled the butler, sweat upon his great forehead. 'You do not belong there, you, *you*, in such a place, the very idea makes me crumble like an ancient ruin, you've stained the marble! Oh, oh, my foundations are rocked, my buttresses bent, there's no true plumb line any more. All fall down!'

'Steady yourself, Olbert, don't you collapse now, where's your medicine?'

'Third floor,' he gasped, 'second chamber.'

Rather than rushing out of the room, the housekeeper sought the address upon the person of the butler, and went straight for the second pocket of his waistcoat, she took out what appeared to me a small nail, though it may have been a little liquorice, which she deposited in the big man's gullet and he sucked upon it and seemed better by and by. She fetched his lantern out from a cupboard too and gave it him, and he held onto it as if for dear life, his birth object. But as he sucked and as he clung on there in the quieting room, the housekeeper turned back to me.

'Look what you have done, thief in the night, to the poor butler, look how you've upset him.'

'She is a death watch beetle,' he mumbled, 'she gnaws at my timbers!'

'We took you in, we gave you a home, this family loved you and cared for you, made much of you. You had a bed and you had warmth and duty and position, much affection was spent upon you. And what did you, in return, what did you do? You spat on our love, you cursed our kindness, you stamped upon it until it was broken. We are sullied by your presence, made ill by it.'

'This house, this whole house,' added the butler, 'every floor, every room, every cupboard, hates you. Every door hates you, every floorboard, every window hates, hates you!'

'You are a blood stain on linen, no scrubbing shall get you out!'

'That's enough right now!' I cried, they'd gone on and I couldn't stand it any more. I was trembling, shaking with fear but also with fury of my own, and I would not let them continue a moment longer. 'You've had your turn and now you're all spent. It's my go now. I'm sorry I saw your precious marble place, I am sorry, I suppose, but there's nothing I can do about that now, is there, it can't be undone. So, there it is, I don't need to listen to any more from you, I've had just about enough of it to tell you the truth, so send me back to Filching, do it, do it now, do it this very morning, I don't care, I'd rather it in fact. I quit this place, I'm done with it! I'm sorry I ever came!'

'She quits!' yelled Piggott.

'Sorry she ever came!' rumbled Sturridge.

'Yes I am, if you want to know. Now I'll have my things back and you can put me on the train and that will be the end of it. But before I go, there's something I need.'

'She has *terms*!' said the housekeeper, her voice very high.

'I want the Iremonger that got lost, the one from my dormitory, she can come with me. Yes, I'll have her with me, thank you very much.'

Piggott's hot face grinned, revealing her worn teeth. 'Which Iremonger do you mean? Who is it you speak of?'

'You know well enough, the one whose bed has been taken out, whose sheets and things have been burnt.'

'I'm sure I don't know who you mean, my dear. What evidence is there of this person you talk of, what proof?'

'She sat beside me at meal times, she was my friend.'

'Proof. Hard fact. Evidence.'

'She had a name.'

'Oh! She had a name did she? Was it, by any chance, could it perhaps have been –' she said all this in a sickly sweet voice, but grated out the last word – '*Iremonger?*'

'No, no, that wasn't it,' I said, 'her name was Florence Balcombe!'

That did it. That did it all right. That took the wind out of her. She stood still, like a dummy, her jaw open, her eyes big and ugly, and she swayed a bit but was otherwise pretty much stopped. I wondered if she was broken like my parents. It was the butler's time to help now, he came to the rescue of the housekeeper. She had a pouch-purse hanging from her belt, Mr Sturridge hurriedly opened it, and he pulled out a metal bottle – it had BRASS POLISH written upon its side – and he pulled out the stopper and waved it under the woman's snout and she came to. Then the butler went behind her back, he untied something there, I thought he was undressing her, loosening her a bit so she could breathe, but what he was actually doing was unfastening a corset she had strapped to her back, beneath her apron, her own birth object, he gave it her and she breathed long and hard and she was back then, her head snapped forward, her face poisonous.

'I throw you out,' said the housekeeper, 'you are so much rubbish to me now.'

'Yes, Claar,' said the butler, 'that's quite right, dump her.'

'Oh yes, all right!' I said. 'Throw me out, shove me on the train, but I shan't go without Florence.'

'Florence? There is no Florence, I tell you!'

'We don't know of such a one.'

'What have you done with Florence? She'll come with me on the train. She will, you know.'

'The train? Take the train?' said Piggott. 'There's no leaving here. There's no going away. This is not a place that people can come and go from as they please. This is no public house, run for your convenience.'

227

'There is no leaving,' said the butler. A statement, a fact.

'No serving Iremonger quits this place,' said Piggott. 'Once here, here you stay, there are only different stations, different positions, going downwards. There are dark places in Heap House, dark and deep. There are gloomy chambers down below where people can be quite lost and forgotten.'

'There are certain places in this mansion that only the butler knows,' said the butler. 'Certain deeps, where only I wander. I go to see how the house is far underground, it used to be deeper, but it was flooded. The heaps do bleed in upon us. This great house is very vulnerable, there are cracks, cracks everywhere, I know them all like old friends, and take sharp note of their progress. A person could fall through those cracks, Iremonger. Have a care.'

'There's another name for Heap House, you might call it "The End". That's where you are and that's where you'll stay. At the very pitch black bottom of The End.'

'You can't keep me here!' I screamed.

'We can keep you here.'

'We shall keep you here.'

'I want to go. I demand to be let go!'

'Then let her go, Claar. Let her sink.'

'Yes, Olbert, I'll let her go, tumbling, falling, thrown all the way to the bottom.'

'Exactly right, Claar, as I said, dump her.'

'Iremonger,' she said, looking hard at me, 'consider yourself dumped.'

'What does that even mean, what are you talking about?'

'Dumped!'

'Dumped!'

'Dumped!'

'Dumped!'

'What are you saying? Speak English!'

'You're going out in the heaps, you're not to work in the house any more,' said Claar primly.

'I'm going home,' I said.

'If by home you mean the heaps, then yes indeed, you're going there, it's all you're good for.'

'You can't make me,' I said.

'Wrong!' grinned the butler. 'Can! Do! Will!'

'I'll tell. I'll tell them above. I know some of them above, what do you say to that? They'll help me. They won't stand for it. I demand to see him, yes, that's it, take me to him now, he'll explain, he won't let it happen. He'll have me put on the train.'

'Who,' said the Butler, trembling now, 'who he?'

'An Upiremonger!' I cried.

'You talked to an Upiremonger?'

'Many times, every night! We even held hands. We even kissed, Mrs Piggott!'

'I don't believe it,' said Piggott.

'And I liked it!' I cried. 'And I liked him! I like him very much.'

'Name the superior,' said the butler, 'name please.'

'Clod!'

'Master Clodius?' gasped Piggott.

'Clodius, Ayris's son, his own grandchild! I don't believe it,' said the butler.

'His birth object,' I declared, 'is a bath plug!'

'I shall give in my resignation!' the butler groaned.

'You shall do no such thing, Olbert.'

'It has never happened before, Claar.'

'It shall never happen again, Olbert.'

'I am very much afraid,' the butler stammered, 'the horrible child is telling the truth.'

'I believe it too, Olbert, Master Clodius has always been slightly suspect, despite his blood, like Master Rippit before him. But it is no matter, true or false. No one shall hear of it.'

'If only it could be so.'

'She shall be sent out, Olbert. Three hundred yards?'

'In this weather?'

'Why not?'

'Yes, Claar, call her three hundred yards, no five hundred! Start her at five hundred, and if she comes back, let it be a mile, two even; give her a lead as long as the Thames, and lose the end of it. Atlantic her! Whoever is her anchor, make that anchor small and weedy, a thing of no weight or character, a feather of a person.'

'Well spoken, Olbert, there's your spirit back. What a character!'

'I'm not frightened of you,' I cried, 'either of you.'

'Be frightened of the heaps then, Five Hundred.'

'I want go back to Filching.'

'Then cut your line,' said Piggott, 'and walk there yourself.'

'Out you must go, Five Hundred Iremonger,' said the butler, ringing a bell. 'You are dumped.'

'No!' I cried. 'You cannot do this. You cannot!'

'Have,' said the butler.

'You will be lost, deary, you're big enough, and lord knows loud enough here, but out there you will seem neither big nor loud. You'll be a grain of sand out there. Lost under a sudden wave.'

A knock at the door.

'Ah, here you are,' said the butler.

'Mr Sturridge,' said two body Iremongers, nodding. 'This Iremonger is to be sent out into it. Five hundred yards.'

'Five hundred, sir?'

'That is what I said. And now. By the noon bell.'

'Yes, sir.'

'Let me go!' I cried.

They didn't.

The body Iremongers passed me quickly on to two heavy, stinking Iremongers who I hadn't known before, these were Iremongers in soiled leather aprons, and they in their turn marched me upstairs to two black doors. The doors were opened and a foul stench rushed at us, and clothed us in

231

itself, and all seemed fogged over and very, very close. I was shoved out. Into a courtyard. The air was cold but thick, my skin was suddenly so sticky. Never get clean, I thought, I'll never be clean again. I looked up there, high up there between dark rain clouds, was just a little, a very little, sky.

'I'm outside!' I said. 'Outside. That's something. That's something, isn't it?'

'There's worse places than the darkest house cellars,' said one Iremonger. 'Didn't you know?'

'Shut it,' said another. 'Not to talk. Strictly not.'

It was very noisy in that courtyard, strange sounds coming from beyond the wall, out of sight for the moment, the heaps smashing against each other. The wall in front was very high and thick, with glass on its top and wire and sharp things.

'The noon bell shall sound shortly. All ready?' the leather man called.

I saw now that there were already many Iremongers outside, all dressed in leathers, wearing helmets, holding buckets and pitch forks, with great nets and shovels, and all with heavy gloves. They were large these Iremongers, big men and big women, thick with muscle, with creased faces, broken noses, scars on them, some with thick scabs.

'Now listen up,' called a leather man, 'stay close to the wall. Not to pass out of sight today. Check your harnesses. Double-check your harnesses. Anchors pull back at the slightest hesitation. Don't go far, stay close. Your leads must be no greater than thirty yards, but don't stretch them.'

''Nother one here for you, express from Sturridge.'

'This? This isn't much. She'll be thudded and pitched. You're new, aren't you, I haven't seen you out before.'

'Yes,' I said, 'I'm new, yes, sir, and –'

'Not a good day to start out, just take it slow, all right? And stay by the wall.'

'Excuse me, Captain, she has particular instructions. She's to have a lead. Five hundred yards. Captain, express order, and a particular anchor too.'

'Five hundred? In this?'

'Yes, Captain, 'fraid so.'

'Well, Iremonger, if you must be Five Hundred, then Five Hundred you'll have to be. I think it stinks myself, but no one cares what I think. We'll have to suit her. And get her a strong anchor.'

'Beg your pardon, Captain, the anchor's been chose for her.'

'Really? Someone strong I trust, strong and heavy. Who is her anchor?'

'This one.'

'That one, you sure?'

'Quite sure.'

'It's murder!' he said. 'Make sure the ropes are secured, tie them yourself, Lieutenant.'

'Yes, Captain.'

'Well do it, man!' said the Captain, marching down the line.

'Step up then, Anchor. Let's get you attached.'

The Anchor was a child, no more than ten at my reckoning. A greasy, skinny thing, very unhappy, shaking a little.

'I only lifted up a saucepan, that's all I did. I just wanted to see it, can't be blamed for that, everyone wanted to see it, didn't they? Just to make sure it really was moving, and it was. A cup. I'm out in the heaps for letting a cup free–! Is it fair, is it right?'

'Did you?' I asked. 'Were you the kitchen boy?'

'I was, I did it, and so what. I let the cup free.'

'Will you shut your filthy gob?' said the Lieutenant, 'I couldn't care if you'd let all of Newgate free. Point is, you're the anchor. That's what I'm told that's what it'll be. Here's a helmet, tie it tight. You're small though, aren't you, and light? I'd take a weight. If I was you, I'd drag this ten-pounder along with you besides. I'll help you with it, some of the way. How's that for caring?'

'I'll weep with gratitude,' said the boy bitterly.

'I'm trying to help!' said the Lieutenant.

'Who am I anchoring for?' he asked.

'Me,' I said. 'We'll be all right. It's not so bad, is it? Out there?'

They both laughed at that, without mirth.

'What's your length then?' asked the boy.

234

'She's Five Hundred Yards,' said the leather man.

'No!'

'Yes, Five Hundred.'

'You've made some friends, haven't you?' said the kitchen boy. 'What the hell did you go and do?'

'I kissed an Upiremonger.'

'I should think you did,' he said. 'Wait a minute, you're not joking, are you?'

'No, I'm not.'

'It's not right,' he said, 'why should I pay for it? Why should I go out in this, I didn't kiss anybody. I haven't kissed anybody. And now most likely I never shall. Where's your bloody boyfriend now, darling?'

'Shut it, Anchor, do your straps up.'

'If you start pulling me out,' the boy said, 'I'll have to cut the rope. I'll have to do it. Same as anyone. No hard feelings. I'll take the weight and I'll hold on. But if you pull me out, I'll cut on you.'

'Will you all stow it!' roared the Captain, tramping up. 'Now you,' he said, pointing to me, 'get in your togs. The bell will be sounding quick enough.'

Suspended on hooks in the courtyard were huge brass helmets and beside them what at first looked like the bodies of some strange deflated men but I soon understood were kinds of rubbery leather body suits, much thicker and grimmer than the ones I knew in Filching. I was to put one on. I could see thick stitching upon it. There were many scratch marks all over it, as if some beast had gone

235

for it, ripping at the suit with sharp nails. There were many patches too where, I suppose, the attacking thing, whatever it was, had managed to bite through the suit, had managed to get through the thick skin of it, and what, I wondered, what happened to the person that was in the suit before me?

'No,' I said then, 'I won't! I won't do it!'

'Don't think about it. Better not to think, just go to it.'

The Lieutenant lifted me up, he dropped me into the suit like a kitten into a sack. I fought, I shrieked but I couldn't get out, he took up the helmet and screwed it on top. I was inside then, there was no getting out. He knocked on the glass of the helmet, and he grinned and waved at me. He unhooked me then and carried me in the leathery suit that was wet at the bottom, in the boots of it, and stank inside of dead animal. I couldn't see very well, everything through the round glass of the helmet was misty. He tied something tight around my waist, I couldn't see it. He knocked on the helmet, opened the round glass window of it.

'Five hundred yards!' he yelled. 'You must come back with salvage. Must! And quick as you can. Then you shan't have to go out again. But you come back with nothing and you'll have to go right back out into it. Understand?'

I nodded.

All the other heap Iremongers were lined up and I was pushed amongst them; behind me was my anchor carrying all the rope, so much smaller than the others, and behind him was the Lieutenant with a weight in his hands.

236

'All ready?' called the Captain.

'Heap! Heap!' called the Iremongers.

'Be strong, lads. Keep close to the wall!'

He held a long metal whistle, I could just see the writing on it – it said THE METROPOLITAN PATENT METROPOLITAN POLICE. J. HUDSON & CO. 244 BARR STREET, BIRMINGHAM. This wasn't his then, not originally, it was taken from someone, or found out in the heaps.

'Steady! Steady!' he called.

All were ready with raised sticks and buckets.

'Steady!'

A bell was rung back inside the house.

The Captain blew his whistle.

'Tally ho!' the Captain cried. 'Open the gate!'

The gate was opened. The heap Iremongers charged forth, and I stumbled and trod with them as fast as I could, and somewhere a little way behind me was my anchor.

Out into the heaps.

The Patriarch Umbitt Iremonger

16

A SILVER CUSPIDOR (FOR PERSONAL USAGE)

Clod Iremonger's narrative continued

The Visitor in the Corner

My plug was resting on my chest when I woke. It was whispering very faintly as if it was frightened. I opened my eyes. I found I was in a bed. In the Infirmary. I thought of Lucy at first, then I remembered Robert Burrington amongst the chimney stacks, the screams of a tea strainer called Percy Detmold and then, worst of all, a bucket in a bed, and . . .

'Alice Higgs!' I called.

'No one here of that name.'

Someone was sitting in the corner of the dark room. A big man in a black suit, wearing a top hat like Robert Burrington's chimney. It wasn't him though, not thin enough, not tall enough either.

'Who's there?' I asked.

Then I heard the birth object.

'Jack Pike.'

Jack Pike was the particular call of a silver cuspidor. Umbitt. My grandfather, all laws, all terrors. Grandfather to us Iremongers was the planets and their movements, no sun could ever come, no morning, no colours, no movements, no breath without his say-so. He was permission to exist got up in dark garments, in a black, black suit.

'Is it,' I whispered faintly, 'is it he?'

'Do you not know your own grandfather?' came the thick voice.

'Grandfather! Oh, my grandfather!'

'Is it so strange,' he said, deep in his corner still, 'that a grandfather should visit his poor grandchild in distress?'

'Yes, sir, I mean, no, sir. I mean, how do you do, sir.'

'Clod, don't be a stranger.'

'It is very kind of you to visit, Grandfather.'

'Yes.'

'Have I been ill? Have I been ill a long time?'

'In the history of the world, no. In the history of Clod Iremonger, a few hours.'

'Is it dark yet? Is it night again?'

'It is dark in this room. It is night here. Curtains and shutters alter time.'

'It is still day then? What o'clock?'

'It is time for a talk, Clod. That is the exact measure.'

'I saw a girl, Grandfather, a starving girl and a bucket.'

'Clod Iremonger, concentrate! Do you see what is on the table there beside you?'

I felt a brown paper parcel.

'Do please to open it,' Grandfather said.

I lifted the parcel, pulled the string and opened the paper to see what was inside. It was something folded up, something new and clean and dark. I pulled it out a little, and just by touching it I knew what it was.

'Trousers!' I called.

'Your trousers have come,' he said.

'So soon?'

'You sound disappointed.'

'No, sir,' I said. 'I thought I should not be trousered for six months.'

'Time has been moved forward,' he said.

'And I am to marry Pinalippy?'

'Soon enough, quite soon enough,' he said. 'You are called now. You are to be made ready. You shall be required in the city.'

'The city! But I was told I should stay here, that I would never leave Heap House. That my illness –'

'You have been told a great many things,' he said, 'for your own protection, and for others'.'

'Grandfather, may I ask something?' I said, my head spinning and aching and pounding with buildings of thoughts inside coming down and going up again.

'Ask.'

'Who was the girl I saw, the ragged one in Rosamud's room?'

'Not that, not yet. Ask another.'

'Grandfather, if I am to go to the city am I well then?'

'No,' he said, 'you are fragile, Clod. You are not like other children, you break easily, you may shatter. But, unlike other children, you have certain sensibilities, a certain understanding, a different, shall we say, outlook on the world.'

'Because I am ill?'

'Because you hear things.'

'Yes, I do hear things, sir, I do truly.'

'What do you hear?'

'They said I was not to listen.'

'But you cannot help it, can you?'

'No, sir, I cannot help it one bit.'

'And what do you hear?'

'Small voices.'

'Where from?'

'All over, so many places, here and there, when it's quiet, so many whispers, not always easy to hear. Things, sir. They can speak, but it's not right, I shouldn't listen, and it hurts to listen sometimes.'

'Tell me, tell me, what speaks?'

'It might be anything, anything at all.'

'For example?'

'It might be a shoe, it might be.'

'A shoe?'

'A shoe, yes, sir, it might be, or a plug. It may be a plug that says, "James Henry Hayward," or something else that calls, "Jack Pike," or, "Alice Higgs."'

'This,' he said, 'tell me, what does this say?'

Grandfather took a coin from his pocket and tossed it onto the bed. I picked it up. I looked at it very hard. I listened to it.

'It is a coin, Grandfather,' I said, 'it doesn't say anything at all.'

'And this?' he asked, tossing a small pebble onto the bed.

I put it to my ear. 'It says, "Peter Wallingford. Mondays to Fridays ten a.m. to four p.m., by appointment only, knock three times." That's what it says. I'm not making it up.'

'I know you are not.'

'My plug talks, your cuspidor talks.'

'Of course it does, Clod. We know all about it. We knew you were a Listener since you were a baby. Some babies can never sleep for all the yelling of the objects. We always knew about you; it was not necessary for Aliver to make such a business of it, we hardly needed his interference. We knew already.'

'And Uncle Idwid can hear too. Sir, Uncle Idwid –' I couldn't stop myself then – 'Percy Detmold . . . sir, Alice Higgs is a girl and not a door handle! Did I see those things? Oh what has happened to Aunt Rosamud and to the world?'

'Peace! Peace, Clod. Let me enlighten you. It is time.'

243

Things Are Not What They Seem

There was a hissing and a gas lamp was lit, I did not see how Grandfather had managed this, he barely moved in his corner, but a lamp was lit. Cold and dank and blue the room was now, a little place at the bottom of the ocean, smelling of gas and fat air and danger. And that great dark figure, that mountain of scree, the greatest of all dirtmounds, Grandfather himself, still in his top hat, his face, an old man's face, smashed rubble, withered and worn, the emperor of rubbish, spoke again. 'Now we shall begin.'

All was suddenly movement. Things began to fall from his pockets, they began to pour out of him, they rushed hither and thither on the floor, scurrying and hurtling, all manner of objects. These were not beetles and small creatures, they were *things*, objects, little pieces of this and that, rushing about Grandfather's feet, walking hurriedly down his trouser legs, over his shoes. Whilst Grandfather sat so still, so upright, so many other things moved and hurried about him. Small cups, knives, forks, napkins, needles, pins, screws, nails, buttons, leapt into life, and at last lined themselves up on the floor either side of Grandfather's large boots and waited there, peaceful once more.

From out of an inside coat pocket a large black slate began to appear, a tile from somebody's roof. Grandfather's thick fingers did not touch it, the slate moved of its own accord, turning over and over in its progress across the floor and up the bed frame, and laid itself down upon the foot of my bed.

'But how,' I said, 'how did you . . . ? What have you . . . ?'

'Things,' said Grandfather, 'are not what they seem.'

'They move quite by themselves!'

'This oblong,' said Grandfather, 'this same field of darkest slate, shall be our theatre, our stage, our scene. I shall show you a story of your family and its objects. Do you attend, boy?'

'Yes, sir.'

'Once upon an object,' said Grandfather in his corner, 'there was a folding pocket knife.'

An object matching that description now came forward, it hauled itself like an old man dragging a leg, pitching its blade first and heaving its handle afterwards. So doing it quickly achieved the slate and stood there a moment before marching back and forth, scratching upon the surface as if the penknife were a man deep in thought marching backwards and forwards.

'This object, first of all birth objects, for it was presented as a christening present, way back, belonged to your Great-great-great Grandfather Septimus Iremonger.' At this instant the penknife appeared to bow towards me. 'He was the first bailiff of our family, which before had been ragpickers of no estate. He took up the unpopular position and squeezed people and squeezed money and property from them. He was a genius for it.' At this, many small objects – clay buttons, cloth buttons, very sorrowful-looking – jumped up from the floor and moved around the penknife, which harassed them, poked them, scratched them and sorted them in piles. 'Where people failed, we, under Septimus's guidance, rose higher; where they came undone we were done up nicely. We grew, they shrank, we bought up more space, they lived in less, we had more children that lived, they had more children that died. We were not loved for this. And we did not care. We bought up all the debts, any debts, every debt, we bought them, they became ours. People have wept at us, we are no stranger to tears, people have begged us, let them beg: it shall prosper them nothing, they have spat at us, they should be fined for that, they have cursed us, they have been fined for that, they have struck us, they have been imprisoned for that. And worse. It was Septimus that started it, so, so long ago, and great Septimus it was that found money in a dirtmound, deep in a London heap, searching about in the muck that others were too proud to touch, finding small things of value that others had tossed away; he cut himself with his knife and Iremonger blood mixed with the filth. And so it has ever since.'

In reaction to Grandfather's last line, a series of other penknives appeared upon the handkerchief, some large, some small, some rusted, some polished, each bowing before me and then all quitting the stage, so that the slate was completely empty once more.

Do Not Trust a Thing

'Under Septimus's declaration, it was his dying wish, we bought up all the small dirtmounds of the city and had them moved here,' said Grandfather, and as he spoke a small mound of dirt formed in the centre of the slate. 'We took on all broken things. We, unwanted ourselves, the Iremongers, abandoned, despised family, took on all the equivalent in object terms.' The dirtmound was the size of the slate now and spreading beyond its borders, covering much of the bed blankets and growing yet. 'The disgusting and malodorous, the shattered and the cracked, the rusted, the overwound, the missing-parts, the stinking, the ugly, the poisonous, the useless and we loved them all, with what great love did we love. No greater love is there than the Iremonger love of spurned things. All that we own is brown and grey and yellowish, and tainted and dustful and malodorous. We are the kings of mildew. I do think actually that we own that: mildew. We are moguls of mould.'

Now the dirtmound was over much of my bed, my legs already covered, and spreading yet, pouring over the sides of the bed and threatening to fill the whole room, I couldn't see Grandfather any more but I could hear him.

'We took up home here in the centre of the heaps,' he said, 'we made this mansion out of broken fortunes; as people shrank so we grew, as they threw away so we grew, as they begged, so we grew. Every time any person in

London threw anything away, we profited it by it. Every chicken bone is ours, every spoiled paper, every unfinished meal, every broken thing. And they look at us, the people beyond, and they hate us, they find us vile and Iremon-gerish, ogreish and goblin-grubbing, foul of thought and small of love. They ban us from the rest of London, they passed an official law that no Iremonger is to leave the borough of Filching. So be it, in Filching we stay, within the borough walls, thick with our dirt. Do you know, Clod, what the Londoners say? They say that all London shall fall if the Iremongers leave Filching. In short, they hate us, in short, to their thinking, we stink of rot and death.'

By now the dirtmound was so huge it was swarming all over the room and still it grew on and on, all the space either side of the bed was now thick with dirt, dirt bubbling up, and still it was rising, beyond the bed level and lapping around me.

'And you smell of it too, Clod Iremonger, you stink.'

'Grandfather, help! Stop it!'

'Here we have grown up amongst foul things, here where the objects move in the shadows, where they creep like animal life.'

The dirt was up to my chest now, all those filthy bits, all that scree, smashed rubble, broken shards, stinking old things, pressing hard against me, into me.

'Grandfather!'

'Here in Filching, the poorest, dirtiest, most mysterious

of all boroughs, here in Heap Deep, Heap House, London, here we are and here you are.'

It was up to my neck now, and still rising, still rising.

'Grandfather, I shall drown!'

To my chin and rising, still rising.

'Grandfather!'

'Here where things must go bump in the night!'

And all at once all the dirt was gone and it was only Grandfather and me again, in an infirmary room.

The Way of All Things

'Clodius Iremonger, attend this last please, and with great concentration,' said Grandfather, in a gentler voice, 'it was not just the rubbish that came to Filching. Many of the poor were rounded up and brought to us here, the malnourished, the luckless, the criminal, the indebted, the foreign, such people, the very worst of people, tired and wretched, drunk and moaning, little people, who scrub about in the mounds for us, shifting and sorting and giving up. The poor, the unfortunate. There have always been poor and unfortunate.'

In response to this speech, small unhappy pieces of rags knotted into shapes that vaguely resembled buckled human forms and came and huddled upon the slate.

'Iremongers of wisdom, born before you or me, helped these people. They could earn money in the heaps, but such a little money to keep them heapbound. And these crouched ones had such a business with the objects, were so thick with them, breathing them in, cutting themselves upon them, mixing them with their blood, that something began to go wrong.'

One of the small bundles now opened up and within a moment was nothing more than a dented brass button.

'Sometimes they woke up to discover deep creases upon their faces which seemed on closer inspection to be cracks, and sometimes, later still, they just stopped working. People froze up, like pieces of rusted machinery, and no one knew why or what was happening, only that they were never well again. To begin with we put it about that these stopped people had just disappeared. We let loose rumours of murders and we lowered the price of gin. But then the stopped people did more than just stop, they turned, they grew, they morphed into things. Often enough a person should go to bed entirely well, his grimy spouse beside him, but when she awoke he would be gone, and there should be nothing in her bed beside her but a washing paddle. More people disappeared. A murderer is amongst us, we told them. But why then, some of the more inquisitive of Filching asked, why in those cases, if a proper inventory was done of the disappeared person's possessions, why was there always to be found one thing extra, a pot, or a plate, a cup or an enamel bowl, a candlestick or a glove? How were we to answer that? There were waves of this disease, sometimes two people a month might shift from being a person into an object. And then there might follow whole seasons when not a single disappearance – or transformation – occurred. But we knew it, we Iremongers, we knew it: people, Clod, ah, dear Clod, were turning into things.'

Two more rags shifted now, they opened up like flower petals and became in one case a modest andiron and the other a joint stool, these larger objects moved off the slate and from my bed, padding about like domestic animals before disappearing beneath the bed.

'To mollify the heap workers, to help them in their distress, for so many were struggling so, we became a sort of charity. Some desperate families, of which there have never been a shortage, had such an excess of family members, too many children, and, less often, too many old, for it is an exceptional heap worker that celebrates his fortieth birthday. They did not know what to do. There was such a crowding of people, such slums, such thickness of humans, that it was announced that swollen families might give up some of their number and should in return be rewarded for it. And so many children, and some old, and some infirm, were delivered to Bay Leaf House and the family was given money for them in return and a ticket. They were told to take especial care of the ticket, for should the ticket be lost they should not be permitted to redeem their person at a later date, whether they had the money or no.'

'It is terrible, Grandfather.'

'It is business, Grandson.'

The remaining huddled rags now somehow shifted from disorderly lumps to crisp cardboard tickets. On each a name was written in neat ink and beneath it a signature and a number. I stretched forward to read one closely.

RECEIVED: *Thomas Knapp (aged 4)*
FOR THE SUM OF: *£11 2s. 5d.*
RECUPERATION COST: *£31*
SIGNATURE: *Frederick Knapp (father)*

'Thomas Knapp!' I said. 'I know that name.'

'Do you, boy? It is not impossible.'

'Thomas Knapp is what underbutler Briggs's shoehorn says! I've heard it calling.'

'Have you indeed?'

'I am certain of it, but why, Grandfather, why would it say that?'

'Patience, child, we are proceeding there.'

'Thomas Knapp, that's what it says.'

'Pawned people were taken from the slums, so that they might be put to great use. The first were taken up to Bay Leaf House and, after a time there, some skilled Iremongers working with these pawned ones (known often enough simply as "tickets"), feeding them scraps, discovered that there was a simple way of keeping people benumbed, useful and hard-working, but unthoughtful. A certain amount of London dirt ground up into a powder or paste can stop a person thinking too much, can unencumber him of memory. A mixture of castor oil, engine oil, ground London dirt, Thames water, oakum, saltpetre. This powder can be easily put in poor food, in bread, or simply, if sweetened slightly, just portioned out upon a spoon. This has been very advantageous for us. And yet.'

'And yet, Grandfather?'

'And yet. There have been complications, there is a great problem.'

The tickets flew away now. The slate picked itself up and returned itself to Grandfather's coat. The old man looked very troubled.

'A leakage, a leakage that has lately started in our region but is spreading beyond. People taking in different air, drinking Thames water, inhaling certain dirts, people from Chelsea, from Kensington, from Knightsbridge and the city have fallen to heap illness. There has been great distress and many fingers have been pointed at the Iremonger family. And so we have had to tell them how to protect themselves. The disease, like any other, does not affect everyone. There is a way to safeguard against it. It has been discovered that the disease passes by a person who keeps close to them an objectified person. It will not turn them object as long as that person keeps that object beside them, or has it to hold now and then – to be in proximity is normally enough. There is a way of connecting a person of flesh and a person of object. A portion – a mere crumb shall suffice – of the object person must be dissolved into liquid form and then injected into the flesh person, and a drop of blood of the flesh person be absorbed into the object person. Thereafter, these two must be kept relatively close to each other, then the flesh person shall be safe from the foul illness, but only if he keeps his particular object about him.'

'Our birth objects!'

'Indeed, young Clod, our birth objects.'

'And so that, oh heavens, is why it is Thomas Knapp that . . . but then . . . James Henry! Then he *was* a person! *Who* was James Henry?'

'Someone, no one, it doesn't matter. You matter, Clod, James Henry does not. Uncle Idwid is not young any more. And so we need you, a new Listener, to hear which objects have . . . had a history, shall we say. To separate the mere object from the talking object. To keep us safe.'

'I wish very much to return James Henry Hayward to his family.'

'Clod, Clod, you may not.'

'No, Grandfather, I insist on returning him.'

'Birth objects and their holders, Clod, over time, over generations, in this great family of Iremongers, have developed strangely together. As they have grown together it has been discovered that one or the other must remain an object. Should you return your plug to its family–'

'*His* family.'

'. . . you should very likely become an object yourself.

254

Should you let your plug get the better of you, it might well be James Henry Hayward carrying a Clodius Iremonger in his waistcoat pocket.'

'What am I to do?'

'Look after him, perhaps. Treat him kindly.'

'I feel sick.'

'Yes, yes,' said Grandfather, yawning, 'I am sure you do. And I am sure you trust your plug, don't you? But the truth is we cannot know who this James Henry Hayward is and how he may react if given the chance. How you may grapple with one another, which of you shall be dominant. Your own dear Cousin Rippit was stolen from us by his birth object, by a letter opener called Alexander Erkmann, he stole Rippit from us.'

'But Rippit died in the heaps.'

'That is what we told you, but no, he was stolen by his letter opener, which, in human shape, hid in our train and took Rippit, in what form we cannot know, away from us into London. It was his body servant, a mongrel creature, who quite from grief lost himself in the heaps. My poor Rippit has never been found, and all because he let his object get the wiser of him.'

'Poor, poor lost Rippit.'

'Thus, Clod, never trust a thing.'

'And, Grandfather, if we are separated from our objects, what then, what shall happen?'

'Why, death, Clod, only death. Death for both the person and his object. When one dies, both die. We are stuck with one another, only one may be about at a time. That is how it is.'

'And so Aunt Rosamud is a bucket.'

'No, Clod, no, Alice Higgs is a door handle once more, and your aunt is recovering, you returned the handle to her just in time; I was quite able to persuade Alice Higgs back into brass.'

'Alice Higgs is a small girl.'

'Alice Higgs is a brass door handle. There was time to put it right. But you must not let this alarm you. You would not know this but you have an uncle who is an inkwell upstairs, and my own brother Gubriel is a potato peeler. My mother, my own mother, a tooth mug. And my former teacher, so free with his punishments, is now no more than a length of bending cane. It is the way of things, Clod, nothing can be done about it.'

'It's horrible! It's monstrous!'

'It does seem so at first. And so, we keep it from our young, to a point, but then if a young Iremonger is deemed promising he is moved to the city, to Filching, only to Filching, no further, and he is informed and he becomes an important part of the great Iremonger machine.'

'I want nothing to do with it!'

'You are something to do with it. Your help shall protect our family.'

'I shan't do it.'

'Oh, you shall, you shall do it. And you will learn to love it or you shall be crushed. How do you think my uncle, my brother, my teacher, my own mother became what they became. They did it with my help. I have an understanding with objects, I can smash them as you have seen. I have never yet met an object I could not smash. Nor yet a person, Clod, nor yet a person. People think they have volition, they do not.'

'I'm frightened, Grandfather.'

'And that, Clod,' said Grandfather, rising, 'is an excellent place to start. I shall leave you now, I am very late to take the train and business waits for no man. You must dress yourself, Clod, and you must visit your grandmother.'

'I must see Granny? Are you quite sure?'

'Dress yourself in your new clothes. Your grandmother wishes to see you. And tomorrow morning, without fail, you shall come with me to the city. In trousers.'

'Tomorrow!'

'I'm so glad we had this talk, Clod, so very glad. Do get dressed.'

'Jack Pike.'

'James Henry Hayward.'

And he was gone.

A half hour later the train screamed for London.

The Quiet Child Ormily Iremonger

A TIN WATERING CAN

A letter written by Tummis Gurge Oillim Mirck
Iremonger, departing resident of Forlichingham Park,
London

To my dear family and friends, this letter list.

*To my mother and father, my drawings and paintings,
my bird articulation.*

For my brother Gorrild, my opal cufflinks.

*For my sister Monnie, some feathers and the ribbons
you so liked.*

For my brother Ugh, my books Robinson Crusoe *by D.
Defoe,* The Pilgrim's Progress *by J. Bunyan,* The Rime of
the Ancient Mariner *by S.T. Coleridge.*

*For my brother Flip, my lead soldiers, all but the Cold-
stream Guards.*

*For my sister Neg, the Coldstream Guards and my cricket
bat.*

For my Cousin Bornobby, a release of the debt of ten

shillings and four pence you owed me, and a return of the corset catalogue of Jos. Horle & Sons, Burlington Arcade.

For my Cousin Clod, my stamp album, my bird books (Familiar History of Birds *by* E. Stanley, Birds by Land and Sea *by* J.M. Boraston, A History of British Birds *by* T. Bewick, Harmonia Ruralis *by* J. Bolton, *unless Ormily wants one – perhaps you might share), my lintel (and his matchbox), please to look after.*

For my Cousin Ormily, my love and this single feather from my seagull, Wateringcan (I do think it was his). Dear Ormily, dearest Ormily and your lovely tin watering can, I kiss you both.

I don't have anything else.

So sorry.

T.

The Indifferent Student Tummis Iremonger

18

A TAP (MARKED 'H' FOR 'HOT')

Lucy Pennant's narrative continued.

The Captain blew his whistle.

'Open the gate!'

The heap Iremongers charged forth, and I stumbled out with them as fast as I could.

Into the heaps.

I kept falling. I got up but then I tumbled down again soon enough. I told myself there was strong rope behind me and that at the end of that rope, hard by the wall, was my anchor and all the other anchors, holding on, keeping us connected.

For a little while we stumbled beneath the shadow of the house. There was protection there, but out from the shadow, well out of it, you were naked, weren't you, more alone. Only I didn't feel so alone, not at first, because there were all those other heap Iremongers ploughing along

263

beside me. I wasn't alone then. Look down. Don't look down. Look down.

There I was.

I was in the heaps. They stretched before me, into the distance. The heaps were shallow by the wall, you felt you were on hard ground there, and for those first couple of yards the heaps weren't very deep at all, you waded a bit, and I thought, I'll be all right, you'll be all right, but then those shallows were left further behind, and you had to keep moving, you had to keep walking or you'd sink, you'd sink down, each stop sank you a bit, you had to keep climbing up afterwards and keep moving. And still then we weren't very deep at all, and if I stopped for a moment then I sank up to my shins, and must scramble up, try to find something to step onto, a bit of wood or metal, some brick, to get my boots out again. Keep moving. Keep moving. Don't look down. Look down.

It was like walking upon a creature, that's what I thought. Only the creature, whatever it was, wasn't living, it had died some time ago and we were out picking upon its great rotten body, it was hard in one place, soft in another, you slipped about, and sometimes just plunged a bit. But still the wall was behind us then and I wasn't alone.

The heap Iremongers swung themselves about, picking stuff up in their big mittens or stabbing at it with their sticks, leaping from spot to spot as if they knew all the stepping stones, as if there was nothing random in this ground, as if it were solid and trustworthy and well mapped. With each small timid step I slipped and slid. I saw two of the heap Iremongers lugging some beam, already heaving it back to the wall, another had an old engine of some sort, and one held nothing more than an old soap dish. And he seemed quite happy with that. Keep moving. Keep moving. Don't look down. Look down.

The thing about the rubbish was that it didn't keep still. I could see it bobbing up and down in front of me. There was a large cupboard of some kind, some old dresser I think, I could see it in the distance, one of its doors flapping open and closed. Sometimes I could see it but at others it went down and I couldn't, it dipped deep, one moment high on a mountain top, the next sunk down a valley. The further out you got the more the objects shifted. There were fewer Iremongers with me soon enough, fewer and fewer, and after a bit there were probably only five of us, and I could see the others around me had ropes that had begun to stretch out full, that they were at their limit already, but not me. I had far to go yet.

The birds were thick about, swooping around, some of them found it hard to wrestle with the wind and kept plummeting or were swept far away. I saw one dive down and come up with a rat in its beak. On I must go, keep the line free, don't let it get snagged. Now and then I must turn around and lift up my rope to make sure it was all right. And then I'd tug on it twice so that the anchor should know I was still there, and then so *I* should know the anchor was still there he'd tug back twice and that was good. That was something. He was still there, then.

I couldn't hear much of anything, the helmet was too thick. I was certain the gulls who flew around me waiting to see what I might tug up from the heaps were probably screaming, but I couldn't hear them. All I could hear was my own breathing, my own laboured breaths. The further I struggled on the more I heard myself. Each exhalation fogged up the glass of the helmet for a moment, so that only when I breathed in did the steam go down a bit and I could see the swirling swaying mass before me.

I was hit several times. I hadn't realised it was the rubbish at first. I thought it was the heap Iremongers beside me, bumping me, but then I saw that what had knocked against me was actually an old wooden chair frame, rotten and chewed through, damp and useless. Once I got tangled around some chain and fell down and as I tumbled the ground beneath me opened up for a moment and suddenly I caught a tiny sight of a great cavern beneath me, a break in the heaps, a crack, and in between the crack I could see down and down into some great hollow where the objects tumbled about fathoms below. Keep moving, keep moving. Don't look down. Don't. Look down. Down there. Look.

For a moment, deep, deep down under, I saw old bits of houses and even a whole dented carriage, a door, and I was right on the edge of this widening gap, staring in. Looking down and down. Leaning into it. Down and down.

It was then that I think I saw someone. Some person deep down below, moving in and out of the drowned rubbish. Someone alive down there. Was it an animal, or some sort of dark fish, or was it a person?

Smack! Something was grabbing at me, tugging me away.

A heap Iremonger had hold of me and wrenched me back. I knew I should have gone in there, deep underground, but for him, I felt it calling to me. But I was pulled back, and the heap Iremonger that did it punched me hard on the arm to wake me up and I could see but not hear that in his helmet he was shouting, his fog inside big and white. And on I went then, stepping far around the crack, still on. Twice I saw the same old boot just by me, as if it was following me, I think it was the same boot, it was black and its toe was slightly open so that it looked like a mouth. On, I must go on, on into the muck or be cut loose. I pulled myself one leg after the other, each foot going deep in. Up again, down again. Then I saw something small and shining skimming along the surface, it was a little watch I think, on a chain. I tried to grab it but it kept dancing ahead of me. I heaved after it, so close, so close, spinning in the wind. I dived for it, nearly had it, I touched the chain, but it was gone again, no sight of it, suddenly lost beneath the surface. Then, turning round, I saw that I was on my own at last, that the other heap Iremongers were far behind me. That was a bad moment that was. I screamed inside my helmet. The glass was so fogged I couldn't see for a few moments and when at last it cleared, I thought how much darker it had grown. The sky so black. The storm closing in.

Dark. Darker than any coal hole I've ever seen, so little light from the clouds above. And cold with it, colder than any winter day when your breath makes thick clouds and the puddles have all iced over and it hurts to touch metal and you're huddling and shivering though you've put so many layers on and you think you'll never ever get warm again. Colder than that. And hopeless, without any hope at all. And the feeling of being dead. Of being lost from everyone. Buried alive deep down and no one to know it. And the feeling of uselessness, of being broken and alone. In the cold darkness. That's how it felt.

I've been put out, I thought.

I've been snuffed out.

I'm not alight any longer.

It was like being lost, dropped out, thrown out, spat out, shovelled under, dropped down a great hole. Small. Very small. Knowing then in the black coldness how small I am, that I'd never be anything big. Crumb. Splinter. Lost thing. Little lost thing. That's how it was. Something like that. Only that doesn't quite do it either. Not yet. It's like you're dead, being out alone in the heaps, absolutely dead, extinct, done in, never remembered by anyone ever, never existed even, not ever, not known anywhere at all. Like that. Except you're alive, except you're breathing, except you're there in this dead place, alive with all the thick deadness about you, on top of you, all around, moving in.

268

That's where I was. Out in the deep of it. There I trod, panting and miserable in the thick leather suit with my hulking metal helmet covering my noggin and all of it so big for me that I had to shuffle up inside of the suit to see out of the helmet window. Me and all those dead things. Hundreds and hundreds of different sized things, all smacked up together. Load of rubbish, wasn't it.

I'm sorry, I thought, I'm so very sorry. For all the broken things. Ugly objects, how did you get like this, who did this to you? I'm sorry no one cares for you. I am sorry. But I can't care for all of you, there's not enough of me. I can't. I don't. You'd snuff me out, soon as anything. You'd have me in an instant.

Just ahead of me was an old wooden staircase, broken and cracked, with some steps missing. It must have been a long staircase, once upon a time. I wonder where it went. Now it climbed up to nowhere, but it stayed where it was, waving a little bit in the growing wind, but not sinking. A bit of a place, it was, I thought. As much of a place as you're ever likely to get out here. Not very solid perhaps but more solid. I reached for it and dragged myself up it and clambered and heaved up its steps, the banister shuddering, until I was higher than the heap ground and I could see then that it was still connected to some building and that for the moment, it was on top of the heaps, the highest bit, like a mast of a ship. There I scrambled and there, on a step, I sat. Feeling sick. Gulls about me. They're living they are, I thought, hallo to you. I'm here. I'm still here. Still alive.

So I took a breather, didn't I. While I could. On some-one's old staircase. From there I could see Iremonger Park in the distance, a black island it was, the very darkest great smudge, and even, when I squinted, a few figures hanging around the wall, like ants, like flies, I could see the gate, still open. Don't close that bloody gate, I thought, don't you dare. Not with me out here, you bastards. That would be me done for, for good and all. Well then, I sat there. That's when I saw him.

There was someone else in the heaps, not the deep dark shadow down underneath, but someone other entirely. He was very smartly dressed. Like he was going somewhere special. It took me a moment to think how strange it was to see someone so well dressed out here in the middle of the rubbish heap. Top hat, tails, bow tie, white shirt, quite the gent. Something strange about his trousers though, they were very tight the bottom half, and I couldn't make them out at first. Who's that, I wondered, what the hell's he doing out here? He'll sink, I thought, if he doesn't watch it. He was tall, I could tell that even out there in the heaps, so tall I thought at first that he must be an adult. Some crazy Iremonger full-blood out for a stroll in the heaps, storm coming on. It was only when he got closer that I saw he was a boy, a tall child. I only figured that out by the strange trousers, they weren't trousers at all, they were shorts, dark shorts like what Clod wore and naked skin beneath the knee. Oh, Clod, I thought then, Clod, who is this fellow here dancing out in the heaps, you'd know, wouldn't you. You'd say. Oh, tell him to go back in, I thought, oh, tell him, do tell him, he shouldn't be out there in this. He'll catch his death. *I've* done something wrong, something very wrong in their books, but even me they thought to cover up, to give this helmet and these leathers, and to give me an anchor, no matter how weak, to give me this line and all. And then I finally realised it. He didn't have a line. If he didn't have a line he didn't have an anchor. There was nothing tying him to land. He wasn't connected. He'll die. I think I actually said that, those words, moving around in my leathers, making steam on my helmet glass, 'He'll die.'

Still the figure moved on, and seemed to make light work of the heaps to skip from place to place, taking great long strides, rushing forward, now left, now right, as if he hadn't a care. If he gets beyond me, I thought, if he keeps on going past me then he's totally had it, then there's nothing between here and Filching itself and that's miles away, and, lord knows, he'll never make it that far. He waved his arms about as he leapt on, as if he was a great long bird trying to gain flight, but not making it. Some seagulls swarmed around him, diving about as if playing with him. He seemed at times, caught up as he was in a mass of white feathers, to be greeting them, to be playing with them. But each time the seagulls swooped down I could see, for he was closer now, that he was dirtied by their attentions, that his clothes were getting fouled, there was filth on them and rips. They're

271

diving him, I realised, they're biting him. They mean to do it.

'Hey! Stop that!' I called. 'Leave him alone!'

They couldn't hear me. He couldn't hear me. Only I could hear myself. I've got to get to him, I said, I must get to him. The storm's coming on, the heaps are getting up, they'll be boiling in an instant. I must get to him, I must make him hear me.

I tried to twist my helmet off, but it wouldn't come, I tried to open the window of the helmet but my thick gloves were too large and fat, too greasy and slippery to unfasten the bolt, and I couldn't take the gloves off, they were part of the suit, stitched on they were. I must smash it, I said, before it's too late. Look, look at him. He was opening his arms out to the gulls. They flew up between each attack, and he would stand again and open his arms to them, waving out for them to come back. And they would. There must have been a hundred of them, swarming, nipping and scrapping in the air, and each time they came back they barrelled into him, winding him, lifting him for a moment up off the ground, into the air, only to be dropped once more in a heap. A pale, torn scarecrow, bloodied now in parts, and still – how ridiculous this seemed – still with his top hat on his head, as if it was right to be properly dressed for such horrors.

I waved my arms at him, even jumped up and down upon the stairs as much as I dared. But he, so taken up with the seagulls, never looked to me. I threw things at the birds, but whatever I hurled was way off, nowhere near. I must smash the helmet glass, I thought, I have to smash the glass. On the top right at the tip of the staircase, at the end of all the treads, was a sharp broken one, with a metal brace. And against this now I banged my head and the glass. Smack! Smack! Smack! Nothing. Not a scratch. And I mustn't do it too hard or I'll bring the sharp edge right through my own face and have me impaled for ever on top of a stairway that leads nowhere. Smack! Smack! Smack! A crack now, a good crack! Smack! Smack! Crash, the edge goes through and slices at my cheek. But it's done! It's done, the window's broke. I pulled the bits out with my thick gloves. I called then, I called for all my lungs' worth.

'Halloo! Halloo! Out there! Over here! Over here!'

He didn't hear me. Though now I could hear him, as he jumped about between the gulls' return, he was singing, he was singing in this foul weather, in this foul place.

'Homily, homily, homily, homily!'

That's what I thought it was.

'Halloo! Over there! Can you hear me?

'Homily, homily –' but that wasn't it, that wasn't quite it – 'Ormily, Ormily.' Yes, that was it, 'Ormily, Ormily, Ormily!'

'Hallo! Hallo! I'm over here!'

He did stop a moment then. He looked out at me. I waved madly at him. He waved back, even took his hat off in salutation, and the moment he did some great gull plundered it, carrying it off for ever. Then I saw his hair.

It was fair and fluffy and so light. Then I knew him.

He was Clod's friend. He was called Tummis. This was Tummis Iremonger so far out in the heaping land.

'Are you Tummis?' I cried.

'Who are you?'

'A friend of Clod's, of Clod Iremonger's! Hang on a minute, hang on there!' I cried. 'I'm coming over to you. I've got a line.'

'No!' he shouted. 'I don't want it! I'm not going back.'

'You can't stay out here. The storm!'

'They won't let me marry Ormily! Won't let me!'

'I'm coming over!'

'And Clod's being sent away!'

'I'm coming to you!'

'Oh, my Ormily!'

'Here I come!'

'I shan't go back!'

The storm was getting up behind him, a great wave rising up in the distance, a great black billowing wave of bricks and glass of bones and rubble, all coming this way.

'Hold on, Tummis! Nearly there!'

I was nearly at him, I was so close, just a few more paces, but then as I struggled on, I felt something pulling me back, tugging me back from my waist, stopping my progress, dragging me back towards the house. I was being pulled in, my anchor and surely not just my anchor but other stronger people than my anchor were hauling me back to the safety of the wall. I reached out my hand for Tummis.

'Grab on, Tummis, the wave, the wave!'

And he looked behind him and then there was fear about him and he reached out at last, he reached out as I was being dragged away, he stumbled towards me.

'Come on! Come on!' I cried.

He stretched something out to me, not his hand but something shining, something to extend his arm.

'Come on! Tummis! Quick!' I cried, because then whoever was tugging was tugging hard, so hard I could barely keep my feet on the ground.

I stretched my hand out, caught hold of the shining thing, felt metal.

'I've got you!' I cried. 'Hold on, they'll tug us in, only hold on!'

He stumbled a bit towards me, but then he fell. He was down in it. He was caught on something, his foot was trapped, he tried to wrestle it free.

'I . . .' he called, 'a post office box has me,' he said, 'by the ankle. I can't free myself.'

'Tummis! Tummis! The wave!'

And then there was an almighty tug on the lead and I was dragged, pulled, heaved away from him, with only the metal thing in my hand. I was rolled over this way and that, smacked into things, but pulled and dragged on. And there he was further and further away and then a great shadow came over him and then a fearsome crashing. And that was it. I was turned over and could see nothing. When I could at last look back again he wasn't there any more. He'd gone under.

I was still screaming when they hauled me in, by the time they got me safe to the wall. I was still holding onto that metal thing. It was a tap, a useless bloody tap. With an H on it, for hot I supposed. That was all that was left of him. Just that. A bloody tap. What was the use in that?

It had been several of the big anchors that hauled me in, they were in a panic over the storm and all were trying to scramble back in through the gates because the heaps now were getting up proper, and waves had begun to break against the house wall, it was much deeper there now than when I first came out.

'In! In! In!' they screamed. 'We must get inside!'

The Captain was running around blowing his whistle, panic on his face.

'It's a big one, a really big one. Haven't seen one as big as this in ages!'

'There's someone out there,' I cried, 'there's someone still out there.'

They were carrying me in through the gate, they wouldn't put me down.

'Please!' I cried. 'We have to go back! We have to find him!'

'No, no,' said the Captain, 'isn't safe, far from it. Got to come in now. Not a day to be outside, not at all.'

'But he's still out there,' I yelled, and then I thought of what they'd listen to. 'A full-blood,' I said, 'a real proper Iremonger! Tummis Iremonger he's called. He's out there! Look, this is his! His birth object I think.'

'Give me that!' said the Captain. 'Oh dear. Oh lord.' But then he said, 'Close the gates!'

'You can't do that!'

'Must! Must do it! Or the walls will be breached. Got to. For the house!'

'An Iremonger!' I screamed. 'Tummis Iremonger!'

'Shut it, little miss,' cried the Captain. 'It's too late. Nothing to be done.'

'Tummis Iremonger's out there! Listen, please!'

'No, you brat,' he said, 'no, he isn't, not any more. Anything that's out there is dead, done with, ended. I'm sorry, I'm really sorry, but that's it. Nothing can make it through that. Not when it's up, not when it's really up like this.'

'Tummis!' I wailed. 'Tummis Iremonger!'

'I wouldn't go out there now for my own mother, not even for Umbitt Iremonger himself, not for the ruddy Queen if you want to know. Now get in, will you, and be reasonable. Who knows who else will get it in a storm like this. More than just one, I'd bet on that. There'll be more dead before the day is out. We better hope the house stays up, it may not, some of it shall come down. I guarantee it. You just have to hope you're not in that part, don't you? Look out!'

At that moment some rubble came flying over the wall, landing in the courtyard. Glass shattered in front of us, and there lying where we had been just a moment before was a twisted and rusted iron bed.

277

'In! In! And slam the door behind us! Slam it and bolt it!'

We were in then, all the heap Iremongers and all the anchors and me all still wearing our leathers and helmets, downstairs, beneath ground, filth all around us, dripping off us, on the Heap House service corridors.

'We'll have a mop down here,' announced the Captain, 'a mop this instant.'

But rather than a mop and Iremonger coming running, instead there was Piggott and there was Sturridge, and there was Idwid Iremonger, his ear facing outwards, tugging on his own lug, and just by him another little man just like him to look at, only this one had eyes that worked and his clothes were less smart and there was a whistle hanging from his neck, and there were other Iremongers in suits, official ones I did not know, all anxious, all trembling. Then, actually, after all, I did recognise one of the official Iremongers, one with a red bay leaf on his lapel. I'd seen him somewhere before. I knew I had. Yes I had! It was the one called Cusper Iremonger, the one that took me from the orphanage. Hullo, what's he doing there?

'There's been a breach,' said the butler.

'No,' said the Captain, 'maybe later. Not yet. Begging to report, the gate bolted and the wall's holding well. At the moment. But, regret to report, been a loss out there. Don't know how he got out, a family member with no lifeguard, but out he went, so I've been told, and yet to confirm; I have this. But not, so it seems, the one that belonged to it.'

He held out the tap. Piggott snatched it.

'That's Master Tummis's! How did this ever happen!'

'Don't know how, not for me to look after those ones. He must have slipped out. Very sorry, very sorry, not my department. But no breach, door fastened and holding! No, you see, no breach at all.'

'Not the storm,' snapped the one with the whistle, 'not the weather, dumbmuck!'

'Regret to say it, would rather not,' said Cusper, 'I let one in.'

'Go on, you pissbucket!' ordered the one with whistle. 'Go on and tell them!'

'That's not the way, dear Timfy,' said blind Idwid, 'not helpful in the least. Tell them, Cusper, if anything can be heard above this storm, this constant shrieking in my ears.'

'I shall have my say, brother!' cried the one with the whistle.

'Please, Cusper,' prodded Idwid.

'I think it may be with you, think it might, one of your number, Captain,' continued Cusper, 'under a helmet, between leather, one of . . . those there. Let in. My fault. Most awfully.'

'What exactly?' asked Idwid. 'What did you let in? Tell the heap Captain. Oh, my ears!'

'A . . . a . . . a non-person, a, well, a not one of us, a . . . erm . . . other.'

'Spit it out, man,' yapped the one with the whistle, 'let's

279

get this done before Umbitt's back. I shouldn't want to stand in your shoes, not for love nor money; he'll throw you from the building. He'll cut you loose. I know *I* would. Yes, I would!'

'Steady, Timfy,' said Idwid, 'steady now, baby brother. Oh, my ears!'

'Baby, he says! He said "Baby"!'

'I . . . you see,' trembled Cusper, 'I . . . took the wrong one. Was in a hurry. Shouldn't have been. Wrong. Wrong. Oh, stupid. I . . . names . . . those ugly names . . . not good with . . . looking for a girl, I said, in the orphanage . . . with red hair . . .'

As he stammered his explanation, his head held low, sweat on brow, he gestured to someone behind him and then a girl stepped forward, one not in a serving Iremongers' togs at all but in the old orphanage uniform with a leather cap upon her head. It was her, of course. I'd know *her* anywhere and instantly. The bully from the orphanage, the one I fought with, the one who said it wasn't right that there were two redheads, the one I bit, the one that scratched, her, her, that one for whom I'd always have to look over my shoulders. That one. I never knew her name.

So it wasn't supposed to be me all along, I'm not an Iremonger. I'm not Iremonger at all, never have been, never will. Not a drop. Mother wasn't, she wasn't at all. I shouldn't have come. They made a mistake. The other redhead was an Iremonger. Well she would be, wouldn't she, let's face it. Iremonger through and through that one.

'I'll find her! I'll point her out,' she said. 'Let me! Let me! I'm the one to do it.'

'Be silent!' shrieked Piggott. 'It will be done, and swiftly too. Minimum of fuss. Never been an un-Iremonger in Heap House, never meant to be one all the way out here, spreading disease. Family here. Family only. Intimate. Come now, deary, come now, my chick, step out. Come to Claar. Which one are you?'

I couldn't go back, not back out there. The door was locked behind me. I couldn't go forward. There were all those Iremongers waiting for me and some of them were keeping one hand behind their backs – what were they holding there? – whatever it was that they held wasn't good, I was certain of that.

'Take your helmets off!' said Piggott.

'Excuse me,' said the Captain.

'Do it now!' called the one with the whistle.

'Come on, girlie, come on now; step out, let's see you.'

'My ears!' cried Idwid.

'Please excuse me,' said the Captain, 'they cannot hear you. They cannot hear through the helmets. They don't know what's being asked.'

'Then get their helmets from them, man! Now!'

'The anchors will do it! The anchors are the swiftest. Each knows its leather so well. They're all so different, you see, the helmets are, particular –'

'I don't want a lecture, I want the helmets off!' bellowed the butler.

281

'Come here, child, come to Claar, I'll have you. I mean to have you.'

The cook's wife, Mrs Groom, licking her lips, showed for an instant a long shining thing that must've been a knife.

'I mean to skin you,' she said. 'I'll bake you, boil you, poach you, pluck you! Gut you!'

'Odith!' snapped Piggott. 'Not yet!'

'My ears!'

I was on the floor, ducked down between the other leather ones who were now twisting and turning with their anchors and helmets all in a struggle to pull theirs off first. I'm not taking mine off, I thought, not if I can help it, even with the glass broken. Protection of some sort, that's what it is. I saw my anchor beside me, the kitchen boy, staring at me, frowning. I shook my head, please, please don't tell. He didn't. He didn't call out.

'Mrs Groom!' he whispered. 'She will cook you! If she's a mind to do it, she'll do it!'

'Help me.'

'She's a fishwife, she is. She'd gut her own baby.'

'Help me.'

He didn't help, but he didn't tell. He might have perhaps, I can't say, because he didn't really have a chance, because then one of those heavy helmets put down on the ground didn't stay on the ground, it started, all on its own, to skid along the floor, faster and faster, to rush down the corridor into something in one of the kitchen halls, onto a wall of the kitchen hall. All eyes followed it, all eyes saw it connect to something that was moving on the back wall. No, it wasn't just something, it was the whole wall that was moving. Was it the storm? Could it be the storm breaking through? No, no, that wasn't it because now I saw the little man with the whistle shriek because his whistle was trying to pull away from him and if he hadn't had it on a string around his neck it would have been lost by now. Then another freed helmet rushed away and then a whole big heap Iremonger fell down and started slipping towards that back kitchen wall. That did it. That did it for all of them because then Idwid screamed, 'A Gathering, a Gathering, quieter than the storm!'

And then they were all screaming, 'A Gathering! A Gathering!'

And then I ran.

The Matriarch Ommaball Oliff Iremonger

19

A MARBLE MANTELPIECE

Clod Iremonger's narrative continued

Grey Flannel

I sat in the Infirmary with James Henry in my lap, apologising to him, asking him who he was, promising to find his family, tapping him a little and then begging its, *his* I must say, begging *his* pardon.

'I do beg your pardon, I truly do. I'll get you home, somehow. I'll get you back. Where are your people? What are they like, those Haywards of yours? If I get you there, shall I become an object? And what, James Henry, dear fellow, if I may, do you suppose I should be were I an object? Should I be something grand, like a lucifer, or something useful like a plunger? It speaks well of you, I think, that you're a bath plug. It's a fine thing to be a bath plug. Very pleasing, good to hold. Oh sorry, James Henry, I'm at it again, of course you'd rather not be a bath plug at all, would you? You'd rather be James Henry Hayward, himself in his own outfit, kitted out, at home with your own. I *do* so wonder what you look like. Do you have a round face, or do I only think of that because of the roundness of the plug? I am sorry, I'm so sorry, James Henry. I didn't know before, but I do know now. And, by heavens, I wish it wasn't so.'

'James Henry Hayward.'

'I know, I know.'

There I sat, taking it all in, head in a spin, wrung out, all those words of Grandfather's and things of his and smell that's his, still in the room somehow. Should get out, I thought. Should get out and far away, go somewhere. But where is there? And what to do with my plug? And all those other things up and down the house, the east of it and the west of it, the whole crammed prison of it, all those people stuck in objects, a fire bucket that's a person, a sofa that's a person, a tap that's a person, a newel post, a barometer, a ruler, a whistle, a cuspidor, a box of matches, all people, all people! A box of matches! Lucy Pennant!

Lucy Pennant, they're sending me away. I'm called to the city. I should have been proud of that. If Grandfather had only visited me a few days earlier I'd have gone with a hop and skip. But not now. Not any more. They were sending me the very next day. I should get on the train. That train that I'd heard so often screaming in and out, always wearing at me, always sending the house Iremongers into shock though they knew it would come. Oh, Lucy, Lucy Pennant.

I should have been up already. A matron had come in and told me to make myself smart. I was to go and see my grandmother. I was supposed to put on trousers. Grey flannel trousers. Goodbye, knees! Goodbye, shins and calves! I should have been happy before, I had so longed to touch my own grey flannel, to look hard at it and to say with manly pride: 'Herringbone.' I should have been a happy one to say: 'Farewell, corduroy.' Not now. Oh, my objects! But what, I thought, what if Grandfather was right, what if James Henry was a little villain, a bully in plug form, who, given the opportunity, should shove me in his pocket and pinch and bite me?

I was to be ready, to be dressed, combed, my hair parted, my teeth picked at, and to be up on the upright corridor. But I sat there, plug in lap, trousers folded beside me. I was to visit Grandmother, the old lady of the mantelpiece. And later, I thought, later on, I'd go to the Sitting Room and I'd sit on Victoria Hollest who no doubt would be wondering where Margaret was and so, a real person, both of them. I'm so sorry. And just for a while, I'd sit with Lucy; she'd be safe now, wouldn't she, I'd tell her not to worry any more, now that Alice Higgs was a doorknob once again. (Oh, Alice Higgs, I am so sorry, what a thing to have done. What sort of person am I after all?) But to lose Lucy!

I picked up the trousers. What should happen, I wondered, when I put them on?

I supposed I should start growing whiskers very like,

just after wearing my trousers, perhaps the moment grey flannel touched Clod-skin. That then I could do mutton chops and sideboards, that I could be bearded and hirsute in a suit, like so many of the city Iremongers that allow themselves to be so hairy that their faces look like a house overgrown with ivy. Shall I hairy me? Shall I grow so beardsome that my own furriness will be a fence between me and the world? Shall I be so long and thick of hair that for Lucy Pennant to kiss me again she, like the prince in *Sleeping Beauty* before her, should have to hack at me with a scythe because finding me in a room all she'd see at first was a forest of beard? There was but one way to find out.

I trousered me.

I pulled them on, like cutting off my own legs.

All the world, I thought, will be in grey flannel for you now. I had dragged it over, put out the nursery with it. How did I feel? Superior? Old? Wise? Heavier? Stronger? Did I find myself upright and forthright and big of birthright, broad of chest, and much impressed?

No, I cannot say that I did.

Truth is, I felt much the same. Only difference was, a tiny bit warmer.

But, I thought then, give it a while. An hour or two, or a week; that grey flannel is upon me now, and means to enter me, to somehow drown my former corduroy self, so that my own skin shall grey and flannel. There's worsted in my blood, threads of it sewing its way through me.

Soon there I was complete: brushed, cufflinked, hair parted (no beard yet), shod, waistcoated, jacketed, tied and strangled in all the usual ways, done up and beribboned, an Iremonger parcel. Poor James Henry in pocket.

Well then, I said to myself, delay no further, you must go to Granny now.

Blood and Marble

I left the Infirmary, the nursing Iremongers that saw me bowed to me, which they never had before. One, a little lippy to do such a thing, even clapped me in my new attire but was soon hushed by a matron. Now that I was trousered I was a big thing of terror and respect; before when I was in corduroy, well then I was only a little chap and could even have my chin pinched and my hair ruffled. No longer. I was a big man now, and I stepped out into the world fully grown and feeling morbid.

Out in the house corridors a few cousins here and there stopped and stared at me, most perplexed as if they'd never seen trousers before. That felt quite fine. I admit it. I went down the main stairs to Grandmother's wing. I was expected, otherwise the porter Iremonger at the door should never have let me pass into Grandmother's territory.

I was seeing her once more, my grandmother.

When Grandmother was born, back so far in history that people were surely very different to the modern people we are now, back then it was Great Grandfather Adwald who was head of the family. Adwald was a hard one. It was known right from the start that Grandmother, Omma-ball Oliff Iremonger, should marry Grandfather, and Adwald wanted everything to be right and proper for his heir, he wanted no complication of wife, no womanly disturbances. So he put Grandmother where Grandfather would always find her. He proclaimed that her birth object, which I had always heard call itself Augusta Ingrid Ernesta Hoffman, would be a large marble mantelpiece. The mantelpiece was, to my knowledge, the largest birth object ever given out. It was such a large thing, this mantelpiece, that it had taken a small army of Iremonger muscles to shift it (and one of those it was rumoured even perished in the process, quite crushed underneath it). The mantel-piece shelf was supported by two caryatids, full of bosom they were. Beautiful maidens, a little sleepy, with thin dresses that were slipping off them, but never, not ever, actually achieving a fall. They were one and a half life-size those figures, oh big and beautiful ladies. That such pretty women should be locked in marble was not right, I always thought. I used to long for them, to dream of them waking up and stepping out, of finding me wherever I was in the house, of visiting my bedroom.

Strange, I thought, that such lively-looking forms, that such beauty should be so heavy. I know they had never lived, and yet they always seemed to me so lifelike. Sitting as a child in Grandmother's room, condemned to silence, to sitting upright and not making a sound, I thought I caught them breathing once or twice. I should dearly have loved to have spent some time with them alone, but Grandmother was always there. And that was the point: Grandmother never left that room.

It was a large room with six full windows. Grandmother was born in this room, and shortly after, the great marble thing shoved in with her. During her long, long life she had never left the room, never once. In that room, in that single space, was all that Grandmother could ever need: her bed was there, her water closet discreetly hidden behind a panel, and all the things of Grandmother's life, her infancy, her childhood, her schooling, her marriage, proof of her children, her old age, all of her living, every shade of it. Since she couldn't go out into the world, then the world must come to her. All the best bits of Iremonger pilfering came to Grandmother, she had the finest porcelains, she had a Qing vase from China, she had Russian silver and Gobelins tapestries from Paris, she had so many famous Victorians in her room. The wallpaper was by William Morris, there was a large painting of a young woman in a large dress by Lord Leighton. She wasn't all modern grandmother in her room, she had older things too: a painting by Joshua Reynolds, a Van Dyck portrait of a doomed cavalier, she had a drawing of a courtier by Hans Holbein. She had all time, I used to think, kept with her in her room. She grew bored of objects soon enough, some things were only played with for a day or two, others stayed for years, and she was always redesigning her rooms; she'd call for a painting of Venice, she'd call for Chinese silks, she'd demand things, and Grandfather should do his very best to please her, for she would be in a temper until her demands were met. And though she could never leave the room on account of her massive marble mantelpiece, still her fury was felt all about the house; it was a temper as big as a mansion. She'd demand things, she'd pull on her bell pull and pull and pull, have the butler with her all day and the housekeeper, demand to have sixteen servants in her room, call in all the uncles and aunts from London. So Grandfather always did his best for her.

To please her, early on, it was Grandfather who bestowed upon his wife the business of choosing birth objects for each of the family members. And how she had relished this occupation. She complained about it often enough, of how it exhausted her, of how it was wearing her down, of how it should be the very death of her, but, under all that, she loved it, she loved it, for then she chose the life – she whose life had been so confined – of all the members so great and so small of Iremonger Park. Thus had my grandmother handed out hairbrushes and bath plugs, whistles (and matchboxes, Lucy so dear to me), eggcups and doorstops. It was a certain thing that, since Grandmother had come into her portion, she had delivered very ordinary things here and there, everyday bits and pieces, commenting on the very average nature of her family, never impressed, dismissing, condemning for example, poor Uncle Pottrick with a noose for a birth object, thus she ruined the man's life. She felt no remorse, why should she, she was stuck for ever in a single chamber; how could any pain ever be greater than hers? At times, so I have been told, when she was younger, she would be so furious at her confinement that she would throw great valuables out of her window, that she would smash crystal glass and grandmother clocks and alabaster busts. The only constant in that constant room with her was the great marble mantelpiece. All else was in a state of flux. Once, after a long and loyal service, Grandmother, her mood – like a tempest – up, and, having scratched at the floorboards in her misery until her fingernails were cracked and bleeding, had opened a double set of windows and propelled her own beloved body servant from her room down, down onto the cobbles below. All was for ever changing, only Grandmother and the mantelpiece remained the same.

It seemed to me that Grandmother was long at war with her mantelpiece, it was always youthful, always beautiful. Grandmother had been a child, looking up to that great thing, playing around it, dressing like it, and, with the aid of stepladder, arranging things upon its shelf, then Grandmother had grown up and had married Grandfather, and then Grandfather visited and I do think then that there were moments when Grandmother was very jealous of her caryatids, that their voluptuousness mocked her, for she was always so thin, Grandmother, flat-chested, narrow of waist, and all bone. Grandmother, day by day, had grown old and had grown frail and had shrunk but those marble girls were still as big and powerful and so rounded and she stooped and brittled and took her teeth out and hurt here and there with her aging. For months at a time Grandmother would have the mantelpiece covered up. Once, for a year or so, it was even bricked over. Later she would scratch at it with things, she marked it and she dented her own birth object. Taking up a hammer and chisel, she added wrinkles here and there to her nearly naked ladies, and yet, despite all this, I think she loved them. For that great marble thing, unlike all our foot pumps and hot-water bottles, unlike our shoes and folding pocket rules, unlike our watering cans and footstools, was a thing of startling beauty.

I had not visited Grandmother for several seasons, the last time I was there, she had been very short with me, had called me a tremendous disappointment. On that occasion, she had blamed my father; she said that my father had never been much of anything, that he had been a terrible mistake for my mother, even that he had killed my mother, that, if it wasn't for Father, Mother would still be alive now. How right she was, she had told me, to have given him a chalkboard rubber, so that he might rub himself out. She had said, crying then, that she could see something of Mother's face in mine, but it was a dismal version of it, a bad imitation, a flawed mimicry. She had packed me off then, saying she never wished to see me again, that I was horrible history, that it was better for her to suppose that my mother had never been born, because the agony of the loss of her was too, too sharp a thing to bear.

And so I was not to visit Grandmother and I was not to go near her wing. It was to be, for Grandmother, as if I wasn't about at all. Instead she liked to have Moorcus and Horryit beside her. They were frequent visitors. She gave them many treasures, she called them beautiful and made so much of them, she said they were the future of the Iremonger family, she said to Horryit, so Moorcus liked to relate, that one day, not a soon day it was to be hoped, but one day inevitably, Horryit should be the one to choose birth objects, and what a marvel she would be at it.

And there, once more, I stood. Trousered now at Grandmother's door. I knocked, but the noise I made was so feeble I feared I was not heard. I stood outside a little while. Get this over, I thought, and then, later on, you may go to the Sitting Room and find Lucy Pennant there. Still no answer. I knocked again, louder this time.

'Who is it?' came Grandmother's impatient voice.

'It is Clod, Granny, your grandson Clodius, Ayris's boy.'

'Wipe your feet.'

'Yes, Granny.'

'And step inside.'

'Yes, Granny.'

Grandmother's Footsteps

The room had changed a good deal since last I saw it. There were new curtains and some new paintings. Her bed was different, and it seemed to me her bathtub too – there were steps up to it. She was sat up in a high-backed armchair, she looked very small in such a thing. She was dressed all in black and in thick black boots which were very worn; there was nothing unusual in that particularly, she often had a serving Iremonger wear her shoes in for her, so that the shoes might go about the world even if she didn't. She wore a complicated white cap which made her head twice as tall. She was wearing at least ten strings of pearls, some tight around her thin wrinkled neck, others pooled in her lap; the weight of them made her head bow forward, not unlike a tortoise I thought. I could hear the storm outside, see the last bit of light still out there. Small objects were being pelted against the glass of her windows: pebbles, broken straps of leather, little shards of porcelain, pages of newspaper. But my grandmother sat oblivious to all the snaps and clinks upon her windows.

'Hullo, Granny, how are you?' I said. 'It's so nice to see you again.'

'Come forward, child, kiss me.'

I stepped forward, my shoes creaking on her floor, across her floor, to the very feet of her. And then that smell of old and of damp, slightly sweet, something a little mouldy, something gone off, my grandmother.

'Kiss me,' she said again.

I leant down and gently kissed her cheek and though my lips touched the surface of something, that something, the corrugated pelt of old Grandmother, seemed barely there at all, as if I'd kissed a cobweb. Brussels sprouts. That was the smell, mostly.

'Sit, Clodius, sit.'

I sat on the edge of a neighbouring sofa, an empire sofa all upright and hardness and no sink to it at all. I perched there and tried not to look into those old yellow eyes.

'Sit up, Clodius.'

'Yes, Granny.'

I looked about the room, most specifically at the mantelpiece, at the marble ladies there, still lovely. And, between the moans of the storm and the tics and the tocks of Grandmother's many timepieces, I heard the marble tell me, 'Augusta Ingrid Ernesta Hoffmann.'

And so, I thought that early evening, you're a person too, Miss Hoffmann – I could certainly not think of you as plain Augusta; to be so familiar to my grandmother's own birth object couldn't be done. What sort of a person were you before you became a marble mantelpiece? Quite some person, I thought, quite an extraordinary thing to have turned out so striking. Outside, an old empty dress, stained and ripped, slammed against the windows, and I shook. Grandmother paid it no heed.

'Well, Clodius, how good of you to visit your old grandmother. How long has it been, pray tell, since last you came?'

'It has been a good few seasons, Granny.'

'It has. You have grown. Not well perhaps, not exactly upright, at an angle shall we say, like a truculent plant seeking out the sun through a crack in a curtained window. So long it has been.'

'I should have come sooner, Granny, but –'

'You should *not* have come sooner. You should *not* have been received. But you are here now, because you have been sent for. I wished for it. I wished to see you before you go away. To catch again some hint of Ayris's face. My daughter. My own dead daughter.'

She was silent again a while and so I sat, upright, and listened to all those clocks and their marking, to the storm outside whistling and cackling, and to the mantelpiece telling its name in a clear young voice. Tic. Tic. Tic. Smack. Tap. Crack. Was one of those tics the ticking of Grandmother's old heart pump, thrusting and sloshing the old, but so pure, Iremonger liquid all about her, to every Iremonger corner of her? Tic. Tic. Tic. Crack. Plick. Snap. There was a whoosh as some old blankets were blown up by the storm and hovered a little before the window, as if they wished to take a peek, before falling down again, actually falling, unlike the cloth around the marble women.

'You are wearing trousers, Clodius.'

'Yes, Granny, new today.'

Tic. Tic. Tic.

Plick. Plack. Crack.

'How do they feel?'

'A little prickly, Granny, to tell the truth.'

'You are given your trousers, early too, and all you can

say on this momentous day is: a little prickly. It's not good enough, Clodius. You must try better.'

'Yes, Granny. Sorry, Granny.'

Tic. Tic. Tic. Smack! Crash! A small book hit the window, as if it were a bird desperate to get in.

'Pinalippy, Clodius. You have seen Pinalippy, I think.'

'Yes, Granny. We have had our Sitting.'

'I know you have, Clodius, I know everything about you. Just because I don't see you doesn't mean I'm not told. How was she? Pinalippy?'

'Ah . . . very nice, Granny. Thank you.'

'Very nice! Very nice, he says! She's plain, Clodius, as plain as a mop. The skin is not pleasing. Hair on her lip, dark hair on the arms. The movements rather masculine. Tall too and thick with it. No grace. No music there at all!'

'No, Granny.'

'Well, you're to marry her!'

'Oh yes, Granny, I know.'

'Rather you than me. But she's loyal I think. And durable. She won't die on you, Clodius. Things like that live long. She'll outlast you.'

'I'm very sure of that, Granny.'

Tic. Tic. Tic. Smack. Tinkle. Crack. Things were pelting against the window very often now, making me jumpy.

'How's your bath plug?'

'My bath plug? Do you wish to see him? It, I mean.'

'Don't be disgusting. Of course I don't wish to see such a thing. It was I, Clod, that picked that out for you.

Especially so. There were a great many objects brought before me that I might have chosen. But I pointed out the bath plug for you.'

'Yes, Granny, I thank you.'

'It was a hard one. I thought over it a very long while.'

'Did you, Granny? Thank you, Granny.'

'Very tiresome.'

Tic. Tic. Tic. Crack. Crack. Crack. And then an almighty wallop as what appeared to be the remains of a cat smacked into the windows.

'Fearful weather, isn't it, Granny?'

'Of course I was in no state to be choosing birth objects. Not so soon after Ayris's death.'

I said nothing to that. Tic. Tic. Smack. Whoosh.

'Some days I remember her so clearly that I can almost see her. She played here in this room. She was a little girl standing over there in that corner. I see her now, almost, leaning against my mantelpiece.'

Tic. Tic. Crack. Tic. Smack. Tic. Howl went the wind. I'd better speak, I thought, I'd better say something to that.

'I'm very sorry I never knew her. My mother.'

Grandmother made a noise as if she were blowing out a very stubborn candle. And then she was silent again for a while and the noises were left to fill the room. I shall go to the Sitting Room soon, I thought, I shall see Lucy before the sun comes up again. It's so dark out already, it is such a bad storm to have taken all the light with it. Tic. Tic. Crack. Snarl. Scream. The door opened, and I jumped, but it was only five maids stepping in, bowing at my grandmother, one of them asking, 'May we, my lady, if it is quite convenient, close the shutters now?'

'So early?' she asked. 'Why?'

'It is gone seven, my lady.'

'Already?' She regarded a clock. 'I had no idea.'

'And the storm, my lady . . .'

'Get on then, don't make a fuss.'

They went about their task, nervous and fretful; each time a window was opened – for the windows must be opened in order for the shutters to be folded out and the bolt-slides to be dropped down – each time this happened the storm entered the room and danced about it. It leapt and laughed and set the room in disorder, it picked things up, hurled them the length of the place, it shivered all the paintings. Even Grandmother's great mobcap was ruffled by it, such was the storm's cheek. My own new trousers flapped about me with the weather, and my parting was unparted. The storm spat at me, there was rain on my cheeks. It filled my head with its noise and its foul breath had me wincing. But most of all, of course, was the noise of it.

At last all the shutters were shuttered up and the windows closed behind them and the room quite sealed in, and, as if in happy victory, the clocks were much louder and more confident. Tic! Tic! Tic! I mopped at myself with my handkerchief, Grandmother looked disapproving. The maids lit my grandmother's lamps, then went about righting the place, and at last, with their bows and crouching down and my-ladying, left. And we were together again, and it was only then, for the first time, that Grandmother showed some hint of disquiet.

'Your grandfather's late,' she said. 'I have not heard the train yet. I do not think I could have missed it.'

'No, Grandmother,' I said, 'I don't think it has come back yet.'

'He is late then. I do not like him to be late.'

'Perhaps it's the storm, Grandmother.'

'It is not like Umbitt to be affected by a storm. Though I must own that it is a bad one. No doubt he'll be home again soon enough. And tomorrow, Clodius, you are for the city?'

'Yes, Grandmother, I am to take the morning train.'

'I have never been to the city.'

'No, Grandmother.'

'I should not like to now. What could there be for me in the city, what might I gain from it, over there, all the way over there? I can't see the point of it at all. I'm much better off here, I've everything I need here. There have been times, long gone now, when I thought I might like to see it, but not now, never now. I curse my former foolishness. Even I, Clodius, was young once. Does that sound strange to you?'

'No, Granny, not at all.'

'It sounds strange to me.'

Tic! Tic! Tic!

A knock on the door, Grandmother looked as if someone

had shown her something very ugly, something lewd perhaps.

'What now? Who is out there?'

'It is Mrs Piggott, my lady,' came the housekeeper's voice from the corridor.

'Piggott? Why, Piggott? What, Piggott?'

'Might I come in?'

'I am being visited by my grandson, Piggott. We are having such a merry time.'

'Please, my lady,' said Piggott, still corridor-side, 'I should very much like to inform you of the news of the house.'

'It is hardly the hour for my gazette.'

'Circumstances, my lady, unforeseen circumstances.'

'Oh, stop nibbling at the door, Piggott! Step in then, be present!'

The Piggott that appeared in the room in no way resembled the Piggott that I knew. This was no starched and ironed Piggott, this was a very rumpled one with smudges upon her, and most notably of all, a slight gash upon her forehead.

'Piggott!' struck Grandmother. 'How dare you!'

'I'm so sorry, my lady,' she said, 'but I felt that I must, I felt it my duty . . .' She saw me then, and rather than giving me the usual bow, let out a small scream. 'Master Clodius! You are here, are you! You yourself! My lady, oh my lady!'

'Piggott,' said Grandmother, 'don't be messy, it isn't like you.'

'No, my lady.'

'Be a good woman.'

'Yes, my lady.'

'What is the passion for?'

Mrs Piggott, her hands fluttering about, playing the piano though there was no piano before them, was at my grandmother, upon her knees and delivering her information, sotto voce, to my elderly relative's right pinna. There was only the quiet rustling of her whispering for a little while, I could not hear her above the racket of the timepieces, though occasionally Grandmother would comment.

'I know the train is late, woman!'

More whispering.

'I also know there is a Gathering!'

More whispering.

'How large?'

More whispering.

'It must be split up. Tell those gentlemen from the city that I shall have their bodies fractioned if they do not break up the Gathering instantly. I don't want to hear about it any more. No excuses!'

Yet more.

'Tummis?'

Yet more.

'You are certain?'

Yet more.

'On his own?'

Yet more.

'In this?'

Yet more.

'Oh, weak stuff! Un-Iremonger!'

Yet more.

'And Iktor and Olish?'

Yet more.

'They have it?'

Yet more.

'Well, I am sorry. I am sorry for that.'

A small pause, and yet more.

'What?'

And more.

'No!'

Still more.

'Can't be.'

A touch.

'How did it?'

Some.

'Among us?'

A bit.

'It *what*?'

Some.

'Our own!'

Some.

'Which one?'

Some.

'*Him!*'

A nod.

'*Alone!*'

A mouthful.

'They what!'

Again some.

'No, no, *no!*'

Silence.

'Where now?'

A very little.

'*Lost!*'

A very little.

'Then find it!'

'Yes, my lady.' Mrs Piggott spoke louder once more.

'Then trap it!'

'Yes, my lady.'

'Then kill it!'

'Yes, my lady.'

'I don't care about the Gathering, I don't care about the storm! I want it trapped and I want it killed. At once, Piggott. Do not show your face to me until it is done. I'll have you bleached, my woman.'

'Yes, my lady.'

'I'll have you eat lye.'

'Yes, my lady.'

'And, Piggott?'

'My lady?'

'The other involved, the other one.'

'My lady?'

'I shall see to that. Personally see to it.'

'Yes, my lady.'

'And Piggott?'

'Yes, my lady?'

'There must be order, I'll have no chaos under this roof. Bells to sound quite as they always do. But, perhaps, under the circumstances, an early bed bell.'

'Yes, my lady.'

'Go then, go!'

Mrs Piggott, so trembling, so shaken about, shook herself from my grandmother's presence.

'Ineptitude!' hurled Grandmother at the exiting housekeeper with such force that it seemed her voice itself had closed the door. Grandmother was silent for a little while.

'Did you mention Tummis, Granny?' I asked. 'Is all well?'

'Do not concern yourself with Tummis, Clodius.'

'I do hope he shall be trousered soon.'

'Do not concern yourself.'

She looked at me for a long time, just looked. What a look it was. That look, I thought, was entering into my nostrils and through my earholes, and peeking about there, gathering information. Then she breathed in with great force, as if recalling that expeditionary look back to herself, back into her own body, where she inhaled it and considered it, before saying something in a way that was by no means quiet or peaceful but rather unhappy and, I rather thought, full of repulsion.

'What shall you do out there, Clodius, in the city?'

'I do not know precisely yet. Whatever Grandfather wishes of me.'

'A good answer at last. You are an Iremonger, Clodius.'

'Yes, Granny.'

'I trust you shall behave like one.'

'Yes, Granny.'

'You must make our family very proud. You have it in you, I think, Clodius, somewhere within you, though you do disguise it so. If only for your mother, you must be a great Iremonger. You shall not let us down.'

'No, Grandmother, I shall do my best.'

'You shall do a deal more than that, for that is not half enough. You will start again this very day, this very moment. A new chapter! You must give your every thought to the family. Every little inch of you, Clodius, is for the Iremongers. You have a talent, I am told. And it is right that you do, it is exactly correct that Ayris's son should have a talent. You have the breeding, Clodius. But you have much yet to do to be worthy of your blood, Clodius Iremonger. You must love it, love it, love that blood. Do you, Clodius? Do you love it?'

'Yes, Granny,' I mumbled, 'it is good blood, is it not?'

'The best! None better! Not even the Saxe-Coburg-Gothas can boast such liquid. Their blood is thin enough stuff. Ours is thicker. You cannot escape your blood, Clodius. Try it and it will go wrong in you, turn against your family and your own body shall go foul and fester.

308

I know an Iremonger, a lesser Iremonger, struck out on his own. And do you know what happened to him?'

'No, Granny, I do not.'

'His own legs went septic on him. He puffed up with pus.'

'Poor fellow.'

'There are great secrets hidden in our blood. Deep mysteries. You cannot escape your blood.'

'No, Granny.'

Tic! Tic! Tic!

'Do you know why I chose a plug for you, Clodius?'

'I do not, Granny.'

'Because, Clodius, it all depends on you. Your family's fortune rests on your little shoulders, did you know that? No, no, I should not think you do. It's been kept from you for a good while now. Too long, I thought. You, like any of the great Iremongers, have a particular way with things. One in every generation or so has usually bubbled up with it, with some particular gift, and they have always kept us going. For there are many beyond here that want us crushed. Your perpetual screaming as an infant marked you out so very early. Personally, I wanted you drowned at birth for what you had done to me. But Umbitt would not have it, and so you lived. You lived and you grew – grew badly – and here you are now in trousers and being sent away from here. I gave you a plug, Clodius Iremonger, as your particular object because, blood of mine, you shall do one of two things. You shall, like a plug, keep us in,

309

keep us safe, be a barrier between us and the threatening sinkhole. Or, conversely, you shall, like a plug that is pulled out, let us fall and tumble away, let us flow out to nothing, let us flood and gush and drip and be all gone!'

She paused for effect. Tic! Tic! Tic! Are the clocks, I wondered, are the clocks getting louder?

'To end such a family,' she continued, trying a smile now, 'is a terrible thing, Clodius, to do that you should be emptying out your own mother, your own father, your aunts and your uncles, spilling them, your playmate cousins, your own Pinalippy wife, abandoning them to nothingness, and all this fortune and all this property so carefully amassed should be lost, should fade away, should be destroyed, and our people should be chased here and there and cursed at, spat at, reviled, broken, if you did it. If you betrayed your own blood.' She leant forward now even further, her face reddened, her hands shaking, the pearls clinking. 'Don't pull out the plug, Clodius, don't do it!'

'I shall not, Grandmother, I will not!'

'You mean to pull out the plug!'

'I do not!'

'You shall do it!'

'I shall not!'

'To your own family!'

'No, Granny, no, no!'

'Then kiss me, child, kiss me.'

Again I made the horrible journey across the carpet, and again as I leant forward, my lips touched upon very little indeed. But while I was so close, she took hold of my hand, and then, our faces so close together, she said, 'Do not forsake us, Clodius.'

'No, Grandmother.'

'Do you love me, child?'

'Yes, Granny, I do.'

'Do not hurt those you love.'

'I promise . . .'

'You promise!' she said with something like happiness. 'There, then. That is what I needed. For you to promise me, here in this room, here before my marble mantelpiece about which your own mother has played, a solemn promise that Clodius Iremonger shall promise to support his family, to serve that family to the best of his abilities, to dedicate himself to them. Do you swear?'

'I do.'

'Say it then, swear it.'

'I do swear it,' I said, trembling and sweating.

She let my hand go. I returned to the sofa's edge thinking what a very long time it was since last I was there. The storm was getting loud again, or was it my own heart sprinting, thumping to be out of its cage? I had sworn, and as I swore to my grandmother I had meant it all. I was an Iremonger then, truly an Iremonger, it was all that I had ever known. I should strive every day for the family. But why had Grandmother persisted so, why had she bullied and talked and spent so many words on me; it was as if she knew I doubted. I *had* doubted, I had for a little.

As if she knew everything inside me: my fears for James Henry, my sorrow for the objects, but most of all my feeling for Lucy Pennant, a mere serving girl, a firegrate. Grandmother, all-seeing, was telling me I must put all that away, I must grow up at last. I was trousered now, I was going to the city. I shall not go to the Sitting Room, after all, I told myself, it's wrong to go to the Sitting Room. I decided at that moment that I should not go.

'I shall do well, Granny,' I said at last.

'You're a good boy,' she said.

'It is very fine to be wearing trousers.'

'It is, Clodius, indeed it is. Well done. I have something for you before you go, Clodius. For such an Iremonger as you. A little going-away present. A parting gift.'

She pointed to a round table on which rested a small package wrapped in tissue paper and tied up with a ribbon.

'Take it, child,' she said, 'open it up, tell me what you have there.'

I unwrapped the little object. It was a small silver hand mirror.

'Thank you, Granny,' I said.

'It is inscribed,' she said. 'Read it to me.'

'SO THAT I MAY ALWAYS KNOW WHO I AM.'

'That is it, quite right,' she said. 'I was going to give it to you today anyway, though I had no idea quite how appropriate it should be. You shall always know, Clodius, that you are an Iremonger of the best blood.'

'Thank you, Granny.'

'It is my pleasure, darling boy. You may go now.'

'Thank you, Granny. Goodbye, Granny.'

'So eager to leave your old grandmother? That is youth, is it not, always moving.'

'Goodbye, Granny.'

'Goodbye, Clodius, do great things.'

I was at the door then and in an eagerness to be the other side of it and far away from my grandmother and all her things and all her words.

'Oh, Clodius?' she called.

'Yes, Granny,' I said, very desperate now.

'I love you.'

Must she say that? Must she nail me for ever to Iremonger property? Yes, yes, she must.

'I love you, Granny,' I said.

'Off you run then,' she said, and she smiled such a kind, loving smile that for a moment all I could think of was what a sweet old woman she was, how dear, how fragile, and for a little while I lost sight of the other grandmother, the unforgiving one, the unforgivable one, the fierce limiter of people's lives. She even had tears in her eyes. My own grandmother.

It was noisier yet away from Grandmother's room. Out in the house again, the roar of the storm everywhere about. All the shutters had been closed but things could be heard smashing against them. There was some broken glass along Grandmother's corridor. The whole house was rumbling.

'Has the train come in yet?' I asked Grandmother's porter on the main stairs.

'Not yet, sir,' he said.

'It's very late then.'

'Yes, indeed it's late, sir, very.'

'Has there been much damage yet?'

'I shouldn't like to be in the attics now, there was a tumbling up there. There have been rushes of dust, sir, descending, even here upon the main stairway. You see a pile there, sir, 'bout halfway down.'

I saw it, a small mass of dirt and chippings, there was something of a crack in the ceiling, not very large, nothing to worry about probably.

'I heard there was a Gathering, has it been caught?'

'Not yet, I think. There are many noises all around the house tonight, and some of those might be a Gathering, and some might be the storm, I couldn't exactly say. There are city people about the Gathering in any case, so it cannot last long.'

'And tell me, porter, have the rats come down yet?' I asked.

'Yes, sir, two hours since. Just after you went in to see my lady. There was a great parade of them, never seen so many. All of one opinion, all going down, down the stairway. I stood here, out of their way, even upon the desk. It took them twelve minutes to quite pass through. Didn't know we had that many.'

'Where are they going?'

'Oh, out, I would say, sir, shouldn't you? They don't want to stay in here.'

314

'Where out?'

'Out in the heaps of course.'

'In the heaps, during a storm like this?'

'Certainly, sir, they'd rather take their chances out there than be stuck in here. There's nothing should keep them in the house tonight. T'ain't safe, they think. What a fuss they made about it, skittish I'd call it. Didn't let off their screeching. They didn't want to stay here. Wouldn't for anything. T'ain't safe. T'ain't safe. They think.'

'Do you think it's safe, Iremonger?' I asked.

'Me? You ask me? I'm no expert in it, sir, far from it, but what I say to myself is, don't go up to the attics, not the higher-most floors, no, don't go there, nor the east wing that wobbles enough even in a mild wind, and do not go down, I'd say, don't head down, it shall be flooded down there after a time, bound to be. As for myself, I'm staying here. Mid-house. Safest, I'd say. How about you, sir, if I may ask, where might you choose on such an evening?'

'I don't know, Iremonger, whether to go up or down and that's the truth of it.'

'Better not stay here, that might be considered loitering, sir. Best not to loiter, sir, in my opinion. Not becoming of such as yourself, sir.'

'I think I'll to my Cousin Tummis, porter, I must say goodbye.'

'Very good then, sir.'

'Goodnight, porter.'

'Goodnight, Master Clodius, let us hope it is a safe one.'

My Friend Tummis

There was more Iremonger traffic than usual, some liveried Iremongers rushing about, and along Tummis's corridor, aunts and uncles looking sombre. The carpet runner was damp underfoot from the storm leaking through, there was a definite puddle around the door that was the entrance into the rooms of Tummis and Tummis's family. His parents, Second Cousin Icktor (ballcock) and Olish (carpet rod) and Tummis's sibs, all younger than him, (U-bend, lavatory brush, doorstop, hatpin and mezzaluna) were all gathered outside. What's all the fuss? Perhaps he's been trousered too, I thought. That must be it, there was always a deal of fuss over trousers. Oh, how wonderful, I thought, that Tummis has been trousered too, we must shake hands, praise each other's new togs, the feel of his herringbone, the wonder of turn-ups. He won't quite look himself out of corduroy. I wonder where they'll be sending Tummis, I wonder what they've found for him.

'Good evening all,' I said, wearing my best Iremonger frown on this moment of high family business.

'Oh, Clod, this is not the place for you,' said an aunt.

'May I see my Cousin Tummis? I should like to shake his hand.'

'No, Clod, you may not, run along now.'

'I have been trousered too,' I said, 'as you can see. So I'll not be dismissed.'

'Oh, have you? That was well done then. But please, Clod, not now.'

'I should like to wish him all the best and everything.'

'No, Clod, enough with you.'

'I should like to, why may I not? It isn't usual.'

'Clod, how many times must you be told?'

'Just a nod then, on such an auspicious occasion.'

'What occasion, Clod, what are you talking about?'

'I'm talking trousers, Aunt Pomular.'

'Trousers? Trousers? What have trousers to do with anything?'

'Tummis is wearing trousers today, is he not? How does he scrub up? Nicely?'

'Clod, oh Clod, Tummis is not wearing trousers.'

'No?'

'What then?'

'Oh, Clod!'

'What then, what?'

'Tummis is lost, Clod.'

'Tummis is lost, Aunt Pomular?'

'Yes, dear Clod, I am afraid so.'

'Then we had better find him, hadn't we?'

'Lost in the heaps, Clod, quite lost, in the storm. He went out on his own. They told him he was not to marry Ormily. Moorcus told him, though it wasn't true. He heard you were in trousers. He went out. Smartly dressed. Singing even, I am told. And the heaps, the heaps, in such a turmoil, pulled him under.'

'No,' I said, 'no and no.'

'Yes, Clod, I am afraid so.'

'No.'

'I am afraid so.'

'No, no, it isn't true!'

'Please, Clod, best leave him now to his close family. They're going to place his tap – that at least was found, some serving Iremonger tried to help him – they have that and that is something. A comfort.'

'Oh, Tummis,' I whispered, 'what a thing to do.'

'It is a time for the closest family.'

I saw then through the crowd of adult Iremongers Second Cousin Olish, Tummis's mother, red-eyed and miserable, holding in her lap a tap, a tap which I knew without looking would be marked н for hot.

'We're going to Marble Hall now,' said Aunt Pomular, 'we're going to go with Icktor and Olish, to put Tummis on his shelf.'

'Oh,' I said, 'my poor own Tummis.'

'Best, Clod, if you make yourself scarce. It would only upset Iktor and Olish all the more to have you there, and in trousers too.'

'I think I shall quite murder Moorcus.'

'No you shan't, Clod, don't talk like that.'

'What punishment shall they give him?'

'Clod,' said Pomular, 'what punishment do they ever give him? Besides, it wasn't entirely Moorcus's fault that he went out in the storm. Tummis chose to go. He let himself out. It is not Great Chest we are processing towards, it's Little Cupboard.'

'Oh Tummis, how could you?'

'Please, Clod, go home, go home.'

'Wait!' I said. 'One moment! Aunt Olish, Uncle Iktor, please, for a moment, may I hold his tap?'

Aunt Olish held the tap very particularly to her breast; she looked most offended by my question, as well she might, it was a terrible thing to ask. You must always leave a grieving Iremonger alone with the birth object of their deceased, it is particular etiquette, and yet, I must hear it, I had to hear it.

'Clod!' screamed Pomular. 'Whatever do you mean by it!'

'Please, Aunt, just a moment. I fear it may turn into a person any moment. Or . . . or otherwise . . . no, it's better if it turns . . . far better.'

'How dare you!' cried Uncle Iktor.

But I had seized the tap out of Olish's hands and I listened to it, I listened out for it. Come on, come on. Speak up. Let me hear you. But it didn't say anything.

'You can talk,' I said, 'I know you can. Hilary Evelyn Ward-Jackson, that's what you say, come on. I've heard you often enough.'

'Clod Iremonger, give it back this instant!' wailed Aunt Olish.

It didn't say anything.

'Oh, be careful with that!' she cried. 'Give it back!'

It didn't say anything at all.

'Oh, Aunt Olish,' I whispered as she snatched it from me, 'it's just a tap now.'

'It's our Tummis's birth object!'

'Aunt Olish, Uncle Iktor,' I said, 'Tummis *is* dead.'

And I ran away.

An Engine Inside Me

The house was full of storm, and something else beside that. Mourn, mourn, you Iremongers. The house was full of guilt. Everyone was white and shivering; it was always like this when an Iremonger went missing in the heaps. But this missing of all missings was my missing. Tummis. Tummis gone. And with him the person that was once Hilary Evelyn Ward-Jackson.

I never wanted to hear the objects' names. I never asked for that. I so hated it then, all those muttering pieces, I so despised that I could hear them, all those locked things. How I longed just to be like anyone else, just to hear what everyone else heard, not the names of all those lost people. I didn't want to know that Tummis was dead, I wanted there to be hope that he might yet be found. I wanted him to come back. But I knew that he shouldn't.

I knew that he couldn't.

To make things worse the storm was so loud it got into my head; it sat and swirled with my thoughts, played with them, took them over, scratched inside me. I could still hear the movement of objects out in the heaps, those murderous heaps. Some objects made it over the walls and hammered against the shutters, as if they were mocking the loss of Tummis.

Maybe I'd kill Moorcus. Maybe I should. What should I do?

I went home.

Doors all over the house were closing. I moved around my small chambers. Everything was wrong, everything itched. All offended. I'd rip my own heart out. I must govern myself, I thought. I must think of my trousers. Truth is, I couldn't bear myself, I hated my trousers. The storm droned on, it wouldn't let you forget, not for a moment, but must mock, mock, mock all the time, knocking on your head, wrapping upon you. I thought about smashing a window and letting it all come in. Oh, Tummis, Tummis. I'm sorry, so very sorry. He was my Tummis, wasn't he, mine and poor Ormily's. How was poor Ormily that night? What to do? What's ever to be done now? Whoever should I ever be without Tummis to tell me? I remembered Grandmother's mirror then. I took it out. SO THAT I MAY ALWAYS KNOW WHO I AM.

Thank you, Granny.

I remember now. I hadn't for a moment. There's an engine somewhere, firing up. Steam. There's steam coming out of me.

The Prefect Moorcus Iremonger and
the Unwelcome Rowland Cullis

20

MOORCUS'S THING

Lucy Pennant's narrative continued

I ran. That great clanking monster turned them all around and I ran. I couldn't see where I was going, on account of the leathers, and that helmet still atop of me. I crashed into things, was nearly impaled once or twice, fell down stairs, down and down, bruises all over me. But I was still there and breathing and couldn't hear anyone else about. So I stopped then, I didn't know how far I had fallen, I didn't know where I was, but wherever I was it was certain I wasn't going to get anywhere in leathers and in that helmet. I crawled under a table, a little shelter, and I tugged the damned thing from me. The leathers were cut in a few places and from those cuts I managed to make tears until at last there was a hole and that hole with effort became bigger and bigger and then I could crawl through and I was out of it. Deflated. Nothing inside it any more.

I was in the kitchen, great pans on hooks, so many knives hanging there. I thought of Mrs Groom and her knife then, she'd skin me, that's what she'd said. Got to get out, I thought, got to keep going out of here, otherwise might just as well lie me down in a roasting pan and call out to them all: 'Here I am! Tuck in!' I left my leathers and helmet behind me, it felt somehow right to leave them there: choke on that, I thought, season that. I rushed and panicked on. I heard people coming closer, talking. And these words, 'This way, Odith, I'd bet on it. Have you the cleaver?'

'Look at the skin! The skin of it!'

I found brief refuge in a pantry, quite penned in, so many jars upon shelves up and down, so many different colours. I could imagine a demijohn labelled LUCY PENNANT and myself, murky, swimming inside. People ran past, but no one came in. There were great noises in the distance, back down the cellar lanes where no doubt that great thing – *what was it?* – was preoccupying them very much, and suddenly there was an enormous crash, so large and loud the whole house seemed to rumble from it. I thought I should be pelted by the jars, they jumped and clinked on their shelves so. A jar of piccalilli mustard danced towards the edge and before I could get to it, it smashed maliciously to the ground. That did it. I got out and found myself very shortly in the servants' dining hall. No one else there, only benches and stools. I thought then that that clanking thing, whatever

324

it was back there, it must have pulled the roof down. And sure enough I heard several people screaming for a while, screaming and not stopping screaming, from bloody hurt or from sheer shock I couldn't say. Perhaps it was just at the sight of it, such a queer unnatural thing as it was. Lots of footsteps, so many people rushing about, I thought surely, surely someone will catch me any moment. I couldn't think what to do. I fumbled and I panicked. I'll get out of here. I'll stay here. What to do? What to do? I found myself a cupboard. It was one of the store cupboards in the dining hall for tablecloths and such, all very dusty there and unloved and abandoned, that was the place, for a bit, for a moment. So I might think.

The cupboard was deep and quite high. I put myself in there and just breathed, that was all. If they find you, I thought in that small space, if they find you they shall certainly tug you out and do their skinning, for they want you dead, Lucy Pennant, they're coming after you. That noise was them probably seeing to that great thing, so now it's you they'll come hunting for, now it's your turn. Strange to be so important suddenly.

Think of it, I thought, like a game, like a game back in Filching, hide and seek. I always knew where to hide then in the old boarding house. Well then, there are many places to hide in this old palace, hundreds must be. You'll be all right. Most of all, calm, calm yourself.

I don't know how long I stayed there, cramped in.

Maybe only a half hour. I kept an eye out through the keyhole and that's when I saw it. That's when I saw *them*. Things. Things were coming in. Just a few old coins and nails at first, trickling in, bouncing along as if someone had tossed them, but then larger things smacking along and soon a great deal of stuff, an old tin bath even, things, *things* moving by themselves. I saw a tea cup coming spinning in, it had a strange lip to it. The cup! There, there was the moustache cup they made such a business over. Other things followed it, and once a huge mass was in they all grouped in a corner and an old kettle rushed over, closed the door, quite quietly, and then other things wedged it shut, clothes and planks and such. More noise and skittering and now the objects started to swirl around to be picked up in some sort of whirlpool of objects, all twisting and rushing around each other, round in circles, climbing higher – cups, saucers, old pans – and very shortly after it had assembled itself into one great thing, I saw two legs of it from my hiding place, legs made of this and that, but moving like actual legs. Feet, one with a ladle for the shoe end, the other with an old colander. I could see up to its midsection, the legs were made of long thin things, poles and pipes and rods, but amongst them knives and forks, old busted pairs of glasses, pencils, pens, all shaped together, all got together like a person, the belly I could just make out was the bathtub. But this person of objects, now united, screeched and whined and made sorrowful noises as if it was very scared. There was a noise outside and the thing backed away towards a wall, flinching and shaking, making creaking, groaning sounds. The back wall was shelving, top to bottom, where plates and bowls, tin mugs and cutlery were kept, and other stuff of use in the dining room. The topmost shelves I remembered being quite twelve feet high, they were pretty much empty, to reach those you should need a stepladder. The object-man, that thing-person, stood by the shelves, quivering and whining, and then someone was at the door trying to get in, pushing hard at it. That thing, that being made of so much, let out a high whining noise, and then seem to somehow detonate itself, for all those consolidated bits were all apart again, and were spread out here and there, all over the shelves. It was hiding itself, separating itself and hiding. There was the moustache cup again, upon a shelf, the last to stop moving.

The door was heaved open. I could see many Iremonger clogs now, rushing in, making a fuss. They didn't notice all those new things on the back shelves, not even the bathtub which had managed to get itself under a serving table. Then I saw amongst all those clogs, new feet, two pairs, wearing scuffed boots, I heard them, whoever they were wearing the boots.

'It's escaped, the thing's escaped.'

'Where is it? Where could it have gone?'

'Hiding somewhere but we'll find it.'

'Do you think, Odith, that it used the dumb waiter?'

'Well it may I suppose, Orris, and if it has it's uphouse now.'

'I wanted you to have first cut of it, Odith. What meat there, eh? We'll find it yet. We'll hook it up in the cold room, let it drip a bit. Shall we hang it, Odith?'

'They'd let us, wouldn't they, a thing like that?'

'Bound to.'

'I'll have the soup brought in.'

'What an evening!'

'The Gathering's dispersed, at least there's that.'

There were sounds of soup being poured out and tables being laid, and then I heard the procession of so many Iremongers coming in for their supper, same as usual, as if nothing had happened. But the blessing this night was led by Mr Briggs and not by the butler and I heard no noise from Mrs Piggott at all.

All those serving Iremongers muttering amongst themselves, talking about the dispersed Gathering, which, little they knew, was still about them, in that very room, a part of it, still there, ungathered at the moment, but lurking. They talked about poor Tummis too, lost outside. And that in turn got them talking about other Iremongers who had been lost in the heaps before him. When they tried to describe the lost serving Iremongers they could only mumble, 'Short Iremonger,' or 'Iremonger with the limp,' 'Iremonger with the mole on her cheek,' 'Iremonger who had once worked on the laundry mangles.' And all their words got out between slurps.

'There'll be some shovelling to do in the morning.'

'The door's fair dented already. It'll hold, won't it?'

'It should, it should.'

'Even if it doesn't they'll just block the passage off, let the rooms around the doors fill up with the heaps but we'll be fine, we'll be safe, it shan't reach us.'

'It'll never break through the second doors.'

'Never has.'

'Nor will tonight, I'm certain.'

After a bit, I could hear that the redhead from the orphanage was there, just a few feet away from me.

'I'm to do firegrates, they say, is that good?'

'Oh yes, very good, that's a fine situation.'

'We're so glad you're here.'

'You've come home, ain't you?'

'Yes, you're home now.'

'I think I might just be,' said the redhead. 'I am an Iremonger. Cusper said so. Oh, and he's for it. Not my problem. Brought it upon himself if you ask me. But I'm here at last. I do feel an Iremonger. I really do. I wonder if they've caught that little red rat yet. I wonder what they'll do to her.'

'She's for it all right.'

'I think they'll do for her, won't they?'

'I shouldn't wonder.'

'Who could blame them. Asking for it.'

'Trespassing like that.'

'Disgusting I call it.'

'To think I talked to her.'

'To think she talked to me.'

'As if she were one of us like everyone else.'

'Made me want to take a good wash. I scrubbed myself when I heard, I don't mind telling you. I even ate a bit of soap.'

'Quite right.'

'Makes my skin itch just to think of her.'

'Still, we have you now, and that's a comfort.'

'Will you tell us about yourself?'

'What do you want to know?'

'Everything.'

'Oh, everything, everything.'

'All about you.'

So it went on like that, making me ill, until Briggs rang his bell, early I think. The spoons all eaten, and licked clean I supposed, the tables were cleared and at last the final footsteps died away and all was quiet again.

I stayed put a while. The door was left open and once or twice some Iremonger came in for a moment, and put down plates, before wandering off again. But I couldn't stay there for ever. I knew that. I had to get myself up the house. Those downstairs rooms were too dangerous for me. Better further up, further up there'd be a chance out. And Clod was upstairs. I'd find him in the Sitting Room just as we said we would, just as planned, before everything got ruined.

I opened my cupboard door, slowly crept out.

The other one was there before me.

It had got itself together again. It had reassembled its bits. It had come together so quietly. It was much shorter now, like a child. A child of bits. And it grunted and scraped a little. It heard me, I don't know how, but it turned to me and its face, which seemed to be made of a dented tea tray and with all sorts of nails and pins and bolts and screws and nuts and chips of glass and pottery, moved around in a great swirl, never keeping still, and for a moment I thought I could almost see a face fully there, eyes and nose and such, but it was only things, just things.

'Don't you hurt me,' I said.

It tilted its head.

'They're after me and all. They want me in pieces too.'

It came forward a bit. It made sounds, there was an old rusted fork that was scraping against a small rusted pan lid, making scratches that were like talking, something like talking, as if it was trying to say something to me. There was the moustache cup again, in the centre of its chest, spinning round and round and round, faster than all the other objects.

'We should get out of here,' I said. 'It isn't safe for us down here.'

Some lids, pan lids, tops of pots, bottle caps, about its person snapped up and down, like many mouths opening. Was it hungry?

331

'I don't have anything,' I said, 'nothing on me. I had a door handle once but that's gone.'

It came closer, there were knives, I saw now, small dirty knives where its hair should have been were it human, and these were striking against each other, making a slashing, scraping sound. I thought, it's hungry, it's hungry and it doesn't understand. It held out a hand to me, a hand wriggling with old piping and handles and bits of old brush, a comb or three, a finger made of an old ointment bottle, another of a teapot spout, one was a bit of pipe stem, its neighbour most of a penny whistle, the thumb was the brass lens of a magic lantern and the little finger the shell of a shotgun cartridge.

'What do you want?'

More scraping, more whining, more lids snapping, knives snipping. I've got to go, I thought, it'll keep me here too long and then we'll be found. How to get rid of it, such a sad, longing collection as that? I pulled open a drawer. Nothing much there but a few napkins. A napkin flew out, a saucepan lid opened and the napkin rushed inside. I opened more drawers, I opened drawers all along the dining room wall, and soon the air was thick with things rushing towards the staggering person-thing, and that thing was growing larger. And it seemed to me to be clacking in approval, as if it was laughing. That's it then, I thought, now's your moment, if it follows you they'll have you in an instant, get out now while it's growing, run, run. Uphouse. Clod.

Footsteps. People coming. I ran. Downstairs then. Down-stairs away from them. I could still hear them, getting closer – down I went and down. Where was I, I couldn't say – deep down, deeper than I'd been before, under the station for sure. Down away from the footsteps. And calling, there was calling too.

'Closing up! Closing up! Hatches down! Hatches down! Shall be flooded, come up! Come up!'

I ran further along, deeper, deeper into the back rooms.

'Out! Out!' I heard. 'This side! Come up! Hatches down! Hatches down! Come up! Come up!'

On I went, on and on, away from the words.

Everywhere I ran was just me, only me. No one else there. So. So. So at last I stopped. I was alone, quite alone. In the long distance I heard one last, 'Closing up!'

And then the noise of doors being shut, of hatches being slammed down, and then hammering, and then nothing, just a distant rumble. I understood it then. The first double doors, where I'd gone out to the courtyard, had broken through, bits of the cellar were being shut up now, they were blocking off the whole stairwell and if you were the wrong side well then, bad luck for you, wasn't it. I was the wrong side.

That's why I hadn't been found. These rooms were empty now, empty of Iremongers who were all thinking themselves safe, barricading all the doors. I couldn't get out. There was no way to get out. These rooms would be flooded by the heaps any moment. I could hear banging and pelting and smashing and rumbling, and I knew then that those sounds were not the Iremongers battening down the doors. Those were the sounds of the heaps, of the heaps coming in.

Think, Pennant, think you, Lucy, there must be a way.

Loads of them. Loads of them actually. All over the downstairs darkrooms. Fireplaces. Must have been ten of them at least down there. I'd climb up a chimney flue, that's how I'd get out and get up.

There was a lonely, cold fireplace made of slate, a dismal-looking thing, it was in the Prussian Blue Room, where old boots and shoes of London taken from heaps were brought and there cooked up to make the pigment called Prussian Blue. It was a dark, sticky room, all slip and shine and stink, as if the whole place had been lacquered and quite japanned over.

The Prussian Blue Room had such a sharp stench, like swimming in vinegar. I stood by the miserable fireplace. Its big mouth was wide open. Well then I let it swallow me, eat me up. In I went, in and up, between the walls, within the house.

Not much to see. Not much to breathe. No light, none at all. Slow progress. Cut all over. But shunting upwards, small ledges in the brick to scratch onwards with bleeding fingers. Storm noise whistling down from above, trying to spook me. A long wail, very human sounding, as if there were a broken woman stuck and screeching above me, wedged in the chimney.

'Shut it,' I said.

'Whoooooowheeeeeeeee!' came the answer.

'Don't scare me.'

'Whooooowheeeeeeeee!'

It did.

I slipped a good deal and lost my progress, sticking out my knees to stop me from falling all the way back down. Bloody knees, bloody arms, bloody elbows, bloody fingers. But up I went, up and up. Moving up the house. Way back down where I started there was banging now and swooshing and I knew that the heaps must have broken in and that if I slipped I'd likely go under, I'd be tugged under by the heaps. And those heaps, I thought, those heaps will be climbing up the chimney too, climbing up from down below, and from up above me I felt some rain falling down, but not just rain, the plip and plop of nails and screws of small heapbits making it down from the sky, a bullseye into the stack and onto my head. Cutting me, little slits. Heap below me coming up, heap above me dripping down, and somewhere in between: me, bloodied and sooted.

Then something else. Some other black thing upon me, pouring onto me. A new black in that other blackness. Black smoke. Someone had lit a fire to warm themselves on this howling night and that fire was beginning to cook me. How the Grooms should love that, to find me tumbled down the flue ready cooked. They'd pick off my crisp skin then, no doubt, have themselves some Lucy crackling, some

335

smoked Pennant. The smoke wanted to fill the black passage, it wanted to be there all on its self, it was a thick fat thing crowding me, dressing me, covering me, taking me over. Only smoke to breathe now, nothing but black inside me, turning me black. I kept going up, coughing and steaming. I felt a sudden draught and went for it, and clambered into the cooler air, I was horizontal now not vertical, I was in a different chimney tunnel, away from the central flue, a branch of it. I crawled along it, cutting myself again, but I didn't care. The flue went down suddenly, but I wasn't ready for it and was rushing, tumbling, falling downwards and could not stop myself. There was light, light coming forward in a great rush, or me hurtling towards the light. I landed in a firegrate. Ironic that.

I was in someone's bedroom.

Someone, some full-blooded Iremonger, was asleep in bed just a few feet in front of me. My tumbling in had not woken the sleeping mound. An adult I presumed by the size of it. And wearing a nightcap. I couldn't see the face. Couldn't tell man or woman. Sleeping away, despite the storm rattling the windows and house. I went into the room very carefully.

She had called me 'the red rat' and that surely was what I looked like then. Red of blood and hair, dirt and soot all about me, very ripped for certain, but still going on, still breathing, a bit of life.

It was a woman I think. Some sleeping Iremonger lady.

There was a night light on, dimly lit, giving me a little show of what was about. Neat place. Nothing out of order. Only strange thing was a small skillet on her bedside table. A small skillet beside a silver hairbrush and mirror, and a photograph of some fellow in a top hat holding a brass bedpan; the frame was silver. So what's a cast iron skillet doing there then, ruining the display? Then I had it. It was her birth object, must be. This old woman under her covers kept her skillet with her day and night, she slept right by it, to feel that it was safe. What an Iremonger.

Well, I don't love the Iremongers do I, I thought, can't say that they've done right by me, can I? And I said to myself, I'll have that. I'll take that, thank you very much. I can hit with that, it's a weapon of sorts, and it's your bloody birth object, you snoring Iremonger, you dumb lump you; yes, by God, I'll have it. I picked it off the night stand. It was quite heavy for a thing that size. I liked the weight of it. It felt like I'd got something. I possessed something right enough. Mine. And I left the woman fast asleep, what a chicken screech she'd give in the morning. If there was a morning, couldn't be certain of that any more. Right then, Clod. Where are you, Clod, where are you this night? Which door shall I find you behind? Sitting room? Sitting room.

Sitting Room. Just as it always was. Up the staircase. Easy to find. Victory, I thought. No one there though. Just the red seat, nothing else. Well, wait then. Just wait. Wait for a while. He'll come. Sure to come.

I found my place behind the sofa. On the floor. Put my skillet down. On the floor. Under the sofa. And now to keep a look out, look out from under the sofa.

The storm smashed on. Bringing noises everywhere. House shaking. And me just waiting, waiting in the Sitting Room, behind the red sofa, on the floor. Come on. Come on.

Door opened then. Here he is! Up I get! No, no, Lucy, you fool, make sure it's him. Let him show himself. You, Clod? Is it you?

Steps closer. Coming in. Clod? Is it? No, isn't. Not Clod. Someone in grey trousers. Standing in the room, just by the sofa. Walking up and down now. Waiting. Go on. Go away. But the trousers didn't. They stopped there, even sat down on the seat. Got up again. Knelt down. Trousers put his hands under the sofa, he's got me, he's found me! Only not. He pulled out my skillet, he took my skillet. Trousers sat down again, my skillet on his lap. Trousers got up again, paced the room again. Once even kicked the door. Scuff on shoe from that. Sat down again. Patted the sofa. But then, at last, one more pacing and then out. Gone. Door closed again. I got up. I'm not staying here. Clod, where are you? The door opened again. I ducked down. Looked out from under the sofa. Clod? The same shoes, the same trousers. As if the trousers were watching the room. Isn't safe here, isn't.

Then trousers were gone again. I waited. Nothing but the storm. I got up around to the door and opened the door and went out of that trap. Footsteps behind me? Thought so. On! On! Another door. Which one? This one. Get in. In I was. Footsteps going past, someone running. Safe. Close. Very. Must find Clod. Where is he? Find him. Room to room if necessary. Well then, first this one.

I hadn't meant to do it at first, it wasn't my purpose, I think the skillet would have been enough, but I didn't have it any more, someone had taken it from me. I was looking for Clod but then there I was in a room with a different sleeping Iremonger, so I took, didn't I, I just took, shoved it into my uniform pocket. When I opened those doors after, so quietly, so carefully, and seeing those heads that could not possibly belong to Clod, all sleeping, there beside the sleeping figures, upon all those night-stands, were things. Objects. Birth objects. I did not exactly mean to do it, not at first. Something incredible. Lucy Pennant, I said to myself, you're a very bad one. Yes, so what? I went from bed to bed, collecting. I had four before I loved the idea, a tiepin, an eggcup, a noose, a darning mushroom. Then I had a passion for it. I stuffed them deep in my pockets, what a feeling, what a weight. They do things to you, these objects. I moved from room to room so quietly, so carefully, and I took the objects, one by one. All those sleeping Iremongers, so vulnerable in the night. One boy's object I couldn't find until I saw that he was wearing it, a woman's shoe, that must be it, I thought, and it slipped off well enough. The storm was furious busy outside. Every now and again I should have to stop my lifting and wait in the darkness as something fell down one of the flues into a firegrate, just like I had, or outside the shutters rattled so much that the Iremonger in bed suddenly sat up and called out, 'Who's there?'

And I, so very close, my hand upon the night stand touching a particular thing, would see that Iremonger's dozy hand come up, pat the object once or twice, seeking solace, finding solace, and go to sleep once more.

I was bitten as I worked, there were bugs all about, sometimes as I took hold of an object some roach should flee from it. I'm very brave, I said. And the storm kept on. Pipes rattled about, it seemed to me the more I went on in my game the more the house shook and gurgled. Once I heard an enormous crash and saw a couple of servants run along the landing, a great banging and thumping. Some shutters had come unfastened and smacked against the walls. The window lasted only a very little time, there was a huge crashing as it broke and then as the poor servants battled on, seagulls, a whole flock of them, came careering in, yelling and cursing and shitting, and objects flew in after them. At first just some papers, some newspapers and a few books whose covers seemed to be flapping in the tempest, but then larger things, great bowls and bricks and hats, shoes, bits of other houses, a broken window frame came in through the window, rubble, a saucepan, a seat that looked as if it belonged in a music hall, all came crashing through, and the servants retreated then, they could not stop it, hiding behind a curtain, peeking out, I saw them barricading the door with an upturned table.

'The house has been breached!' one of the servants screamed. 'Get help! I shan't be able to hold this for long!'

The other ran off, seagulls hopping and flying all about. One gull, a large one, with a red tip to its beak, stood in front of the poor servant as he pressed himself and the table against the door, which had begun to thump now as if there were a person, not a thousand objects, trying to smash through from the other side. The seagull waddled up to the man in an appallingly good-humoured, slightly lazy way; it put its head to one side, and then it leaned forward slightly and began to peck at his shoe, then it waddled forward a little bit more and its beak snapped at the man's shoelace.

'Shoo!' the man called.

With the next peck the seagull had undone the shoelace and was now tugging on it, trying to haul the man with his foot with all its might.

'Get away! Get away!'

But the gull pulled all the harder and now other gulls came to watch this sport and one, cawing and screeching, waddled over to the other foot and began to peck at the neighbouring lace.

'I can't hold it! Help! Help ho!'

The other servant came back and I shuddered to see Sturridge who heaved all his colossal weight against the door and kicked one of the seagulls so hard that it burst against the wall.

'Awaken everyone on the corridor,' thundered the butler, 'get them safely beyond. This landing must be sealed off! Move! Move!'

In all the commotion I slipped away then and to a lower floor.

I crept down the main staircase. There was a man in official Iremonger uniform, with gold-braided bay leaves, fast asleep at a desk. He'll drown in his sleep if the heaps have anything to do with it. I heard footsteps on the marble stairs. I ducked down behind the man's chair, behind him at his desk. Someone ran past, stopped for a moment before the desk, and I saw the trousers again with the same scuffed shoe. Trousers stopped a moment then hurried on. Official uniform still sleeping, I entered his corridor. This must be an important place, I thought, let's see what's within. The door handles were porcelain with pretty flowers on them, I turned a handle, stepped in. Treasure room! Paintings in gold frames, polished tables and all manner of stuff on top of them. A huge marble fireplace with marble women, naked nearly, holding up the shelf. What place is this? I hadn't gone two steps before an old voice called out to me, 'Who is it, who's there?'

An old woman was inside a great four-poster; she was awake but her bed curtains were drawn. I couldn't see her and she couldn't see me. I hid behind a great ugly seat; after a bit looked out above it.

'Someone's here, I know it.'

A head came from the curtain, an awful withered face, old and lean.

'Who's there? Show yourself.'

No, no I shan't. Can't make me.

'Who is it?' called the old woman. 'Is it you, Iremonger, have you come to check upon me? If it's you I shan't be angry. Declare yourself. Has the train come in yet? Who *is* there? I shall not be angry, only show yourself this instant. Piggott! Is it you again, Piggott? Have you found it? It's not good enough just to disperse a Gathering, that won't win you any medals. Is it you, Piggott, come to tell me how useless you are? No, no, you wouldn't do that, would you? You wouldn't come up again until you've found it. It's not you then. Someone else? But who? Is it, could it possibly be . . .' Her voice was quieter, then, 'Is it . . . the it? It's got lost, hasn't it? Somehow stumbled its way in here. That's it. The it.'

The old woman was silent a while and then the emaciated figure came out from her bed. On her night stand, I saw, but a glass of water, no birth object at all.

'Who is it please,' said the old woman, in a very different voice, weak and frightened, 'there's only me, me and my memories. What have you come in here for, who are you in my room? I can hear you breathing. Why do you not answer me? I don't see well but I can smell you and hear you, come closer, come to me, visit me. Won't you please? No one comes to visit me. Only the Iremonger with the food, it's so nice to have someone new, someone young. Can I touch you, may I feel your skin? The Iremonger who comes does not have nice skin, do you?'

As she said this, very slowly she crept towards me, and I just as slowly crept away. I moved to the side of the seat, and then, that no longer being safe, crawled out until I was behind a great black armchair.

'Was that you moving? Did I just hear you? You're very shy, aren't you? Don't be shy. There's just me here, an old, old woman. Have you seen my fireplace? It is a magnificent thing. There's nothing so fine in all Heap House. Would you like to see it properly, why not step close to it? I was given it when I was born. We have stayed here together, my marble fireplace and I, in this room. When I was a child I should dart out of the corridor, even go down a stairway a little before running home, but that was long ago now, I haven't seen the staircase for so many years. I used to open the door every once in a while and look at the different weather of the landing, but now, generally, I just lie here, in my bed, facing the fireplace.'

Something clattered down the flue into the firegrate, I saw it as the ash settled, an old and filthy dress, someone's old clothes. It lay in the grate and the old woman said, 'Such a storm, blowing filth into my room, dirtying my fireplace, perhaps tomorrow I'll have my Iremonger open the shutters and I'll look out and see how the storm has moved everything, where the rubbish has piled up. Oh, it wasn't someone come to visit us after all, fireplace, it was just the storm, only a storm.'

I thought the storm had fooled the old bird then, but a moment later I heard a key in the lock. She'd locked me in with her.

'All right you, you creature. I've locked the door and pulled the bell rope, there'll be a dozen Iremongers here any instant. You filth! I shall have my carpets burnt. I shall have my seating thrown through the windows. You filthy dirty bitch! Come on, come here, come up, come out! Come out I say!'

No escape. The old woman had got hold of a fire poker and was waving it about. Coming closer, banging the furniture. No way out. And then people at the door, banging on the door, calling, shouting, 'My lady! My lady! My lady!'

'It's in here!' she answered. 'I've got it trapped. The foreign thing is in my room. I've caught it, I've found it. What you lost and could not find, *I* found! Here! In my room!'

'The key's in the lock, my lady. We can't get in! Turn the key and we'll be with you instantly, only hurry, my lady, hurry, do hurry, lest you be harmed!'

'I harmed? Very unlike!' she spat. 'That it thing! Toss it out! I'm at the door now. See that it doesn't try to run

345

past you! I want it ripped apart in front of me, hell to the furnishings! Ready? One, two, three! Get it!'

But while the old lady was at the door turning the key and giving instructions, I was at the marble fireplace and scrambling back up into the wretched black passages, leaving so many marks behind me, sooty hand and footprints upon her marble fireplace. No matter that it hurt, so what that it hurt, good that it hurt, I bloodied myself upwards back into darkness and dirt. For a moment, looking down, I saw a torch shining beneath me and heard cries of, 'It! It! It!'

And then, 'Light a fire!'

On, on, I scraped my way. But I smacked into something just a moment later, the flue was bending. I followed it along and then I must have lost my way somehow, got confused by the passages, because there were different openings now, different holes and somehow I slipped and went smashing down another black tunnel and landed all the way down in some other Iremonger's firegrate. You should get out of this habit, Pennant, I told myself, or you shan't thrive long. This time I fell hard and smacked my back bad, and when I tried to get up I couldn't, I just couldn't. I'd wedged myself somehow between the grate and the andirons and the fireplace, it was a small fireplace it was, and I was stuck in it.

No one was coming. At least there was that. But I couldn't shift. I couldn't heave myself up. I kept trying.

Before me on the floor were all the birth objects I'd picked that had all tumbled out of my pockets when I landed. Where was I? What room was this? Some sort of store room I thought at first. I could see a door and there were five different locks to it. Somewhere important then. All sorts of things here. Shelves full of different objects, but no logic to them, bits of ribbon, and yet silver things, a catapult, some stamps in a jar, a mouth organ, buttons, toy soldiers, pipes, but also cigarette cases, but then a wooden sword, a mousetrap, flypapers, ink bottles. Whose stuff was all this?

I heard movement, someone coming. I tried to pull myself free. Couldn't. Couldn't do it. There was someone there then. Someone looking over me.

It was a man, youngish, maybe eighteen. Dressed in black, grim-looking. His skin very yellow, a sour face. Didn't like the look of him much. He had a slight moustache, a smudge of one, spots on his forehead. And then I saw around his ankle a metal cuff, and from it a length of chain. Some young man on a chain. Who chained him up?

'Sir! Oh, sir,' he called to his master, 'you may as well know it. There's something new in here. Something quite new.'

A voice in a room further back replied, 'Oh, for God's sake, Toastrack, what is it now? I'll beat you!'

'And I'll kick you back, you turnip.'

'What was that?'

347

'Words, I should think, so many words from my own hole.'

'What did you say, Toastrack?'

'Stuff, wasn't it? Wouldn't you like to know.'

'You said you'd mind your manners.'

'And you said you'd cut me free, but you didn't, you chained me up. We're all liars. Born to lie I shouldn't wonder. Cretin. Come on in then, Sir Mucus, and have a gander at this. Look what the storm dragged in.'

'I am trying to be nice to you, Toastrack.'

'Don't much see the point in that myself. Why bother?'

'We must attempt to be civilised, to make the most of the situation.'

'I hate you. You hate me. That's about the picture of it.'

'No, Toastrack, I don't. I'm fond of you. You mean much to me.'

'Well, I loathe you, sir!'

'I will beat you, you know.'

'No, no you shan't. I'll smack you back, just like I did last time.'

'I broke your nose.'

'I gave you a headache that lasted a month. Next, I'll crack your skull.'

'Please, please, can we try to be pleasant?'

'You started it.'

'Then I apologise.'

'Big of you.'

'Come, Toastrack, let us shake hands. I'll find you something new and precious. Something for your collection.'

'Already have that by the looks of things.'

Another young man came into view, wearing a silk dressing gown, a medal pinned to his chest. This one, unlike the other, was handsome.

'Well, well, what have we here?'

'Tumblebum,' said the one called Toastrack, 'mine, I reckon.'

'I'm stuck,' I said, 'help me out.'

'What have we here and what shall we do with it?' said the handsome one.

'I said, help me out. I'm stuck!' I cried.

'Shouldn't want to eat it,' grunted the ugly one.

'I'm stuck!' I cried.

'So it would appear,' said handsome, 'and then, my next question would be, do we want to unstick it? Would that be to our advantage?'

'I'm hurting. This hurts, stuck like this! It bloody hurts!'

'Couldn't say,' said Toastrack, 'might be diverting.'

'What's that on the floor there,' said his unchained companion. 'An ashtray, not your ashtray, I've seen that before. And what's that? It's a tiepin, where did that come from, that's familiar too. And what's that? A shoe, a lady's shoe! That's not just any shoe, is it? I'd know that shoe anywhere on earth. That's Bornobby's that is. But how did it come to be here? Hang on a minute. You're a thief, aren't you? A little bloody thief. You've stolen all those birth objects. I see that now. Why would you do such a thing? Who are you? Hang on a minute, hang on a bloody minute, you came in here to steal mine too.'

'No, no, I didn't.'

'You came down here to steal my own birth object.'

'Well,' said Toastrack, 'here I am.'

'Be calm, Toastrack, nobody's going to take you.'

'So grateful,' he moaned, 'my hero.'

'He's your birth object?' I asked. 'He is? But he's a person.'

'Oh, aren't we observant?' Toastrack said.

'Yes, he's a man, if you'd call him that,' said handsome.

'I'll thump you!' said Toastrack.

'But he didn't use to be. Did you, Toastrack? He used to be . . .'

'A toast rack!' I said.

'Well, of course a toast rack! What else!'

'A toast rack!' I cried.

'A silver toast rack,' Toastrack said. 'Silver, I was silver.'

'But how did he, how was it, how did he become a . . . man?'

'Never you mind.'

'We don't know,' said Toastrack.

'Shut it, Toastrack.'

'Not Toastrack, is it?' shouted Toastrack. 'Not actually, not any more Toastrack. I'm Rowland Collis. That's my name. Rowland Collis. But he'll never say it. He'll never call me Rowland. Never say Rowland Collis!'

'You're Toastrack, Toastrack. Learn your place.'

'I shall break things! I'm going to do it! I'm in the mood. I need to break things!'

'Be calm, calm yourself now.'

'Can't! Can't!'

'Here, have a little medicine. Have a draught of this.'

The smart one handed over a bottle. Rowland Collis snatched it away and glugged deeply. I smelt it then, it was familiar enough. Gin.

'Grandmother said he must be kept like this,' said the one with the medal, 'until it's understood. He just stays here. My thing. No one knows. Only Granny, and now, it seems, you. Who are you anyway and what are you doing in my room and how did you get all these things?'

'I fell.'

'That much I can see.'

'Can you help me?' I asked. 'Please help me out. I think I might have broken something.'

He stood before me, puffing his pipe, shaking his head, then he stopped, then he looked at me closer, even reached out to tug a little on my hair.

'Oh . . . my . . . lord!'

'What?' I said. 'What? What?'

'I've just worked out who you are.'

'No, I'm not . . . whoever it is you're thinking . . . I'm not what you think. I'm a servant, true, I'm a thief too. A servant and a thief.'

351

'You don't belong here, do you?'

'No, no I don't and I'm trying to get out of here. Can you help me? Please?'

'No, no I couldn't possibly. Toastrack, get my shoes!'

'Should make my day, sir.'

Rowland Collis seemed quite calmed by the gin now, and slouched off to return shortly after with a pair of polished gentleman's lace-ups.

'Put them on me.'

Rowland Collis did so.

'Where are you going?' I asked.

'Out, you foreign thing. I'm going out!'

'Please help me! Please!'

'Oh, I'll fetch help soon enough. Toastrack, stand guard, when I come back in get into your place, not a sound. I'll make it worth your while.'

'Two bottles!' said Rowland Collis.

'Yes, at least.'

The smart one went to the door, he took keys out and unlocked all the locks. He opened the door and the moment he did another foot from the other side wedged itself in so that the door must stay open now.

'Who's there?' the handsome one called. 'Who's at my door? Stand back! I'll have you whipped!'

I recognised the shoe in the door, I knew it from earlier, from the Sitting Room, it was scuffed. I recognised the trousers too, and following the trousers up I saw at last the person that was inside them.

352

Clod.

'Clod!' called the handsome one.

'Clod!' I shouted.

'Rowland Collis,' moaned Rowland Collis, 'that's who I am, if anyone cares.'

And then Clod hit the one with the medal square in the head with a skillet, with my skillet.

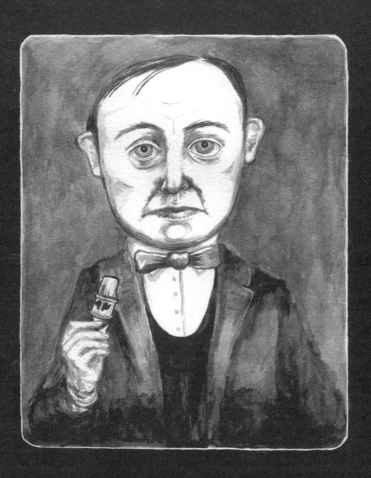

The House Uncle Timfy Iremonger

21

A PIGNOSE WHISTLE

Clod Iremonger's narrative continued

I Make an Entrance

I hit Moorcus, I hit him with hate, with hate and with Cousin Gustrid's skillet (Mr Gurney) and he hurt and he fell down, holding his own pretty head. And it felt good. I admit it freely. And I was glad of it. And with that hit just a little of the hate came out from me.

'That,' I said, 'is for Tummis and for Hilary Evelyn Ward-Jackson. And it's not enough, there'll never be enough denting of you, Moorcus, not all the smashing of all the world, not all the bullying from every country on the globe brought down upon you would be enough.'

'Please,' wailed Moorcus, 'my head! I'm bleeding. You'll murder me.'

'I think I will indeed if you don't shut up this instant.'

'Clod! Clod!' cried Lucy from the fireplace.

I pulled Lucy free. What had they done to her? She'd been so scraped and bloodied and smeared with soot, what a sad sight she was, but it was her. Actually there before me. In truth. Lucy.

'Lucy Pennant, at last! What a dance you've led me on.'

'What, Clod, have I?'

'In the Sitting Room, up and down the house, I should never have found you if you hadn't found Granny, she made such a fuss even I heard it. All those servants to her and then you'd gone somehow, up the chimney, and I calculated what other chimneys should share that flue and figured Crosspin and Flippah, but I heard sleeping at that door, so I figured Moorcus, and what voices I heard here at this door. I heard Moorcus saying he was going out so I waited just close by until the door opened and then shoved my foot in and then the skillet, Mr Gurney, which I found, for some reason, in the Sitting Room. But so here I am, and there is Moorcus, and here are you, and there, somehow, is Bornobby's Cecily Grant and Onjla's Henrietta Nysmith, and Aunt Loussa's Little Lil, all gathered here, collected somehow, but, then, who is he? I have never seen him before.'

'Toastrack,' snivelled Moorcus, 'but please don't tell anyone.'

'He's Rowland Collis, Clod,' said Lucy.

'I'm Rowland Collis, Clod,' said the strange fellow.

'He's Moorcus's birth object,' said Lucy, 'somehow made . . . flesh.'

'Rowland Collis! But how can he be . . . how can they be . . . together! It doesn't make sense.'

'We don't know,' groaned Moorcus, 'and how I wish it weren't so, he was much nicer as a toast rack. How I wish he were again. He was such a good toast rack, but such an indifferent person. Granny said in time he should probably grow back into smart silver, but he hasn't, he stays here day after day, plaguing me. There's been doctors come in from Filching, special ones, but they're useless, they can't toast rack him. I'm to be trousered soon, very soon, and then to marry my Horryit, but whatever shall she say when she sees a toast rack like this one?'

'But it's wonderful!' I cried. 'The very best news!'

'It's terrible,' said Moorcus, 'the very worst.'

'It means,' I cried, 'it means, James Henry Hayward, my very dear plug, and I might be about in the world at once. It means that there is some way of breaking the business of birth objects. How, Moorcus, how did you do it?'

'I didn't do anything,' he said. 'I went to bed, just as I always did, but then in the morning, where my toast rack usually was . . . my toast rack wasn't, and *that* was there in its place, which was quite a shock I can tell you.'

'But you must have done something different, think, Moorcus, think!'

'I tell you there was nothing different.'

'There must have been.'

357

'Nothing at all.'

'Think, Moorcus,' I cried, 'would it help if I used the skillet?'

'Yes, use the skillet,' said Rowland, 'use it by all means. That's sure to help.'

'Please, please, Clod,' begged Moorcus.

'Rowland Collis, did you do anything else?'

'Can't remember and there's the truth on it.'

'Do you remember how it was, being a toast rack?'

'Can't remember. And there's the truth on it.'

'Do you remember who you were before you came to be a toast rack?'

He paused a while and said sadly, 'Can't remember. Can't. And there's the truth on it.'

'Perhaps it shall come back to you, Rowland, in time.'

'Might I have a turn with the skillet?' asked Rowland.

'Don't give it to him, Clod, please,' pleaded Moorcus. 'How fine you look in your trousers. What a figure you cut.'

'Don't you try it on with me, Moorcus,' I said.

'Clod,' said Lucy, 'we shouldn't stay here. Surely we shouldn't. Let us go, Clod. If they find me, Clod, and they mean to find me, they shall kill me, they've said as much.'

'Kill you?'

'Yes, she *is* right there,' said Moorcus, 'they will kill her. I heard Sturridge saying so.'

'Help me, Clod, get me out.'

'There is no way out,' said Moorcus, 'not from here.

358

The only way out is by train, through the tunnel, but the train hasn't come back yet and so the tunnel has probably collapsed. And that means that's it. You're stuck here. Everyone is. Until the storm's done and the tunnel's repaired.'

'Is it true, Clod, is he right?'

'There must be some other way,' I said.

'There isn't,' said Moorcus, 'and you know it.'

'Strike him! Strike him!' called Rowland. 'I can see you're thinking about it.'

'Rowland Collis,' I said, 'I'd like you to have this.' I gave him the skillet.

'Much obliged.'

'Lucy, come along. Can you walk? Let me help you.'

'They'll find you,' said Moorcus, 'they'll catch you, and when they do, they'll do for her. And you, Clod, I don't know what they'll do to you, but I shouldn't like it myself, it's certain to smart.'

'Is this the key to your chain, Rowland?' I asked, pulling the key from Moorcus's waistcoat pocket.

'The very same, I suppose,' said Rowland, 'though I don't see it much myself.'

'No, Clod,' cried Moorcus, 'I warn you, give that back.'

I gave Rowland the key.

'Much obliged.'

'No, Toastrack, no,' said Moorcus. 'I'll have that please. At once. You are my toast rack!'

'Rowland,' I said, 'if you please.'

Moorcus yelped.

'Thank you,' I said.

'Don't mention,' said Rowland.

'Where are we going?' asked Lucy.

Down-house-drown-house

To have her beside me again. To feel her, warm and moving. Battered, yes, bruised and tattered, but here with a limp and some cuts, my heart. What a lucky thing, what a life I'm leading. I'm alive, I thought, I'm living now. We shan't die, shall we? I wondered suddenly, not now surely, that would be too cruel. Not now she's beside me again. We'll get out and we'll shout and dance and be ourselves. I'm fifteen and a half, and trousered what's more.

I thought we must go down to the bottom of Heap House, that we must get closer to the outside. I thought that there might be some way along the tunnel, to walk along that dark route, then at least we should not be here in Heap House; that was the first thing, not to be in this place that shook and wailed and protested at the weather. Heap House, our mansion, was built as I saw it finally not with bricks and mortar, but with cold and pain, with malice this palace was made, with black thoughts, with aches and cries and sweat and spit. Other people's tears stuck the wallpaper on our walls. When our house cried it cried because someone else in the world remembered what we had done to them. How the house wept and screamed and howled that terrible night, how it pitched and groaned, how it cursed and blamed, how it hurt in that terrible storm, as the heaps hit it and hit it and hit it again. We must get out.

Down below, we'd go down below where Lucy Pennant's birth object was. We'd need that. Somehow we'd make it live again, and James Henry too. If Rowland Collis could, well then there must be hope.

'We'll go down, Lucy. We'll find the tunnel.'

'It's probably flooded, Clod. It was pouring in when I was last there.'

'But still the central part of the cellar was safe?'

'It was a while ago.'

'Then we'll go down, Lucy. We'll try it. And, most of all, please to remember, your birth object is still down there.'

'A box of matches, I'm not going to drown for a box of matches.'

'It's not just a box of matches, you must believe me. My own plug, here, is a person, truly, a person trapped in the shape of a plug. And I don't know what will happen to you if we don't get your box of matches. You'll get ill, I think, you won't last long.'

'I'll take my chances if it's all the same to you.'

'I saw my own aunt turned into a bucket because she didn't have hers.'

'But the Grooms are down there, and Piggott, all of them! They know me down there.'

'No, Lucy, no, they won't be there any more, they will have come up, no one will stay down there, it isn't safe.'

'Then it can't be safe for us either. I shan't go back down.'

'And, Lucy, there's something else.'

'I'm not going, you cannot persuade me.'

'I think that Florence Balcombe is down there.'

'Florence is?'

'Only she's not what she was, she's only a cup now, and, you must believe me, a moustache cup I heard them saying, and I've heard her, I heard her calling. Her voice, among all the others, she is a part of the Gathering.'

'But I was with her then! So close! I saw her!'

'And she, Lucy, I do believe, is in the cellar.'

'Well then, Clod,' she said, taking a breath. 'All right then. Come along.'

She looked so bullied already, so beaten and scraped. As if they'd got to her, pulled some of the Lucy from her.

'We'll get out,' I said, 'and we'll never come back.'

'You're coming with me?'

'I shan't leave you. We'll smash our way out if we have to.'

'What made you so tough of a sudden?'

'You did, Lucy, you did.'

'I'm not an Iremonger, Clod, not even a bit of one.'

'I know, I know, and I love you for it.'

'I'm a thief, I always have been I think, I stole those objects.'

'I know it and I love you for it.'

'I was out in the heaps, I saw Tummis going under. I tried to get him, I didn't though, I didn't manage it.'

'Oh, Lucy, you tried, didn't you, you tried your absolute best.'

'I did, yes I did.'

'And I do love you for it.'

'Do you?'

'Yes, I do.'

'Albert Powling.'

'Oh no.'

'What is it?'

'Little Uncle.'

On Our Way

Little Uncle Timfy was before us, his face illuminated by a gunny lamp, making it shine like a little moon, a small planet of malice. His nostrils flaring in the pride of our discovery, so eager, so hungry to damage.

'Stop, stop you right there, I've got you now. I'm the one to do it. Not Idwid. Me. I'm in charge here, not him. He's been smashed about. How he bleeds! That wiped the smile from his face. Well, good, I say. I'm in charge of this house. I'll be Governor some day. Why not! Stand straight now! Clod Iremonger, you ruin your own blood.'

'Leave us be, Uncle Timfy.'

'Not likely, never likely is it? Give her, give it, up.'

'No, Uncle, step back.'

'I mean to take it from you.'

'I'll hurt you, Uncle, I shall hurt you.'

'You, Clod, you're made of nothing but foul air. What hurt could you do?'

'You will not touch her.'

'I shall, I shall touch that. Watch me at it!'

'Don't kick me, Uncle, I'll smash you, I swear I will.'

'Do it then, you bit of nothing. You're not worth my spit, Clod, you've no use at all. I'll end this now.'

He blew hard on his Albert Powling and in response there was a sudden crash further along the corridor.

'What's that?' Lucy cried. 'Who's he brought?'

'I don't know,' I said, 'something large, or some army of servants. What on earth is it, Uncle? Who is that coming?'

But Timfy didn't seem to know either, there was terror in his face, but he blew on his Albert once more, and a great rumbling answered it immediately, the noise growing now, coming closer.

'What is that? What is coming, Uncle Timfy?'

'I . . . I . . . I don't know. I cannot say.'

Something was coming, something large running our way. No place to hide, all the doors were locked, and that running was getting louder and louder. We couldn't see who it was, whether just one person or several, the corridor was so dark.

'Help!' called Timfy. 'Help me.'

'What is it? What could it be?' Lucy cried.

'Is it a Gathering? Who goes there?' Timfy screamed.

'Back,' I called. 'Stand back.'

I pushed Lucy against the wall as the thumping came closer and closer, Uncle Timfy was still in the middle of the passageway, his face, in a horror mask, illuminated by his lamp.

'Help! Help ho!' Uncle screamed. 'What devil are you?'

A great stomping, a horrible screaming, a quick rush of raw, wrinkled pink skin, and with it a great mass of thick black and white feathers, huge claws on the ground, slamming to a halt, a creature, some monster. It smashed into Uncle Timfy, sending him flying and his light crashing against the wall and igniting some torn wallpaper, the flames spreading upwards, fire licking the ceiling, so that now with this great new light we could see suddenly everything. Timfy on the ground staring up with all horror at an impossible creature bent down before him, snapping at him with a huge angry beak. An ostrich! Tummis's ostrich!

'Murder!' shrieked Timfy. 'Oh, murder!'

He stumbled up, dodging the flames, and rushed in his agony out of sight, deeper into the darkness, the ostrich screaming after him, both so terrified, both so terrifying. Tummis, after so much cruelty, was having his revenge.

'To think it was with us all along! Tummis's ostrich! Thank you, Tummis, a thousand thanks!'

'The fire, Clod, the whole place will be alight in a moment.'

'Then down we'll go, down where it's dampest.'

We went along the landing. On we went, Lucy hobbling but keeping up. There was a service stairway just off the landing. A cold stairway, no carpets, no pictures there. It was the serving way down to the Marble Hall.

'There'll be people at the bottom,' I said, 'almost certain to be. We must try further along.'

'As long as it's not in the chimneys, I don't think I could do that again.'

'We'll find another way.'

'Is the dining room nearby?'

'The Great Dining Hall is. Why?'

'Does it have a dumb waiter? I heard the Grooms talking about one. Could we get down that way?'

'Yes, Lucy, well done, we might, we might.'

In the Great Dining Hall

The Great Dining Hall, all flock wallpaper and cut glass, chandelier and shining light, polish and sparkle, but dark too, and deep, as if rather than being in a grand setting for the purpose of eating, you were already in the stomach of some leviathan. That's where we tumbled, and, tumbling in saw suddenly that we were not alone.

Birth objects all around, birth objects mumbling, hushed, in terror whispering. All the names were questions, every speaking object spoke with a question mark. My own plug was wondering too, very quietly, timidly, 'James Henry Hayward?' So many Iremongers had gathered themselves here in the Great Dining Hall. We had run straight into them. My relatives, the whole place thick with them. Iremongers all around.

'Oh, Clod,' whispered Lucy, 'help me! What now?'

And all I could say was, 'Oh!'

'Please, Clod, you must do something.'

All around Iremonger eyes upon us, everyone looking up. How to explain? How to make right again?

'Dreadful night,' I said. 'How do?'

All the eyes kept upon us, they did not look away.

'I've just seen an ostrich. True as life, running down the way. Tummis's ostrich, as I live and breathe. There's fire, there're flames down the midway corridor. How you stare so.'

They stared still.

'How are you all, what's new?'

Still they stared.

'What a night it is!' I said, not able to stop talking, because when I stopped, I felt certain they'd come for her. 'What a night when the Iremongers go dumb one and all. I've been about tonight, seen such weather. I'm sure you all have, same as me. Well then, it's a terror to be certain. Do I sound excited? Well, I am excited. I came upon this creature here beside me, this rag person. You may not recognise it, but I'd call it human. Lo, people, it is a serving Iremonger. I found her lumped in a corridor, so many things heaped on top of her. Took a while to dig her out. Couldn't say what it was at first, wouldn't gamble upon it. But there then I found this dishrag, this sink thing, and I thought, well, I thought, I thought . . .'

'Oh, do shut up, Clod!' came the voice of Uncle Aliver over in a corner. 'What a fuss you make. This hall has been made a makeshift hospital, the Infirmary is closed off by the storm. Look about you, everyone's hurt. Be useful. Find some use.'

I could understand then, the panic slipping slightly away, that these before me were not dining Iremongers, though Uncle Aliver had a knife in his hand and was at table, but he was standing, not sitting, and the knife was a scalpel. The other relatives were dressed in Aliver's clothing, they wore bandages, they wore sheets of finest linen tablecloths, and these ripped coverings had about them here and there red blossoms spreading through the bandages. So many cut, so many purpling with bruises, so many weeping and groaning. So many sad white faces watched the chandelier of the Great Dining Room pitch and swing now, watching for it to come down upon them. The house, I thought, the house will go tonight. But no one, not a one of them, thought Lucy was the searched-for party, the object of the Iremonger manhunt; no one pulled her down, no one screamed murder. So I got a bit braver then (I'm fifteen and a half, I'm trousered), I stepped in a little bit, looking about me, and over there, in a far corner, sure enough, there was the hatch of the dumb waiter, but between that hatch and us were so many Iremongers, each one primed, each one, if they understood Lucy properly, liable to erupt and then with a clarion screech of, 'It!' blow us and our hopes to nothing.

Step. Step carefully.

'This way, Iremonger,' I whispered to Lucy. 'You may rest over by the wall there. Follow on.'

There was such clinking from the chandeliers and such crashing heard from the outdoors danger and such moaning and begging for mercy from so many timber joists all around us, and, even more yet, such mumbles of help and mercy and God save us from so many buckled and hurting Iremongers (and such questioning, such whispering from those birth objects) that we had got about half the way to the hatch before someone called.

'Stop! Stop right there!'

And so we must.

It was a matron from the Infirmary, full of bluster and business, big lady, big mouth, big lungs beneath them no doubt.

'You there!' she called. 'You there, answer me!'

'Me?' I asked.

'Not you, Master Clodius, excuse me. The other one, behind about, what's your station?'

'I work with oakum, miss, downstairs,' said Lucy, thinking quickly, 'been a wool carder in my time. Came up with the flooding.'

'This Hall is for the blood, girl, not for servants, it's not for you to come in here. You're not to be in here at all, storm or no storm.'

'Very sorry, miss, I'll leave right away. Didn't know.'

'Wait a moment!' said the matron again. 'Oakum, you said, wool carding, well then you've got fingers haven't you, you can bandage then can't you? Come here and be useful. Here. To me.'

Lucy followed the matron, her head down, trying not to be noticed. Wait a moment, Lucy, I thought, I'll tug you back, tug you back and through the hatch. Give me a moment, then amongst all the moans of family and all the questioning of birth objects, I heard one that wondered familiarly, 'Gloria Emma Utting?'

Ignore it, walk on.

'Clod, Clod, what's happening?'

Pinalippy was calling. She was huddled among other of her schoolgirl cousins, holding a napkin to her smacked head.

'Clod, I've never seen anything like it. So many fallen down! I saw Cousin Horryit washed out into it, screaming as she went. Oh Clod, what's to become of us?'

'Hullo, Pinalippy. Poor Horryit, I can hardly believe it,

she was never kind to me but I shouldn't wish her dead. And Tummis, Pinalippy, Tummis has drowned.'

'Grandfather's not come back, has he? Have you seen him?'

'No, Pinalippy, I have not.'

'Grandfather should know what to do.'

'He should indeed.'

'Who was that with you, Clod? Who did you come in with?'

'Just a serving Iremonger,' I said, 'some nothing from down below. I found her, caught under things, dug her out.'

'You are good, Clod, to take such trouble over a servant. I'm not sure I would have done it. How like you.'

'I wonder if I shouldn't help Uncle Aliver.'

'Will you sit with me, Clod? I should feel better for it.'

'Well . . . yes, Pinalippy, of course I shall, but first I should probably see if –'

'Let somebody else help. I need you.'

'Do you, Pinalippy?'

'Clod! Clod Iremonger!'

'Yes, Pinalippy.'

'You're wearing trousers!'

'Yes, indeed, Pinalippy . . . I've been trousered.'

The discovery of this was, unfortunately, enough to get Pinalippy fully perpendicular, she stomped over to me, looked me up and down, shook her head in disbelief, and then, ah heavens, Pinalippy grasped me to her, and

371

I was somewhat crushed by her affection. Lucy was further off then, I couldn't see her among all those Iremongers.

'I'm proud,' said Pinalippy, 'so proud.'

'Thank you, Pinalippy, very much. I shall be back in a moment.'

'I'll think of you differently now, I shan't take you for granted again.'

'Pinalippy, I –'

'Foy! Theeby! Come look, Clod's been trousered!'

'Please, please, Pinalippy!'

But it was too late, other cousins were upon us in a moment and though some of them were scraped and bandaged all took time to look at me in my new clothes and to smile at me and give me much encouragement. I couldn't see Lucy. I couldn't see her anywhere.

'He does look grand, doesn't he?' said Pinalippy.

'Yes, Pin, what a fellow he is all togged up.'

'You'll be married soon, then, Pinny, any day now.'

'If there is another day.'

'Oh, Pinny, don't be like that. You've got your man, and he's been trousered!'

'That's something to hold onto, isn't it, Pin?'

'Pinny, I shouldn't let go of that in a hurry.'

'Yes,' she said, 'you're right. I'll hold on tight,' and saying so she squeezed my hand till I thought it should be nothing but pulp. 'He's mine!'

I couldn't see Lucy.

'How did it happen, Clod, so early? Was it a surprise, did you know all along?'

'Grandfather,' I stammered, 'Grandfather gave them me.'

'Grandfather!' they cooed. 'Grandfather himself!'

'Yes,' said Pinalippy, 'very proud.'

How, how I wondered, might I pull myself from this, and where had Lucy gone?

'You're a dark horse, my Clod Iremonger,' said Pinalippy, stroking one of my trouser legs.

There Lucy was! Not so far away either. Bandaging.

'Uncle Aliver,' I said, 'I do believe that Uncle Aliver needs my help. He was waving to me just now. I'll be back with you ladies, by and by.'

'Ladies,' said Theeby, 'he calls us ladies.'

'Clod,' said Pinalippy, 'you are to come right back as soon as you are done, is that clear?'

'Yes, Pinalippy, crystal.'

'Be swift then, I shall be missing you.'

I started towards Uncle Aliver whose hands were very crimson, he had just taken some shards of porcelain from out of some family member or other. I hoped very much to steer from him before getting too close and thus make my way back around the room to Lucy, then to use the authority of my trousers to get her free, but Liver saw me and he did wave me over.

'Clod, Clod, do you have a steady hand?'

'A little wobbly actually, Uncle, I'm rather nervous. My head, you see, it hurts chronically. There are so many noises inside it, trying to shout each other out. I can barely hear you at all.'

'This before me,' said Aliver, 'is your Uncle Idwid, he's been very punctured. Many things have flown into him, as if they were aiming for him most particularly. A quantity of china have I plucked from his chest, there was a whole tea service for all I reckon all about him, sticking in. And what's more a tea strainer cut into his left ear as if it was attempting to burrow itself inside.'

'Poor Uncle Idwid, he does indeed appear much perforated. Is he awake, Uncle? Is he sensible?'

'The Governor was in such an agony and making such noises of discomfort that I thought it sensible to put a little chloroform on some wadding to have him passive as I removed the china and stitched him up. But he shall be with us again very soon, I am sure. Indeed, Clod, he is stirring now.'

Uncle Idwid shivered a little upon the dining room table, his scratched hand reached out to the nasal clippers that lay beside him. His broken eyes remained closed, but his mouth opened a crack to whisper, barely, 'Hayward . . . is it . . . Hayward?'

'Hullo, Uncle, how do you do?'

'I am a colander, dear Clod,' he whispered.

'Nothing like so bad, sir, more a pepper pot, few holes, just a few, closing up now.'

His smile was back with him. 'You're a good boy, Clod. I love you.'

'Thank you, sir.'

'The Gathering, Clod, the Gathering down below has grown so very big again, it is trying its hardest to get out. But you must not let it! If it gets out, if it joins with the rest of the heap beyond it shall become such a thing, such a huge monster, that it shall bring us all down.'

'It shall be kept in. I am sure, sir, perhaps it has already been dismantled.'

'Is Umbitt back?'

'No, sir, I fear not.'

'Umbitt, Umbitt would know what to do.'

'There is a portion of a saucer, Cousin Governor,' said Uncle Aliver, 'still lodged inside your knee, I mean to take it out now. Clod, will you hold your uncle still?'

'Clod, my love,' said Idwid. 'Clod, my ear, come close, come close now.'

I found myself very close to Uncle Idwid then, so much that his mouth and his teeth were just by my ear. I had seen him pick up Geraldine Whitehead and move it towards his own face, but I thought that was only for comfort's sake.

'This shall hurt a little,' said Aliver further down.

'Do not hesitate!' called Idwid.

Aliver dug his knife in.

Idwid cried out and as he cried, Geraldine Whitehead closed its long jaws tight upon my ear.

'Ah!' I screamed.

'Nearly there,' said Aliver, 'a little more.'

'Ah!' shrieked Idwid, clamping down all the harder on his Geraldine so that it began to cut into me now.

'Uncle, please, sir!' I cried.

'Where is it?' whispered Idwid into my clamped ear. 'Where is the it? It's with you, I think. It is known that you had a liking for it. What have you done with it? Tell me, dear, tell me, Clod, now!'

'Hold tight!' called Aliver.

'Ah! Ah!' shrieked Idwid and to counter his pain dug in the deeper with Geraldine. 'Where now,' he whispered, 'have you put it? Is it here? Is it in this room even now? It is! It is, I'm sure of it! Under our noses! It! It! Get it out!'

'Last bit now, and then all done. Once more!' called Aliver.

'It! It!' cried Idwid, cutting my ear. But he had cut too far, Geraldine had slipped, it had torn my ear a bit and so doing lost its grasp. I had the wadding then in a moment and stuffed it over Idwid's wide moon face, and the hand that raised Geraldine Whitehead withered slowly and cluttered bloody upon the table and Uncle Idwid was asleep with the chloroform.

'All done,' said Aliver, 'well then, that wasn't so bad after all, was it?'

'I fear poor Uncle Idwid has fainted with the pain.'

'I thought he was made of stronger stuff.'

'Apparently not, Uncle.'

'What's happened to your ear?'

'A little nick, Uncle, nothing to speak of, well, I must go on, glad I could be of help.'

'Yes, thank you, Clod. Sure I can't do anything about that ear?'

'No, thank you, Uncle, no need.'

I was around the Hall, stepping over Iremongers, nodding at relations; there she was in her spoilt uniform, her hands shaking, Lucy finishing wrapping a smashed leg. I pulled her up.

'Iremonger,' I said, 'I need you. You're to come with me.'

'She's working here,' said the matron, calling over, 'attending to the sick.'

'Don't argue with me, matron, I'm in trousers now and not to be spoken to.'

'You might be in ermine for all I care, Master Clodius, I need her help.'

'You have no authority over me.'

'Over you, no, over her, yes.'

'She's coming with me.'

'She stays here.'

'Do you argue with a full-blood?'

'I argue with the circumstances, with medical emergency. That's my beef.'

I had hold of Lucy by the right hand, the matron, up now and with us, held her by the left. Lucy stood in terror in the middle.

'Let her go!' I said.

'I shall not,' called the matron.

'She's coming with me.'

'She stays in this room until I'm done with her.'

'Listen, matron, be sensible, I must have a word with you.'

'I thought we were doing that already. You've got everyone's attention.'

Indeed now so many people were looking up at us, wondering at our argument, no doubt at why a true Iremonger should be making such a fuss over a servant. In the distance Idwid was beginning to stir upon the dining room table.

'Listen, matron,' I said, quiet now, so that only she and I and Lucy might hear, those Iremongers all about us watching the swinging chandelier again, 'please to listen. Do you know who this filthy creature is?'

'Some skivvy, what does it matter?'

'Please, matron, I want you to stay calm. I want you to take a deep breath. Now listen carefully. This ugly wraith is something more than you suppose. Consider now who she might be. Her hair beneath this filthy bonnet is russet. There is a clue in that. Take a look at her, do but properly observe her muddied phiz, and you shall see soon enough what I'm talking about.'

The matron dumbly looked, but saw – for her face betrayed her mind entirely – nothing in particular.

'I did not wish to say it,' I continued, 'for fear of causing great alarm. I did not wish to tell you for fear of upsetting you, now I see that I must.'

'Well then, you must,' she said, 'go on do.'

Lucy was all the while staring at me, most perplexed.

'Well, then, this person whose wrist you are holding is none other than the one they are all searching for. I did not want to raise alarm. People here have been hurt enough already. I merely mean to proceed with her under my custody to the hatch over beyond, and there to take her downhouse where she is waited for, waited for and expected by my Uncle Timfy himself and Sturridge and Piggott, and there I, the one who caught the vermin, must move her, and quickly too, before more harm is done. Do you understand now? Must I make myself clearer? This, what you hold, is it, the it, the unblood. It itself.'

The matron stood very still now, her hand still grasping Lucy, no words coming out, just looking, just standing, and then in time with the clinking chandelier she began to shake a little, in her eyes a moisture grew and then some tears began to fall down her cheeks and very soon she was sobbing.

'I . . . I didn't know,' she wept.

'Come now, matron, no one's blaming you.'

'I touched it . . . I'm touching it,' she said, hurriedly letting go.

'And all shall be well again after a good wash.'

'I'm ever so, I'm ever so, I'm ever so sorry.'

'You're in shock, matron, understandable that you are.

Perfectly sensible that you are. Indeed, who wouldn't be. Here's a chair for you now, sit you down.'

'Bless you, Master Clodius, oh dear, I don't feel well.'

'Shall I take it away then?'

'I wish that you would.'

'Are you all right; are you safe to leave now?'

'Oh, don't worry after me, master. Please get it away. Please do. So terrible having it so close. Oh, my heart!'

'Off we go then, and quietly too, not wishing to cause any alarm.'

'Yes . . . yes,' she wept, 'I quite see that now.'

So I pulled Lucy away from the unhappy matron, and walked with her as quietly as we could, towards the hatch. On the dining room table Uncle Idwid was trying to sit up.

'Oh, Clod,' said Lucy, 'have you done it?'

'Not yet, Lucy, not yet.'

'I think I might scream from fright any moment.'

'Best if you don't, I think, on the whole.'

We reached the hatch, and under the cover of the swaying chandelier we slid the serving hatch upwards, the dumb waiter was in place, we did not have to heave it up ourselves and so we crept in. We were very close, very tight together in there. I slid the hatch down and there then we couldn't see the Great Dining Room any more, the ropes were either side of that tiny shelf-room, we must pull it up bit by bit to let us go down bit by bit. And so we pulled and we started our descending. We bumped and stuttered as we moved. The sounds of the dining room were going away. We could just comprehend, 'Clod! Clod Iremonger, where are you? I want you!'

Pinalippy's voice, diminishing.

Little Room Descending

'Clod, I thought I was dead.'

'Not dead at all, you see. Down we go.'

The further away from the din of the Great Dining Room we went the closer we grew to the abominable noise of the rooms under the house. The vaulted ceilings echoed noises there at the best of times, but now, on such a night, it could be guaranteed to thunder. And if all those things clamped around the name of Robert Burrington were shifting below, bloat and great, fat with possessions, all with names sounding like the report of fusiliers, then, once down there, I should not hear a thing, I should be very deaf, and only have sight to help me. And then, of course, in addition, there was the flooding.

'She did seem keen on you, your Pinalippy,' said Lucy.

'It's just the trousers, she never liked me much in shorts.'

'James Henry Hayward,' my plug was calling out.

'All over you, wasn't she?'

'Well then, perhaps she was a bit, Lucy.'

'Enjoyed that?'

'Are you jealous?'

'James Henry Hayward,' he called, growing louder.

'Certainly am not.'

'There's one thing I must tell you, Lucy, before we get very much further.'

'James Henry Hayward.' Louder yet. My plug was calling out to down below. He was calling to it, calling.

'If the heaps have broken through to the centre of the cellars,' I said, 'then it shall be too loud for me. The noise of it all. Those names calling out. I shan't be able to hear anything. Just a great roar. I shan't be able to hear you.'

'We shall manage.'

'James Henry Hayward!'

'I mean, Lucy, I shall have to rely on you very much. I shan't be able to hear anyone coming, I shan't be able to hear anything at all.'

'James Henry Hayward!'

'I'll keep you, Clod, I'll watch out for you.'

'Not even if you shout at me,' I said.

'James Henry Hayward!'

'The noise is coming now, Lucy, I hear it rising, and my plug calling back to it!'

'James Henry Hayward!'

'All those names shouting upwards,' I cried 'It's coming! It's coming, Lucy!'

'JAMES HENRY HAYWARD!'

'Lucy! Lucy, it is here!'

I couldn't hear any more then, not a thing. As if we

were both already drowned. She was talking to me, saying something, but I couldn't tell what it was. My head, oh my head. What a head, quite filled up, a drowning head. No pocket of peace. All full up, drowning, drowning.

The Heap House Serving Girl Mary Staggs

22

A WOODEN TOOTHPICK

Concluding the narrative of Lucy Pennant

I have thick red hair and a round face and a nose that points upwards. My eyes are green with flecks in them, but that's not the only place I'm dotted. There's punctuation all over me. I'm freckled and spotted and moled and have one or two corns on my feet. My teeth are not quite white. One tooth is crooked. I'm being honest. I shall tell everything how it occurred and not tell lies but stay with the actual always. I shall do my best. One of my nostrils is slightly bigger than the other. I chew my fingernails. Sometimes the bugs do bite and then I scratch them. My name is Lucy Pennant. My name is Lucy Pennant and I shall never forget it.

'I do love you I suppose, Clod Iremonger, you idiot.'

'Lucy! Lucy, it is here!'

'I do love you,' I said.

He couldn't hear. He'd gone all strange on me. His hair

was up and he was sweating, his teeth clenched. He had all those noises in his head, eating at him. Only part Clod, then, the rest of him not available, not for now. I grabbed his chin and made him look at me.

'We'll be all right,' I said, 'we shall be. If you get lost I'll find you. No matter what. I'll find you. Do you hear?'

He nodded, but I couldn't be certain. All right then. I pulled the ropes along, he did his side. And then with a great smack that took the wind out of us, we were done and down. We'd reached the bottom. We were in the cellars again, the other side of the hatch was the kitchen of Heap House, right then. I looked at him, just once more. On we go then. No fumbling. I shoved up the hatch. Out we scrambled.

No one there, and everything smashed about. So many broken things. The kitchen, this cooking place, the site of some battle. Clod behind me? Clod behind me.

'All right, Clod? All right?'

He nodded a bit.

Right then, Piggott's room, first off. I knew the way. Clod kept behind me, but his walk was wrong, staggering like he was drunk or something, dried blood around his ear. Is he going under, I thought, even as I speak? No, no, can't think like that. Quick as you can. Get everything, get everything and then onwards, and it will be all right, because if you say it will be and he says it will be and so it bloody will be.

'Come on, old Clod, keep up.'

The ground was covered, Clod stepped and slid over things. Scrapes, great gashes along the wall. All the noises were storm noises from outside, I couldn't hear any human sounds. Come on, Clod. Round we go. Along the corridor, slipping but up again. His ear. Up you get.

'All right?' I shouted.

He put his hands to his ears.

'All right,' I said.

On we go. Round the corner, up the stairs. I could hear it then. Piggott's room, sounds to make you want to run away for all you're worth. Bells. It was bells. Bells sounding, all the bells of the birth objects of the serving Iremongers all ringing out. Getting louder.

There.

Piggott's door. Open. Good then.

Don't think, just do it. Here we are, Clod, in we thrust.

'Lucy!' he called.

She was there. Piggott. She would be, wouldn't she? She was at the back of the room. She was pushing herself against all those bells and drawers, she was forcing herself against them. Some of the drawers were opening, and when they did, Piggott, in her fury, slammed them shut again. She was very ripped, her bun had come loose, her clothes were very torn, I could see her petticoat, her white skin beneath it. Skin of Piggott, not something to dwell upon.

She hadn't heard us, not with all that noise. Piggott slammed the drawers shut, she was wailing, weeping to keep all those things in. Look at that, I thought, that's her authority spilling out all over the place. She was wailing, moaning, groaning, awful deep groans like what a cow should make in agony, trying to slap those drawers shut. She couldn't keep every drawer closed, she couldn't cover the whole wall up, some things must slip out. There was a boot suddenly out of her grasp and free, there was a pillow, a lice comb, a bicycle wheel. Those free things tumbled to the floor and ran free, they made for the doorway and out to freedom. Moving things! It was such a sight to see! It was beautiful, that's what it was, so, so beautiful!

'Go on then,' I cried, 'go on, things! Lovely things, go on! Get out! Fly free! Get away! Be gone! Be free!'

'Look!' cried Clod. 'Look at them go!'

Piggott turned around, all insult and disgust, and as she turned to me so many drawers seized their chances and cannoned themselves from the wall, so much spilling out now.

'You! You again!' screamed Piggott. 'You've ruined everything! All I ever had!'

Drawers took their advantage, so many breaking their locks, so many shooting out, all those things rushing past her.

'Come back, come back! Come you all back to me!'

They didn't though. They kept falling out, tumbling everywhere. Clod, wide-eyed, watched it all and grinned now at the lovely storm of it. Looking at all those things running free, so lovely, so lovely. A floating, flying tape measure eeling in the air! A chair, its legs kicking up dirt as it ran! A boot scraper, upturned, clockworking its way out.

'Matchbox, Lucy!' cried Clod. 'Find the matchbox!'

I couldn't see it. It wasn't there.

A thumping behind me then, and I was slammed to the ground, someone was rushing by. It was the great lock-woman, Mrs Smith, agony on her flat mug, smashing through those things, crushing whatever was underfoot, fumbling with all her keys. But which keys now? Which to use? How to keep all those locks closed, locks that were bending, snapping, breaking? Her world, just like Piggott's, was coming unfastened, was getting out.

Smith soon gave up with the keys and, turning around, flattened her great back against the drawers, so doing covering a good portion of the back wall, she was herself a lock. She grinned then, a great happy, simple grin, full of triumph. But it didn't linger long. Smith looked up, she saw it before I did. The great tall safe of Piggott's sitting room was wobbling, it was wobbling and also it was leaning forward, tilting itself forward. Now Smith, grinless, looked up at it, and that great lead thing looked down upon Smith, it looked down and down upon her like its own metal child. There was a screech of metal, Smith's face very white now, and then Smith's face was not there at all, nor the rest of her neither, the great safe had fallen upon her and taken her quite out. The lock of Heap House was no more and, as if in answer, as if in glorious salute, the remaining drawers smashed open and all the disobedient objects hurried out. Piggott, in her loud misery, snatched at the air, trying to grasp them back, she had hold of a wax crayon for a little moment, but it soon slipped her grasp. Then I was being pulled at. There was Clod, tugging at me, smiling and holding something in his hand: a box of matches.

'I have it! I have it!' he cried.

'My matchbox!'

His ear was bent over it, he called out, 'It has a name, I can just hear it if I'm so close. I think it says it is Ada Cruickshanks. Yes! Ada Cruickshanks she's called, Lucy! Your own Ada Cruickshanks!'

But as he showed me, holding his hand out, it leapt from his hand and, rolling itself with great speed, rushed from the room. Clod and I looked at each other for the tiniest of moments and fled after it.

All those escaped objects were rushing pell-mell in the same direction. They were skittering, thumping, crashing along the cellar walls, all speeding the same way. All hurrying to the same meeting. To the Gathering itself. But some of them did not make it, some of them tumbling forward suddenly grew larger, changed shape. A kettle skittering along, rolling, rolling, stopped being a kettle at each turn and grew bigger and greyer and became all of a sudden an old woman in a filthy floral print dress, thick legs, she sat there upon the ground and screamed and screamed.

'Mary Staggs! Mary Staggs!'

Mr Briggs was at her in a moment, he had a swinging bucket and a spoon and he rushed to put the spoon to the poor old woman's mouth, he shoved it in her and she stopped her screaming. Further along a bicycle wheel circled into a young boy with missing teeth, looking about him most peculiarly and wobbling upon his legs, very unsteady as if he'd quite forgotten how to walk, and he, coming to himself, hollered out, 'Willy Willis! I'm Willy Willis! Mammy, Mammy! My mammy!'

The boot scraper waddled no further but suddenly stopped in a heap and was a fat man in a dented straw hat, mutton chops, looking most confused, and weeping, 'Brian Pettifer, sea captain. Baltic. Kattegat. Gulf of Riga.'

Mr Groom was upon him and giving him grim physic as fast as he might.

All was confusion down there, a battle scene, objects rushing into people, and also serving Iremongers, upright and hollering and falling into objects. I saw a parlour maid fall to the ground and in an instant become a creamer jug. A leather Iremonger, a heap worker, leant against the wall and was very sudden a ladder. A body Iremonger, tall with shining hair parted exactly in the middle, was in a moment reduced to a leather satchel.

People dropping down around us, people pulling up.

And still rushing past all these people turning into objects and objects turning into people were so many other things, mostly sprung from Piggott's room, all hurtling forward, towards, towards . . . I saw it then. Clod did too.

'Lucy! Look, Lucy!'

Huge it was.

That Gathering.

Bigger than rooms, howling and smashing, many mouths, a thousand thousand things all got together. It was all of the servants' dining room, the kitchen, the polish room, the cold room, all of those places. A great creature taking over so much space. Hungry for more. So hungry, so hungry. So many mouths, so many dark deep holes in it, eating up. It'll never have enough. And so sorrowful, so needing, so hurt and wronged, and mad with it all.

Serving Iremongers were about it, prodding it, poking this and that into it, some of them falling into objects even as they laboured, others maybe cutting a few things from it, but only ever angering it more. Wrong to do that, surely, I thought, to upset it so. Iremongers in brass firemen's helmets with poles and hoses, with ladders trying to climb up it, into what exactly, and losing their grips, falling in, crushed by it. And the noise of creaking and snapping, of the house itself crying for mercy, cracking and breaking under the size of the great creature. The ceiling was breaking, great rents appearing, it will bring the whole house down.

As we came closer, close to that terrible end, we passed the butler's Sitting Room. Sturridge was in there, he was just standing there. What's he doing there, just standing like that, great bulk like his, why doesn't he lend a hand? Then I saw that he was, he *was* doing his bit. Sturridge was holding up the ceiling, sweating so. Or was he weeping? Couldn't tell. He had the weight of the house upon him, and was just, just, just keeping it up, what a pillar, what a column!

'Clod! Clod! Look at me, can you hear me?' I held his face to me. 'Listen to me, Clod, if we get separated, if anything should happen, I will find you. Wait for me. I shall find you.'

'Filth! Gut it out!'

Mrs Groom had seen me now down the cellarway and, raising her great cleaver in one hand, her jelly mould swinging from her belt, rushed at me.

'Cut you! Cut you!' she wailed, but then quieter, 'Cut you?' as she suddenly flipped over, swung a somersault, and tumbled exactly at my feet, a mere cheese grater, so many sharp holes in it, the cleaver useless beside it. The grater lay over a shoe of mine, I hurriedly kicked it off. Beside her, where her jelly mould might have been, was a fat baby, quiet and naked.

'Ada Cruickshanks!' cried Clod. 'There she goes!'

The matchbox was ahead of us, rushing forward. I tried to catch after it but then suddenly came a terrible sound and I thought the whole house was smashing down.

Screeeeeeeeeech! Screeceeeechh! Scraaaaaaaaaaatch!

What was that? What was that? Even Clod heard that, even Clod turned to that. What was that? What was that?

'Lucy,' he cried. 'Oh no, Lucy, no!'

Then the shouts, the great calling from the Iremongers.

Agony? Are they in pain? No, no, not pain. They were cheering. Why? What for?

'What is it? What is it, Clod?'

'Grandfather, Lucy, Grandfather is coming!'

The train.

The train had made it back. Smashed its way through the tunnel.

'Hold on! Hold on!' called the butler. 'He's coming! He's coming now!'

'Here! Here! To us! To us!' yelled the Iremongers.

The great Gathering seemed to be understanding something too, for it moved and scraped with greater agitation. And then there he was. The old man. The old man but rushing now, a swift walk, ploughing through the rubble. The old man, big old man in his top hat and a great coat. Rushing down the cellar passage, coming forward, and the Gathering made a huge mouth and it spat at him – a great wall of things flew out from the Gathering, nails and glass shards, broken bits, sharp pelting – but he kept on marching towards it, the old man kept on. He walked right on. He walked right into it, throwing bits and pieces of it behind him as he entered. He just walked through it, and anything in his way, he tossed it out. He made a great path through the creature. We could see him, we all just stood there watching. His great old hands were out then, feeling inside the gathering, his whole arms went deep inside it, and the creature seemed to groan and screech in pain, it swung around him, trying to drown him, all its mouths snapping around him, but the old man only carried on searching through all the things, like he had an ash pan, sifting through it, looking for something specific, something he'd lost and needed back. Old man in the thick of that, what have you lost, what are you looking for? Go on, creature, drown him, drown him, bite him! The old man, big old man, ugly old man, his hands scrabbled about under the surface, searching around, feeling through all the objects. It was up to his neck by then, it'll drown him, it'll surely drown him. Good then, let him drown. But then the Gathering stopped still, it seized, it shuddered, it didn't move any more, it stayed so still. Horrible still. So still we could see at last all what it was made of, see all those things that it was, just things, this and that, everyday things, just things, nothing special. It stayed like that a moment and then, and then, all dropped. All found gravity again, all smashed to the ground, a sudden raining of all those things, down upon the flagstones. All dead once more. Just things again. Only one thing upright, just one from all those thousand thousand things. Only one. Him. The old man, big old man, ugly old man, standing, vertical. Holding something. Holding in his hands just one thing, a thing, a teacup it was, with an extra lip, a moustache cup. Florence Balcombe.

With that cup in his hands, my Florence Balcombe, he, like all those other things just a short while before it, he let it drop, it fell to the ground. It didn't smash. Amazing that it didn't. It landed upright, Florence did, like a cat might. Well done, Florence. It rolled around a little, Florence did, but just a very little. And then the old man, crazy old man, ugly old man, lifted up one of his great black boots and he brought it down hard upon Florence Balcombe and he smashed her, he smashed her, she was broken now, she was in pieces, and he lifted up his boot and he brought it down again.

'Florence!' I screamed.

'Lucy!' Clod screamed. 'Lucy, don't!'

I ran at him.

He looked up then, he saw me coming, cold, cold those eyes.

And I –

The New Governess Ada Cruickshanks

23

A CLAY BUTTON

Concluding the narrative of Clod Iremonger

How It Ended

I could hear more, after the falling of the Gathering I could hear a bit. I could hear. Hear Lucy calling out, 'Florence!'
I called after her.
And then her falling. Lucy fell. She was running towards Grandfather, and then she just stopped, she tumbled to the ground, rolled on the ground, and as she fell, as she rolled, she got smaller and smaller, until she was nothing more, I couldn't see her.
'Lucy! Lucy!' I screamed.
'Lucy Pennant.'
'I hear you! I hear you! But I can't see you. Where are you?'
'Lucy Pennant.'
'Lucy! Lucy!'

'Lucy Pennant.'

On the ground, where she fell, where she stopped falling. There she was, there she was, a button. Nothing more than a button. A clay moulded button.

'Lucy, my Lucy Pennant! I've got you.'

'To me,' said Grandfather, and she flipped up into the air, as if I'd tossed her, flicked her, like a coin, only I had not. She was in Grandfather's great hands.

'Please, please,' I cried, 'let me have her.'

'This, Clod, even this is the cause of our recent misery, the reason the heaps had grown so disturbed, this guilty button, this Un-Iremonger, this wrong of blood. Objects were ill at ease even before it came, but when it came it did by its arrival so upset everything, so spread disease, so excited that cup, that it, turning cup-like, called all the other things to it. This thing is going back, back out now, into the deep of it, let it feel lost there and abandoned, missing without hope, let it suffer so. You – are you there, prefect, Moorcus? Strong of blood!'

There was Moorcus, a little bruised and creased, but there with his medal shining.

'Here, sir, here, Grandfather.'

'Take this thing, this button, and run you as fast as you can into the heaps.'

'Out there, sir?'

'It is quite becalmed now, the storm has blown itself out, do it, take it quick, throw it, throw it far out, *lose* it.'

400

'Grandfather, no!' I cried. 'Grandfather! Moorcus, stop! Grandfather, please!'

'You, Clod! Be still!'

'No!'

And I –

The Ticket James Henry Haywood

24

A HALF SOVEREIGN

Beginning the narrative of ticket no. 45247, property of
Bay Leaf House, Forlichingham, London

My name is James Henry. My name is James Henry Hayward. I'm on a train. There's an old man beside me. A nice, grand old man. He holds my hand. We're on a train. Going to London.

I can't see much of anything through the windows, it's all very dark out there. I don't know if I should be worried or not. I look at the old man and I think, not. It is light here in the carriage. The old man is good to me. I don't know if we're going to see my family, I think I should like to see them. The old man says that he shall do his best to find them. I wonder where they can have got to. I cannot remember them very well. I wonder how I lost them. Or how they lost me. I do feel a bit worried. It worries me that I don't remember them. I look up at the old man, he smiles down at me. That feels better. It is a kind old face.

There is a woman sitting a little further away from us, she keeps to herself, she sits bolt upright. She has a large black bonnet with a veil over it, I cannot see her face properly. I hear her coughing, a horrible dry cough that gets inside my head. I far prefer the old man. I do prefer the old man but I shall be seeing a deal of the strict woman, for she is to be my companion for a while, the old man has told me, I am to live with that dry cough. I cannot say I like her. I have heard the old man calling her by name, Ada Cruickshanks.

James Henry Hayward. My name.

I'm in a new suit and cap. New shoes, new everything. I feel very smart. Quite grown up. I wonder if I am rich. The old man is very rich, I think. He must be. He owns the huge faraway house we've just left. He shall look after me. It is a nice story in the end, having a guardian like him. I think he shall adopt me. I hope he shall. Yes, I feel better now, despite the strict woman Ada Cruickshanks, I didn't earlier, but I can't remember that so well.

I slip my hand in my pocket. There's something there. It's a half sovereign. My own. A golden half sovereign. All ten shillings worth of it. My own. The old man gave it to me. But I am not to spend it, he tells me. If it is mine, I wonder, then why can I not spend it? I should like to spend it. I should be able to buy such things with it. But the old man is very strict about this, it is the only thing that stops him smiling.

The old man has told me I must look after my half

404

sovereign particularly. He has asked me several times whether I still have it. He asks me to bring it out into the light and show it to him. I do. And each time he says, 'Very good. Well done, James Henry.' I like it when he says that. I feel the coin around my hand, warm it up a bit.

I hear a sharp loud whistle now calling out, gave me quite the shock. The train is slowing down. We're coming into a station.

'We're here, James Henry,' says the old man.

I smile back and ask, 'London?'

'London,' he says, 'Filching.'

ACKNOWLEDGEMENTS

I would like to thank Sara O'Connor, wonderful editor, and everyone at Hot Key for all their enthusiasm and help, for being who they are – they are an extraordinary team. Very many thanks are due to my long-suffering agent Isobel Dixon, whose faith never wavers, and who keeps me buoyant. To Elisabetta Sgarbi at Bompiani for always being there. To the marvellous Christopher Merrill who sent me to China and to a museum of rescued objects that gave me the first inspiration for this book. To Elizabeth Butler Cullingford and James Magnuson for letting me teach fairy tales and creative writing, and providing me with wonderful students, and for all their support. To my mother for so very much (and with apologies for stealing family names). And most of all to my wife Elizabeth and my children Gus and Matilda for everything.

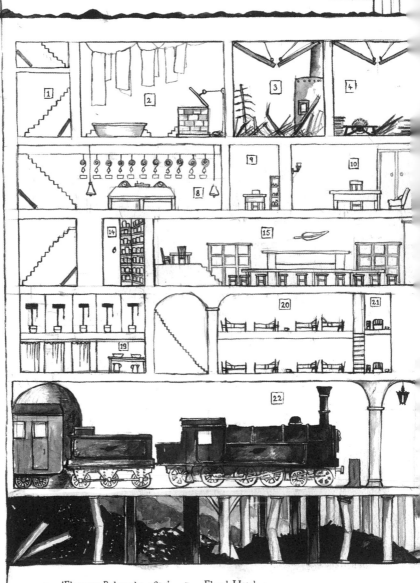